Black Cockles

(Ed Case: Book 1)

John Moritt

DEDICATION

This book is dedicated to everyone who has given me the support and inspiration to continue to write. Special thanks to my golden retriever, Connor, who recently passed away and was the inspiration behind Fat Boy.

OTHER TITLES BY JOHN MORRITT

Nine Lives (Ed Case: Book 2)

Inglorious (Ed Case: Book 3)

Vengeance

AUTHOR'S NOTE

Black Cockles was originally published in paperback form in 2010. However, the original manuscript was heavily edited, removing significant content. I was never comfortable removing so much content but had little choice in order to publish at a competitive price. Recent advances in publishing have made it possible to release the original, unabridged version in paperback and e-book format. It has also given me the opportunity to rewrite and reword much of the original manuscript. I hope anyone buying this book for the first time, or those who have read the previously published version, enjoy this full-length, re-edited version.

.

CHAPTER 1

The shadowy figure walked slowly and stealthily down the narrow, tree-lined path towards his destination, despite being encumbered by the heavy load he carried. The half-moon shone brightly in the cloudless sky, guiding his way. He sweated profusely beneath the dark boiler-suit and black ski mask he wore; not through exertion but from fear-tinged excitement. He fought to keep his breathing even and under control, fearing he would be heard, although confident at this late hour he was completely alone.

When he reached the end of the trees, he placed his burden on the ground and removed his mask to wipe his brow with the back of his gloved hand. His eyes darted left and right, looking for any signs of danger, his ears attuned to any sound that was out of place. Hearing nothing but the gentle lapping of the ebbing tide on the sandy beach, he replaced his mask and continued with his load, across the sand dunes towards his goal.

The shifting dunes sucked at the flip-flops he wore, which were two sizes too big for him, his only concession to his otherwise black appearance. They slowed his progress but were a necessary requirement a part of the plan he had gone over in his mind, time and time again. This time it was for real and he could not afford to make a mistake; he would not allow himself to make a mistake.

Before emerging onto the beach he stopped once more to wipe away the sweat that stung his eyes. Once again, he held his breath and listened. The beach and the dunes in particular were notorious haunts for young couples who came down to fornicate. They were no better than animals; he despised them all.

He stared down the beach in both directions, just to be certain he was alone and unobserved. He smiled to himself, certain he was. He picked up his load and took the final steps towards the high tide mark on the moonlit sand, his excitement almost overwhelming. His heart was racing. His blood pounded in his ears so loudly it almost drowned out the sound of the waves gently kissing the beach.

Time was now critical, now he was exposed. He carefully laid down his load just above the high tide mark in the soft sand and pulled the tarpaulin open to reveal the naked body of a young woman. Her body stood out starkly against the dark shroud she was encased in, shining reverently under the bright moon. He gasped at the beauty of it as he lifted her off and placed her on the sand.

He didn't know her name but he knew her kind, nothing but a common tart. He had seen her two days earlier, sunbathing topless on the beach. He approached and told her what she was doing was immoral and she should be ashamed of herself, despite the fact she was well away from the crowds and unlikely to cause offence. She smirked, taunted him and made fun of him but he didn't care, he would have the last laugh.

He watched her for two days, remaining out of site, watching, waiting, full of hatred, biding his time. Tonight she left the pub alone after closing time and made her way home. He already knew where she lived, alone, and waited until she was inside. After making sure he was unseen he knocked confidently on the door. When she opened it he barged in and immediately pressed the chloroform-soaked cloth over her mouth and nose, stifling her screams.

He carried her upstairs, laid her on the bed and stripped her with trembling hands, his excitement mounting. He photographed her many times from all angles. Unable to control himself, he dropped his trousers and masturbated furiously into his handkerchief, being careful not to spill his seed on the carpet.

As she began regaining consciousness he put the nylon cord around her neck and strangled her, staring into her frightened, bulging eyes. He smiled broadly as her tongue protruded from her mouth and her life slowly drained away. He felt no remorse only his growing erection.

Big Mouth Billy from Brisbane found the body early that morning.

Billy, over from Oz on a two year working visa, resigned from his job so he could spend his last few months in the UK enjoying some of the world's best surf on the North Cornish coast. Billy earned the nickname "Big Mouth Billy" on account of not being able to keep anything to himself and was certainly not someone to be trusted with a secret.

Knowing his time in the UK was limited, he would be the first on the beach every day, no matter what the weather, determined to catch the first waves of the day. Today, however, he was second on the beach. He jogged down the same narrow path as the killer the night before. Once he reached the dunes he sprinted towards the beach and the beckoning waves. He slowed when he saw the woman, thinking she was just sunbathing, despite the morning chill and the fact the sun was just a yellowy haze behind a diaphanous film of grey cloud that covered the entire sky. Billy, as well as not being able to keep a secret, was also not the sharpest tool in the box and possessed an IQ only slightly higher than that of plankton.

Billy planted his surfboard in the sand and walked cautiously towards the prone woman. His initial excitement of finding a naked woman of the beach quickly evaporated, once he noticed her pale skin and bloodless lips. It was when he saw the black cockle shells placed over each of her nipples and the vivid mark around her neck that the bile began rise. Not wanting to vomit over the body, he staggered almost drunkenly to a nearby rock pool and emptied his stomach into it. The crabs and small fish were more than grateful for the free meal.

After retching the entire contents of his stomach into the rock pool, he took out his mobile phone and called the police. He sat down on the edge of the rock pool, shivering, and waited for the police to arrive, oblivious to the feeding frenzy taking place in the water behind him.

CHAPTER 2

Ed wasn't happy. It wasn't even seven o'clock and Fat Boy, his ageing Golden Retriever, had just woken him by licking his ears. To make matters worse, Fat Boy was huffing his halitosis into his face and thumping his tail excitedly on the bed. His tail seemed to beat in perfect synchronisation with the pounding in Ed's fragile temples, because Ed had a hangover. He pushed Fat Boy away and stretched, his joints popping audibly, like that of an old man's. Disgruntled, Fat Boy jumped off the bed, farted and padded his way across the room and downstairs to wait for his master to serve breakfast.

The room was stifling. In his drunken state last night he forgot to open the window. It also stank of sweat and dog. Spurred on by the need for fresh air, aspirin, water and the need to urinate, Ed swung his legs onto the floor and took his first tentative steps of the day, naked across the landing to the bathroom.

Once in the bathroom Ed flopped down onto the toilet, certain prolonged standing was neither advisable nor possible in his current state. He put his elbows on his knees, cupped his head between his hands and squeezed, trying in vain to alleviate the stabbing pain in his temples, which seemed to be increasing exponentially each time he moved. After urinating for what seemed an impossibly long time, he shuffled over to the sink and drank greedily from the tap before swallowing four aspirins. OK, it was twice the recommended dose, but, he decided, was fully justified as he felt twice as hung-over as he usually did after a heavy night.

A look in the mirror was not encouraging. His short, dark-brown hair looked greasy and was plastered to his scalp, resembling a flattened bird nest. His face sported thick, dark stubble, and what skin was visible, looked waxy and unhealthy. His eyes usually bright and alert and often referred to as "come to bed eyes" were dull and bloodshot; so much so he screwed his eyes shut fearing he may bleed to death. He massaged his temples again, willing the aspirins he recently struggled to swallow to work. His bloodshot eyes travelled over the remainder of his wiry, thirty-three-year-old, five-foot-ten frame for signs of damage. Every limb and muscle seemed to ache, and therefore the absence of cuts and bruises was perplexing. However, pleasing, meaning he managed to arrive home without falling over or getting into a fight. He stood there a while longer, staring moronically at his own unpleasant reflection until the dog barked and broke the spell. Ed donned his dressing gown, which was hanging on the back of the bathroom door and made his way slowly and carefully down the stairs, wincing with every step that created fresh waves of pain in his temples.

Fat Boy was waiting patiently by the back door, staring longingly down the garden beyond the glass pane. Ed unlocked the door following him out hoping the fresh air would do him some good. It was yet another glorious morning, a light breeze and hardly a cloud in the sky; unusual for mid-May. If the weather forecaster was to be believed, it was due to last at least until the end of the month, which probably meant it would piss down with rain by evening. Ed stood, inhaling deeply in an attempt to clear the fug from his head. He watched Fat Boy, who blissfully unaware of his master's condition, circled the garden before selecting the right shrub and urinated, copiously over it. Fat Boy came bounding back down the garden and jumped up at Ed, putting his paws on his chest. Ed stroked him and lowered him to the floor, cursing him silently for the dirty paw-prints he left on his freshly laundered dressing gown.

After feeding the dog, Ed looked in the fridge and found the remains of a sliced loaf. On opening the plastic bag he was disappointed to find just two crusts, each sporting a healthy smattering of green mould. He spent a few minutes picking off the mould and put the slices in the toaster, only to find he had no butter. Cursing his poor housekeeping, he made do with a mug of strong, black coffee and started to feel a little better. After brushing the fur from his teeth, gargling a hefty swig of mouthwash for good measure and showering, he was beginning to perk up a little. He dressed and headed out with Fat Boy for a nice, refreshing stroll.

Around the same time Ed was sitting on the lavatory, his stomach in turmoil, his mouth and lips dry, and feeling altogether sorry for himself, a second body was discovered on another deserted beach in North Cornwall. The body was discovered less than a mile from the first by a man taking an early morning jog before work. The victim was another young woman who had been placed in exactly the same position as the last, her head towards the sea, legs together and arms at right angles to the body, resembling a crude crucifix. She was naked and, as with the first body, black cockle shells had been placed over each of her nipples, and death was by strangulation. The police found no forensics, although there was a partial flip-flop print in the drying sand, just below the high tide mark. The police were not making too much of this, as millions of flip-flops were purchased and worn on these beaches by tourists and locals alike. Tests carried out later would reveal that they were a size twelve, indicating the killer, who they undoubtedly belonged to, was likely to be in excess of six foot tall. The body, as with the first, revealed no clues to the killer, only that he had used chloroform to render the victim unconscious before killing her. They were able to ascertain the time of death as being around midnight, about the same as the first victim, although that was never an exact science. The two women were unconnected other than they were undoubtedly killed by the same person.

Attempts to keep the black cockles out of the public domain failed miserably, this largely being attributable to Big Mouth Billy, who told everyone he knew. Very shortly it came to the attention of the local press, who were all over it like a cheap suit and already began calling him "The Black Cockle Strangler". In some respect the local papers were slightly reserved as they were all aware of the importance of tourism to the area. After all, even local newspaper sales were affected by slumps in tourism.

CHAPTER 3

The five mile walk across the fields and along the river did nothing for either of them. Fat Boy beached himself on the cool, tiled floor in the kitchen, while Ed, sweaty and still feeling nauseous, was slumped in the armchair staring at the TV. He had no idea what the programme was, but it was one of many mindless shows, which Ed thought of as chewing gum for the eyes. The format of the show was the same, day in and day out, where emotionally crippled members of the public, with IQ's at the bottom end of the spectrum, were dragged off the streets to air their dirty laundry in public. The smug host would usually goad and provoke both parties until a fight broke out and they would cut to a commercial break. Today was no different and Ed wasn't left disappointed. When he realised he was jeering and clapping along with the audience, he picked up the remote and switched the television off, disgusted with himself.

It was late afternoon by the time Ed felt sufficiently recovered and sober enough, thanks to a near lethal cocktail of coffee, aspirin, paracetamol and ibuprofen, to drive into town. He contemplated walking down with Fat Boy but decided against it as he was curled up on his bed, fast asleep and snoring. He got behind the wheel of his car, waited until the air-conditioning chilled the interior, setting off on what would prove to be an eventful trip.

He had only travelled a few yards along the main road, when a dull-blue Fiat Panda pulled out in front of him, forcing him to brake hard. Ed swore out loud at the driver and again, after looking in the rear-view mirror to find he was the only other car on the road. Rather than being in a hurry as the Fiat's hasty manoeuvre suggested, it pottered along, never edging above twenty-two miles per hour. Ed glared at the back of the drivers head, urging him to go faster or turn off, to no avail.

Ed could tell the driver was a pensioner as he was driving just inches from his rear bumper, still trying to urge him on without success. Typical bloody pensioner, Ed thought. Just because they fought in the war to ensure future generations didn't have to endure a life of tyranny under a German dictator, it didn't give them the right to continually irk the future generations whenever they took to the road. It was ironic really: they may have won the war but what was the European Union, if it wasn't living under the tyranny of a German dictator?

Ed decided long ago that dying of old age wasn't for him. No, he was going to die young from a combination of drink and sexually related diseases. After the amount he drank last night, he was fairly confident of drinking his internal organs into submission but not so on the sexually related diseases; after all, how often did you hear of anyone dying of a sprained wrist or serious friction burns?

It wasn't that he was completely unattractive to the opposite sex; although, he would be the first to admit he was no Brad Pitt. He didn't have jug-ears or a huge nose. He didn't have acne and wasn't fat. It was more a case of not trying hard enough or not trying at all, if he was completely honest with himself, which, like most men, he wasn't. A few years ago he got his fingers burnt, which hit hard and he still hadn't completely recovered from it. He kidded himself he was still searching for Mrs. Right but the truth was he was happy the way things were, just him and Fat Boy - well happy-ish.

It was becoming clear the driver in front was heading into town and probably to the same multi-storey car park as Ed was. Unfortunately, he was right and, to make matters worse, the old fart stopped a few feet inside the car park to wait for a space. Ed gripped the steering wheel so hard his knuckles turned white and his head began to throb again as his recently cured headache threatened to make an encore. He took a deep breath, exhaled slowly, forcing himself to relax as he watched a middle-aged woman load enough food to feed a small army into the back of a 4x4, which looked equally capable of transporting a small army. Each time she bent over her T-shirt rode up and her pink jogging bottoms slipped in the opposite direction, revealing what Ed affectionately called a "tramp stamp" on her lower back. Anyone who could think that a bluish-black tattoo, that would not look out of place on a New Zealand rugby prop-forward's forearm, emblazoned across the top of their arse was a good look was seriously delusional.

After a further delay while the woman took her trolley back to the collection point and walked back, blowing like a buffalo at the exertion, she finally got behind the wheel of her over-sized vehicle and reversed out. The old man in front executed a perfect reverse into the recently vacated space, on his fifth attempt, and very nearly parked straight and between the lines. As Ed passed he noticed the old man give him a military salute and a friendly smile. Ed felt compelled to acknowledge and gave a grudging wave, muttering obscenities under his breath as he smiled back politely, before hurtling off and taking the turn to the upper levels. Ed ignored the numerous available parking spaces on the next levels and sped up to the roof, where his was the only car. He sat there for a few minutes composing himself and massaging his jaw, which was aching, having spent the last twenty minutes with gritted teeth.

CHAPTER 4

The town was busy, considering it was late afternoon on a Wednesday. The crowds seemed to be made up mainly by pensioners pulling baskets on wheels who seemed to stop in the most inconvenient of places to gossip with one another. The conversations were always the same, each trying to win the bragging rights of who had the most grandchildren and the worst ailment. The loser walking away disgruntled and cursing her children for not being sufficiently prolific in the bedroom and wishing for a condition that could top her friend's prolapsed bladder.

Ed ambled along the streets, wishing the shuffling herds of pensioners would go a little quicker. Quite why the old women had to walk arm in arm like ageing lesbians was beyond him. The old men didn't do it, but then as a general rule, a man would only ever touch another man if he was drunk and couldn't stand up or, of course, if he was gay. The idea of the two old women approaching him being gay was not something he wished to contemplate. It was clear that these two old dears were either ignorant or possessed no spatial awareness and showed no signs of moving over or unlinking arms. Ed thought about standing his ground and making a point but took the path of least resistance and walked in the road to continue his journey. It went against his nature to do so but he was in no mood for confrontation and quietly seethed as he approached the bank.

With a wallet full of cash, he headed back the way he came and made towards the supermarket, the only reason he had ventured out in the first instance. Basket in hand, he weaved his way through the sloth-like pensioners towards the bread counter. When he finally arrived he was immediately disappointed at being faced with row upon row of empty shelves. It was either a small, sliced granary loaf or go without. His day was slowly but surely getting worse, as was his mood. In need of some comfort food he went in search of cake and selected a slab of angel cake. It was on special offer and seemed to be screaming 'eat me'. Ed hadn't eaten angel cake in years and could never resist a bargain. The thought of tucking into it when he got home cheered him slightly.

At the checkout, a terminally bored teenager, who was only working there after school to earn enough cash to spend the weekend getting pissed on cheap cider, asked him if he wanted any help packing. Ed fought back the urge to tell her it wasn't exactly a difficult task and politely said he could manage. He stuffed his few provisions roughly into the carrier bag, paid and began making his way back through the crowded mall towards the car park, with thoughts of gorging himself on angel cake.

It was when he was half way down the mall that disaster struck, in the form of a self-destructing carrier bag, which he must have ripped as he packed. One minute the bag was full, the next it was empty, the contents seeming to take on a life of their own, scattering over the entire mall. Cursing himself for not allowing the checkout girl to pack for him and realising it was a lot more difficult than it looked, he bent down to pick up his groceries. As he retrieved his carton of milk, which fortunately hadn't split, a large boot launched his angel cake even further down the mall, where an equally large shoe trod on it. The events of the day came to a head and Ed finally lost it.

'That's my fucking tea you're playing football with, you prick!' he bellowed down the mall, making him the centre of attention. The man came striding towards him, nostrils flaring eyes boring into him. Bloody hell, Ed thought, now I've got to have a fight over a piece of bloody cake. His would-be opponent stopped a few feet away at the same time a hand was placed on Ed's shoulder from behind.

'Calm down, sir and watch your language,' a soft female voice said.

Ed turned and looked up into the face of a policewoman. 'Sorry officer. I've had a really bad day and this was the final straw,' he said apologetically.

'What about I help you with picking this lot up and you tell me all about it?'

Bloody hell a copper with compassion, Ed thought. After retrieving all the items, including the angel cake, which was now shaped like a wedge of cheese, they sat down on a bench that wasn't occupied by exhausted pensioners or loitering school kids.

'Thanks for your help and for not arresting me for foul and abusive language,' he said, thinking that she was quite attractive.

'So, why has your day been so bad, then?' she asked, trying to stifle a smirk.

'You sure you want to know?'

She nodded and gave him a smile, 'Go for it.'

'Well, you asked for it. I woke up this morning. Correction, my dog woke me up at the crack of dawn, by licking my ears. My own fault as I forgot to shut him in, on account I'd had a few beers. Needless to say, this morning I had the hangover from hell. When I eventually start feeling well enough to go out, I get cut up by some old fart, who proceeds to drive at 20mph. I couldn't over take and sat behind him all the way to the car park. Then, he had the audacity to wait for hours to get the first available parking spot. I had to wade my way through a shuffling mass of pensioners to get to the bank, where I'm forced to walk in the road by two fat geriatrics. Then my shopping bag breaks open and some bugger uses my angel cake as a football. But you know what really concerns me? I think I'm turning into my dad! Jesus, what a thought. I'm Ed by the way,' he said, extending his hand.

'PC Moore,' she said, giving him a firm handshake.

'And does PC Moore have a first name?'

'Angela. And does Ed have a surname?'

'Case. Are you a real policewoman or one of those community support officers?'

She gave a friendly laugh. 'I'm a real one, why do you ask?'

'Dunno. You seem too nice to be a real one. You didn't arrest me, you smile and laugh and you're actually human.' he said, smiling back.

'I'll take that as a compliment,' she said 'Not everyone in the force is a baton wielding, officious, egomaniac you know. And who knows I may still caution you.'

'I know you're not. I've got a mate, who's a DCI,' he informed her.

'DCI?' she replied, sounding impressed. 'You could put a word in for me. I could do with losing this uniform.'

'I could do that but you'd have to emigrate to Cornwall, though. He's ex Met and got shipped out to the sticks, because his bosses didn't like his lack of political correctness. He's what you'd call "old school," but not in a corrupt way. Anyway, his bosses in the Met decided he was a bit of a throwback and suggested he might like a less high profile place. This was when the Met were under pressure to clean up their act. He moans like hell about being stuck in the back of beyond, as he calls it, but I think he secretly likes it. And by the way, I'd like to see you out of that uniform, too. Something tells me that uniform is hiding the body of an angel,' he said, hoping he hadn't gone too far. She laughed, which was a good sign.

'Are you flirting with me, Mr. Case?' she asked with a smile.

Ed gave her his best smile back. 'Could you do me a favour and wait here, while I go and beg the card shop for a new carrier bag?' he asked.

She said she would and Ed wandered into the shop, returning a few minutes later with a carrier bag.

'I was wondering. Would you like to come to dinner with me tonight?' he asked, once he had sat down.

'How do you know there is no Mr. Moore waiting for me at home?'

'I don't but you seem too happy to be married so I'm taking a chance,' he replied grinning.

She smiled kindly. 'No thanks. I've been on my feet all day. When I finish my shift I'm going to have a nice long soak in the bath and relax with a book and a glass of wine.'

'Ok, another time maybe?' he said, giving her his best cheeky grin.

'We'll see.'

'Well, that's not quite as bad as no, I suppose. I'll ask you again next time I see you. Enjoy your night in,' he said, standing up with his new bag of shopping and walking off. He turned round to see her walking off in the other direction and noticed he was right, under that uniform was the body of an angel.

By the time he reached his car, his hangover had gone

completely and he felt extremely pleased with himself. Considering he was a little ring rusty, it wasn't a bad effort at chatting her up. He decided then he would venture up the town again tomorrow to renew his acquaintance with PC Moore. Attrition, that's all it would take. Keep asking and eventually you get a result, even it is just to shut you up.

CHAPTER 5

Ed unlocked the boot of his car with the remote and threw his shopping in. He turned towards the driver's door and noticed a young woman sitting on the railing of the car park perimeter wall, her legs dangling over the side into eight storeys of nothing. His first instinct was to ignore her, let her sort out her own personal demons, just as he had once. Guilt, however, wouldn't allow him to, so he closed the driver's door and walked towards her, cursing under his breath.

He wasn't quite sure how he would handle this one. Should he go for the no nonsense approach and tell her to stop being stupid, get over it and move on, or go for the softly-softly approach? Unsure on what would be best, he did neither. Looking over the edge to the road below, a respectful distance away, he turned and faced her. From what little he could see, it was obvious from the red rimmed eyes and streaked face, she had been crying, something that most men are ill-equipped to deal with. Ed was no exception, falling squarely into that category.

'Jesus Christ! That's a long way down.' he said loudly, looking down to the street below. No response. No acknowledgement he was even there. She just stared straight ahead, unblinking, absorbed in her own little world. Undeterred, Ed carefully put his leg over the wall and sat astride the railing. She definitely had the right idea sitting facing out. The square railing was digging painfully between his cheeks. He tried to lean forward to relieve the pressure by taking his weight on his hands, which proved impossible as his cheeks were gripping on like limpets in case he fell. He tentatively inched his way forward and put his hand out.

'Hi, I'm Ed,' he said, his voice shaking slightly.

'Piss off,' she told him quietly.

'I'd love to but unfortunately, my arse is gripping this railing too tightly. I'm afraid to say, I'm not going anywhere.' Again this didn't gain a response. It was time to try a different approach. What that would be, he didn't have a clue. 'Quite a crowd you've got down there. See that fat bloke from the building site? The guy with the wispy, ginger hair, with no shirt on under his fluorescent waistcoat. You can't miss him. He's the one shouting something, beckoning you down with his hands, trying to get you to jump. Do you really want to give him the satisfaction of seeing you throw yourself off?' Very slowly he placed his hand on top of hers. She didn't jump, which was a relief and she didn't move her hand away, which could only be deemed as progress.

'Look, I won't pretend to know what's gone on in your life to make you want to kill yourself but believe me, if you jump, it'll be worse. You'll launch yourself off and immediately regret it. You're still young. What are you, early twenties, something like that? You've got the next fifty or sixty years ahead of you, if not more. OK, you might be really screwed up for a while. Who knows, you may never get over it completely but isn't that worth a risk, rather than ending it all now?' Ed was quite pleased with that. Not that it seemed to have any effect but he hoped she was at least thinking about it. 'What about, you get down and I'll drive you home or wherever you want to go and we can talk about it?' he said, not knowing if mentioning home was a good move.

'My mum told me never to go with strange men,' she said quietly.

This wasn't the response he was hoping for but speaking was definitely a good sign; unless of course she said goodbye and jumped.

'I'm not strange. I'm one of the good guys. Look, what's the worst that could happen? I take you back to my place and stave your head in with a hammer and bury you under the patio. No worse than jumping, I'd say, but at least you'd get a nice cup of tea out of it. You still get to die, without having to think about jumping. A right result all round, I'd say,' Ed said, hoping it came out as jokily as he intended it to sound.

'You're weird.'

'Probably, but what about it? The cup of tea, forget about the hammer. I promise only to stave your head in if you ask me nicely. Come on, my arse can't take any more.'

'Come on, weirdo,' she said and jumped down into the car park. Ed's heart leapt, thinking she was jumping the other way. As it was, he was left sitting there looking foolish. He glanced down at the crowd, which was now already slowly dispersing. The boisterous, ginger bastard, looking more than a little disgruntled as he sloped off back to the building site.

She was already sitting in the passenger seat as he climbed into the driver's seat and wriggled around, relishing the soft upholstery as his buttocks slowly lost their right angles.

'Do you have a name?' he asked her.

'Emma James. Just shut up and drive, you talk too much.'

Ed could do shut up and drive. This one was going to be a right bundle of laughs, he thought to himself, as he turned on the ignition. He switched off the radio, just in case, by some uncanny coincidence, the theme tune from M.A.S.H. came on the radio. The last thing he needed was someone singing about suicide being painless. He put the car in gear and headed for home.

CHAPTER 6

They drove home in silence, which Ed found uncomfortable but constantly remind himself conversation was not an option. Fortunately, it was only a short journey home. He pulled onto the drive, turned off the ignition and sprung the boot. Emma exited the car without saying a word and stood with her back to him, facing the front door. Ed retrieved his shopping from the boot. Despite the short journey the contents of his carrier bag, once again, had made a bid for freedom and were scattered across the entire area of the boot, a reminder of his less than satisfactory excursion.

He took the opportunity to appraise Emma whilst re-capturing his groceries. He started at her bottom, which looked to be quite pert under the crumpled, white, cotton skirt she was wearing, which finished just above the knees, revealing a rather shapely pair of calves. The heavy, white trainers she wore were dirty and didn't really go with what she was wearing but then what did he know about ladies fashion. He worked his way back up, lingering on her bottom and deciding that it was indeed pert, before appraising the top half. She was short, very short in fact, around five-foot-two-inches. Her hair was auburn, just about shoulder length, which rested on a white, three quarter sleeve, V-neck T-shirt. Further inspection was thwarted as Emma turned round and gave him a look that conveyed, get a move on. Ed closed the boot and joined her at the door.

'I've got a dog, by the way. His name's Fat Boy and he's rather friendly. Just thought I'd warn you. Not everyone likes dogs.'

As expected this didn't prompt a response so he put the key in the door and pushed it open, allowing Emma to enter first. Fat Boy could be heard before he was seen. He hurtled from the kitchen, through the dining room and into the living room, skidding across the wooden floor, before finally arriving into the hallway, where he promptly stuffed his nose into Emma's crotch and took a deep sniff, wagging his tail dementedly.

'He does that to everyone. It's just his way of saying hello,' Ed told her, slightly embarrassed by Fat Boy's behaviour. He was actually very well trained but this was one habit Ed hadn't been able to break. Ed thought about making a joke about how hard it is to rehabilitate a crack addict but decided against it.

Emma stroked the dog and made a fuss of him, before he lost interest and went to see his master or, to be exact, went to his master's carrier bag to inspect the contents. Unimpressed, he turned around and trotted back out to the kitchen. Ed walked into the living-room, uncomfortable that Emma still hadn't said a word.

'Do you want tea, coffee or something stronger?' he asked, pleased she would have to break the vow of silence she seemed to have taken since getting into the car.

'Coffee please,' was her quiet response.

'OK. Make yourself at home. I'll go and put the kettle on.'

Once in the kitchen he opened the back door to let the dog out and let some cooler, fresher air into the house and emptied the carrier bag onto the worktop.

'Do you want milk or sugar?' he shouted, hoping it was loud enough to travel through to the living-room.

'Just milk,' was the quiet response from behind him, making him jump and throw a spoonful of coffee granules across the work surface.

'Jesus. You're a bit light on your feet. You nearly gave me a heart attack,' he said, his heart racing.

'Can I have a glass of water, please?'

Ed got a pint glass from the cupboard and filled it up from the tap and handed it to her. She drank it down in one go and put the glass on the draining board, smiling.

'Want a piece of cake?' he asked, holding up the battered angel cake.

She shook her head and wrinkled her nose up at it. To be

honest, Ed couldn't blame her. It really was a sorry sight, and he knew that he probably wouldn't bother either so unwrapped it and threw it out for the birds. Unfortunately for the birds, Fat Boy's reaction time hadn't diminished with age and they never got a look in, as he devoured it in two greedy bites. Ed finished making the coffees and handed one to Emma.

'We can sit in the garden or go into the living-room. It's up to you,' Ed said and immediately cursed himself for not asking a question that had to be answered. Emma turned and headed back to the living-room and sat down in one of the armchairs.

'You're a woman of few words,' he said, taking the armchair opposite. This was answered with a shrug of the shoulders. The silent routine was beginning to annoy him but what did he expect, it was only a few minutes ago she was going to kill herself.

'I'm not trying to pry but if you want to talk about, you know, what you were going to do, I'm happy to listen. If you don't, I'm happy to talk about anything, because not saying anything is doing my head in,' he said with a smile.

At least she appeared to be thinking about it. Her brow did seem to furrow ever so slightly, but before she did say anything, Fat Boy came trotting in and stood in front of her, demanding to be stroked, and was not disappointed. He flopped down contentedly at her feet and rolled over on to his back, trying his luck for a belly rub and, again, was rewarded for his efforts. Ed looked on smiling, amused at how few people could resist a cute dog, Emma being no exception. He also couldn't help but notice she was flashing quite a lot of cleavage as she bent forward and couldn't stop himself from staring down her gaping top. Unfortunately for Ed, Emma couldn't help but notice either and sat up quickly, snapping her legs together and putting her hand across the top of her T-shirt.

'Sorry. That obvious, was it? I couldn't help myself. When I said I was one of the good guys earlier, I didn't say I was perfect,' he said in lame defence, feeling like he just been caught shoplifting.

'Where's your wife?' she asked coldly, looking round the room. Ed hoped, not for an escape route.

'You can tell I'm married, just from looking at the colour of the walls and a few ornaments?'

'No. I can tell all that from the wedding ring you're wearing,' she told him in a firm voice.

'I'm not married,' he replied in a see, you're not so bloody clever tone.

'I see, so you just wear a wedding ring as a deterrent because you get so many women throwing themselves at you, is that it?' she said, taking offence to Ed's tone.

'Actually, my wife's dead,' he told her, thinking it would mellow her, which it did.

'Oh. Look I'm sorry. I'm being a right cow. You must have really loved her if you still wear her ring.' she said sincerely.

'It's OK. I hated her,' Ed began. Enjoying the look that Emma gave him. 'I didn't shed any tears when she died. Everyone told me she was only interested in my…well, everyone told me I was making a mistake and they were right. I only wear the ring as a reminder not to get taken for a mug again,' he said bitterly.

'How long ago was this?'

'She's been dead four years now. We were married not even two years and she had an affair with the fitter who was putting this wooden floor down. He wasn't happy just to lay the floor; he had to lay the wife as well.'

'How did she die, if you don't mind me asking?'

'Don't worry, I didn't kill her if that's what you're wondering. Infidelity killed her.' On seeing her perplexed look, he continued. 'One evening, they drove out to Epping Forest in his van and whilst they were in the back doing what lovers do, the handbrake broke. The van wasn't left in gear and it rolled down a gulley. The police aren't entirely sure what happened but they think some of the lacquer or other flammable stuff he had in there spilt and probably got ignited by a cigarette. The van when up in flames along with my marriage.'

'Wow! You're not joking?' she said with a look of incredulity.

'No. Her death certificate is framed and in the downstairs toilet, if you want to have a look? What really galled me was paying for the cremation, when she was already burnt to a crisp. I was at least expecting a discount,' he said with a chuckle, although Emma didn't seem to appreciate his dry sense of humour. 'Just me and the dog since,' he added with a smile, noticing her discomfort.

Well that seems to have killed the conversation, Ed thought, as they both sat there in silence. Emma bolt upright and knees seemingly super glued together, in case she gave him another opportunity to leer over her, which suited him as he was still feeling suitably embarrassed.

'How come you're not working today?' she asked, breaking the deafening silence.

'After my wife died, I had a life style reassessment. Perhaps a premature mid-life crisis; who knows?' He did, but it wasn't something he wanted to go into. There were some aspects of his life even those closest to him didn't know about. He wasn't about to pour his heart out to a complete stranger. 'I decided I hated commuting to London every day, getting squashed against the train window by some lard-arse who needed a seat and half and working with a bunch of people that, on the whole, I didn't like. Too busy looking good and kissing the right arses to care about doing a good job. You know the sort? I took voluntary redundancy and decided to do something I wanted to do and enjoyed. I now buy up houses that can't sell because they're in such a state. I do them up and sell them on at a bit of a profit. It's great fun, and the beauty of it is, I do what I want, when I want. At the moment I don't have one on the go. I finished one last month and haven't seen anything suitable to buy yet. What about you?'

She paused as if calculating the response to give. Whether she was looking for a suitable lie or not Ed didn't know and wasn't really bothered. Even a lie would be better than silence.

'I finished university last summer and decided to take a year out before looking for work. I studied art and am a reasonable painter and would like to do that for a living but it's not something that will make enough to live off. To be honest, I haven't got a clue what I'll do,' she said eventually, not enjoying the silence either.

Ed decided that it was probably the truth, unless she was an accomplished liar, but first impressions told him she wasn't, just economical with the facts. Not so different from himself, really.

'Are you hungry, by the way?' Ed asked, deciding he was getting peckish and regretting throwing the angel cake to the birds.

'I'm starving. I haven't eaten since breakfast yesterday,' she replied.

'Good. Me too. I'm not going to insult a guest by giving them pie and chips from the freezer and I don't have any meat that doesn't need defrosting but there's a nice pub five minutes away that does fantastic food. How does that sound?'

'Sounds great but I'm not going anywhere looking like this. I'm filthy and I stink. I spent last night sleeping rough in an alleyway, using black sacks full of rubbish to keep warm. Thanks but no thanks. Can't you get a take away?'

Ed tried not to look surprised and decided to ignore the remark on where she slept last night, thinking she would have elaborated if she wanted to. He looked at her more closely and noticed she did look a bit on the dishevelled side. Her hair was in need a good wash and brush, her face was streaked from where she had been crying earlier and her clothes were grubby. Ed had missed all this previously, as he only really looked at her bum and cleavage. Everything else had evaporated from his vision as he focused on the interesting bits.

'Say no, if you like but my wife was about the same size as you, I think. A couple of inches taller but slim, like you.' It always paid to creep. 'All her stuff is still where she left it. I moved out into another bedroom as I had less stuff. The room is en-suite so you can shower and pick a new wardrobe and we can go get a nice steak or something. How about it? Don't worry, there isn't a Bates Motel hole in the shower wall that I can spy on you through and the bedroom door has a lock on it.'

Emma seemed to study him before she nodded, which surprised him as he was expecting a refusal. He took her upstairs and showed her the room and where everything was. The room had been untouched, apart from being cleaned once every couple of weeks and was exactly the same as the day his wife had died. He meant to take all her belongings to the charity shop but just hadn't got round to it. That was four years ago and it didn't seem important now but one day he would, maybe. The small en-suite still contained all the toiletries that any woman could possibly need and a whole selection of those that every woman has but never uses. After giving her a spare toothbrush and toothpaste, which he knew weren't in there, he left her to it, lingering on the landing and smiling as he heard the bedroom door being locked. He took a quick shower and shaved himself. Thinking perhaps he'd better make an effort he put on a clean pair of trousers and shirt and went downstairs to wait.

Emma walked into the living-room, closing the door behind her and stood looking at Ed, who was sitting in the armchair with his mouth open, hardly believing the transformation. Ed felt compelled to stand up when she entered the room, which made her laugh. The early evening sun was streaming through the window making her hair seem almost ablaze, like a fierce Caribbean sunset. She was wearing a tailored black skirt, with a cream silk blouse tucked into the waistband, which accentuated her curvaceous hips.

'Please don't tell me I remind you of your ex-wife,' she said almost apologetically. 'I knew this was a bad idea. I'll go and get changed.'

'No!' Ed almost shouted. 'I was staring because you look great, not because you remind me of the wife. I don't think I ever saw her in what you're wearing. She had so many clothes; it was one her vices,' Ed said, biting his lip wanting to add 'and cock' but managing not to. 'I'm just glad you got something to fit'.

'It wasn't easy. All the trousers were too long but the skirts were OK. The sleeves on a lot of the tops were too long. The shoes I'm wearing have toilet paper in the toe, as they're a size too big and none of her bras fitted but I manage to find a tight fitting vest to keep it all in place,' she said smiling.

'Well, I must say, you scrub up very well,' he said and he meant it, she looked very good.

'Thanks,' she said clearly pleased with the effect it had on him. 'Are you going to sit there all night with your mouth open or are you going to take me to dinner? I'm bloody starving.'

Ed disappeared into the kitchen, locked up and came back with Fat Boy at his heels. Since his wife had met her untimely demise, Ed and Fat Boy had been inseparable and generally wherever Ed went, Fat Boy went. He tended to sulk if he didn't. The pub had a large beer garden, which meant Fat Boy could come and, as he hadn't been for his afternoon walk, it killed two birds with one stone.

'After you,' Ed said, opening the living-room door for Emma.

'Generous and with good manners,' she complimented him.

'I think you'll find that most men only open doors and let women through first so they can check out their bums. Good manners don't come into it really. It's just a great excuse,' he told her, with a grin. Ed did the same at the front door as Fat Boy, ever eager, decided that he would go first.

'You just want another look at my bum, you pervert,' she jested.

'Don't flatter yourself, it wasn't that good,' he joked back and was rewarded with a slap on the arm. They set off down the road and Emma surprised him by linking her arm through his. It felt good to Ed. It was a long time since he last walked arm in arm or hand in hand with anyone.

CHAPTER 7

The beer garden was empty despite the warm evening, everyone having either eaten earlier or deciding to eat inside, knowing it would quickly cool down. They found a table and within a couple of minutes a waitress brought them menus and took their drinks order. Ed looked at the menu and decided he would have the mixed grill; that being the biggest plate on the menu. It wasn't because he was hungry but if Emma hadn't eaten since breakfast yesterday, she was probably starving and he didn't want her to feel uncomfortable if she chose a big meal and he didn't.

The waitress soon returned with their drinks, both having elected to go for a white wine, and asked them if they were ready to order. Emma chose the mixed grill so clearly she was famished and Ed ordered the same.

'Anything else?' the waitress asked.

'Yes please,' Ed said 'I'd also like a medium 16oz rump steak.'

The waitress stared at him as if to say, "Well, aren't you a greedy, fat bastard, sir" but didn't.

'Would you like chips or potatoes with that, sir?' she asked politely.

'Neither thanks. It's for my dog. I'm not that much of a pig. I saw the way you looked at me then.'

'I did wonder,' she said, obviously embarrassed. 'Lucky dog,' she added before walking off.

They spent their time making small talk. Ed found out that Emma was twenty-two and lived in Cambridge. However, she didn't seem to want to talk about her and steered the conversation back to Ed at every possible opportunity.

'So, why did you name your dog Fat Boy? He doesn't look fat

to me. Has he been on a diet?'

'Well, a friend of my parents had a Retriever bitch and decided to breed her. She sold all the litter bar Fat Boy, who she intended to keep. It turned out he had a really bad case of worms and would probably need an operation. She didn't have insurance and couldn't afford it and was going to have him put to sleep. My parents got to hear of it and couldn't bear the idea of a healthy dog being put down so they took it off her hands. He was a right state, really weak with a big, fat belly full of worms, hence Fat Boy. Anyway, to cut a long story short, he had a course of treatment, which didn't solve the problem, and finally an operation, and here he is.'

'That's really nice. How come you have him now?'

'My parents died in a coach crash when I was twenty-five. They were on the way back to the airport whilst on holiday. I was looking after him so he was part of my inheritance. He was only about a year old at the time. He's nearly ten now.'

'Sorry. I seem to be asking all the wrong questions. You've not been very lucky, have you?' she said, feeling awkward.

'Don't worry about it. I was devastated at the time but it was a long time ago and I'm over it. I still miss them but hey-ho, life goes on.'

The waitress arriving with their meals saved any prolonged silence and further awkwardness. They ordered more drinks and she brought those back, along with the extra steak for Fat Boy. She waited and watched as Ed picked it up and dropped it into Fat Boy's salivating mouth. Ed was sure she only stayed to watch, just to ensure he wasn't lying and trying to cover up his own greed. Satisfied, she walked briskly back to the bar, leaving them to enjoy their meal. Ed was hungrier than he thought and demolished his, leaving nothing for the expectant Fat Boy, who finished his steak in seconds and was looking for more. He was even more disappointed as Emma did likewise, leaving nothing for him; so he resumed his position curled up at his master's feet.

'Having a dessert?' he asked.

'No thanks. I couldn't eat another thing. I'm struggling to finish my wine. That was great by the way, thanks.'

'That's OK, you're welcome. I'm off to the gents,' he informed her and headed towards the bar leaving her and Fat Boy behind.

After visiting the gents, he settled the bill at the bar and headed back outside, having made up his mind to find out why she had almost taken her own life, earlier that day.

'Tell me to mind my own business, if you like. I won't be offended. I'm just curious what were you doing in the multi-storey earlier, apart from the obvious.'

Emma looked at him and nodded, deciding whether or not she wanted to tell him and if she did, how much. In the end, she thought, perhaps she owed him that much. After all, he had been kind and she had been a bit of a cow.

'I was living with my fiancé. He lost his job became a bit depressed and started becoming abusive. At first it was just verbally, which I could handle. Then it became physical. He could be so cruel one minute and the next he was full of regret, telling me he loved me. I was torn between trying to help him and leaving. In the end I stayed, which turned out to be a big mistake.

I think he knew I was on the verge of leaving and he begged me to stay, which I did. He became paranoid and locked me in the bedroom so I couldn't leave. I was a prisoner in my own house, only allowed out the bedroom to go to the toilet or take a shower and always with him standing guard. He used to bring me meals, when he remembered. Some days he wouldn't even do that. Then, the day before yesterday, I pulled myself together and managed to escape. I couldn't go to any friends as he knows them all and would come and find me. I've no relatives as my parents moved back to South Africa a couple of years ago so I had nowhere to go.

When I got outside the house I just ran and ran and ran. I don't think I know where I was going or what I was going to do. I just wanted to be as far away as possible. I ended up in the centre of Cambridge and slept rough in an alley at the back of some shops, trying to keep warm between the rubbish bags.

In the morning I headed for the station and jumped on the first train that I saw, which just happened to be going to London. I noticed the ticket inspector walking down the train so I moved to the carriage furthest away but it wasn't a busy train and he was just coming up to my carriage when we stopped. I got out quickly, not even knowing where I was. It all got a bit much for me and, well, you know the rest.'

Ed was shocked. He looked at Emma, who sat there

impassively, no tears, only a sad look on her face. Ed was lost for words. How anyone could be so cold and callous was beyond him. Instinct told him there was a lot more to this story than she was telling but she was holding back. What she left out must be pretty horrific, he thought, as what she told him was horrific. His own marriage had been a complete sham but he never raised a hand to his wife, despite her infidelity. It was bloody hard. There were days when he could have throttled the bitch but he was taught never to hit a girl, even when provoked.

'Do you think you would have jumped?'

'I don't know. I wanted to. I came close but lost my nerve and had to build up the courage again. I'd been there about half an hour and must have changed my mind a hundred times. I glad I didn't, though.'

'Me too. The road below would have been sealed off and I'd never have got home.' Ed said, trying to lighten the mood.

'You're all heart,' she said with a weak smile. Clearly not yet used to Ed's sense of humour.

Ed looked up and noticed two men looking in their direction, talking animatedly. One was tall and lean, wearing a black, leather sports jacket. The other was a bull of a man, shorter than his companion, and wore a grey hoodie with the hood down. His shaved head seemed massive and sat on a neck as thick as one of Ed's thighs. They looked like trouble and were heading his way. Here we go, Ed thought, the perfect end to a perfect day.

'I know you, don't I?' the taller one said.

'Don't think so,' Ed replied.

'I wasn't fucking talking to you, was I? I was talking to her,' he said pointing at Emma, which as far as pointing went was quite menacing.

'No,' she replied 'I'm just up for the day visiting my cousin.'

'I know you. I never forget a face or a pair of tits,' he said, sniggering and leering at her.

Ed was marvelling at his memory. In his youth he would try and sleep with anything that moved, no matter what size, colour or age so long as it was legal but he couldn't remember what any of their breasts looked like. He was also bristling, knowing that this was quite possibly going to get messy.

'Look mate....' Ed started but never finished.

'I ain't your fucking mate. Get it?' he fired back quickly, giving Ed his most menacing look yet.

'OK. All I was going to say is that I think you're mistaken. She's just up from London for the day. She doesn't live round here,' Ed finished.

'So, now you're calling me a liar? My friend here takes offence at things like that and is liable to cut you open, so you wanna watch what you're saying.'

Ed looked at the other man, who had his hands in the pockets of his hoodie. He looked capable and dangerous, despite the fact a lot of his muscle had gone to flab. He heard a metallic click and watched as the thug in the hoodie smiled maliciously. Ed knew he just opened a flick-knife, which was concealed in his pocket. He heard that sound once before. It wasn't a happy memory and he had the scar to prove it. His mind was racing now, assessing the situation and what to do next.

The taller one clicked his fingers several times before announcing 'You're Danny's girl. I knew I recognised you. Danny isn't going to be happy, knowing you're seeing someone behind his back. Wouldn't like to be in your shoes mate,' he said looking at Ed.

Ed fought the urge to tell him, calling him "mate" just contradicted his statement earlier of Ed not being a mate but held his tongue. Instead he pulled his mobile phone out and began to dial.

'What the fuck are you doing?' he spat.

'I'm just phoning a good mate of mine who just happens to be on duty tonight. He's a DS in the police.' The phone picked up and Ed spoke loudly. 'Dave, its Ed... Yeah I'm OK, it has been a while... I know you're probably busy but I need your help, I've got a bit of bother...Nice one appreciate it. Look can you send someone down to the Fox and Hounds...That's right, the one on the London Road...Got two guys here, one with a knife so it's quite urgent or I wouldn't be bothering you...OK, thanks mate. I owe you one...Cheers. Bye.'

Ed kept his eyes on the two thugs throughout his conversation. He gave them a smile that said, what are you going to do next? They looked at each other and shrugged. The distant wail of a siren approaching seemed to help them decide.

'I'll be sure to tell Danny where to find you' he said, looking at Emma. 'And next time I see you' he added staring at Ed 'I'm gonna enjoy taking slices off you, so watch your back.'

They jogged over to the car park and got in a black BMW with tinted windows, which made Ed smile; he hadn't expected anything less.

'Time to go, Emma,' Ed said with a degree of urgency.

They walked home in silence, each with other things on their minds. Ed opened the front door and didn't even bother to make a joke about allowing Emma to go first. The happy mood from earlier had faded and been replaced by sombre reflection. The answerphone was beeping when they walked into the living room, which Ed ignored.

'Don't know about you but I could use a drink. Nightcap?'

'OK. White wine, please. Aren't you going to listen to that? It could be important.'

'It won't be. Can you push play and I'll do the drinks. If you think it's important let me know and I'll come and have a listen,' he said, walking into the kitchen.

Emma pressed play and listened to the message. 'Dave, its Ed... Yeah I'm OK it has been a while... I know you're probably busy but I need your help, I've got a bit of bother...Nice one appreciate it. Look can you send someone down to the Fox and Hounds...That's the one on the London Road...Got two guys here one with a knife so it's quite urgent or I wouldn't be bothering you...OK, thanks mate. I owe you one...Cheers. Bye"

'I suppose you think you're clever?' Emma stated, slightly annoyed.

'Not really. There's a joint fire brigade and ambulance depot at the top of the hill. I hadn't heard one go by for a while so thought it was worth a stab,' he replied, laughing at the unintended pun.

'And if that didn't work, what was plan B, smart arse?' she said, now quite annoyed.

'Well, there were two options. The first would have been to take out the guy with the knife, as he was the immediate danger. Then take out the one in the black jacket. Option two, of course, would have been to run away screaming like a big girl's blouse,' he said, grinning from ear to ear.

'Option two, more like,' she said, back to just slightly annoyed.

'Why's that, then?'

'You're built more like a run-away type of person.'

'I'm deeply hurt that you think I'm built like a wimp. I'll have you know, I could have taken them out any time. Here take this,' he said, handing her a glass of wine 'Inside or out?'

She took the glass of wine and stepped out into the garden. Ed switched on the patio lights and followed her out. Her mood swings were beginning to annoy him a little bit but he could understand the reasons a little better, since she revealed what she had been through in the past few weeks. It still didn't make it any less annoying though. Ed sat opposite her, not wanting to sit next to her and make her feel claustrophobic or intimidated. Despite not representing a threat, he thought, maybe she didn't trust him enough to know that. She looked very fragile with her arms crossed, almost hugging herself, as if she were cold. Her face was blank and emotionless. Ed walked back inside and returned, putting a fleece jacket over her shoulders before sitting back down opposite.

'You looked cold,' he said by way of explanation.

'Thanks. You're sweet.'

Well, at least she doesn't seem mad at me, Ed thought, unless she was a very good actress.

'I've been thinking what to do about you. I can't take to you to one of your friends, because Danny will find you there. I'm assuming those two thugs back at the pub were right and Danny is the fiancé?' When Emma nodded, he continued. 'OK. Your parents are in South Africa and I assume your passport is with all your other stuff at Danny's so I can't buy you a plane ticket and send you home.'

'You'd buy me a ticket to South Africa, just like that? You hardly know me,' she said, looking at him suspiciously.

'I told you, I'm one of the good guys. If white hats were fashionable I'd be wearing one. Unfortunately, these days a white hat usually means you're a poof. Anyway, until about half an hour or so ago, I was going to suggest you stay here for a few days or as long as you like, come to that. As long as you need to or want to but, potentially, Danny could be sniffing around in a few days so it might not be a good idea.' Emma nodded again 'So here's an idea. I have a caravan in Cornwall, something else I inherited along with Fat Boy. These last few years I've spent the entire summer down there. I work all winter and spend summer there. I've got a few really good friends down there from way back and I know you'll like them. How do you fancy a couple of weeks or longer, if you want, in Cornwall?'

'Sounds nice but aren't you forgetting something really important here? I don't have any money. In fact, I don't have anything, apart from the clothes I walked in here with. I can hardly spend two weeks in Cornwall sponging off you and wearing the same clothes for a fortnight. Get real,' she replied, unimpressed.

Ed nodded and smiled broadly 'Do you trust me? Maybe not entirely but maybe just a little bit. Maybe just enough take a leap of faith, leave all the arrangements to me and don't worry about trivial things like that.'

There was a long pause as Emma narrowed her eyes and looked directly in Ed's, who was still smiling back.

'I think so,' she finally said, although there was a hint of suspicion in her eyes, which Ed ignored. If he was in her position, he too would be slightly suspicious.

'Right sorted. We leave as early as we can in the morning as we need to make a stop off to sort you out,' Ed said, more than a little pleased she had agreed.

Emma laughed and gave him a smile. 'You're weird,' she said. 'Very sweet but very weird. I think I'm going to bed now, if you don't mind. Nice wine by the way.'

'Before you go, and please don't take offence, I've left some money on the radiator shelf in the hallway. If you decide you want to leave during the night, please take it. I won't be offended and I'll know you only took it because you need it. OK?'

Emma walked round the table, kissed Ed on the cheek and smiling, told him she would see him in the morning.

Before turning in himself, Ed switched on the computer and sent a few e-mails, arranging to meet up with Chris and Jack on Friday night at the clubhouse and another to the site manager, to ensure that the caravan was cleaned and aired in the morning. Next he printed off street maps of Cambridge and spent a few minutes trying to memorise some of the areas and streets. He had two pieces of the jigsaw but needed another two. He would get those in time and then, Danny would be history.

CHAPTER 8

Ed was having trouble sleeping and lay there with his eyes closed counting sheep, glad he wasn't Welsh. What the hell did they count when they wanted to get some sleep? He heard footsteps on the landing and hoped it wasn't Emma making a midnight flit. He was quite looking forward to Cornwall with some company for a change. The footsteps stopped outside his bedroom door. He held his breath. The door opened and the footsteps continued to the far side of the bed. Emma climbed in next to him. His heart began to race. Happy days!

'Hi,' he said quietly.

'Sorry, did I wake you?'

'No, I couldn't sleep.'

'Me neither. Look, I'm not... just hold me,' she said, moving closer to him.

Oh great. Just hold me, she says. Christ. She needs to hold on to me before I pole vault myself out the window, Ed thought.

'Are you wearing anything?' he asked.

'I found a nightie in one of the drawers,' she informed him. 'Why are you wearing anything?'

'Only a bloody big hole in the mattress, at the moment,' he mumbled.

Emma giggled and apologised.

'I was hoping you'd be awake. I wanted to tell you something, which might explain my behaviour. I really appreciate what you've done today, you've been really kind and generous and, well, I've been a pain.'

'You've been OK, considering what you've been through. I think you've handled things pretty well.'

'There's more to tell. What I told you was the truth,' she said snuggling into his body, placing her head on his chest. Ed tried to manoeuver himself into a position where his groin was as far away from Emma as possible, not wanting to embarrass himself – four years was a long time. 'Danny lost his job through drugs. He started taking a little cocaine, just recreational after work and at parties and clubs but it took over. His work was affected and he got sacked. He couldn't get another job, got depressed and took more and more cocaine. Before he knew it he was up to his eyes in debt and his supplier came calling, threatening him with all sorts. He was a mess and even asked me to go on the game to bring in some money to pay him off. I refused, of course. That's when the abuse started. Him saying I didn't care about him and if I did, I'd do as he asked.' Ed could feel her tears trickling down his chest as she spoke. He stroked her hair and pulled her closer to him. 'Then the abuse started getting physical and after a while he kept me locked in the bedroom, like I told you. I think he drugged me. I don't know what with but I remember coming round and he was on top of me raping me, while his friend was recording the whole thing. It started becoming more regular, every night towards the end and not just Danny. Some nights there would be three or four of them, taking it in turns and making me do things. It was so humiliating and I hated myself for it but I couldn't do anything about it. I overheard them one night talking about it. They were streaming the video onto a special website, as well as making DVDs of the whole thing to pay off his dealer. Although, by this time the debt was already paid and he was in partnership with him, as he was making so much money using me. That was the final straw for me. One afternoon, when I knew he was out, I smashed the window and used a couple of sheets tied together to make a rope. I climbed out and got as near to the ground as possible before I jumped and ran. The rest you know. I just wanted you to know. I think I owe you that.'

Ed didn't know what to say, his eyes were stinging with tears on the brink of spilling down his face. He said nothing but hugged her and kissed the top of her head. When he stopped stroking her hair, she asked him not to carry on. Ed was so angry that anyone could be so cruel; especially to someone they loved or once loved. Danny was in for a shock when he finally caught up with him. He was going to wish he had never been born. Ed would make sure of that. He lay there and continued to stroke her hair until sleep finally came.

CHAPTER 9

Ed awoke, stretched, yawned and farted loudly, muttering 'shit' when he remembered he might still have company, something he wasn't used to unless you included Fat Boy, of course. He opened one eye slowly and gazed across at the bed, thankful it was empty and he hadn't woken Emma. His elation soon turned to regret, as he realised the possibility Emma decided to make a run for it in the early hours.

He threw on his clothes that were heaped on the floor beside the bed and made his way to the bathroom, where he urinated and splashed some water over his face to wake himself up. The door to the guest room was wide-open and he noticed that the bed was remade. On reaching the bottom of the stairs, he saw the money he placed on the radiator shelf was missing, which seemed to confirm that she decided to go. He was surprised he felt quite sad about it, despite having only known her a few hours. He liked her and was looking forward to spending some time with her in Cornwall.

When he entered the living room, his sadness turned to panic as Fat Boy wasn't there to greet him as he usually did. Surely she hadn't taken the dog with her! His heart was now beating out of his chest as he hurried into the kitchen. The back door was wide-open and he looked down the garden and saw Emma playing with Fat Boy or the other way round would be closer to the mark. Emma would throw a tennis ball, Fat Boy would run after it and then run away when she tried to take it off him. Ed smiled to himself, marvelling at how resilient she was. At this moment in time, she looked like she didn't have a care in the world, a far cry from the traumas she had been subjected to by Danny and his so called friends over the last few months.

Just thinking about Danny spoilt his mood and he began thinking very dark thoughts on how he could extract his revenge for what he done to Emma. Should he do this directly or indirectly? The direct approach would be far more satisfying but probably not the most sensible thing to do and could lead to a lot of unpleasantness. There was plenty of time to work out what to do, because at the moment he only had a first name and the city he lived in. When he had the last two pieces of information he needed, he would decide.

Emma saw him standing at the door and ran down the path towards him, Fat Boy bouncing around at her heels. She was wearing a loose fitting, white summer dress, which had a full-skirt. She looked almost childlike running towards him. Runs like a girl, Ed thought. When she reached him, she threw her arms around his neck and gave him a hug and a kiss on the cheek, completely taking him aback.

'I thought you'd gone,' he said to her.

'Don't worry. The money's on top of the fireplace. I moved it there in case the wind blew it all over the floor when I opened the front door and went out for a walk with Fat Boy,' she replied smiling.

'I wasn't worried about that. I was more concerned you'd left and even more concerned that you'd taken Fat Boy with you, when he didn't come to see me when I walked into the living room.'

'You really think I would've taken your dog?' she said in mock hurt.

'Of course I didn't but it's unusual for him not to jump up at me the minute I come down. Thanks for taking him for a walk by the way. What time did you get up?'

'Don't know. You were snoring like a pig, though so I thought I'd get up. You did say you wanted an early start.'

'I did and I do,' Ed said, realising he was still holding on to her and releasing her. She wasn't what Ed would call beautiful but she was certainly pretty. She had a small, thin face, which tapered to a pointed chin. Her cheekbones were prominent and flushed from running round the garden with Fat Boy as was the tip of her small, sharp nose. She was more what he would call cute, like a little pixie, rather than beautiful, he thought. A combination of her vulnerability and cuteness made him feel very protective towards her, which took him by surprise, having only known her for such a short time.

'Earth calling Ed. Hello, anyone at home,' she asked, waving her hands in front of his face.

Ed smiled at her and kissed her on the forehead. 'Sorry, I was miles away. Just thinking about Cornwall,' he lied 'I don't suppose you fed the dog did you?'

Emma said she hadn't so he fetched his food and fed him, much to Fat Boy's relief, who normally got fed before going for his morning walk, not that he was in any danger of wasting away.

Ed took a quick shower and put on some fresh clothes and was ready to go. He kept a full wardrobe and all other necessities he needed in the caravan so didn't have to pack a bag. He did this for two reasons. One, if he didn't need to pack, it meant he couldn't forget anything and two, he was an idle bastard. The only things he needed to take were a couple of cases of wine and some water for the dog to drink, when they stopped half way.

'Right,' he said to Emma. 'Don't know if you want to take any of the stuff upstairs or not? There is a hair dryer at the caravan but not a lot else so you might want to take the hair straighteners, I noticed you used them yesterday and this morning.' Emma seemed impressed he noticed and it was always good to score the odd brownie point. 'Don't worry about clothes or cosmetics we'll pick them up on the way. Help yourself to any of the jewellery if you want. It's all going to the charity shop when I get round to it and we don't have time to take in the jewellers. OK?'

Emma gave him a quizzical look and sensing that she was going to start asking awkward questions, Ed said 'Don't ask questions. Last night, you said you trusted me so here's the deal. We jump in the car and stop and get what we need. No arguments and no questions or the deals off and I drive you back to Cambridge. How's that sound?' he said, giving her one of his big grins.

Emma wasn't totally happy but agreed. She also wouldn't take any of the jewellery, despite Ed's protest it was all going to charity so she might as well make some use of it. Emma had already looked it over and knew it was expensive from the boxes they were kept in. The diamonds were real as were the sapphires on the rings and necklaces and probably worth a fortune. As much as she liked some of the pieces, she couldn't accept any of it, not even as a loan, in case she lost or broke it.

They were in the car and on the road by eight o'clock, which was better than Ed had hoped for, as he hadn't expected Emma to be up so early. Fat Boy, bored before they even got to the bottom of the road, was curled up in the boot, bracing himself for a few hours sleep.

The conversation flowed as they each tried to find out as much as possible about each other's likes and dislikes, schools, food, music; they explored them all. Ed laughed when Emma said she had never heard of The Bay City Rollers, who were number one in the charts when he was born with "Bye Bye Baby" and laughed even harder, when she said Nick Berry was number one when she was born, with "Every Loser Wins."

When the conversation lulled, Ed sang along to anything on the radio, humming or la-la- la-ing when he didn't know the words, which was quite often, especially when it came to anything too recent. Emma seemed to favour dance music, which Ed hated with a passion, much preferring proper music with real drums, real keyboard and real guitars. Funny, he mused, how age gaps always became more apparent when it came to discussing music from your youth or musical tastes. Right now the eleven-year difference seemed like the Grand Canyon to him.

The journey was passing quite quickly. Even the M25 was relatively free of traffic and Ed managed to average around 70mph, when the signs allowed him and the average speed cameras were not present. Just as they turned onto the M4 the news came on the radio. The newscaster was just getting started on a story about Lord Peter Mandelson, when Emma reached over and switched it off.

'He's not my cup of tea either,' Ed said, slightly perplexed. He looked across at Emma, who was now staring moodily out the window. 'What's up?'

'I never want to hear that name again,' she replied bitterly.

It then clicked with Ed. 'Mandelson. That's Danny's surname, I take it?'

Emma nodded and Ed said a little prayer. Danny Mandelson from Cambridge. Three down, just one to go. Thank you very much. Lady luck was really shining down on him today. He was finding it hard not to shout out or pump his fist in the air. In the end, he did neither and gave her hand a squeeze, more as a thank you, than for reassurance.

At around ten-thirty, they pulled off the M4 and parked up in the multi-storey for the Oracle centre in Reading. Ed made his way to the very top so there was a nice breeze for Fat Boy to enjoy, as he was being left in the car. Ed was initially worried about parking on the top floor, hoping that Emma didn't get upset at revisiting the scene of the crime so to speak. If she was upset, she didn't show it. He reassured her it was safe to leave Fat Boy in the car with all the windows down and nobody would steal it with that smelly old mutt in it. If they did try, they would be in for a shock. Although he looked a placid old mutt, he was quite protective. Not so much with Ed but he loved riding in the car and would make a scene if anyone tried to come to close. He wouldn't bite but he would snarl and bark, which was an excellent deterrent.

A couple of years back, he parked up outside the bank and left the car unlocked. While he was getting his money from the hole in the wall, two opportunist youths decided to try and make off with his car, not noticing Fat Boy in the boot. As soon as the first youth got behind the wheel, Fat Boy was over the back seat and snarling inches away from his ear. The second youth hadn't even got in the car and was already running down the road. Unfortunately, the would-be driver froze and Ed had to physically extract him from the car. Ed thought about giving him a good kicking but the poor lad was so frightened it didn't seem to be appropriate. He laughed all the way home and, if dogs could laugh, he was sure Fat Boy would have been, too.

That sorted, they headed into the shopping centre. Ed told Emma that they could get everything they needed in Debenhams so it should be a quick trip.

'Think of it as being a bit like Supermarket Sweep. Even you must remember that crappy daytime programme with Dale Winton?' he asked her. She did so that was a good start. 'OK. There's only one rule and that's don't look at prices. If you like it, we buy it. Actually, there are two rules. The second is no arguing with me. Any mention of price or sneaking a look at a price tag, and the deals off, I turn the car round and drive you back to Cambridge. You OK with that?'

She was but didn't look too convinced. Ed thought about a strategy on the journey down and decided the only way to get this done without any questions, was to go round quickly and keep the enthusiasm up. It would be interesting but he should get away with it. At least he hoped he would, but wasn't sure how she would react to somebody buying her enough clothes to last for three weeks, without the need to do any washing and ironing.

They reached Debenhams and Ed picked up four of the shopping baskets, which resembled keep nets fishermen use and gave two to Emma. Ed set off at pace, almost dragging Emma along behind him like a petulant child, until he reached the ladies department. After taking a quick look around, he dragged her over to the jeans section, where three pairs later they were off. So far so good. Next were six jumpers of various colours and styles, where Emma took a sneak at a price tag and got a first warning, although she protested she was checking the size. He pulled her round to the next department, where they picked up a dozen T-shirts and Emma picked up her second and penultimate warning. She picked up her third and final warning, when she decided she didn't like a dress because it was overpriced but Ed put it in anyway.

'Ed…' she began but wasn't allowed to finish.

'You've had all your warnings so unless you want to go back to Cambridge, I'd keep quiet and just shop,' he said, giving her a smile and a hug.

Eventually, they reached the department every man hates and always feels conspicuous in, lingerie! Emma wasn't slow on the uptake and could tell Ed was a little embarrassed about walking round the lingerie department and laughed at his discomfort. While Emma was looking at a bra and Ed was pretending to look at something important under his fingernail, anything other than the lingerie, she embarrassed him. Emma held up a sexy, scarlet bra with black lace, wriggled in a very suggestive manner and asked him if it turned him on, as she knew how horny he got when she wore red. This caused everyone in the immediate vicinity to laugh, with the exception of Ed, who went as red as the garment she was holding up.

They had a disagreement on the number of bras and knickers. Ed said she needed one for every day and she said not. In the end they agreed on ten bras and to double up on the knickers, which seemed like a good compromise. They had everything they needed from shoes, coats, jackets, dresses, shorts, sunglasses and handbags and proceeded to the check out. Ed left her there while the assistant scanned the items, returning short while later with a huge suitcase and instructed the assistant to throw them all in there. The bill was just over four thousand pounds, which seemed fairly reasonable to Ed but Emma gave him a look of horror. Ed wagged his finger and reminded her of the agreement.

After paying, they headed for the escalators, Ed grabbing her arm and pulling her along again. Downstairs he headed for the cosmetics department and looked for the assistant wearing the most make-up. Ed was positive anyone who couldn't smile without sloughing would be perfect to ensure Emma didn't skimp on the necessities.

Ed spotted her straight away, sitting on a stool behind the counter, filing her nails. A genuine aeroplane blonde, bleached on top with roots coming through, a sure sign there was a black box down below. Ed told her Emma needed absolutely everything and he would be disappointed to come back in ten minutes to find she only had a lipstick and hairbrush. Ed walked off and returned ten minutes later, not to be disappointed. How women could need so many creams, lotions and accessories was beyond him but he paid for it on his credit card with a smile.

Back at the car, Ed let Fat Boy out to stretch his legs. He trotted over to the nearest 4x4 and urinated against a tyre - good Lad, Ed hated 4x4's. He ambled back and put his front paws in the boot, waiting for Ed to give him a leg up as he wasn't as young as he used to be. Ed duly obliged and got a handful of ginger scrotum for his trouble.

CHAPTER 10

They were back on the M4 around twelve thirty, which was far better than Ed expected. Emma hadn't said a word since getting back to the car, which worried him. He stretched one hand behind him and pulled a carrier bag to the front and gave it to Emma, telling her to put her new mobile phone on charge, using the in car adaptor. She gave him an exasperated look, which Ed saw out the corner of his eye and braced himself.

Emma was brooding over their shopping trip, which all told must have cost Ed around five grand. She had to admit he was clever, keeping the banter up all the way round the shop, sucking her in like a timeshare con artist from the Costa Brava and she had fallen for it. That alone annoyed her but she was becoming suspicious. Why would anyone spend that sort of money on a stranger? Was he some kind of saddo, who fell in love with every woman he met and felt the need to impress her? Well, she didn't feel impressed, she felt smothered. Was there some more devious motive behind his generosity? No normal person, no matter how generous, would go to that length and she wished he would wipe that stupid, grin off his face.

'What do you want from me, Ed?' she asked.

Ed knew from past experience that any question that began or ended in his name, was a sure sign the shit was about to hit the fan. That much he did remember from his short and unhappy marriage.

'Not sure I know what you mean,' he lied.

'Well, where I come from, it isn't normal behaviour to spend that kind of money on a perfect stranger,' she said with an edge to her voice.

'It is where I come from. I thought you'd be pleased. You've got a whole wardrobe and you won't have to do any laundry for the entire holiday. Seems to me like a right result,' he said cheerily.

'Don't pretend you don't know what I mean. Personally, I find it a bit creepy. What the hell do you want from me?' she screamed.

'Nothing, just for you to be happy,' Ed said softly.

'Happy? You want me to be happy? Then tell me, what the fuck is going on?'

'There's nothing going on. What, you think I'm some loser, who thinks he can buy you a few clothes, just so I can turn round to you and say I bought those, now get down and suck my dick, is that it?' he asked, raising his own voice.

'I don't know but it's not normal and you're freaking me out,' she replied, raising her own voice again.

'OK. Calm down,' he said quietly, deciding he had no option but to tell her the truth, now. 'I'm a millionaire.'

'Bullshit,' she spat back. 'You're forgetting I've seen your house and what's in it. Yeah, it's a nice little detached house, in a nice little part of town but it's not a millionaire's house, and you drive a fucking Mondeo!'

She had a point but he wasn't about to concede. 'Just because I don't have gold plated taps and butlers crawling out of every orifice, doesn't mean I'm not a millionaire; and I like my Mondeo, it's practical for the dog.'

'Bullshit, you're a lying, creepy bastard. Yesterday, I said you were weird. Well, I've changed my mind, you're fucking scary. I'm getting out the minute we stop. I don't give a shit where it is. I'm getting as far away from you as possible. You're making my skin crawl.'

Ed was shocked and hurt. He was also angry with himself for kidding himself he could get away with it. He should have been honest with her from the start and avoided all of this bullshit. All he wanted to do was what he thought was the right thing and he'd screwed it up, big time.

'Right, shut up and listen and don't interrupt. Got it?' he shouted at her. He looked over to catch her eye but she was looking out the side window. 'I am a millionaire, OK. My parents died when I was twenty-five, like I told you yesterday. Fact! They left me a caravan in Cornwall and old ginger bollocks in the boot.

Fact! After the solicitor sold off the house, sorted out the life insurance and bank accounts and paid the death taxes, I also inherited just over half a million. Another fact! Losing my parents hit me hard, very hard and I didn't want anything to do with the money, I just wanted my parents back. Just for a laugh, I bought shares in the company I was working for and one a mate was working for. Both these shares were falling like stones and I bought one lot at thirty pence, when they were at seven pounds, a short time before and the other at three pounds when they had been eleven. I thought it was a great way to lose it all and at the time it made me feel a whole lot better.

Shortly after my parents died, Dawn, my now very dead, ex-wife, turns up. I'd known her for years and we had an on-off relationship. When she wasn't with me, she was off with someone else and it was like that for about two or three years. When she turned up this time, things seemed different and we were married just after my twenty-seventh birthday. Everyone told me not to as she was just after my money. I hadn't told anyone I'd deliberately invested badly, you see. Pretty soon it was obvious she thought I was loaded and kept asking about it. When I told her I'd lost it all in a bad investment, it all started to go wrong. I knew she was having affairs but couldn't prove it. Towards the end of our brief and unhappy marriage she didn't even have the courtesy to try and hide it. She died, as I told you yesterday. Fact!'

Ed was trying to not raise his voice but a combination of being angry and dragging up the past, made it impossible and he couldn't stop himself shouting.

'A month or so after she died, I was down the pub and was just starting to feel a little bit better about myself. While I was waiting to get served, I overheard a conversation behind me. One guy was telling the other, what a shame it was about Steve dying but hey, what a way to go. It would've been the way he wanted it, stuck between the legs of the town bike. He then began telling him Dawn put it around quite a bit and only married her sad fuck of a husband because she thought he had money and it turned out the stupid bastard didn't have a pot to piss in. He said I must have been a right tosser, to have been taken in by a slag like that.

I felt so humiliated. I wanted to rip that bloke from limb-to-limb but didn't have the stomach for it; I felt physically sick. I went home and drank. I don't think I've ever drunk so much in my entire life. It was then that I started to feel a bit sorry for myself and decided my life was just one big fuck up. I staggered round the house and got every pill I could find. Pain killers, a few of *her* sleeping pills, some unused antibiotics; Christ, I think there was even some bloody birth control pills in there. I put them all in a big pile between my legs and stared at them for ages, trying to get drunk enough to take them. Just when I thought this is it, that stupid bastard in the boot back there came walking in, flopped down on the floor beside me, put his big, fat, stupid head in my lap and looked up at me with his big sad eyes and thumped his tail on the floor. I couldn't do it. I just couldn't do it. I couldn't leave that soppy bugger behind, could I? I picked up all the pills and washed them down the sink and sat down and drank and drank and cried like a fucking big kid. When I saw you sitting on that wall, I thought, I've been there, I know what it feels like. OK, my problem was nothing more than self-indulgent, self-pity and yours was something a whole lot worse but I've been there all the same. That's why I wanted to help you.

Anyway, a couple of days later when I was sober, I decided to get my life in order and start living again. First thing I did was hand in my notice and got lucky there, getting offered voluntary redundancy and a nice cheque for eighty grand. A few weeks later, I got two more cheques. One from a life insurance policy I had out on Dawn, for a hundred grand and another for two hundred grand from her works pension scheme, death in service. I looked up my shares and found that the ones for thirty pence were now just over two-fifty each and I had about eight hundred and fifty thousand of those as I took the dividends in shares. The others, which I bought for three quid were up at seventeen something. I cashed them all in and, after tax, plus the money I already had, I was sitting on just over three million. I couldn't believe it, twenty-nine years old and a millionaire.' He laughed dryly 'I couldn't even lose half a million without fucking it up.' Emma was still staring out the window as Ed continued, in a softer voice.

'I know what you're thinking but believe me, it doesn't make you happy. There are days even today, when I despise every last penny. I've done some good with it. I paid off the mortgages of my closest friends. I've given to local charities. I've given to appeals that have been in the local paper. You know, some kid needs to go to the USA to have treatment, because he can't get it over here or some kids got leukaemia and wants to go to Disney Land before he dies, so I've paid for him to go. Does it make you feel good? Yes it does but it's so impersonal. Do I get to see that kid's happy smiling face as he comes off some roller coaster in Disney Land, having the time of his life? No! Do I get to see how happy the parents are after their kid pulls through his life saving operation? No! Can I treat my mates or their kids? No! Buy too much and you're a flash bastard, don't spend enough and you're a tight bastard. You can't win.

You ask me, what I want from you? That's what I want. Just for once, I wanted to do something for someone I know and to make a real difference to their life and be around to see their happy smiling face. Is that too much to ask for, is it?

Anyway, now you know what a fuck up my life's been and how fucking sad and empty it is. Happy now?'

Ed was gripping the steering wheel so hard his hands were hurting. His head was also pounding, the veins in his temples throbbing. He knew he screwed up yet again and he was angry. Angry with himself for not being up front with her, ranting at her as if it was all her fault, angry he let her get under his guard and angry she was about to walk out of his life.

After driving in total silence for what seemed like a very long time, Ed pulled the car into the service station just outside Exeter. He was now feeling rather guilty about his outburst earlier but, being a bloke, didn't want to apologise, even though he knew he was in the wrong. In hindsight, he knew he should have been up front with Emma about his financial status but had his reasons not to.

After filling up with petrol, he drove round to the car park and backed into a space at the end. He took a furtive glance at Emma, who was still busy looking out the passenger window, deliberately ignoring him and he couldn't blame her. He sprung the boot and headed round the back of the car. He lifted the up the tailgate and released Fat Boy, who ran to the thin row of trees separating the car park from a farmer's field and urinated copiously, before heading into the field beyond. Ed sat down on the edge of the boot and lit one of the cigarettes he purchased when he paid for the petrol and blew out a long, satisfying stream of smoke. Fat Boy was running round the field sniffing and urinating on anything interesting, until he found something of real interest and curled down a turd of biblical proportions, which would probably warrant a new contour to be added to the ordnance survey map of the area.

Emma approached the rear of the car and stood in front of him. Ed braced himself for a well-deserved bollocking for his behaviour earlier, which, although he felt was justified at the time, he could see how it must have looked to her. She was right; he was weird, but he would dispute creepy all the way. He looked up at her and saw she had been crying and felt even worse than he already did.

'I didn't know you smoked.'

'Only when I'm really pissed, really stressed or have made a total arse of myself,' he said apologetically, looking up at her. 'I've made you cry, I'm such an arsehole. I'm sorry,' he said and meant it.

'It's OK. It's my fault. I said some really hurtful things earlier. I don't blame you for being angry. I just wish you'd told me before,' she replied, giving him a sad smile that didn't help at all to ease the guilt he was already feeling.

'I know,' he replied dolefully. 'It's just people treat you so differently when you tell them you're a millionaire so now I don't bother. Either people try and take advantage, which to be honest I don't really care about. They're the ones who have to live with their conscience not me. Or you get the complete opposite, where people won't even let you buy them a drink because they don't want to be seen to be taking advantage. I just want people to accept me for what I am and not what I have.'

She seemed to be studying him, thinking on what to say next, which she was. She was feeling ashamed of some of what she had said, even more so after his explanation, which surprised her on two accounts. One, the fact he was a millionaire, and she knew from the passion in his voice that he wasn't lying, and secondly, he wasn't quite as carefree, happy-go-lucky as he portrayed himself to be. In a way, it was comforting to know in some ways he was just as screwed up as she was but didn't have him down as a the sort of person who would try to commit suicide, which really shocked her.

Ed gave a shrug, stood up and ground his half smoked cigarette into the tarmac and, after looking to make sure Fat Boy was still in the same county, looked into Emma's eyes to try to get a feel for just how much damage he had done. She took a step towards him and put her arms around his waist and hugged him, resting her head on his chest, which Ed took to be a good indication that either everything would be OK or she was saying goodbye.

'Are you still coming with me to Cornwall?'

'On one condition,' she said staring at him intently. 'No more secrets. OK?'

'OK. Unless they're embarrassing ones, of course, or irrelevant.'

'Deal,' she said and stretched up and kissed him quickly on the lips.

Fat Boy returned and after being given some water, was back in the boot, and they were ready to leave, neither of them wanting to use the service station facilities nor wanting anything to eat. Ed also bought a couple of bottles of water when filling up with petrol, which they drank and would probably regret, as the service stations were few and far between. Ed looked across at Emma, who nodded as if to say what are you waiting for?

'Its 77 miles to Cornwall, we've got a full tank of gas, it's sunny and we're wearing sunglasses,' he said mimicking the famous scene from the Blues Brothers.

'Hit it!' Emma replied, which Ed was thankful for. If she hadn't seen the Blues Brothers, he would have looked a prat. As it was, they both laughed as Ed over revved the car and performed a lengthy wheelspin, before shooting off to re-join the M5. Not bad for a Mondeo, he thought.

The rest of the journey was completed in much the way it had started, a number of hours ago. Singing along to whatever was on the radio, humming when they didn't know the words or making them up. The conversation flowed, which was far more preferable to the cold shoulder treatment they gave each other earlier. At one point, Emma even held his hand and gave it a squeeze, which made Ed think that everything would be OK.

CHAPTER 11

By the time they arrived at the caravan park, both were in dire need of the toilet, which wasn't helped by the numerous speed bumps on the narrow road that snaked around the site. Ed pulled up adjacent to his caravan and let the dog out, who immediately urinated against the dry-stone wall in front of the caravan as Ed fumbled with his keys, hopping up and down, in extreme discomfort. When they finally made it in, each was being magnanimous and allowing the other to use the toilet first. In the end, Ed did the honourable thing and decided to toss for it. He lost. Emma went in first and seemed to take ages, as he stood outside clutching his crotch. When Emma finally vacated the toilet, Ed couldn't get in there quick enough but saved a vital few seconds by unbuttoning his fly whilst waiting for Emma. It was a close call and he stood there for ages, eyes closed and rolled back in their sockets, finishing with an ecstatic sigh.

'There's no milk,' he told her as the kettle boiled 'We can go and get some from the mini-market before it shuts.'

'I'll have my coffee black, same as you,' she said, walking up to him and giving him a hug, which Ed returned with interest.

'I've got house rules,' he told her. 'Anything in the caravan is yours, as much as it is mine, so use it, eat it or drink it. Don't ask permission or I'll be offended, as it says you're not comfortable. It's your home, as much as mine, for the next two or three weeks or however long we stay for. OK?' Emma nodded and he continued. 'The only exception to that rule is my razor. No using that on your legs or armpits or anywhere else,' he informed her, raising his eyebrows. 'It's gotta go round my chin after. OK?'

'You are so gross,' she told him, laughing.

'Finally, it's a small caravan and can get quite ripe, if you know what I mean? So when you use the toilet make sure you open the window. Believe me, it can get very unpleasant. Apart from that anything goes.'

'You have a lovely choice of phrases and words. Your mother must be so proud of you,' she said, before you realised her mistake. 'Shit. I'm so sorry. I forgot.'

'That was a long time ago. I'm over it. You don't need to tread on eggshells on my account. I'm sure I'll put my foot in it at some point,' he gave her a reassuring squeeze, which was abruptly ended by a jealous dog, joining in for a group hug.

Ed gave her a quick guided tour of the caravan, showing her all the facilities, which didn't take long. She seemed impressed he had Satellite TV, a DVD player, iPod docking station, shower and her own room, which Ed hoped she wouldn't use too much - ever the optimist.

After, the three of them went for a walk round the campsite so he could show her where the shop, reception and the clubhouse with restaurant and fish and chip shop were. The first port of call was reception so Ed could pay his ground rent and maintenance fee for the year, which had become something of a tradition on his first visit of the year. Eric, who ran the site, was in his late sixties and refused to retire. He was in good shape for a man of his age, as he jogged every day and lifted weights. He was permanently tanned with a flat nose, from when he used to box in his youth, and loved to talk about his fights and how he was Cornish champion for three years, retiring undefeated. He was also one of Fat Boy's best friends, on account of the endless supply of custard creams stashed under the counter. In all the years he had known Eric, he had never seen him with any other type of biscuit. Ed often thought about buying him a selection box one day, just to show Eric that other types of biscuits existed.

'Hi Fat Boy, come for a biscuit, have you?' he said as the dog entered and put his paws on the counter so Eric could give him a stroke and to be nearer the biscuit when it arrived. He wasn't disappointed, as the custard cream was handed to him and he ate it, getting crumbs all over counter. Fat Boy, promptly licked them up, leaving behind a pool of saliva.

'Hi Eric. I'm here too and this is Emma,' Ed said as a reminder.

'Yeah but you're not as cute as old Fat Boy here. Nice to meet you, Emma,' he said shaking her tiny hand with one of his huge shovel like hands, which Ed could imagine inflicting a great deal of damage in the ring. 'So, I take it you heard about our strangler, then? Two bodies so far in a week, both young girls, found on the beach. Nasty business and not good for business either.'

They told Eric they hadn't heard about it; Emma looked worried. Ed was far from impressed, removing her from one nightmare to somewhere that could be just as unsafe as the last.

'Strange thing is,' Eric continued, 'He leaves them on the beach, naked in the shape of a crucifix and puts painted cockle shells over their nipples.' He said the last word with a hint of embarrassment. 'Bloody strange, if you ask me. The Police don't seem to be doing much either. They interviewed Bob on the local news and it doesn't seem like they've got very far. They just gave out the usual old flannel about pursuing a number of lines of inquiries, blah blah blah. Just hope they get him soon, before peak season.'

'You're all heart, Eric,' Ed said light-heartedly, writing out his cheque. Ed wanted to leave quickly before Eric spooked Emma even more. He left with Emma, giving the excuse of needing to get to the shop before it shut, which was partly true. As usual, Eric's parting words were 'Don't forget, if there's anything you need, just ask.'

The same conversation took place in the shop, with Eric's wife, Maureen. By the time they got to the chip shop, they'd both heard enough of the Black Cockle Strangler to last a lifetime. Fortunately, the chip shop was busy, leaving little time for the staff to gossip.

After finishing their meal and mopping up the lake of slobber deposited by Fat Boy, who drooled continuously from the first chip being eaten until the last, Ed suggested they walk it off before heading to the clubhouse for a few drinks.

'Before we go Emma, take this,' he said handing her a wad of notes. She looked about to protest but Ed held his hand up and stopped her. 'Look, I don't want you constantly asking me for money if there's something you need and feeling embarrassed about asking,' he said, smiling awkwardly, hoping he hadn't embarrassed her.

'Ed, what could I possibly want? You've bought me just about everything I could need,' she replied, trying to hand back the money.

It was Ed's turn to be a little embarrassed. 'Well, you know, girly type things.' Emma smiled at his discomfort. 'And I don't expect you to stick around with me all the time. Obviously, you can if you want to. I'd like you to but you might want to go off on your own for the day and you'll need money for food and drinks.' Ed knew he was floundering. The way Emma was smiling at him confirmed that. He gave a nervous laugh. 'Look, just take it will you.'

Emma smiled at him and flicked through the wad of notes. 'There must be...'

Ed cut her short. 'Enough for two weeks,' he said, giving her another smile. Emma conceded and reached up and kissed him on the cheek and thanked him.

From the caravan they took a narrow, rutted track that led to the low clifftop. Here it merged with the coastal path and a natural slope that led to a small sandy beach, which at low tide linked up to the next bay, where there was a nice pub. They took the path to the left, which would eventually lead in a circular walk to the opposite side of the headland, where they could cut across inland, back to the caravan park.

'So, where are we, then? And don't say Cornwall. I know that much. I'm not that thick,' she asked.

'When we walked down the track from the caravan, if you turned right, that eventually leads to Padstow, which I guess you've heard of as it's now infamous for being the home of Rick Stein's gourmet empire. The headland we just walked round is Trevose Head and if you keep going this way, it leads to Newquay,' he enthused.

'It's nice,' she replied.

'Nice. I've never heard anything so understated in all my life. This is one of the most beautiful places in Great Britain and the best you can do is nice. You take a lot of impressing.'

Emma laughed. 'OK. It's beautiful. Happy now?'

'Not really,' he replied. 'As much as I could stand here all day, listening to the waves crashing on the rocks at the bottom of the cliff, relishing the feel of the sea breeze on my face, admiring the unspoilt scenery in the one place I feel truly at peace with myself, I'm gagging for a pint so get your arse in gear,' he said giving her a slap on the backside.

'There was me thinking you were being all nostalgic and romantic but you're just full of shit,' she told him, slipping her hand into his as they headed back to the clubhouse.

Before they entered the clubhouse, Ed stopped her and turned to face her.

'Just so you know, as it may or may not come up in conversation, I'm officially the joint owner of this fine establishment. There, no more secrets. I forgot about that one. Not that it's a secret as such.'

'How come, couldn't you afford the other half?' she joked.

'I didn't want any half. Sue, who is the real owner, used to run a pub in Padstow, which I used to go to a lot. We became friends. Don't look at me like that, she was married and there was nothing going on. Anyway, she caught her husband in the cellar giving one of her barmaids a knee trembler and kicked him out. After, she didn't want to stay in the pub anymore and this place became available. She couldn't afford it and was too proud to let me give her the money or even lend her the money so we went into business. I've never taken a penny out of it, mind you. I just tell her to put my share back into the business. Deep down she knows it was a gift but she's too proud to admit it and so the pretence continues. Now, can we go in and have a drink?'

She gave him a look he couldn't quite work out what it meant. It didn't say I'm pissed off with you and it didn't say I want to have your babies, therefore, it meant something else his limited capabilities as a man couldn't understand, so he just shrugged and opened the door to let Emma through.

The clubhouse was relatively empty as it was still only early evening and it was a Thursday. Out of season, it only really got busy at weekends, when the caravan owners descended like locusts. Ed knew quite a lot of them, mostly just to nod to and say hello. Some had been coming as long as he, if not longer, and he had been coming for twenty years.

At the bar, Sue was nowhere to be seen but Lisa, Ed's favourite barmaid was, as she always seemed to be. She was the only item from the pub in Padstow that made the transition to the clubhouse. Lisa was always ready with a smile and knew how to pour a decent pint. She was married to Colin with whom Ed also got a long with quite well. He owned a couple of speedboats he moored in Padstow harbour and took tourists on trips round the coast at twenty quid a go. Ed had been in one of them once but only the once. After hitting a particularly big wave, he was suspended in mid-air. The boat landed back in the water, with Ed following shortly behind, squashing his balls. They'd ached for weeks afterwards, completely ruining his holiday and he vowed never to go in one again. Colin thought it was funny though, so that was OK.

After introducing Emma to Lisa, who greeted them with one of her genuinely warm smiles they ordered their drinks and took a seat, Fat Boy flopping down between them on the floor.

'I forgot to mention, we'll be coming here tomorrow to meet Jack and Chris, two of my oldest friends. We've been friends since I first started coming here with my parents, when I was about twelve. I think you'll like them, they're pretty easy going and will probably spend all night taking the piss out of me but hey, that's what mates are for. Jack was a DS in the police until last year but gave it all up to take over the running of the family funeral parlour and Chris owns an arts and craft shop in Padstow, so might be a good contact for you.'

'You really like it here, don't you? I've noticed since we've been here you've been like a little kid, all excited over anything and everything. It's quite sweet. I'm seeing you in a totally different light. Why don't you move down here? You're obviously happier here.'

'Good question...' Ed began but didn't finish

'Eddieeeeee,' came a wail from behind, reminiscent of a banshee.

'Sue, by any chance?' Emma asked, smiling broadly.

'Oh yeah.'

Ed stood up to get his customary bear hug from Sue, who was striding towards him with real purpose to her step. Sue was originally from Edinburgh where she met her husband, who at the time was working on the oilrigs. He gave it up after making his fortune and having had enough of the hardships and danger. They got their first pub together in Edinburgh and after years of brawls and chasing out the drug dealers, decided to go for a taste of the rural life and came to Cornwall fifteen years ago. She always ran a tight ship and didn't stand for any nonsense. On more than one occasion, Ed had witnessed her breaking up fights by confronting those involved head on, wielding a baseball bat that was ever present behind the bar, sporting more than a few notches in it. She was one of the few people that frightened the shit out of Ed, which was partly why he liked her. After making a huge fuss of Fat Boy, Sue pulled up a chair.

'Who's this pretty wee thing, then?' she asked, looking at Emma and making her colour slightly at the compliment.

'Emma, this is Sue,' he said introducing them.

'I hope you're looking after my Ed? He's my favourite.' Emma nodded. 'How long have you two been an item then?' she asked, still addressing Emma, obviously trying to gauge if she was worthy enough for Ed and to find out if she liked her as well. Ed was used to it. It was all part of her Scottish charm. Emma on the other hand wasn't but smiled back and gave the response they rehearsed earlier, to save any embarrassment.

'I've only known him a short time but I think I'm looking after him OK. I had a few family problems so Ed thought it would be good to come here for a while, to get away from it all,' she replied.

'Well, if you've only known him a little while and he takes you on holiday, he obviously thinks a lot of you. That's good enough for me,' she said winking at Emma, which was a clear sign she met with her approval. 'Right, I'll get the drinks in. Lager and that looks and smells like a Vodka Red Bull, right?'

Emma nodded and Sue disappeared to the bar. Ed sat there smiling at Emma, who shook her head as if to say, who the hell is this mad woman? Sue was soon back with the drinks and immediately launched into her version of the Black Cockle Strangler. Speculating, she thought it was one of the surfers who descended on the North Cornish coast all year round, as they were all on drugs and drank too much but, she had to say, were very good for business in the area. Sue was never short of an opinion.

Two more drinks later and another hour of listening to Sue, smiling during the appropriate pauses in the conversation, adding the odd comment whenever possible, was curtailed by the lights going out, leaving the clubhouse in almost total darkness. They both let out a sigh of relief as Sue yelled out to everyone in the bar the lights would be back on soon and left to reset the circuit breaker, giving their ears a chance to recover. The respite was short lived and she was back a few minutes later, lights restored.

'It's been like this all week,' she told them 'I've had the electrician round and he couldn't find anything and suggested replacing the fuse box or something and if that didn't fix it, the whole place might need re-wiring but he can't do it for another week or so yet as he's got too much work on. More drinks, I think.'

Once again, she refused to allow either of them to buy a drink, which Ed explained was the norm. She didn't pay so why should he? After all, the place was as much his as it was hers, was her explanation and Ed had given up trying. Lisa also tried to take the same stance but had given up arguing with him and now just reluctantly took his money.

Ed was flagging. The long drive and several drinks were beginning to take its effect, so soon stared to make his excuses, yawning to prove a point. He eventually managed to leave with Emma, letting Sue know that they would be back tomorrow with Chris and Jack.

They sat on the built-in sofa that curled around one end of the caravan, drinking coffee. Emma nestled into the crook of his arm and Ed's hand rested on her stomach, feeling more than a little content.

'Thanks for everything,' she said, resting her hand on his and giving it a gentle squeeze. 'Sorry about earlier in the car, I feel really bad about that.'

'We've been over that already. I should've been straight with you from the start about my finances. It was more than a little stupid of me. Still shopping was quite fun. Although, there was no need to make my embarrassment any worse than it already was, in the underwear department. I'm just glad you didn't want to try any on and leave me there on my own like a pervert.'

'I think you were enjoying it, really. You were just putting on a front so you didn't look like a pervert. I saw you eyeing up all the women on the posters, you dirty old sod.'

'Looks like I've been rumbled,' he replied laughing.

'You're bloody uncomfortable, you know? It's like leaning up against a brick wall. I'm going to bed.'

Emma kissed him goodnight and left him alone with Fat Boy, who was curled up on his bed, already in a deep sleep. Ed retrieved his maps of Cambridge and studied them, hoping that some of the street names and places would be locked in his memory, to use at a later date. Then he would have that final piece of information he needed on Danny Mandelson from Cambridge. Quite how he would get this last piece was perhaps going to be difficult but he'd cross that bridge when he came to it.

CHAPTER 12

Ed awoke and opened his eyes and saw it was only just after six o'clock but felt refreshed and ready to go. Emma was in the bed next to him, which startled him slightly. He must have been in a deep sleep when she climbed in next to him. She was still fast asleep, breathing deeply and looked quite sweet. Ed moved across the bed and kissed her lightly on the forehead. She screamed and began thrashing around, lashing out with arms and legs. Ed backed as far away as possible when her knee caught him on the thigh. He grabbed her flailing arms, which were coming perilously close to his head.

'Emma!' he shouted over her screams 'Wake up. It's me, Ed.'

Emma opened her eyes and stopped screaming. She looked at Ed and seemed confused and dazed, before breaking into a smile and saying 'Oops' and giggling.

'Shit. You scared the life out of me. What's wrong?'

Emma looked sheepish. 'Sorry, just a bad dream.'

'Bloody hell. Don't have any more. OK. I don't think my nerves could take it. Are you sure you're OK?'

'I'm fine. Don't worry, just a dream, nothing else. I didn't hurt you, did I?'

'No, you kicked me in the shin, narrowly missing the tip of my penis, but other than that, I'll live.'

'Sorry,' she said giggling but clearly wasn't.

Ed got up, put his clothes on and left Emma curled up in bed. He fed Fat Boy, downed a quick coffee and headed out for his morning walk. When he returned with Fat Boy, Emma was already up and showered and wearing a tight pair of shorts, which looked good on her. She was cooking a fried breakfast. Ed took a quick shower himself and sat down at the table, drinking the coffee that was waiting for him; he could get used to this. He watched as she cooked, marvelling at how calm she was. Whenever he cooked a fried breakfast, things started out calmly enough but always ended in chaos as everything seemed to happen at once. The beans would start boiling, the sausages would turn black in the blink of an eye, the bacon would turn to a fragile crisp and the eggs either split or the yolks turned hard, but she seemed to be in full control.

Everything on his plate was done to perfection. Even the eggs had none of that snotty, uncooked white around the yolk, which he always seemed to manage. The beans were soft but not a thick pulp and the bacon didn't shatter like porcelain when you put a knife into it. Ed wasn't a bad cook. He made a fair bolognese and an edible roast but just couldn't muster a decent fry-up. Smug cow, he thought, as she smiled and gave him a look that said 'I know it's perfect'.

Ed washed up the plates and Emma dried, as they discussed how they were going to spend the day. In the end, they opted to take a walk into Padstow along the coastal path, to have a look round the harbour and shops and grab a pub lunch and a few pints.

It was another glorious day with a slightly cool wind blowing in off the sea, as they walked hand in hand along the coastal path. They hadn't gone far when Ed stopped and studied the path in front and the sand dunes below.

'There's a bloke in the dunes over there with binoculars, spying on that woman sunbathing down there. Wait here with the dog and I'll go down and let her know.'

'Are you sure? He could be bird watching or something,' she replied.

'Could be but I don't think so. Anyway, it could be that bloke with the black cockles. Keep an eye on the pervert and if he makes a run for it, phone the police and report it. OK? If he doesn't do a runner, then it could be he is a bird watcher or something. I'll go over and ask him.' Emma nodded and seemed satisfied with Ed's logic.

Ed set off down the dunes to do his good deed of the day. It was hard work as the sand was bone dry and shifted constantly under his feet. He eventually reached her and coughed politely from a short distance away. He noticed she was wearing in-ear headphones so wouldn't be able to hear him, if she had the volume cranked up as high as he usually did. He walked up to her slowly, not wishing to startle her as her eyes were also closed. He knelt down and gently tapped her on the shoulder. As he did he was hit with force from behind as somebody rugby tackled him. Ed landed heavily in the sand, struggling with his assailant. He couldn't swing his arms to hit him so relied on wriggling and tossing his body around to shake him off, which he eventually managed. Ed was definitely a lot quicker than his assailant and turned this to his advantage, pinning him down on his back, with his hand round this throat. Ed drew his hand back to punch him in the face and it was deftly handcuffed by the woman who had been sunbathing.

Ed turned round and looked over his shoulder at the bikini clad woman, who just cuffed him and saw she was holding out her warrant card in her free hand.

'Bloody hell, last time I got handcuffed by someone wearing as little as you, I paid a fortune. If I'd known it was free, I'd have moved to Cornwall years ago,' he said with a grin, which she clearly didn't find funny.

Before she could say anything, a commanding voice boomed from the top of the dunes.

'PC Walsh, get those handcuffs off Mr. Case now! I think he's getting aroused and DC Murphy is looking decidedly worried. Case, get your fucking arse off my DC.'

'Hi Bob,' Ed said as the cuffs were removed and he extracted himself from DC Murphy, who didn't look pleased.

DCI Bob Brown was a huge man, in both size and personality. Ed had met him some years ago through Jack, who was a Detective Sergeant under Bob at the time. They got on well from day one, sharing similar views on political incorrectness and politics in general and would get drunk and put the world to rights. Whenever Ed was down, he would ensure they got at least one night out on the town together, spending the next day in a dazed fug through over excess.

Ed apologised to PC Walsh, who reluctantly shook his outstretched hand. DC Murphy was less gracious and refused to shake his hand. Ed just shrugged and ignored his hard stare. He couldn't really blame him for being angry, having just screwed up his day's work and made him look an arse in front of his boss.

'Where's that dog of yours?' Bob asked, in his usual growl.

As if on cue, Fat Boy came bounding over the dunes, followed by Emma, who looked worried. After Bob had finished rubbing Fat Boy's belly, Ed introduced him to Emma. Bob towered over her at six-foot-two and stared down at her with his hard eyes.

'Batting well above your average there, Ed. Very nice,' he said making Emma blush, despite enjoying the compliment.

'I take it I've just screwed up your day, then?' Ed said apologetically.

'Don't worry about it. I've only got two dead bodies and the top brass breathing down my neck for a result by the end of the week,' he replied sarcastically. 'Of course you bloody well have, you cretin!' he barked.

They walked the short distance to the beach and headed for the car park.

'I take it it's not going too well, then? It's the talk of the town back at the caravan park. Just about everyone has an opinion.'

'I've always said opinions are like arseholes. You know everyone has one but you don't necessarily want to hear them. Not going well is a bloody understatement. Two dead bodies and forensics haven't found anything. Absolutely fuck all. We've been inundated with phone calls from concerned citizens, to tell us they've seen kids on the beach collecting shells and they're worried they could be the killer. The local press have named him the Black Cockle Strangler, comparing him to Jack the Ripper. Apart from that everything's fucking marvellous.'

'What it is with the black cockles, then? Any idea what the significance is?'

'The Chief Super's got some fancy-arsed psychologist in, coming up with all kinds of theories but if you ask me, it's all bollocks. He's just a sick bastard.'

Ed didn't know what to say and just nodded. He'd never seen Bob so stressed. He was always abrupt and his language colourful but he looked really tired, like he hadn't slept for days. The fact was he hadn't and had been burning the midnight oil since the second body turned up, looking for connections no matter how remote. None had been found. The only connection being both victims were female, both were in their twenties and lived alone.

Otherwise the only link was both being killed by the same person in the same way.

'We're meeting up with Jack and Chris tonight in the clubhouse, if you fancy a few beers?' Ed said eventually.

'I might just do that,' he said.

Ed knew straight away that he wouldn't turn up. There were never any grey areas with Bob. If the answer wasn't yes, anything else meant no, simple as that. They reached the car park and with the promise of a beer before he went back, they parted, Ed and Emma up the hill to rejoin the coastal path and Bob in the direction of the Harlyn Inn for a quick pint. Emma surprised him by stretching up and kissing Bob on the cheek as they said goodbye. Ed was sure Bob was blushing but the look he gave him didn't invite comment.

CHAPTER 13

They walked in silence, both admiring the views, until they reached the top of a steep incline, where they stopped, both out of breath. Ed wished he remembered to bring some water. He was gasping and the temperature was still rising, as the morning began edging towards midday. He took a couple of steps back off the path and sat down on the grass for a breather, resting on his elbows with his legs stretched out in front of him. Emma joined him and sat down at right angles to him putting her head in his lap.

She seemed to be getting more and more tactile with him, which wasn't a problem in itself but he wasn't sure if she was just at ease with him or if it was something more. He put it down to her being a tactile person by nature as it was the easiest option and didn't involve any unpleasantness, if interpreted otherwise. After what she had been through with Danny, he was sure the last thing she wanted would be another relationship, which was a pity as he was getting quite fond of her.

'I think you took Bob by surprise, back there,' he said, stroking her hair.

'He's quite sweet and looked like he needed something to cheer him up,' she replied, like it was the sort of thing she did every day.

'Sweet?' Ed laughed. 'I don't think anyone has ever called him sweet. I've heard him being called a lot of things but sweet was never one of them. I'm sure he wouldn't like it either. It wouldn't be good for his macho, tough guy image.'

'You sound jealous,' she said, looking up at him.

'Jealous? Why should I be jealous? It's not like we're an item, is it?' he said fishing and hoping she would pick up on it, which she did.

'No,' she replied and seemed to want to say more. 'Ed,' she began.

Here we go again, Ed thought. A sentence starting with my name, meaning something profound was about to be said.

'I'm really grateful to you for everything; for stopping me jumping, for dinner, for the clothes, for bringing me here, for everything. Most of all for just being here for me and making me feel special and safe. I really like you.'

Yep and there was a "but" in there somewhere he could tell.

'But...'

Here it is. Just a matter of how big the "but" was.

'I really don't want or need to get into another relationship at the moment. I've been through hell the last few months and I don't think I could have a...physical relationship with you or anyone else. I know I'm probably sending out the wrong messages, coming to your bed at night but that's because I can't sleep. Being alone, gives me time to think about the past and I just lay in bed crying. I wish I could spend a night in my own bed but I get so frightened. God, I hate myself for being so bloody fragile and so dependent on you. I hope you understand. I'm not doing it because I'm a prick teaser. I don't suppose it's easy for you either?'

'It's not a problem,' he lied, 'it's quite nice having someone to cuddle up to. It's been a long time since I shared my bed with anyone and sharing it with a twenty-two year old is certainly good for the ego. I'm happy with the way things are. It's good you feel safe with me. You can share my bed anytime you like. I can't promise to keep my hands to myself, of course, but I'll do my best,' he said with a grin.

She smiled back at him, sat up, hugged him and then kissed him on the lips. She pulled back and inch or so and looked him in the eyes, before kissing him again. Ed gave her an enthusiastic hug, only letting go when he lost his balance, as she put her full weight against his chest. They lay together laughing and holding each other, until two sturdy middle-aged women, clad in equally sturdy waking gear, approached from the opposite direction to them.

'I say,' the nearest woman said. 'You should be ashamed of yourselves, behaving like that in public, it's disgusting. You youngsters, have absolutely no sense of decency or propriety. And you, young man, look old enough to know better.'

Ed was pissed off his moment of intimacy had been rudely interrupted by this frigid, dried-up, rotund, middle-aged, battle-axe and decided retaliation was entirely appropriate.

'You know, you are absolutely correct. It is disgusting and I am definitely old enough to know better. But surely, even you must remember what it's like when you get so horny you can't wait? Right now, I'm feeling bloody rampant so I'm gonna give you a five minute head start and if I can still see you, you're next fatty! How does that sound?' he said rubbing his crotch.

They both stared at him open mouthed, until Ed started counting down, which spurred them into action. They turned and hurried off down the hill, their chubby backsides swinging like oversized pendulums. Emma was in fits of uncontrollable laughter, which excited the dog, who padded over and began licking her ears, before trying to hump her. Ed pulled him away and calmed him down and waited for Emma to compose herself enough to carry on walking.

'You're a very bad person,' she told him 'and you're definitely not going to get to heaven,' she added, giving him a hug and kiss on the cheek.

Ed didn't believe in heaven but didn't want to get into a discussion on his sometimes atheist, sometime agnostic beliefs, depending on whom he was trying to wind up. In truth, he hoped that heaven, if indeed it did exist, turned out to be a sweat shop for the righteous. A place where pompous bible bashers were forced to work significantly harder than they had during their life on earth; eighteen hours as day without pay. Poetic justice for all the religious wars fought over the centuries, to prove that one nation's invisible friend was better than the other nation's invisible friend.

They reached Padstow sweaty and parched around lunchtime. Luck was on their side and a table was available in the small beer garden at the first pub they came to. Emma sat at the table, while Ed went off to get the drinks and Fat Boy emptied the bowl of water put out for patrons' dogs, before curling up in the shade under the table.

Ed returned shortly with two pints of lager and two menus, before disappearing back into the pub, returning with two more pints. Emma told him he was a greedy sod. Ed defended himself by telling her he had a thirst you could photograph so it made sense to buy two, as the first wasn't going to touch the sides. It didn't and was gone in one lift and a few swallows. Emma, not wanting to be out done, tried the same but only managed half, following up with a loud belch, which raised a few eyebrows from other patrons and a nod of appreciation from Ed.

They both decided to have the Cornish pasty, which Ed went in to order and retuned with two more pints. The pasties, when they arrived, were enormous and filled so much of the large plate the chips had to be served in a separate bowl. By the time they finished and downed the second pint, they were stuffed and struggled to get the third pint down. While they nursed the last pint, they looked out across the quaint harbour and engaged in a spot of people watching. The most memorable moment being when a Japanese tourist decided to take a picture of his wife or girlfriend, who was seated on a post, with her back to the harbour. The husband was a bit of a perfectionist and walked backwards and forwards and side to side, to ensure he got the perfect shot. Unfortunately, he was blissfully unaware that a dog turd was close to his feet and each time he moved around he stepped in and out of it, leaving shitty footprints in a wide circle. After finally taking the snap of the century, he walked off with his partner, leaving a trail of fading brown footsteps in his wake. Emma and Ed were laughing so hard throughout they cried, much to the bemusement of the other patrons in the pub who hadn't noticed.

After finally finishing the last pint, Ed showed Emma round Padstow, pointing out the best bistros and restaurants, including Rick Stein's numerous establishments. She seemed fairly impressed with the number of art galleries and wanted to look in them all. Unfortunately for Emma, Ed told her time was limited as they still had to walk back and get ready to meet Jack and Chris in the clubhouse. There was however, just enough time for Ed to purchase a 21 year-old Glenlivet, single malt whisky and a card for Bob. He wrote a brief note "If you can't make the clubhouse tonight. Have a drink on me. Love Emma. XXX." and left it at the front desk of the police station.

CHAPTER 14

Ed purchased a couple of bottles of water before setting off on the trip back, even though they were going to take a shortcut across country, to save a couple of hours walking. The walk back was uneventful and they were back at the caravan in good time to get showered and changed into fresh clothes. Fat Boy went straight to his bed and was snoring loudly within minutes, a nasty reminder to Ed that he was getting old and probably only had three good years left in him, but didn't dwell on that.

Ed showered first, changed into clean trousers and shirt and fed the dog. Emma put the television on and found MTV, which was playing some modern crap, which Ed put under the generic label of dance music. She cranked up the volume and went into the bedroom to sort out an outfit for the evening ahead. Ed turned the volume down on the television. Emma reappeared within seconds, giving him a look that told him, if he didn't turn the volume up his balls were in serious danger of parting company with the rest of his body. Ed, fond of his testicles being attached, gradually increased the volume, stopping when Emma ceased to glare at him, a sign he reached the desired level. She suggested he go for a walk with Fat Boy and leave her to get ready as he would only be in the way, which suited him; anything to get away from the noise being emitted from the television.

Not wanting to go too far as his feet were aching from his walk earlier, and Fat Boy certainly not looking up for anything too strenuous, he walked down the rutted track to the top of the cliff, turned right up an incline and found a nice patch of grass to sit on and stare out to sea.

His mobile vibrated in his pocket, which he retrieved and read the text message.

"Thanks for the whisky you piss taking bastard. PS you didn't happen to see any sex maniacs on your walk did you? Bob."

The two middle aged walkers, who had taken offence to Ed and Emma earlier, were local councillors. They bumped into Bob, who had moved on to the next bay along the coast. After suffering a long complaint from them both, Bob promised to investigate "this serious incident" and deal with the "filthy fiend" severely, when he was apprehended. His day was turning to rat shit and he would have promised anything, just to be left to get on with the real issue of finding a serial killer. The description the councillors gave of the "offensive and dangerous pervert" seemed too much of a coincidence not to be Ed. He smiled to himself, it was just the sort of thing Ed would do. The little shit!

Ed was studying a street map of Cambridge on his phone, as the first drop of rain fell. He looked up at the sky and could tell it was only going to be a brief shower but knowing how the weather could change quickly in Cornwall, decided to head for the clubhouse. The thought of listening to MTV, while waiting for Emma to get ready, appearing a poor choice and, as she said, he would only be in the way. He called her mobile and left a voicemail. Knowing it was unlikely she would hear the phone ring over the din coming from the television, he didn't bother trying a second time.

As he was walking back up the rutted track, he noticed a woman in a wheelchair, struggling with the uneven surface a few yards in front and decided he would be a Good Samaritan and offer to help.

'Hi. Need a push?' he asked, giving her one of his best smiles.

'No!' came the sharp reply. Not the response he had expected. 'I think I'm perfectly capable of getting up here on my own.'

'I'm sure you are but it's raining and if I push, you might get to the top without getting so wet,' he replied, doing his best to remain friendly, despite her rudeness.

'Why is it, whenever anyone sees somebody in a wheelchair, they feel compelled to patronise them? I don't need your help,' she said angrily

'Sorry, I wasn't trying to patronise you, I was just offering to help,' he said tetchily.

'Well, piss off. I don't need your help,' she replied.

'That's nice. I hope you go fucking rusty. See ya,' he replied and headed off up the track.

He felt a little guilty for saying what he did but justified himself by the fact she was rude and ungracious. It didn't work and he was soon feeling rather ashamed for his outburst. As he was nearing the clubhouse, he turned round and saw she was now burning rubber and catching him up; an angry look on her face. Ed stepped up a gear himself and headed for the clubhouse, the last thing he needed before a good night out was another confrontation.

Ed pushed open the door and walked into the clubhouse with Fat Boy at his heel. He turned and saw that the woman in the wheelchair was also coming to the clubhouse. Out of spite, Ed let the door slam shut and walked over to the bar to get a well-deserved pint. Lisa, the ever-present barmaid was working again and walked up to him with a friendly smile and began to pull a pint for him. Ed turned to watch the woman in the wheelchair struggle with the heavy door and almost went to her assistance but thought if he did, he would only get another mouthful. She eventually managed to get through and wheeled her way to the far end of the bar, as far away from Ed as possible.

Ed gave Lisa a ten pound note and told her to have one herself and to buy whatever the woman in the wheelchair wanted. Lisa raised an eyebrow but said nothing. Ed said 'don't ask' and took his pint to one of the many spare tables. A few minutes later, an angry and red-faced woman wheeled herself towards him and slammed a couple of pound coins on the table in front of him.

'So, you think I'm incapable of paying for my own drink as well as getting up a hill, do you?' she spat.

'No, I'm sure you're perfectly capable. Look, it was a genuine offer of help. I'm sorry if I offended you. OK,' Ed said flatly. She was beginning to irk him.

'Well, I don't need your help or anybody's help, come to that. OK.'

Ed let out a long sigh. This wasn't going as planned and he now wished he hadn't bothered buying her a drink.

'Look, I'm genuinely sorry for what I said back there and for letting the door slam on you. Please accept the drink. It's the liquid equivalent of an olive branch, which are hard to find in Cornwall. I'm sorry.' If this didn't do the trick, he was going back to the caravan; even MTV was preferable to this.

'So, you think one drink gets you off the hook, do you. Do I look that cheap?' she said, slightly less angrily.

'No, but it's all I can offer until the shops open tomorrow, when I will be able to buy you a nice diamond necklace,' he said with a smile.

'I prefer sapphires,' she told him, this time without scowling.

'And you said you weren't cheap.'

'Heart shaped pendant, with matching earrings,' she added.

'OK. Consider it done. It might take a bit of time finding one though.'

'Can we start again? I'm being a right bitch. I've had a really bad day,' she said apologetically.

Ed finished his pint and said 'No. Not until I get another round in' and went to the bar, returning a couple of minutes later, with another pint and another white wine.

'Laura Jacobs,' she said, extending her hand.

'Ed Case,' he replied, shaking her soft hand and studying her face. She had a mass of dark-brown hair, scraped back severely into a ponytail, pale skin and the darkest brown eyes he had ever seen, behind a pair of black, metal-framed glasses, and a nice smile, when she bothered to. She was wearing a thin, cream jumper, which clearly wasn't enough to keep her warm as he could see the outline of her nipples. He made a mental note not to stare at them; he was in enough shit as it was. He didn't need the sexist pig tag to accompany his patronising bastard tag. 'And the ginger thing on the floor is Fat Boy. So, want to tell me about why your day has been so bad, then?'

'Oh, it's nothing serious. Just another blazing row with my mother. She keeps fussing round me and treating me like a child. It's so infuriating. I'm twenty-six; she doesn't seem to realise that.'

'Don't be too hard on her, she's only being a mum, all mums do that, it's their job to worry and fuss over their family.'

'I bet your mum isn't like that?' she said with a wry smile.

'Mine was exactly like that. Unfortunately, both my parents died eight years ago, when I was twenty-five but she was, and still would be, if she were still alive. Have you spoken to her about it?'

he added quickly, steering her away from the need to say sorry and getting embarrassed.

'Of course I have. We go over the same ground, time and time again. She eases up for a while, then slowly gets back into being overbearing. Then we have a fight and go round the whole cycle again. It's been worse since my fiancé ditched me. We came down here to have a bit of time away to patch things up. It's so frustrating and I'm sorry I took it out on you. It was uncalled for. I really could've used your help. I was having all sorts of problems keeping in a straight line,' she said, laughing at her own stubbornness.

'You've not been in a wheelchair long, have you?' he said knowingly 'You don't have any calluses on your hands for one and the way you reacted to my offer of help was a give-away.'

'You're a right Sherlock Holmes, aren't you? You're right though, about six months. I was knocked off my bike and woke up after being in a coma for a couple of days and couldn't move my legs. They took X-rays and it turns out I have a tumour on the spine that's pressing on the spinal cord, which has there for ages but was aggravated by the accident. At the moment, I'm having drugs and being zapped with all sorts of things, to try and shrink it and if that doesn't work, they'll operate as a last resort. It's risky and the operation could leave me in a chair for life or I could be back on my own two feet,' she said, giving him a sad smile.

Ed nodded and decided to change the conversation. 'Did you say your fiancé ditched you?' he asked.

'Sort of. He has a good job in the city and is under a lot of pressure at the moment. He said he couldn't handle things as they were and maybe we could get back together if I get better, but right now he didn't need it.' she shrugged and gave him another sad smile.

'The miserable, callous bastard. I'm sorry, I've never met the bloke and I hate him already. I'm with your mum on this one. I assume she doesn't like him either?' Laura shook her head. 'And would you have him back? Seems to me you deserve someone better than that,' he added.

Laura shrugged again 'And who's gonna want to take on a burden like me. I don't blame him.'

'Edieeeee,' came the familiar cry from the bar. Sue had arrived.

CHAPTER 15

Emma was applying the finishing touches to her make-up in the bedroom, when there was a tap on the caravan door. Not that she heard it, as the music was too loud in the living room. She did hear the voices and footsteps outside her bedroom door and was so worried she was almost physically sick. The footsteps became lighter as the intruders entered further into the caravan. The volume on the television was lowered and Emma gathered enough courage to confront whoever it was.

The two women heard the footsteps behind them and turned to face Emma, who stared back nervously.

'You must be Emma?' the shorter of the two said. 'I'm Chris and this is Jacqui.'

Emma laughed. 'Ed never said you were women. He only called you Chris and Jack so I was expecting two men,' she said by way of explanation.

'Bloody typical of Ed. Where is he? Don't tell me, he's forgotten?' Jacqui asked.

'No, I sent him away. He was moaning about the music and would only have been in the way and made me late,' she explained.

'I like you, already,' Chris said 'You've obviously got the measure of Ed.'

The three of them stood there appraising each other, the way only women do. Chris at five- foot-four, immediately liked Emma because she was shorter than her and she hated being the shortest wherever she went. She always admired and looked up to Jacqui, literally, as she was five-foot-nine, but she would never admit to her. Jacqui on the other hand, hated being so tall and wanted to be more like Chris, fed up with always being the tallest woman when she was out, despite always wearing flat shoes. God, she would love to wear some of the killer heels Chris wore. Not that she would admit to her, of course. Jacqui, therefore, wasn't impressed that Emma was even shorter than Chris, emphasising her height even more. Still, she seemed OK. A good grilling from the two of them would find out soon enough.

Emma looked at Chris and Jacqui and immediately felt dowdy. Both were beautiful, Chris more so with her long, wavy, blonde hair. Jacqui was intimidating because of her height but had a friendly smile. Both were dressed immaculately. Jacqui in tight, black trousers and a red, silk blouse and Chris in a knee-length, black skirt, which clung to her hips and she wore a green, satin blouse, tucked into her waistband, showing off her narrow waist.

'Well, if he isn't here, he must be over the clubhouse so why don't we crack open a bottle of that expensive wine of his and get to know each other?' Chris said.

'Are you ready for the third degree, Emma?' Jacqui said teasing her. 'How long have you known Ed?'

'Not long, only a few weeks. I've had a few family problems and needed to get away. Ed suggested coming down here for a couple of weeks, to keep out the way. He's been so nice to me. The perfect gentleman, he's lovely,' she said, giving them the rehearsed response and felt slightly guilty at the lie.

Both Jacqui and Chris were quick to pick up on it but decided not to push. They knew there was something else unsaid but would get to the bottom of it in good time.

'Hmmm, he has his moments but he's no angel,' Jacqui told her.

'Take no notice of her,' Chris said, giving Jacqui a look. 'We've known him for years and he is lovely. She's just teasing you.'

'So how long have you known him?' Emma asked.

'He was twelve, I think. We would have been about thirteen. Our Frisbee went in the sea and was getting washed out. Neither of us were good swimmers and we were too frightened to swim that far out to get it. We asked Ed as he walked by and he shrugged and swam out to get it for us. I remember being so worried, he was so far out. I thought he was going to drown. Eventually, he made it back and we've been friends ever since.'

'We used to tease him something rotten, back then. Didn't we, Chris?' Jacqui said.

'We still do.' Chris replied. 'He doesn't mind though. I think, secretly, he likes it.'

'So, what do you know about Ed? Just so we can fill in the gaps for you.' Jacqui said.

'Well, I know both his parents died when he was twenty-five. He married the wrong person and she died. She got her just desserts if you ask me. He's got a dog called Fat Boy and he's a millionaire. That's about it,' Emma told them.

'He's told you all that already. He obviously likes you. He doesn't normally like talking about money, gets very touchy. OK. So, we'll fill in the blanks for you as soon as I refill the glasses. Nice wine this. It's Chateaux Palmer Margaux. Two hundred quid a bottle he pays for this, you know.'

Ed stood and Sue gave him her customary bear hug and kiss on the cheek, leaving behind a pair of red lip marks, which Ed removed with the back of his hand.

'Where's that pretty wee Emma you were with last night?' she asked.

'Getting ready. I was evicted so I didn't get in the way. I thought I'd grab a quick pint or two. Sue, this is Laura, who I met on the way in.'

'Nice to meet you, Laura,' she said. 'So are Chris and Jacqui still coming?'

'As far as I know.' Ed looked at his watch and saw it was gone seven o'clock, which meant they had gone to the caravan first and were probably tucking into his wine and grilling Emma, which was, of course, correct.

'OK. I'll come back later and leave you to it,' she said, eyeing him suspiciously.

'Who's Emma, your wife?' Laura asked.

'No, she's just a friend. She needed to get away for a few days so I brought her down here. I'm not married.'

'You wear a ring,' she said with a smile.

'I was. It was blissfully short and very unhappy and was a big, big mistake. She died in a car accident, which to be honest was a bloody relief. Not everyone I know dies by the way. I'm not jinxed.'

'Why do you still wear the ring then, if you hated her so much?' she enquired.

'It probably sounds a bit lame but I wear it as a reminder of how unhappy I was and as a reminder never to get caught like that again. Maybe one day, when I feel truly happy, I'll take it off and throw it away. For now, it stays. Another drink?' he said with a smile.

When he returned from the bar, Fat Boy had stirred and was now planted firmly across Laura's lap, making the most of being stroked and made a fuss of, his tail wagging furiously behind him. Ed put the drinks down along with the packet of crisps he brought. Fat Boy dropped his front paws to the floor at the sound of the crisp packet rustling and sat obediently.

'Can I give him one?' Laura asked.

'I'm sure you'd make him very happy but even in Cornwall they have laws on bestiality.'

'You're rude,' she said blushing but laughing at his joke. 'How long are you staying here for?' she asked.

'Don't know. I've only been here a couple of days. The caravan is mine and I don't rent it out so I can stay as long as I like. How about you?'

'Similar really. The caravan is mum's and she paid out for some alterations to accommodate my wheelchair. You know, put in an access ramp and got the shower modified. But the way things are going, we might as well go home. At least at home I've got places I can escape to. There's nowhere to hide in a caravan. I think that's half the problem.'

Ed was at a loss as to what to say and just smiled at her.

CHAPTER 16

The clubhouse doors opened and in walked the three amigos, giggling like schoolgirls, which probably meant they had done some damage to Ed's stock of wine. Not that he minded; it was there to be drunk. He stood up to greet them and smiled broadly, as all the males in the bar turned to stare at the three gorgeous women. He noted their jealous looks as he kissed and hugged them all and smiled even more smugly, if that was at all possible. You either had it or you didn't. Well, they weren't to know, he wasn't romantically involved with any of them.

'Have you lost a bit of weight or has Jacqui put on a few pounds?' he asked Chris as he picked her up and swung her round in an embrace. Something he couldn't do with Jacqui, she was too tall and Chris had always been his favourite.

'Don't start,' she warned him.

Ed introduced Laura to everyone, explaining who everyone was.

'Can't leave you on your own for five minutes, can we?' Emma said.

Ed proceeded to explain how they had met, including his comments about hoping Laura rusted.

'I can't believe you said that, you nasty bastard!' Jacqui said

'Yeah alright. I don't rate it as one of my proudest moments and to be honest I'd quite like to forget it,' Ed said defensively.

'It was my fault,' Laura stepped in. 'He offered to help and I was extremely rude to him and got what I deserved. I think it's quite funny now.'

'Right, who wants to give me a hand at the bar?' Ed said changing the subject quickly.

'They didn't give you too much of a hard time, did they?' he asked Emma at the bar.

'No but they told me lots of interesting things about you though,' she said, with a mischievous smile. 'They're really nice. I wish you'd told me they weren't men though. Chris is lovely and has said I can go down to her shop and use the studio to do some painting, and if they're the sort of thing that sells, she can put them up for sale or put me in touch with one of the other galleries in town. I'm really excited. Laura seems nice; pretty too,' she said, giving him a big grin.

'She is nice,' he said ignoring the pretty comment. 'Come on, before everyone dies of thirst.'

The conversation never lulled. Ed spent most of the time on the periphery of it all, happy to sit back and listen to them gossiping and talking of clothes and hairstyles and so on. It never ceased to amaze him, if you put a group of women in a room, they would immediately find common ground and talk the night away. There would never be a gap in the conversation and not a secret left uncovered. Put a group of men in a room and it was a completely different story. Once the football and car conversations were exhausted and after a brief excursion into the latest gadgets and power tools, the conversation died a death, each being quite happy to stand in silence and get slowly pissed. The mere thought of entering a conversation that encroached on any aspect of another's personal life was a complete taboo. Each would leave at the end of the evening knowing no more about any of the others, other than the football team they supported and whether or not they were a cock.

The karaoke was in full swing and so far those who plucked up the courage to stand up and sing in front of an apathetic audience were quite good. One or two even got a couple of claps, which in the clubhouse was the equivalent of a standing ovation. Ed loved karaoke even at the bitter end, when someone who was waiting all night, knocking back the Dutch courage staggered up to the stage and wailed like a banshee to the Gloria Gaynor classic "I Will Survive." Ed knew his limits and generally, never sang after more than six pints.

'How long have you known Ed, then? Sounds like years,' Laura asked Jacqui when Ed had gone to the gents.

'Twenty years, back when he strutting his skinny arse up and down the beach in his speedos.'

'It's filled out nicely, hasn't it?' Laura said giggling, clearly a little tipsy.

'It's a bit bloody vocal for my liking. This morning he farted so loudly, the caravan shook. I was just surprised when I got up I found him still in one piece,' Emma told her, making everyone laugh.

Ed returned to his seat and looked round the table.

'Why are my ears burning?' he asked.

'It should be your bum-cheeks that are burning,' Emma said laughing.

'Haven't you got anything better to talk about, other than my pert, little arse?'

'Laura seems to like it. Personally, I think it too vocal,' Emma said with a knowing smile.

Ed was saved any further humiliation, by the karaoke host calling his name. Ed looked at Emma, who shrugged and gave him a smile. Chris mentioned while Ed was in the toilet he loved karaoke and used to sing in a band and had a good voice. Unfortunately, their music was mediocre and their fame was short lived but he still liked to get up and sing. Emma wasn't too sure it was a good idea but selected an appropriate song that Chris said he would be OK with and hoped he sang better than his efforts in the car and the shower.

He walked onto the stage, with a ripple of applause and a few whistles from his table, without a clue what he was going to be singing. He just hoped it wasn't anything too cheesy or too modern. When he asked the karaoke host what he was singing, he smiled when he told him and knew in an instant that Emma had chosen the song.

He gave what he thought was a fairly passable rendition of "The Great Pretender" thankful that it was the Freddie Mercury version and not the down beat Platters version. He received the usual smattering of applause and walked off stage pleased with himself. As he approached the table, he saw that three youths were standing around it and none of his friends looked too pleased. He slowed his pace to take it in. Two were young, probably in their late teens. One was standing to the side of Laura and the other to the right of Ed's seat. The third was older and looked to be trouble. His hair was cropped short, almost to the scalp, revealing numerous scars. Ed guessed he was in his mid-twenties and looked mean, which was due to his small beady-eyes, which darted left and right like a bird of prey and was definitely the one to watch.

'Well, how was that then?' he asked as he stood between the two youths looking at Emma. Before she had a chance to answer, the youth in front told him he thought he sounded shit.

'Thanks for your constructive criticism and words of encouragement. I'm sure one day you'll make an excellent manger.'

'You're fucking funny,' he replied, trying to sound menacing and falling short of the mark.

'I think so,' Ed replied.

He looked at Emma and Laura, who both looked nervous and uncomfortable. He gave them a smile to say everything was OK but they didn't look convinced. Jacqui and Chris were both chatting away as if nothing unusual was taking place, which Emma found strange.

'What we wanna know, is why you've got all the good looking birds on your table?' The youth standing next to Laura asked.

'Dunno,' Ed replied. 'One minute I'm sitting there minding my own business, just licking my eyebrows and the next thing I know, I've got four gorgeous women sitting at the table,' he said, chuckling at his own joke.

'You think you're fucking funny, don't you? I think you're a prick,' he spat

'I thought we'd already established, I think I'm funny. You need to eat more food with omega oil in it. They say it's very good for short-term memory problems in children,' Ed said, glancing round to see where everyone was.

Emma now looked extremely uncomfortable with the building tension. Ed didn't seem to be trying to find a way round the conflict that seemed inevitable and she was scared.

'Well, I think we should take a couple of these birds off your hands,' the youth to his right said. 'I'll have the one with the dark hair. The old ones are always more grateful.'

Ed laughed. 'I think they need to be a little older than that to be grateful. She'd eat you alive, mate. Trust me.'

'I'll have this one,' the youth next to Laura said. 'She's got great tits for a spastic,' he added and groped her right breast.

'Didn't want to do that,' Chris muttered quietly, at the same time as Ed muttered 'Showtime.'

Ed punched the youth standing to his right viciously in the stomach, almost simultaneously launching a savage kick to the balls of the youth next to Laura. Then he delivered a right uppercut to the youth to his right, knocking him off his feet, following up with a hard left hook to the youth now doubled over next to Laura, sending him to the floor. Two down and out, in just a few seconds. Ed turned to the older youth and swung at him with a right hook. He stepped back just in time and the punch just glanced off his chin. Ed continued forward, jabbing and swinging left and right hooks, backing him up against the wall. The youth smiled and pulled out a flick-knife, waving it in front of him left to right, urging Ed on, looking at him with his evil eyes and twisted smile.

Two flick-knives in two days. The Daily Mail were right, knife crime really was on the up. Shit. Did that mean the country really was being overrun with illegal immigrants and undesirables from Eastern Europe? He really should have taken that newspaper more seriously.

Sue was on the scene in seconds, wielding her huge baseball bat, like a Viking running through a village on a pillaging trip, screaming at him to leave the club now while his head was still on his shoulders.

Before leaving, he turned to Ed and said 'I'm gonna cut you and your dog. You'd better watch your back, cunt,' before walking backwards through the main doors.

'Thanks Sue,' he said giving her a hug. 'I see you haven't lost your touch.'

'Neither have you, looking at the state of those two,' she said, turning towards the two youths behind him.

Ed walked back to his table and pulled the two youths to their feet, grabbing them round their throats, once they were standing.

'What was that all about, then?' he growled at them, not expecting an answer. Firstly, it was a rhetorical question and secondly, because their windpipes were constricted.

'I think, you two, owe these ladies an apology,' he told them, staring at them with blazing eyes.

They both looked at him defiantly, until he increased the pressure on their throats. He then released them and they mumbled hoarse apologies.

'Who was the other idiot with the knife?' he asked the youth with the swollen gonads.

'Mack. Don't know his real name, only Mack. You were lucky he only pulled a knife on you. He robbed a gun from some old geezer last week. You don't want to mess with him, he's fucking mental. He scares the shit out of me.'

Ed nodded but wasn't too worried. He could handle himself. 'Right, you two, time to leave. If I see you round here again, I'm gonna kick your arses so hard, you'll be shitting out of a bag for the rest of your lives. Got it?'

They both turned and hurried out the clubhouse. Ed turned to Laura.

'You OK?' he asked, although the look on her face told him she was.

'I'm fine. He only squeezed my breast. It's been so long, I'd forgotten what it was like to be groped. If you hadn't kicked him in the balls, I might have asked him back to my place,' she said with a huge smile.

'What about you, Emma? Christ you're shaking,' he said concerned.

'I was worried bloody sick. You could have got hurt.'

'Nah, there was only three of them and only one of them was going to be a problem. Those two were just boys,' he said, trying to make light of it.

'Don't worry about Ed, Emma. He can take care of himself. I remember in my last pub, he took on four guys who were giving Lisa a hard time. Broke all the pool cues in the place, it was awesome,' Sue told her.

'I paid for the pool cues and I only broke one. Three, if you include the two broken over me,' Ed said laughing.

'We've seen him take on five,' Jacqui chipped in, 'A bunch of guys were giving Chris and I grief in a club, until Ed sorted them out for us. Sue's right, you don't need to worry about Ed.'

'Any advance on five?' Emma said sarcastically.

'I did do six once,' Ed said matter of fact.

'You beat up six guys in one go!' Laura said in awe.

'Nah. They beat the shit out of me but I was very drunk at the time,' he replied laughing, despite the painful memory and rubbing subconsciously at the long scar on his forearm, received from a knife that night.

'So you could have taken out those two guys in the pub on Wednesday night?' Emma asked. Ed nodded his head. 'So what was different tonight? Why didn't you try and get out of it like you did then?'

She was getting quite angry with him. Ed wasn't sure if she was angry with him or she was just concerned and it was coming out as anger.

'Sometimes you just know whether you can avoid any unnecessary aggravation. Those guys at the pub weren't interested in having a fight. I could tell they were getting a kick out of playing the bullies. Tonight was different. These guys were out for trouble. Then they crossed the line. I don't give a rat's arse if someone calls me names or tries to provoke me, I'll quite happily take it and walk away. He over stepped the mark when he grabbed Laura's tit. I find that offensive.'

Emma let out a sigh and shook her head. Chris stepped in and suggested she help her get a round of drinks in. Ed was just about to take his seat, when he was tapped on the shoulder.

'I saw what you did to those lads. It was pretty good. You've done a bit of boxing haven't you?'

'I did for a while, until I got asked to leave. They put me in to spar with this huge heavyweight. I was only just a middleweight and he was a right bruiser, fought dirty. Punching below the belt, back of the head, head-butting you name it, he did it. I lost my rag and changed the rules and threw in a bit of kick boxing and that was the end of my boxing days.'

'Was that in the armed forces?' he asked

'No. I thought about joining the Commandos once but didn't like the idea of going to war with no underpants on,' Ed replied, chuckling at his own joke.

'I'm Pete,' he said offering his hand, which Ed took and instantly regretted. It was like squeezing a handful of uncooked sausages. His hand seemed to almost ooze through his fingers. Ed had always been told anything other than a good, firm handshake was the sign of a weak character. Looking at this bloke, he could well believe it. He was around Ed's height and probably around mid-fifties in age but it was difficult to tell, as his hair was very grey but his skin was unwrinkled and waxy looking. He had a pathetic excuse for a moustache, which looked more like an apologetic eyebrow became curious and dropped down onto his top lip for a pint. This sat above a pair of fat, wet-looking lips. If someone had asked Ed what a child molester looked like, he would have drawn a picture of Pete.

'I'm Ed,' he finally said.

'I know. I asked Jacqui earlier. I know her from work.'

'Her new work or old work?' Ed was thinking old work in the police, where she probably arrested him for loitering outside a school, with a big bag of sweets and couple of puppies stuffed inside his coat pockets.

'New work. My wife passed away recently – breast cancer. Jacqui was very good, very accommodating and understanding. She a remarkable woman,' he enthused.

'Sorry to hear that and yes she is. I've known her twenty years and she's one of my best friends,' he told him.

'Nice meeting you. I'll go back and pick up my conversation with her. I just wanted to say, I was impressed with the way you handled yourself,' he said and walked off. Ed thought he was a little strange but dismissed it and pulled his chair up to be nearer to Laura.

CHAPTER 17

At the bar, Emma said to Chris, 'Just when I think I'm getting to know Ed, he surprises me.'

'You shouldn't be too hard on him, you know.'

'I know. I'll apologise to him later. You've known him a long time. What's he really like?'

'Pretty much what you see is what you get. You know his parents died. Well, that hit him pretty hard and he was a bit of a mess. I did what I could to help him but there's only so much you can do to help people; the rest is up to them. Then that bitch of a wife of his came along, just when he seemed to be getting back to his old self and got her claws into him. I tried to tell him she was wrong for him. I'd met her a few times and I hated her with a passion. She was just out for his money; not that he knew he had any, really. He thought he'd lost it all. Anyway, you know all that and when she died, he was worse than when his parents died. Even I don't know what was going on in his life at that time. We've never really spoken that much about it. Normally, he's very candid, so I never pushed him. A few months after she died, he seemed to pull himself together and he was back to his old happy-go-lucky self. Becoming a millionaire came as a bit of a shock to him but he's coping, more or less. He buys up houses, renovates them and sells them on. Sometimes he even makes a profit. The first one he sold at a loss to a young couple who were expecting a baby. They fell in love with the place but couldn't get a mortgage for the amount they needed so that soppy sod, reduced the price so they could have it. That's what he's like. I love him to bits.'

'Did you two ever have anything going on between you? I know he thinks a lot of you and I've seen the way he looks at you.

It's the same look, Fat Boy gives Ed.'

Chris smiled at a distant memory and the fact Emma was very perceptive and picked up on it.

'Yes, a long time ago. We tried to make a go of it but it never worked out. We'd known each other far too long. We made love once and it felt strange. It was like having sex with my brother, if you know what I mean? I told this to Ed and he agreed but made a joke about not being Cornish so he wouldn't know what it was like to sleep with a relative and that was that. I'm just glad we didn't ruin our friendship over it. To answer your original question, Ed is the nicest, most generous and kindest person I've ever met,' she said with a hint of sadness. 'Now let's get these drinks back. The sooner we drink them, the sooner we can get another in.'

Pete was asking Jacqui her professional opinion on the Black Cockle Strangler and everyone stopped to listen, what with it being the talk of the town.

'I've no idea what the cockles are all about. Perhaps nipples offend him in some way. Maybe, he had a childhood incident that scarred him for life? Maybe his wife or girlfriend had a deformity and that's the reason. It could be the murders are for a totally different reason and the cockles are for another,' she opined.

'Do you know what sort of paint it is?' Ed asked.

'I spoke to Bob earlier this week and he said it was just ordinary, black, gloss paint. Why, do you think it makes a difference?' Jacqui asked, not understanding why he was asking.

'Well, how many people do you know who have used or even have a tin of black paint around the house? I've never used black paint in my life,' Ed said.

'So where are you going with this? I don't see how it's relevant.'

'Well, I'm guessing the police have looked into recent sales of black paint in the area and probably come up with not many. If it's masonry paint, for example, perhaps someone had it laying around the house. Stay with me, on this and stop frowning, you'll get wrinkles. So, why would someone have it, you ask? Because they used it to paint their windowsills, window frames or steps even. Maybe the police want to check out all the owners of houses with black window frames or front doors. See what I mean?' Ed said with enthusiasm.

Jacqui laughed. 'I'm sure there must be hundreds in Padstow alone. It would be an almost impossible task. Nice try, Poirot.'

'I reckon that's pretty good,' Pete said. 'What's your theory on the reason for the cockles, then; while you're on a roll?'

'It's a gimmick,' Ed said, looking at the incredulous looks everyone was giving him.

'A gimmick? Come on Ed, you can do better than that,' Chris added to the conversation.

'Why not? No forensics, two bodies and bugger all clues; apart from the cockles. It's to throw the police off the scent and the papers were quick to pick up on it so he gets a thrill out of being labelled with a sinister tag. Maybe I read too much but it seems every serial killer has his calling card. Silence of the Lambs was a moth or something, wasn't it? I've read about the Doll Maker, who slapped make-up on his victims, and the Poet, who left poetry on the bodies. He wanted a tag, simple as that. Better than all that bollocks about witchcraft and childhood traumas. Ah sod this. I'm getting the drinks in, while you laugh at my theory,' he said in mock hurt as they all sat there shaking their heads, chuckling to themselves.

The conversation was still going strong when Ed returned from the bar, everyone having their own opinions and theories and wanting them heard. Ed sat back, listened and watched. Laura looked a bit worse for wear and was struggling to keep awake, her eyes almost as hooded as his were on a good day. She caught him looking at her and smiled, with half closed eyes. She had a great smile he noticed. He wasn't sure if he had his beer goggles on, making her appear more attractive than she was but right now, she looked beautiful. He smiled back and took a few more gulps of beer, to see if she became even more attractive. Emma and Chris were in a deep, almost conspiratorial conversation. Chris would look over at him every few sentences and give him a reassuring smile, just to let him know she was fighting his corner. Typical of Chris, she was always like the big sister he never had. Jacqui and Pete were still ranting about the Black Cockle Strangler. Pete's blubbery lips and stupid moustache were twitching away as he spoke, still giving Ed the creeps.

The lights went again at around half-ten, to a loud chorus of boos as Sue reassured everyone they would be back on soon. When they did, Chris declared she was waterlogged and thought it would be a good idea to go home. Nobody disagreed.

'You OK or do you want a push?' Ed asked Laura.

'You can push if you want. I'm a bit tipsy,' she said with a giggle. 'My mum is gonna be so pissed off with me,' she said looking at her phone and seeing six missed calls, all listed as Mum.

'It's OK. I'll win her over with a little bit of the old charm,' Ed told her and everyone groaned, knowing it was probably not a good idea. 'What's her name?'

'Raechael.'

'OK. It'll be fine,' he leaned over and whispered in Laura's ear, also getting a good view of her cleavage. 'Bloody hell, that lad was right about your tits,' he added and received an elbow in the thigh.

'You deserved that you dirty sod,' Jacqui told him.

Laura thought it was amusing and apologised to him, before directing him to her caravan, which was obvious by the large wooden ramp outside. Ed wheeled her up the ramp, which ended in a decked area, just big enough to turn a wheelchair around. Unfortunately, he pushed too hard and banged heavily into the door. He put his finger his lips and said 'Shhhh,' which made Laura giggle.

The caravan door opened, before Laura could get her key out and the stern figure of Mrs. Jacobs appeared.

'Good evening, Mrs. Jacobs,' Ed began. 'We've brought your lovely daughter home and may I say, what an absolute pleasure her company was this evening. You must be very proud of her. I'm Ed,' he said extending a hand, she had no intention of shaking.

'Thank you Mr...' she said, fishing for a surname.

'Case,' he replied, leaning over and saying to Laura 'Why didn't you tell me, your mother was so gorgeous? Frightened of the competition?' This made her laugh, which was more than could be said for Mrs. Jacobs.

'We had a great evening, Mrs. Jacobs. She knows some great songs but they're very rude. Did you teach her those?' he asked, beaming from ear to ear, hoping he was wearing her down.

She gave him a look that said exactly the opposite. 'Thank you and your friends for making sure my daughter got home safely.

Goodnight.'

Going for one final try, Ed squeezed by Laura and planted a kiss on Mrs. Jacobs's cheek. Needless to say, it didn't have the desired effect. She stood there impassively, willing him to go. He knew when he was beaten and bent down and kissed Laura goodnight, before walking dejectedly down the ramp.

'That went well,' Jacqui said, smiling at him and shaking her head.

Ed said nothing as they turned and walked back past the clubhouse to the reception building, where Chris and Jacqui's taxi would arrive.

'What are you two doing tomorrow night?' he asked.

'I don't like the sound of this so I'm busy,' Chris said.

'Don't be like that. I was going to take you to dinner.'

'OK,' Jacqui replied immediately.

'There's a catch isn't there?' Chris stated, rather than asked.

'A small one. I'm going to ask Laura and her mother to come along, by way of an apology for my pathetic performance back there.'

'Why don't you just buy her a box of chocolates? I don't think it's a good idea and for that reason, I'm out.'

'Come on Chris. As much champagne as you can drink,' he said, knowing she had a weakness for the stuff.

'OK,' she replied immediately. 'But why?'

'Because Laura and her mum haven't been getting on and they came down here to try and patch things up. You know, a bit of girly bonding, that kind of thing. Only it hasn't worked out. I just thought it would be nice and might help.'

'Same old Ed. Saviour of damsels in distress, slayer of dragons.' Jacqui chided him.

'I think Mrs. Jacobs might be a dragon too far!' Emma quipped.

Ed rang the Harlyn Inn and booked a table for six people for the following evening. He informed them one guest would be in a wheelchair so would like a good table and was assured it would be no problem. The taxi pulled up and after prolonged goodbyes, Ed and Emma walked back. Ed kept a watchful eye on the shadows, in case any of the idiots from earlier where still lurking around. He was fairly confident they wouldn't be, but it paid to be careful.

CHAPTER 18

Ed was walking along the cliffs with Fat Boy, having left Emma fast asleep. Last night she hopped straight into his bed without any pretence of sleeping in her own. Ed took this as a good sign she wasn't too pissed off with him for the scrap in the clubhouse. He knew Chris had a lot to do with that and he was grateful. He wasn't off the hook yet and anticipated a lengthy conversation, once he returned from his walk with the dog.

It was a beautiful morning. Not a cloud in the sky with a fresh breeze coming in off the sea, perfect for blowing away the cobwebs and easing the slight hangover he had. It was still only six-thirty when he left the caravan and he had the entire headland to himself or so he thought. In the distance he could see a figure walking towards him, a little Jack Russell scampering around his heels.

As he came nearer, Ed could tell he was a local on account of his attire. It seemed to Ed all locals of a certain age dressed in the same clothes. This as a rule was a check-patterned shirt of some description, made of thick woollen weave, no matter what the weather was like. The trousers were always a French-blue colour and made of the same material as boiler-suits, like heavyweight chinos. He was old, judging by the white hair and had a ruddy complexion, either from years at sea or years down the pub – perhaps both.

'Have you got one of those mobile phones on you, son?' he asked.

'I have. Want to borrow it?' Ed asked, handing him the handset.

'No. I don't understand all this modern technology. No point giving it to me. Can you phone the police for me? I found a body on the beach. Reckon it's that bloke they're after. She's got shells on her nipples, like it said in the paper.'

Shit, Ed thought, a third one and this time right on my own doorstep. He thought about dialling Bob direct but thought better of it and dialled 999 and gave them the details. He and the old man, who introduced himself as Amos, walked back the way he had come and waited near the body.

'First dead body I've seen,' Ed said by way of conversation. It wasn't as bad as he was expecting. She was laid out crucifix style, with her head towards the sea and was stark naked, except for the glossy, black shells covering her nipples. The body was pale but slightly darker towards the bottom, where the blood had settled. Her face was just as pale, the lips almost blending into the face, bloodless. The mark round her neck, where she had been strangled, stood out starkly against the rest of her pale skin. Ed shuddered.

'Seen plenty in my time, whilst working on the boats. That one's a pretty one. Some of the ones I've pulled out the water have been grim, all bloated and white. Even worse if the fish have been hungry,' Amos told him with relish.

'Thanks for that. You'd better get your dog away from the body. The police won't be happy if we contaminate the crime scene,' Ed said a little too late, as the Jack Russell urinated across the dead woman's hip.

'Her muff looks a bit severe. It don't look natural, does it?' Amos said, not at all concerned about his dog. In contrast, Fat Boy was lying obediently at his master's feet.

'It's called a Brazilian. It's so the stragglers don't poke out the top and sides of their bikinis,' Ed said knowledgeably 'Going down on that must be like licking Hitler's face, eh?'

'I wouldn't know about that,' Amos replied. 'Me and the Missus haven't done that in years. We've had four kids and she's like a wizards sleeve down there.' They both chuckled at the joke.

'I went out with a girl once. Wendy her name was but everyone called her Candy. I found out why. She'd dyed her pubic hair pink and it looked like a bloody great big candyfloss.'

'I bet it didn't taste like one,' Amos said with a grin, displaying teeth that hadn't seen a dentist since the war.

'Dunno, I laughed so much she told me to leave so I never

found out.'

'You two, get away from my fucking crime scene!' Bob's voice boomed from the top of the dunes as he strode towards them, followed by a huge entourage of uniformed police, plain-clothes police and men in white suits. Ed noticed dickhead Murphy was among them. Deep joy.

'Fucking hell, Ed. Not you, again. You're like a bad smell. Thanks for the whisky by the way, a nice drop of stuff that. Who found the body?'

'I did,' Amos told him.

'Right, come with me. Murphy, you take a statement from Mr. Case and be nice to him.'

Murphy walked over with a sadistic grin on his face, which said he was going to make this as difficult as possible. Ed gave him a look back, that said he was going to be a complete pain in the arse too, if he dicked him around.

'Name,' Murphy demanded.

'If you'd added please, it would have been better. Ed Case'

'Are you trying to be funny?'

'No, it's my name you muppet, ask Bob,' he replied, impressed he even picked up on it. He didn't seem the sharpest tool in the box.

Murphy gave him a look that said he didn't believe him but carried on regardless. 'What time did you discover the body?'

'I didn't, Amos did. I just phoned 999.'

'OK. What time did you phone?'

'Dunno, ain't got a watch on,' Ed replied, knowing he was trying to wind him up but not being able to help himself.

'If you continue to make this difficult, we can do this down the station. Right?' he snapped, trying to sound officious and failing.

'Wrong. You're just flexing your muscles, because you're pissed off with me for making you look a plum in front of your boss yesterday so you're using your position of power to give me a hard time. Right?'

'I can do what the hell I like. This is a murder enquiry,' he said raising his voice.

'You might want to know that the Jack Russell peed on the body,' Ed said trying not to smirk.

'And you think that's funny, do you? That's somebody's daughter and you think that's funny. You're sick.'

'Oh, just ask the questions and give me a break on the moral high ground routine. Christ you'll be trying to convert me to Christianity next,'

'There's nothing wrong with having morals, you should try it some time, you ignorant bastard.'

'You're just about the most odious policeman I've ever met. You're really getting off on this power thing, aren't you? It's pathetic and so are you.' Ed was pushing as hard as he could, trying to hit a nerve. 'You look quite angry actually. Fancy your chances again, do you? I wouldn't if I was you. I can't see that cute, bikini-clad, PC Walsh anywhere to save your useless arse.' That was the right button to hit.

Murphy threw his notebook into the sand and took a swing at Ed, who saw it coming, stepped back and laughed at him. That also had the desired effect and Murphy launched a second attack but it was uncontrolled, uncoordinated rage and he went sailing by, arms wind-milling as he lost his balance and ended up in a heap in the sand. Ed smirked as Murphy got to his feet, nostrils flaring and his face contorted in rage.

'Case, come here!' Bob shouted from behind him and didn't sound happy.

Ed walked over and Bob put a hand on his shoulder and walked him away from the rest of his team.

'What the fuck was that all about?'

'We were winding each other up and I wound him up more that he wound me up. Sorry Bob but the bloke's an arsehole and I couldn't help myself any more than he could,' Ed said apologetically.

Bob stared at him intensely. 'You're right, he can be an arsehole but he's a good copper; very clever, too. He just wasn't blessed with any interpersonal skills and has a short temper. Anyway, that's my problem. Where were you last night?' he asked.

'At the clubhouse until about eleven and went straight home with Emma, officer,' Ed replied.

'Good.' he replied. 'Now, bugger off and stop winding my officers up. Before you do, what were you playing at yesterday, insulting Councillor Pascoe?' he said with a smirk.

'Not sure I know what you mean, officer,' Ed said innocently, knowing exactly what he meant. The look Bob gave him encouraged him to continue. Ed he told him what happened. 'Sorry, she pissed me off and I thought I'd have a little fun.'

'Well, thank you very much. I got a right ear bashing from her. She doesn't take kindly to being called "fatty" and thinks we've got a sex maniac on the loose, you cretin. You've only been down here two days and have already wound up Murphy and Councillor Pascoe and that's only what I know about. You can be a right pain in arse sometimes.'

Ed nodded and realised Bob was right and for the briefest of moments felt remorse but soon got over it. He decided to tell Bob about the incident in the clubhouse, just to really make his day, which by the look on his face, it didn't.

'And his two mates reckon this Mack character's got a gun. That's all I bloody well need. What is it with you? I've known you quite a few years now and you get into trouble wherever you go. Last time you were down you were involved in a brawl in the pub. Why can't you just walk away, like most normal people would?'

'You mean like you would?' Ed replied, knowing Bob would never back down or walk away if provoked.

'You've got a point there,' he said grinning 'Now bugger off back to that cute little girlfriend of yours and stay out of trouble,' he said, giving Fat Boy a stroke, before striding off back to his crime scene, barking orders all the way.

CHAPTER 19

Ed was disappointed with what was on offer in the mini-market. He now stood, slightly embarrassed, outside the door of Laura's caravan with a box of Maltesers in his hand. It wasn't much to offer by way of an apology but that was all that was available. Before knocking, he checked for signs of life and saw Mrs. Jacobs through the window, pottering around in the kitchen.

'Oh, it's you again,' she greeted him frostily when she answered the door.

Ed gave her what he hoped was a winning smile, which faded quickly, when he saw the stony look on her face.

'These are for you,' he said handing her the Maltesers, sheepishly. 'It's all they had in the shop and I wanted to apologise for my behaviour last night. I'm not always such an idiot,' he said, trying another winning smile, with the same noted lack of result.

Mrs. Jacobs took the offering, with a look of distaste, thanked him and look set to close the door.

'I also wanted to invite you and Laura to dinner tonight,' he added quickly before the door was closed. 'It won't just be me so it shouldn't be too painful,' he said smiling. 'The friends who were with me last night will be coming. I would be extremely grateful if you would accept so that I can apologise properly.'

'Of course, we'll come. Won't we, mother?' Laura said, as she wheeled her way through to the front door.

Mrs. Jacobs nodded and walked off, leaving Laura and Ed alone.

'OK, table booked for seven so we'll come by around six-thirty. It's only at the Harlyn Inn so not far to walk, or whatever you do in that contraption; unless, of course, you want to get a cab?'

Laura smiled at this clumsy attempt to cover his embarrassment and said walking would be fine. 'I must look a right mess?' she told him. She did, Ed thought.

'You look better than I did first thing this morning but I have to say you don't look too good. Hangover?' he told her.

Laura nodded and winced as her fragile head throbbed as a result. 'You certainly know how to make a girl feel good. I'll make such an effort for tonight, you won't recognise me,' she said, flashing one of her killer smiles.

'Good. Wear a name badge in that case. See you tonight,' he said and walked off back to the caravan. He needed caffeine.

'Where the hell have you been?' was Emma's greeting.

'Sorry, stopped off to deliver some chocolates to Mrs. Jacobs and to ask her to dinner. She said yes or Laura said yes on her behalf, to be correct.'

'That's why you took so long, Laura,' she said with a knowing smile.

'And what's that supposed to mean? I was only there a couple of minutes.'

'I think she's got the hots for you.'

'Get out of it. She hardly knows me and vice versa. Stop trying to wind me up. If you must know why I was so long, it was because I had to phone the police. An old boy found a body on the beach and didn't have a mobile phone. Bob turned up,' he said raising an eyebrow at Emma, who gave him a sneer in return.

Emma wanted to know every little detail, which surprised him. Rather than being squeamish, as he expected, she was the complete opposite and wanted to know everything. She didn't seem too impressed with his run in with Murphy but laughed when he said he took a roasting from Bob, for his antics with the local councillor.

'Do you have to wind up or fight everyone you meet?' she asked mockingly, sounding just like Bob earlier and he told her so. 'I must admit though, you seem to be quite good at it. I bet you were the school bully,' she said, scrutinizing his reaction.

'No. Not at all, I was the complete opposite. I don't remember having a fight until I was about thirteen. The school bully decided it was my turn that day and gave me a thump. I retaliated and knocked seven shades of shit out of him and he was two years older than me. That started it all off. I was then the new school hard-nut and everyone else wanted to prove they were better. I always tried to avoid a fight but sometimes you can't so I had to take on all comers and kept winning. By the time I was sixteen they gave up and left me alone, more or less but I never started a fight and used to stick up for the underdogs.'

'My hero,' she said, wanting to wind him up even more. 'I know all that, anyway. Chris told me all about you last night but it's nice to know you're not lying to me,' she said gleefully.

'Great, definitely no secrets now you're in with her. Think it might have been a mistake getting you two together. I have a feeling that you, Chris and Jacqui are gonna make my life hell. I'm off for a shower.'

Emma and Ed took a stroll down the beach and cut through to the village, to get a pub lunch, unknowingly walking the same path the killer had the previous evening. Emma wanted to see where he found the body, which had since been removed and no trace left. Ed was surprised the forensic team had finished already, half expecting the area to be a hive of activity but there seemed to be none.

Once again, the police found nothing at the scene, apart from another solitary flip-flop print in the sand, which matched the one found previously. The body, once it had been thoroughly examined would also yield nothing, not a solitary clue to the killer's identity. The woman had been identified and so far no link could be found between her and the previous two victims. Single, twenty-four years old and lived alone, just like the others but had a completely different social circle with no known common acquaintances. Once again, the police were left with nothing, other than the certainty they were slain by the same person.

The first killing had been for what? For revenge for mocking him, or justice, for her lack of modesty? It didn't matter, it was no longer important. The first victim was difficult, not knowing if he would or could go through with it, the uncertainty of how he would react and feel afterward. The fact was he enjoyed every minute of it. Once he rendered her unconscious it was just so easy and felt exhilarating. The thrill was immense. The power he felt was better than anything he ever experienced. It was like a drug and he wanted more.

The second and third in comparison were easy. He followed the same routine each time, speaking to them and following them home. The abundance of police asking questions made it so much easier, passing himself off as one of them on the last occasion, even getting their addresses, not needing to follow them for the remainder of the day. Knocking on their front doors when he knew they were alone, even being invited in, it was just so easy. Even the killing was easier. He no longer rushed taking his photographs, panicking and blurring the shots like he did the first time. He was in total control and could take his time and savour every moment. No remorse, no guilt, just a hunger for more and there would be more, a lot more.

They only had a light lunch at the pub. Ed ate a tuna sandwich and Emma a plate of chips, while they basked in the afternoon sunshine in the extensive beer garden. Ed couldn't remember a time when he felt so content and was savouring every moment.

'Why didn't you tell me, you and Chris once had a thing going on?' she asked, pleased she knew another secret.

'Didn't see it was important. It was ages ago and I was only about twenty at the time. I've slept with a few women in my time,' he said brushing it off.

'Including Jacqui?' she said, raising an eyebrow. Ed wasn't sure if she was fishing or if Jacqui told her. He didn't think it was Chris, as she didn't know or at least he didn't think she did.

'Yep. A year or so before I got married. She was on a course in London and I went to see her after work and missed my last train home. I stayed in her hotel room and it just happened. We both regretted it in the morning and agreed it was a mistake, a nice mistake but a mistake and it was the one and only time. Story of my life, it seems.'

'Do you sleep with all your friends?' she said laughing.

'Not yet,' he replied with a leer.

'In your dreams, old man. In your dreams,' she told him.

'You make me out to be a right womaniser. I'll have you know,

I can count my conquests on…two hands.'

'Yeah but only if you count in binary.'

'Very funny and very untrue,' he said, genuinely put out by the last remark.

'Come on, let's go. I need to get ready. I've got a lot of competition tonight. I don't want to be outshone by the others and stop sulking, it doesn't suit you,' she added, realising she had hit a nerve and trying to make light of it.

Ed knew that wouldn't be the case. Jacqui and Chris were both extremely attractive but Emma had the advantage of youth and he knew they were both jealous of that; he could tell. He just preferred to play dumb, when it came to matters of the opposite sex. It was easier that way. The path of least resistance was an easy path to walk.

CHAPTER 20

Ed put his iPod into the docking station, selected Elvis Costello and cranked the volume up, much to the disapproval of Emma. Sweet revenge for having to endure the crap she was polluting the air with the day before. He sat there smugly, singing "Oliver's Army" at the top of his voice. Ed showered first and changed into a pair of tailored, black trousers and a clean, dark-blue, striped shirt and even wore a pair of dress shoes. He felt a little over dressed but wanted to make a good impression on Mrs. Jacobs and, if he was honest with himself, which he wasn't, on Laura, too. Above all, he wanted tonight to be a success. It had potential disaster written all over it but hoped Mrs. Jacobs might be a little more amicable than she was on their previous encounters. Maybe after a few drinks she would mellow. He hoped so or everyone was in for a very long night.

Emma finally emerged from the bedroom a few minutes before Chris and Jacqui were due to arrive. She looked fantastic in a little, black, sleeveless dress, which finished a few inches above the knee and went in and out in all the right places. Ed complimented her but knew, she thought, she looked good. He could tell from the way she was smiling and wished he could be that happy when he looked in the mirror. Chris and Jacqui arrived, both looking equally stunning, especially Chris, who had on a white linen dress that clung to her curves and made Ed wish things had turned out differently between them. After Ed warned everyone to give Mrs. Jacobs a chance and to be on their best behaviour, they set off to meet her and Laura; Jacqui reciting the Lord's Prayer out loud as they approached their caravan.

Before he had a chance to walk up the ramp and knock on the door, it opened and Laura wheeled herself down followed by her mother, who had also been warned to be on her best behaviour or else Laura would never speak to her again. Mrs. Jacobs didn't look quite as unfriendly as in the morning. She wasn't exactly oozing friendliness either but it was a start. She was wearing a white, floral-patterned, summer dress and Ed thought she looked pretty good for her age, which he guessed to be around the mid-forties to have a daughter of twenty-six. Just a pity she was unable to smile.

Laura, on the other hand, was grinning like a Cheshire cat. Gone were the glasses and ponytail, replaced by a mane of flowing, glossy, dark-brown hair, which was naturally wavy and ended below the shoulders. She was wearing a black dress with thin shoulder straps and a plunging neckline. Ed stood there astounded by the transformation, his heart beating so hard it almost hurt.

'Ed, stop dribbling, it's embarrassing,' Jacqui said to him quietly, pushing his chin up with the back of her hand to close his mouth. Laura noticed and laughed; pleased with the effect she had on him.

'Told you, you wouldn't recognise me,' she said, smiling broadly.

Ed was lost for words and stood staring for a couple of seconds, before he could find his words. 'You look great, Mrs. Jacobs,' he said. 'You, on the other hand, look fantastic, wow!' he added, seeing the pout she gave him after his first comments. He walked over, bent down and kissed her on the cheek, getting a waft of a very nice and no doubt very expensive perfume.

Laura introduced her mother as Raechael. Everyone smiled politely and said hello, even Raechael. A tepid start but what was he expecting, hugs and kisses all round?

'Right then, shall we go?' Ed asked. Everyone seemed to be in agreement. 'Want me to push, Laura? Don't want you all sweaty and smelly before we get there.'

'A lady doesn't sweat she perspires,' she told him.

Ed laughed, 'Next you'll be telling me you don't fart you do love puffs. Come on, let's go.'

'You're rude,' she informed him.

'Your mum looks good from behind,' he teased. 'You think she'll take it as a compliment if I told her, she has a nice bum?'

'I think she'd be horrified.'

'OK, another day maybe. Some good hip action going on there though.'

'Gross. That's my mother you're talking about. She's forty-six, too old for you.'

'I dunno, ever seen the Graduate? That Mrs. Robinson was a right little minx.'

'Shut up and push.' she ordered him 'Are you looking down my top?' she exclaimed.

'Of course, why else would I volunteer to push?'

'Good. Just don't crash,' she said happily, as they turned onto the narrow coastal path.

They arrived at the restaurant just before seven and were shown to their seats. Ed asked Laura if she wanted to sit in her wheelchair or on the chair provided. It was a carver with arms and she opted for that, as the wheelchair was too low. Ed stood in front of her and bent down and instructed her to put her arms round his neck. He eased himself upright and put his arms around her. He lifted her up, swung round and set her gently down in the chair. Her hands lingered on the back of his neck and she released them, slowly brushing the sides of his neck as she did, causing Ed to come out in goose bumps. Ed was surprised by her overt flirting and sat down with a grin on his face. Emma, who was sitting the other side to him, pinched his leg and in a whisper, called him a tart.

The waitress appeared and for once didn't look like an illiterate, bored teenager and was even enthusiastic, handing out the menus, informing them that the soup of the day was leek and potato.

'Would you like drinks while you look at the menu?' asked the waitress, whose name badge identified her as Sarah.

'Well, I've promised Chris champagne all night,' Ed said, looking round the table. 'So unless anyone isn't happy with that I suggest letting Chris choose as she's the connoisseur and I don't know one brand from another.'

'You certainly have expensive taste, Mr. Case. This could be a very expensive evening for you. Assuming, you're true to your word and will be picking up the bill?' Raechael asked with a not too friendly smile.

'Not me. Champagne, I can take it or leave it and don't worry about the bill, I've got it covered. Eat and drink whatever you like. I might have to spend the rest of my holiday washing up dishes here but I'll worry about that when it comes to it.'

'You must have a very well-paid job in that case?'

'No. I'm what an actor would call between jobs. I took voluntary redundancy a few years ago and decided to do something I like. I buy up properties on the cheap, give them a lick of paint and sell them. Sometimes, I even make a profit,' he replied cheerily. Chris and Jacqui both gave him an exasperated look and he was sure Emma's eyes were boring into the back of his head, but he didn't want to look.

'Probably not the most sensible thing you could have done in the current economic climate, Mr. Case,' she said in derisory manner.

'Maybe,' he said, determined not to let her get to him. He was saved by Chris.

'OK we'll have the Pol Roger Reserve, please.'

'Right, make that two bottles please, Sarah,' he told the waitress, who smiled politely and hurried off.

'So, I'd better introduce you to everyone properly, Raechael. Next to you is Chris Stevens, who I've known since I was about twelve years old, when I used to come down here as a kid. Chris owns an arts and crafts shop in town. Next to her is Jacqui Smith, who was and still is, as far as I know, Chris's best friend, who I also know from when I was a kid. She was until recently a detective sergeant in the police and now runs the family undertaking business. Last but not least, on my right is Emma James, who I've known a very short while but she needed a holiday so I invited her down with me. And then there's me but we've already done me to death,' he said pleased with himself. He was just about to ask Laura and Raechael to fill in a few gaps, when Raechael beat him to it with another barbed remark.

'Yes, Laura told me all about you, Mr. Case, including your penchant for brawling in public, like a common thug.'

Ed could see everyone was getting a little edgy and out the corner of his eye, Laura, staring daggers at her mother. He blew out an exasperated breath, determined to win this battle of wills. Surely she must be getting bored with taking shots and missing the target? Sarah turned up and popped the champagne and eventually managed to fill everyone's glasses, before putting the two bottles into champagne buckets and leaving.

'It's not something I'm proud of, Raechael, but it was unavoidable. I'm very protective towards my friends and those thugs overstepped the mark. Unless, you think, a minor sexual assault on your daughter is OK?' He regretted saying the last remark. She was definitely getting to him.

'How very chivalrous of you or is that just an excuse for loutish behaviour?' she continued. For Emma, it was the straw that broke the camel's back.

'How dare you, sit there on your high horse criticising him,' she said, fortunately keeping her voice at a reasonable level so as not to cause a scene. 'I've only know Ed for three days. Yes that's right, three days,' she said, for the benefit of Jacqui and Chris, who were sitting there wide-eyed. 'And I can tell you, he is without doubt, the kindest and most generous person, I've ever met. Three days ago when we met, I was about to commit suicide and he stopped me.'

Ed didn't like the way this was going. 'Emma don't go there, it's not worth it. It doesn't matter...' he began to protest.

'Yes it does.' she said, as he held her hand under the table. 'The reason I was going to kill myself was because I felt completely worthless, thanks to a violent and abusive boyfriend, who raped me, repeatedly. Sometimes he raped me at knife point, sometimes with this friends joining in and getting it all down on video to sell, to feed his drug addiction. Ed stopped me and took me home, a complete stranger. He took me to dinner and let me stay the night and was the perfect gentleman, who wanted nothing in return. Everything I own, from the make-up on my face to the shoes on my feet, he bought for me. In fact he bought me an entire wardrobe, more clothes than I've ever owned in my entire life. So what gives you the right to sit there and try and humiliate him in front of his friends and your own daughter, when he is ten times the person you'll ever be?'

Emma stopped. Time seemed to freeze. Chris and Jacqui sat there open mouthed. Chris hurried round the table and put a protective arm around Emma. Ed blew out another huge sigh and downed his champagne. Mrs. Jacobs ran from the table and headed for the toilets.

'That went well, then,' Jacqui said to try and break the tension.

'I'm sorry but she was getting on my nerves. Sorry, Laura, but she was being a right pain in the arse,' Emma said, turning to Ed and giving him an apologetic look.

'It's OK. Thanks. I don't think anyone has ever stuck up for me before. I suppose I better go and get her,' he said, giving her a kiss on the cheek.

'Do you think that's a good idea, Ed? I'll go, she's my mother,' Laura said

'Nah, I'll go and charm her back out,' he said, triggering Jacqui to start muttering the Lord's Prayer again.

Sarah, the perpetually smiling waitress, was hovering as Ed got up to retrieve Raechael, the words 'deliver us from evil' repeating over and over in his mind.

'Sarah. I need two favours. What's the biggest tip you've ever had?'

'I got a tenner once,' she said grinning

'OK. Here's the deal. If you keep that champagne flowing and everyone has a full glass and there are no empty bottles on the table when I come back, I'll give you ten times that,' he said to the wide-eyed Sarah. 'And if you take no notice, if someone tells you there's a pervert in the ladies, I'll double that 'cos it'll be me extracting my friend. Is that a deal?'

'You bet!' she said, clearly pleased with the deal and rushed over to the table to top up everyone's glasses.

CHAPTER 21

Ed walked straight into ladies toilets without knocking, which were fortunately empty apart from one trap, showing engaged. When he finally got over the fact they were clean, didn't smell and weren't swimming in a meniscus of piss, he knocked on the cubical door, hoping it was occupied by Raechael.

'Raechael. It's Ed'

'Go away,' was the tearful reply.

'I can't do that. I came in here with the intention of leaving with you and I'm not leaving until I do,' he replied softly.

'Just leave me alone. I can't go back out there. I've made such fool of myself,' she said sniffing.

'Don't worry about that. I do it all the time and that lot are a forgiving bunch.'

'Just leave me alone and go have your meal. You don't need me there. I'm sure you'll have a much better time without a bitter and twisted old woman spoiling your meal.'

'Look, I don't do talking to toilet doors. Either you come out or I'm coming in. It would be easier if you come out.'

'Just go,' she said, sniffing back more tears.

'OK, have it your way,' he replied and walked into the vacant trap adjacent to the one occupied by Raechael. He put the toilet seat down, just in case he slipped in his leather-soled shoes. He gauged there was just enough clearance at the top of the partition to climb over and hoisted himself up onto it with the aid of the cistern. It was a struggle, due to the limited clearance and had to lie flat across the partition. He swung his legs over and slowly slid is legs and torso down the opposite side, until he was clinging on by his fingertips, feet dangling in mid-air. He looked down but couldn't judge the distance to the floor and didn't want to jump. He never had liked heights. The partition was the type that started a foot from the floor and Ed's feet were at the gap level and he couldn't move them to push against the partition as his waist wouldn't bend. He tried to pull himself back up but didn't have the strength in his finger tips to do so. He tried to lower his body but all that happened was his trousers disappeared up the crack of his arse. Not being able to pull himself up, didn't help matters. He was stuck and his fingers were hurting him and his backside was in agony, as his pants and trousers, threatened to split him in two.

Ed didn't know this just yet but his belt buckle was snagged on a screw sticking out of the partition. It once held the toilet roll dispenser, which had long since been replaced with a drum on the opposite side. Ed tried in vain to lift himself up, sweating with the exertion. When he relaxed, another few millimetres of clothing disappeared between his bum cheeks, which were only just recovering from sitting on the railing three days ago.

'Mrs. Jacobs,' Ed said in an agonised voice. 'I'm stuck.'

'Of course, you are. Just get down, get out and leave me alone.'

'Mrs. Jacobs. I really am stuck. Take a look at my backside and ask yourself, would I put myself through that, if I wasn't genuinely stuck? It bloody hurts Raechael, its cutting me in half.' He wasn't joking, his balls were now being squashed by the seam of his trousers and it was no longer funny. 'Help me out, Raechael. Please!'

'It does look a little uncomfortable,' she said, which was the biggest understatement since he heard someone say Hitler was just misunderstood.

'Can you push me up or something, so I can get a better grip with my hands?' He pleaded. Raechael stood up and put her shoulder against his buttocks and pushed up. He didn't budge an inch. Unfortunately, another inch of cloth disappeared, as she stopped pushing, causing Ed to wince. 'I think it must be my belt can you undo it?'

'I don't think so!' she replied, as if he had asked her to perform some abhorrent sexual act.

'Raechael, I'm starving and I don't want my next meal to be hospital food, even on BUPA it ain't that good and I'm in agony. If I could get down on my knees and beg, I would. Just try, please.'

Raechael put her arms around his waist, as Ed breathed in so she could find the belt. His fingers were becoming numb and also very sweaty as was the rest of him, with the exception of his backside, thanks to several inches of cotton underpants being forced up it by his unforgiving trousers. She finally got a grip on the belt and started to feed it back through the belt loop on his trousers.

'Faster Raechael. I don't think I can hold out much longer,' he said breathlessly.

'I'm going as fast as I can. There isn't much room to work with. It's out. Hold on, I'm going to give it a tug and see if I can release it.' She gave a huge tug and the belt came free and Ed was finally able to put his feet on the floor. Ed threw his arms around her and hugged her and kissed her on each cheek, then, holding her head in both hands, on the lips.

'Thanks Raechael. God, I thought I was going to be going to hospital for stitches,' he said picking his trousers out of backside, smiling in ecstasy.

'It doesn't change anything. I can't go back out there now. Not after what I said to you and what that poor girl told me. She's very lucky to have someone who would do that for her,' she said sadly.

'I think I'm the lucky one, for having a friend, who would tell that to a complete stranger to sick up for me. I was quite touched,' he said and meant it. It must have taken a lot of courage to say that. He was genuinely overwhelmed. 'Mrs. Jacobs, if you don't come out now and go back to the table, what's Laura going to think? I know you haven't been getting on with each other; she told me,' Raechael turned her head away from him. Ed put his finger under her chin and turned her head to face him again. 'Wouldn't she think a lot more of you, if you went back and sat down at the table and enjoyed the rest of your meal?' he said, looking her straight in the eyes.

'I can't, not now. You go and enjoy yourself, you don't need me there. I'll make it up with Laura,' she said with fresh tears in her eyes.

'Raechael, the main reason I invited you and Laura here tonight was to try and help you two patch things up. Both my parents died when I was twenty-five, when they were probably not a lot older than you are now. Laura's twenty-six, think about it. You could try and work out your differences today or wait until tomorrow or the day after. Like me, you might leave it too late,' he said staring at her, as tears flowed down her face.

'You're right,' she finally said and gave him a hug, making his shirt damp. 'I think I've seriously misjudged you, Mr. Case,' she said sniffing.

'Maybe, but perhaps not as much as you have Laura. I think she just needs you to let her be a bit more independent.'

'I know but I can't myself. It hasn't been easy for either of us. She used to be so full of life, always so happy and carefree. Seeing her in that chair, tears me apart. I only want her to be happy and to help. Is that so much to ask?' Ed shook his head. He felt sorry for her, thinking how devastating it must be, seeing her daughter like that.

They walked out of the cubical and came face-to-face with an old lady, wearing far too much make-up. She had a look of horror on her face; either that or she had dawn her eyebrows in too high up her forehead. Ed couldn't work out which.

'People like you are disgusting, filthy, perverts and should be locked up,' she admonished them, making Ed laugh.

'I'm sure you came in here for a reason, so why don't you shuffle off into the cubical before you have an accident. I'm sure at your age that happens quite frequently and you don't want to have to go back to your meal stinking of urine, do you? Go, shoo!' he said, urging her on with a wave of his arms. It was the first time he had seen Raechael smile, like she genuinely meant it. It wasn't a patch on her daughter's but it looked good. Ed just hoped the woman he insulted wasn't another local councillor. The last thing he wanted was Bob on his case. This time he might not be as understanding.

'You're wicked. Now give me five minutes to do my makeup and I'll be out,' she said smiling again.

'I'm waiting outside. Please don't make me come back in, my backside's in tatters.'

She emerged a few minutes later and they walked back towards to the table.

'How old are you Raechael, if you don't mind me asking?'
'Forty-six. Why?'

'You've got a lovely bum,' he said, leaning back and appraising it, thinking Laura will never believe me when I tell her about that.

'Don't push it, Ed. I might just change my mind about you,' she said but was obviously flattered and didn't appear to mind and even laughed, which was the sight that greeted the rest of the party. As one they looked up and couldn't believe their eyes. Ed scanned the table and saw all the glasses were full, as were the two bottles in the champagne buckets. He looked around and caught Sarah's eye and gave her a thumbs up. She looked very pleased with herself.

Raechael walked straight over to her daughter and apologised for her behaviour earlier and for causing her embarrassment. Ed couldn't hear what was being whispered but it ended with hugs and kisses so it seemed all was OK, for now at least. Raechael approached Emma and apologised to her, which also ended in hugs and kisses. Ed sat back in his chair and gave Jacqui and Chris a smug look. Chris shook her head and mouthed 'What the hell did you say to her?' Ed just shrugged and continued to be smug.

Laura tapped him on the arm and said. 'How did you manage that? She's like a completely different person.' And she was, walking round and apologising to both Chris and Jacqui.

'I told her she had a nice arse,' Ed said grinning.

'You didn't. Did you?' Ed nodded and carried on looking triumphant. 'You did. Bloody hell, you've got some guts. I'm surprised you got out in one piece.' Not as surprised as Ed was, at one point he was sure he was going to come out in two. That experience took the expression laying your arse on the line, to a whole new dimension. Thank God the chairs were padded.

They finally got round to ordering their meals, along with another two bottles of champagne, which seemed to start disappearing rapidly, on the return of Ed and Raechael. When Sarah came over to take their orders, Ed slipped ten twenty pound notes into her back pocket, thanking her and telling her a deal is a deal. She smiled so broadly Ed thought her face might split.

'Before the food arrives, for the benefit of Raechael and Laura, and following on from Emma's frank revelation, I thought I'd be completely honest with you and let you know, I'm actually a millionaire,' he turned to Emma and said 'There no more secrets,' and gave another of his now, well-practiced smug grins.

'Wow, did you win the lottery?' Laura asked, wide eyed.

'Nope. It's a long story but I'll give you the abbreviated version,' he said, and proceeded to tell everything, pulling no punches. Emma shook her head and nudged him when it got to the part about his failed suicide attempt but he continued, ignoring the shocked looks on both Chris and Jacqui's faces. When he finished, the table was in complete silence. He looked over to Chris and Jacqui and raised an eyebrow, inviting comment.

'Why didn't you tell me?' Chris asked 'I could've helped you if you had. I would've stayed longer, done more for you.'

'What and have my macho image in tatters. Big tough guy like me, admitting he wanted to end his life because his ex-wife was an old slapper and it all got a bit much. Get real. Anyway, once I'd got over that night, I was back on my feet and a changed man. You did plenty to help me, you both did. I'm more than grateful for that but would it have made any difference if I told you? No it wouldn't, except you'd have made a fuss and I already felt like a fraud. Anyway, it was a long time ago. Cheers,' he said raising his glass.

Chris gave him a look that said she would talk to him later. She did, however, by this time she was pissed and compassionate, rather than angry he hadn't told her, so by and large it was a relatively painless conversation.

The food, when it arrived, was excellent and the conversation flowed, as did the champagne and the mood was light-hearted. Ed gave his elongated version of how he managed to persuade Raechael to rejoin the table; not leaving out any of the detail, which gave everyone a laugh. Jacqui said she was just glad she didn't have to wash his underpants. That set the tone for the rest of the evening. Raechael kept them amused with numerous anecdotes about her job as a call centre manager and her dealings with irate or plain stupid members of the public. She really was a completely different person. Even Emma had to admit, she actually liked her by the end of the evening.

Sarah came back with what turned out to be the last bottle of champagne for the evening. When she opened it the cork flew from the bottle and champagne to shot across the table. The cork hit the suspended ceiling, breaking one of the tiles, causing it to shatter and fall onto the table. Everyone thought it was funny. The exception to this was the manager, who was keeping an eye on the table. Ed was sure this was so he could collect the fat tip he was sure would be left at the end of the night and was right. The manager gave Sarah a severe reprimand in front of everyone and told her to go and serve another table. Before Ed could open his mouth, Raechael beat him to it.

'Sarah, stay where you are!' she ordered her, before venting her spleen on the unsuspecting manager. 'I deal with officious, petty minded, bullies like you every day of the week. Do you get a kick out of bullying young girls and humiliating them in public? Do you?' she said, giving him no time to answer, before continuing. 'Sarah is the most competent waitress I have met in a long time. How dare you tell her to serve another table. You've been hovering for the last half an hour and I think you're just waiting to scoop up the tip we leave behind, you sly, greedy, little man. Now why don't you piss off and let Sarah get on with her job.' Everyone at the table applauded as did a number of the other patrons in the restaurant. The manager scuttled off in embarrassment and Sarah stood there, smiling like the village idiot.

The bill came and Ed paid by credit card and personally handed the tip to Sarah, giving her strict instructions not to share it with the arsehole that called himself a manager. Sarah nodded, never breaking her smile as she pocketed the tip and walked with them to the door and waved them off.

CHAPTER 22

When they left, Chris and Emma walked off in front, Chris putting a friendly arm around her shoulders every now and again, like a protective big sister. This was typical of her. She had done the same to Ed on numerous occasions, perhaps as compensation for being an only child and not having a younger sibling to look out for. Raechael insisted on pushing her daughter, which worried Jacqui and Ed, because she was quite drunk, but not as much as it worried Laura. Jacqui and Ed walked a discrete distance behind them, as they both seemed to have a lot to say.

'You must be quite pleased with yourself? They seem to be getting along OK,' Jacqui said to him.

'Of course, I am. She's alright, really. Got a nice bum, as well,' he said, watching her as she pushed Laura, hips swinging side to side. Jacqui gave him a slap on the arm and chuckled. 'It's been a long time,' he said by way of an excuse.

'Tell me about it,' Jacqui replied.

'Anything I can do to help? Isn't that what mates are for?' he said laughing.

'You are incorrigible,' she said slapping him again. 'I think your services are required elsewhere.' Ed looked up and saw that Raechael was almost pushing Laura over the cliff. Laughing, he stopped her and said it might be safer if he took over. She didn't argue, as Jacqui put an arm around her to steady her and continued down the narrow path.

They decided the night was still young, and a nightcap back at Ed's would be a good idea. Once he opened the door, Fat Boy was running around, sniffing everyone, making sure nobody forgot to make a fuss of him, before urinating against the wheel of Ed's car.

Ed wheeled Laura to the bottom of the steps and lifted Laura from the chair and carried her inside. When he got inside, he set her down on the sofa. Once again, her hands lingered and slid from his neck, while she stared at him with those big, brown eyes, her face inches from his. Ed, flustered, said he was going to get her chair and hurried off faster than was really necessary, leaving Laura on the sofa, smiling broadly.

The sofa curled around the end of the living area and could easily accommodate six, which was just as well, as Laura elected to give the wheelchair a rest. Ed was worried she might topple over but she told him she was OK and as he was sitting on the end he would act as a human bookend for her. Once again, the drink was flowing and it looked like being a long night, so much so, that Fat Boy curled up on his bed, bored.

'Come on, Jimmy, don't be shy, get us a top up. I'm parched,' Chris said with a snigger, making Ed cringe.

'Who the hell is Jimmy?' Emma asked.

Chris pointed at Ed and said, 'He is.' Both she and Jacqui broke into fits of giggles.

'Bloody hell, can't I have any secrets?' he said, looking round the room at the confused looks on three of his guest. 'Come on, you don't think my parents were that bloody cruel, they would name their son, Ed Case, do you? My real name is James Case.'

'I did wonder,' Emma said 'but I didn't like to say anything, just in case you were a bit sensitive about it. So why are you called, Ed? Apart from the obvious reason, it's funny and appropriate, too.'

After Ed opened another couple of bottles and filled up their glasses, he explained. 'I was always a bit of a prankster doing stupid things. Like putting cling-film over the toilet bowls in the girls' lavs at school. Shinning up the flagpole outside the school gates, silly things like that and a few of my mates started calling me Ed. When I got picked on by the school bully and gave him a kicking, it took three teachers to pull me off him. One teacher said to me "Who the hell do you think you are?" rhetorically, like teachers do and one of my mates shouted out "Ed Case". There was a big crowd by that time and it stuck. In the end, even the teachers called me Ed and eventually even my parents; simple as that. I prefer it to James or Jim and it's definitely preferable to bloody Jimmy. She knows I hate Jimmy.'

'You were Jimmy when we first met,' Chris continued 'Back when you were a skinny little twelve year-old. Remember that time I asked you to put suncream on my back?' Ed winced at the memory. He knew what was coming but could only sit there and listen to her, embarrassed. 'I started making fake orgasm sounds, you know urging him to rub harder, saying oooh yeah and he got a hard-on and had to lie face down in the sand for half an hour,' she said, howling at the memory.

'I remember,' Ed replied, 'Was that the same day I tickled you so much, you wet yourself? Then ran off into the sea with your towel, to make the whole thing wet, to cover it up,' he came back with.

'Oh, I forgot about that. Let's call a truce. We don't want to embarrass your guests, do we?' Chris said meekly.

'Well, I can't remember the last time I had so much fun,' Raechael slurred.

'Too much more of that wine and I don't think you'll remember much of this time, either,' he told her.

'You're a very nice young man,' she slurred, raising her glass and toasting him.

'And you're what they call a MILF, Mrs. Jacobs.' he replied 'That's mother I'd like to fu...'

'Ed!' Jacqui said, stopping him in mid-sentence, although Raechael seemed quite flattered.

'I'm not sure if I should thank you or slap you,' she said with a sly grin. 'I would imagine you get quite a few of those, Mr. Case?'

'Yep quite a few but then again, I do get the occasional shag,' he replied, making everyone groan. 'The fact that you haven't slapped me, gives me some hope.' He gave her a wink and raised his glass.

Ed carried Laura's wheelchair outside and came back in and stood in front of her. He bent down so she could put her arms around his neck again, lifted her up and carried her outside. He tripped on the last step and staggered into the side of his car, just managing to turn his back to it, before crashing back across the boot, with Laura pinning him to it, giggling. That sobered him up quickly, his heart racing, thinking of the damage he might do if he dropped her.

Laura sensed his panic and whispered in his ear as he lowered her into the chair, 'Don't worry they're broken anyway,' and gave him a sad look.

He locked the caravan door behind him and pushed Laura back home, Jacqui and Chris behind, supporting Raechael on either side. Outside the caravan, Raechael gave him a big hug and thanked him for a lovely evening or at least that's what it sounded like. He leaned down and pulled Laura out of her wheelchair and gave her a hug. As he tried to kiss her on the cheek, she turned her head at the last minute so he ended up kissing her on the lips, once again giving him a hard stare, with those alluring, brown eyes. A cough from behind, pulled him back to reality.

He walked Chris and Jacqui back up to the reception building and waited with them, until their taxi arrived. They both gave him another mild ticking off, for springing his suicide revelation on them and for not telling them, period. It wasn't as bad as it could have been but no harm was done. The taxi arriving probably saved him from a real tongue-lashing. No doubt he would get the full works at a later date. They were like that.

When he arrived back, he locked the door behind him and walked in to find Emma curled up, fast asleep on the sofa. Not just fast asleep but out for the count, in a deep sleep that is only achievable with the right amount of alcohol and, medically, is just one small step away from a full-blown coma. He tried in vain to wake her without success. The only option was to put her to bed.

He picked her up as gently as he could and carried her to the bedroom, using her head to open the door. She would probably have such a rotten hangover in the morning; banging her head on the door would make absolutely no difference whatsoever. He laid her down on the bed, looked down and pondered on what to do next. He would have to undress her or her dress would be ruined. The thought got his heart and mind racing, until his conscience got the better of him and told him to do the gentlemanly thing. With a sigh, he lifted her into the sitting position, unzipped the back of the dress and dropped the straps down her arms.

He then pulled her nightshirt from under the pillow and put it over her head, before easing the straps of her dress further down. Temptation, reared it's not so ugly head and urged him to take a good look but he was strong enough not to. God, it was harder than giving up smoking. Once the dress was down to her waist, he pushed her arm up inside the nightdress and through the arm hole, repeating the process for the other arm. After pulling the nightdress down to her waist, he let her fall back flat on the bed. Then he pulled the dress down, making sure that the nightdress followed, to cover her modesty. He hated being such a gentleman sometimes, when all he wanted to do was get a good look at her lovely, little body. Bloody consciences!

With the dress removed, he lifted her up again and undid her bra through the material of the nightdress, which was no mean feat after what he'd had to drink but he finally got there and the straps parted, with that once familiar pinging sound that still made his heart race today, with the anticipation of things to come. Only tonight, there would be no more to come. He then put his hand up the sleeve of the nightdress and pulled her arm out of the bra strap, repeating the process with the other arm. Next he pulled the bra through the sleeve of her nightdress, finishing by holding up the bra and saying "Ta dah" like a magician pulling a rabbit out of a hat. He saw Jacqui do that on the beach years ago with her bikini top and was so impressed he still remembered it fifteen years later.

What to do about the knickers, that was the question. Should he remove them or not? Once again, the devil on his shoulder egged him on, urging him to get a good look. He was tempted but his moral compass was still in good operational order, despite the alcohol he had consumed. He decided, albeit reluctantly, to leave them on, before pulling up the sheet and kissing her goodnight. Her snoring started long before he began to undress himself.

CHAPTER 23

It was the same snoring that woke him at seven o'clock the next morning. It was loud enough that further sleep was not an option. Not just because Emma was snuffling like a pig searching for truffles but he had a bladder the size of a small country and needed to empty it in a hurry. He padded across the narrow corridor with a mouth as dry as a camels bum in a sandstorm and urinated for what seemed to be an impossibly long time.

On arriving back from an extra-long and uneventful walk with Fat Boy, to give Emma the chance of a lie-in to sleep off her hangover, he found her leaning on the counter in the kitchen, willing the kettle to boil. He gave her a cheery good morning and received a grunt in return. He was feeling ready to face the world now, the fresh morning air having blown away the fug from the night before and was actually looking forward to a good fry-up. One that he would have to prepare himself, judging by the state of Emma, which was a pity; the one she cooked the day before was perfect. No matter how hard he tried, he knew his would be a poor second to hers.

She came up to him and laid her head against his chest and put her arms round his neck, more for support than being affectionate.

'Not feeling so good, then? Don't suppose you'd like to make your best mate in the whole world a fry-up?' he asked optimistically.

'None at all. I've already thrown up once and I think round two isn't that far away. I feel like shit,' she informed him in a croaky voice.

Ed made a few sympathetic noises and put his arms around her waist. He noticed her reflection in the window and saw that her nightdress had ridden up revealing her backside, which was barely covered by her thong. Was this a reward for doing the right thing last night or just plain good luck?

'I'm talking to you,' she said, breaking his daydreaming.

'Sorry, miles away. I was looking at the reflection of your bum in the window. What did you say?'

'It doesn't matter and stop looking at my bum,' she said dropping her arms and sitting on the table so he couldn't. He gave her a sad look, stood in front of her and gave her a hug.

'Had to put you to bed last night, you were crashed out on the sofa. Had to undress you and put your nightie on, too,' he said, giving her a wink.

'Yeah and I bet you had a good look as well, didn't you? You filthy, old man,' she said in jest.

'No, I was the perfect gentleman,' he said but the look she gave him said she didn't believe him, so he explained the intricate process he went through last night.

'Really?' she said, shaking her head and instantly regretting it.

'Of course, I'm sure. You would have done exactly the same if it was the other way round.'

'I bloody well wouldn't have. I would've had a good look at what you've got,' she told him and looked like she meant it. 'I wouldn't have minded if you did, I wouldn't have known about it.'

'That's what I kept telling myself but my conscience wouldn't let me so I missed out. Mind you I saw all I wanted to just now,' he said laughing.

'Pervert. Laura seems to like you, a lot. In fact, I'd say she wants your babies,' she said.

'She doesn't. She was just a bit pissed and is friendly, that's all,' he said, brushing it off.

'Yeah right. Every time you picked her up out of her wheelchair, she sighed like she was having an orgasm and rolled her eyes. When she talks to you or looks at you when you're talking to someone else, she's always touching her hair. She fancies you something rotten.'

Ed gave her a quizzical look. 'What do you mean about touching her hair?' he asked perplexed.

'Oh, come on Ed, everyone knows about that. If a woman touches her hair when you're talking to her is means she likes you

– a lot,' she replied, as if she was telling him something obvious.

'Rubbish. There's a hippy down the pub who does that. Doesn't mean he fancies me, does it. Does it?'

Emma gave a shrug and a smile 'Will you keep your hands still.' she said, because he was subconsciously, caressing her thigh.

'Sorry,' he said embarrassed 'I didn't even realise I was doing it.'

'That's OK. I just don't want you thinking it's getting you anywhere,' she smiled.

'Well, there's always Laura,' he said.

'You're sick. The poor girl's in a wheelchair.'

'It's only her legs that don't work, I'm sure everything else is in perfect working order,' Ed said with a smile.

'That's horrible. Now get out the way. I think I need to be sick again.'

Ed moved aside and watched, as she hurried off to the toilet. Within a few seconds she was retching over the pan, shortly yelling 'Piss off Fat Boy, and get your nose out of my crotch. It isn't helping!' Fat Boy came trotting round the corner, with what Ed could only describe as a look on his face that was the equivalent of a snigger.

Ed was bored. Emma had gone back to bed, still too hungover to take any part in what turned out to be yet another glorious day of wall to wall sunshine. He cooked a mediocre fry-up, of over-cooked beans, brittle bacon, burnt sausages and eggs, crusty on the edges and snotty in the middle, where he had the heat too high. The icing on the cake being he broke the yolks in both of them. The only redeeming factor was he felt a lot better after eating it.

He was now lying on the sofa with his earphones in, blasting out My Chemical Romance as loud as it would go through his iPod. He was still bored and restless and the caravan had warmed up so much, it was like sitting in a blast furnace, despite having the windows open. He had to get out and scribbled a quick note to Emma, informing her he had gone for a walk with the dog. Fat Boy didn't seem too thrilled by the idea and trudged along lethargically at his side. He thought about paying Laura and Raechael a visit but decided it might not be a good idea if their hangovers were as bad as Emma's.

Fat Boy was definitely not up for another long walk, so he walked down the road a short distance, before turning onto the track, which led to the cliffs on the opposite site of the headland. Once there, he walked to his favourite spot and sat down, to stare at the beach below and the sea beyond. Fat Boy seemed quite pleased with that and flopped down next to him, panting and also staring out to sea.

It was relatively quiet, considering it was a Sunday afternoon and the sun was blazing. He made the most of the peace and quiet, as he watched an obese, little boy stalking seagulls on the beach. He was taking little steps towards them, with all the stealth of a bull elephant, before breaking into a wheezy waddle and scaring them off. The seagulls just flapped their huge wings, evolved over years to enable them to beat the gypsies to the rubbish tips, and took off, landing a few yards further down the beach, leaving the kid breathless and red faced. Ed wasn't sure if he was trying to catch one to eat or was just trying to annoy them. Either way, he seemed to be enjoying himself and the exercise was probably doing him some good.

Ed reminisced about the joys of childhood. Not a care in the world, other than worrying if you had completed all your chores for the week and been relatively good, so as not to incur any pocket money deductions. Only to blow the whole lot on the Beano and as many sweets as the change would stretch to. No worries about relationships, work or careers – bliss. He remembered his first career aspiration as a child was to become a coal miner. The thought of getting paid to get that dirty seemed a perfect choice. Little was he aware of the hardships endured by miners and the poor pay. As it was, the government closed all the pits before Ed was old enough to leave school so he ended up in sales. Not through choice, but then, how many people work in jobs they actually aspired to be in when the left school?

Ed finished his 'A' levels and took a job temping in a finance department and was offered a permanent position as a credit controller. He took it, as it seemed like the right thing to do at the time. The work was OK, the pay wasn't too bad and there was a lot of crumpet in the finance department. After a couple of years, he managed to get a move into the sales department, in an account support position and then a year later as a salesman. He was bloody good at selling and was promoted to sales manager. Everything seemed to be going right for him. He was meeting his sales targets, his love life was interesting and the money was excellent. Then his parents died and everything started to go wrong.

At work, he began to turn into one of those arrogant suits you see in every wine bar in the City every night of the week, loud, bullish and full of himself. He wouldn't think twice about walking over anyone who stood in his way, which was good for the company profits but on a personal level, he began to hate himself. It got worse when he married. He was only interested in himself and his commission. Fuck everyone else, and he kept similar company, which only fuelled him on. It wasn't until the death of his wife, and trying to deal with the aftermath that his whole world crashed in on him. He took stock of his life and realised what he had become. It was that, as much as overhearing the conversation about his ex-wife in the bar, which drove him to the brink of suicide. Would he have gone through with it, if it hadn't been for the dog? He thought so.

It was the lowest point in his life and it took him a long time to put the past behind him. Taking redundancy had to happen, regardless of finding out he was an overnight millionaire. It was necessary to break the cycle of self-destruction. Chris and Jacqui had both been fantastic. Both had taken a lot off time of work to stay with him and he felt guilty not telling them about the suicide but it came down to pride. He came down to Cornwall for a few months convalescence, which helped. By the end of his stay, with Jacqui and Chris nearby, he was completely over it. The only problem was what to do next, now he didn't have to work.

The idea of buying up properties seemed a good idea at the time, as he had always liked DIY, and he went on plastering and plumbing courses to bump up his skills, which was also good for his rehabilitation into the big wide world. He brought his first property, which was a repossession and been gutted by its disgruntled, previous owners and spent months carefully restoring it back to its former glory. The valuation by the estate agent would have meant a small profit, but money was not the point. He was doing it to keep the boredom at bay and make him feel he wasn't frittering his life away, which basically he was, just constructively so.

The expected profit never materialized, as the young couple who put in an offer couldn't get the mortgage from the bank. Ed asked them what their maximum was and sold it to them at a loss, as they had a baby on the way and seemed quite nice. At the end of the day, he wasn't doing it for the money so what did it matter? It didn't and he felt good about it.

The money was a problem. He paid off several close friends' mortgages, including Chris and Jacqui's but other than that concession, by virtue of bullying them into letting him do it, he was very much restricted. Nobody wanted to come across as being on the make and taking the piss. Ed just wanted to share some of his new found wealth but respected their opinions. Trying to find a balance was difficult. When his friend's son said he wanted a flat screen TV for his birthday, Ed offered to buy one but his father wouldn't allow it, as he couldn't afford to buy him one and when he could, he would. He didn't want Ed to buy everything his kids wanted, as he wanted to buy them, which was why he went a bit over the top with Emma. What he told her was true, giving to charity was all very well but it was impersonal. His friends wouldn't allow him to treat them and Emma was just too good an opportunity to miss.

His thoughts turned to Emma. Where was that going? He liked her. She was fun to be with and seemed to be dealing with her past really well but was there any future there? He didn't think so. She was eleven years his junior for a start. She clearly wasn't interested in a physical relationship and he couldn't blame her, after all she had been through and he certainly wouldn't try anything on. On the other hand, if she came onto him, he would be all over it like a cheap suit and it would take someone with a bloody big stick to get him off again. He might be a gentleman but he was still a bloke. However, that wasn't going to happen; in spite of the fact she was sharing his bed, which didn't help. Their relationship would only ever be plutonic. He knew it and she knew it; another missed opportunity to put with the others in Ed's tragic love life.

It was funny, he mused, he had met three women in as many days and all three meetings resulted in him getting a mouthful. He had been called weird, a pervert, scary, patronising, a thug, loutish, and two real thugs had threatened him with knives. Who said life was dull? Right now, Ed had had enough excitement for a lifetime, let alone three days. What was it about him that brought out the best in people? He had a lot less bother when he was a real arsehole, working in the City.

CHAPTER 24

Emma had only just dragged her sorry arse out of bed and was downing a pint of water when there was a tap at the door. She tried opening it but it was locked. She had seen the note from Ed but was surprised he locked the door behind him when he left. She shouted 'hang on' and went to find her key. Had he done it just as a reflex action or was he actually worried about repercussions from the night before and locked it for her safety? She hoped not, just the thought made her nervous and brought back memories of Danny, which were always on the periphery of her consciousness and took all her strength to push away. She shuddered at the thought and opened the door to a smiling Laura, who had obviously made an effort. She had her contact lenses in, her hair was immaculate, flowing over her shoulders, and she was wearing a little make-up. Emma smiled. It was obviously for Ed's benefit, not hers and it was for nothing, as he wasn't here.

'Hi,' Laura said. 'I was out and about and thought I'd stop by and say hello and see if your hangovers were as bad a mine,' she said cheerily, despite being disappointed Emma answered the door.

'Well, I think mine was probably worse, I was throwing up all morning and have only just got out of bed. You look like you've been up a while, judging by the look of you. Ed's not here at the moment, he's gone for a walk with Fat Boy. Fancy a coffee?'

She did and a few minutes later, after Emma made herself a little more presentable, not wishing to be outdone by the dazzling Laura, headed over to the clubhouse in search of caffeine.

Emma bought two coffees and a plate of sticky buns; she was starving, her stomach growling with a real purpose. Emma asked how Raechael was and found out she was much the same as Emma and spent the majority of the day in bed. When she did surface she was completely changed and what time they spent together had been great, no more fighting and arguing, and she promised to give her more space, be more understanding and be a better mother and friend.

'She even said, she thinks Ed's a lovely man, which was a big improvement on what she told me she thought of him this time yesterday. So everything's great,' she said smiling broadly.

'I don't think your mum's the only one who thinks he's a lovely man, is she?' Emma said, giving her a knowing look, making Laura blush. 'It's OK. We're not an item or anything. I don't mind, we're just friends. Well, you know our brief history from last night. That's it.'

'I do. I think he's wonderful. He's kind, funny and he makes me feel special. I know that's just the way he is. I don't think I'm anything special to him and I don't blame him. Who wants to be stuck with someone in a wheelchair, having everyone feeling pity for you, because your partner's a cripple,' she said sadly.

'I think you might be surprised. You may have noticed he's not like most blokes, or most blokes I know, anyway. He helped me out and look at my background; that didn't bother him. I think he can see past the wheelchair. He's just afraid to admit it. I think he's afraid of women, full stop.'

Laura thought about this, hoping she was right. 'I don't think he's afraid of women. Look how he dealt with my mother. She can be a right cow when she puts her mind to it and he took it all on the chin and turned her into a pussycat by the end of the night.'

'OK, he's afraid of commitment,' Emma said and told her about his ex-wife and how that affected him and his relationship with Chris that never developed past friendship, albeit almost an inseparable bond between them but no commitment. Emma didn't think Ed would mind her talking about him so openly with Laura, who seemed to find some hope in this.

'Shall we go and find him?' Emma suggested, knowing Laura would jump at the chance.

'OK. I'll have to let mum know, I don't want her worrying again.'

Ed was also on the move. The sun beating down on the back of his neck was too much and it felt hot to the touch so decided to head back. When he arrived at the caravan the door was still locked, meaning Emma was still sleeping off her hangover or decided to get some fresh air. Both bedrooms were empty and a note was left on the table, saying she was out with Laura. Having spent all day by himself, he decided to pay Raechael a visit.

Raechael seemed pleased to see him, greeting him with a hug and kiss, a definite improvement on the last time he stood in the very same spot. She even made a fuss of Fat Boy and invited them both in for coffee. The conversation turned to the events of the previous evening, mainly Raechael thanking him for the meal and his part in patching up her relationship with her daughter. She even asked him how his backside was. He assured her it was still in full working order.

They were on their second coffee when Laura and Emma entered. Emma still looked slightly jaded around the edges, while Laura looked like she had dropped off the front page of Vogue magazine in comparison and was smiling broadly. Raechael put the kettle on again and Ed accepted the offer of a third cup. Laura asked him to lift her out of her chair so she could sit on the sofa. He made a point of listening, to see if what Emma said to him this morning was true. As he lifted her up she did make a little noise, a cross between a grunt and a sigh, obviously he couldn't see if she rolled her eyes but her hands lingered longer than was absolutely necessary, just as Emma described. He looked over at her and gave a slight nod, to let her know she was right. She gave him a shrug to let him know, she told him so.

It was a couple of hours later, when Raechael suggested they stay to dinner, which was music to Ed's ears. He was starving and was wondering what to do about something to eat. The thought of a homemade bolognese was making his mouth water. Emma said she needed to take a shower first and Ed had to feed the dog so they left with a promise to return in an hour, armed with wine.

CHAPTER 25

After seeing what Emma had changed into, it provoked Ed to put on a fresh shirt and swap the shorts for a pair of chinos, as compared to Emma he looked like a tramp. He even shaved and splashed on a bit of aftershave. He was glad he did, both Laura and Raechael had done likewise, although Laura had clearly made the biggest effort, looking ready for a night out, in a blouse with a plunging neckline.

The bolognese was excellent and was even served with homemade garlic bread, which was equally delicious. Ed cracked open a bottle of the red wine he brought back with him. Initially, this was met with groans and protests as memories of the previous night's excess and hangovers of the morning were evoked, but everyone drank it and the second bottle.

Raechael began clearing the plates away and started to fill the washing up bowl. Ed insisted he would do the dishes and physically dragged her away from the sink, back to the dining table.

'Come on Laura, you're helping, too,' he told her. 'You wash, I'll wipe.'

'I'd love to but I can't reach the sink, can I?'

'That's not an acceptable excuse,' he said and lifted her out of her chair and carried her over to the sink. He put her down and wrapped his arms tightly around her waist, from behind and supported her weight, before shuffling forwards until she was in front of the sink. 'Right get scrubbing.' he told her, looking over her shoulder at their reflection in the window.

'Bully,' she said pouting and picking up a plate, making him laugh.

'I feel like Patrick Swayze in that film Ghost. All we need is the soundtrack,' Ed told her and started to sing. 'You never close your eyes anymore, when I kiss your lips. And there's no tenderness...'

'That's from Top Gun not Ghost,' she interrupted him in mid-flow. 'Ghost is Unchained Melody,' she corrected him.

'Really?' he said feeling a bit stupid. 'I always get the Righteous and Walker Brothers mixed up. OK. I'll try again. Oh, my love, my darling, I've hungered for your touch. A long lonely time and time goes by so slowly and time can do so much are you still mine?' he sang, swaying from side to side, making her laugh. He then turned her around, which wasn't as easy as he thought it would be and asked her to dance. He pulled her close to him, with one arm around the waist and the other holding her hand, now humming Unchained Melody as he only knew the first few lines.

'This is the first time I've danced since my accident,' she told him, looking up at him with those big, brown eyes.

'And the first time you've washed the dishes too, no doubt, which you haven't finished so get back to work,' he said leading her back to the sink. 'And hurry up will you, the combination of your perfume, looking down your top and being this close is getting me aroused, and I'd hate to embarrass myself,' he whispered in her ear jokingly.

'I don't mind,' she said looking at his reflection in the window.

'Have you always been such a slut or just since the accident?' he said teasing her.

'That's for me to know and for you to find out,' she said leaning on the sink and pushing back into him. Any more of that and he would embarrass himself.

Later in the evening, when they were sitting on the sofa, chatting away about anything and everything, Raechael inadvertently did him a huge favour, when she asked Emma where she lived and found out she was from Cambridge.

'I've got friends in Cambridge. Whereabouts do you live?' She asked

'To the north of the town,' Emma replied.

'My friend lives just off the Huntingdon Road on Thornton Close,' Raechael informed her, as if Emma should know every street in Cambridge and instantly be able to provide further comment on the area.

'I was quite close then. I lived in Woodland Road, about a mile or so down the road from there,' she said. Ed could hardly contain his excitement and good fortune.

'I bet it was number thirteen,' Ed said dryly.

'Very funny. It was number four actually,' she replied.

Bingo. Ed had all he needed. Danny Mandelson, 4 Woodland Road, Cambridge. The only dilemma now was what to do with the information. Not that there was much he could do with it at the moment so he filed and stored it, to be used maliciously at a later date. Ed was a happy man.

'What are you looking so happy about?' Emma asked.

'I was just thinking about a time I made bolognese for my mum and dad,' he lied. 'I didn't know at the time but I cooked the spaghetti in the saucepan my mum used for boiling my dad's hankies in. She wasn't impressed when she found out,' he added, smiling at the memory.

'Thanks for that Ed. I glad you saved that little gem until we finished eating,' Raechael replied. 'What are you two up to tomorrow?' Emma shrugged and looked to Ed for an answer.

'Thought we could go to Tintagel and, if we get time, to Boscastle. It's quite nice there, although I haven't been there since the floods. Not so sure Fat Boy will be up for it. I think he's struggling with all the exercise. He's not as young as he used to be. Look at the state of him.'

He was knackered, sprawled across the floor in a deep sleep, his front legs twitching once in a while in time with his whiskers.

'I'll look after him for you,' Laura volunteered 'He can keep me company for the day. It'll be nice to have a dog around.'

'That sounds good to me. I think he could do with a day off. As long as it's not going to interfere with any of your plans?'

Laura looked at Raechael for confirmation and, seeing the look on her daughter's face, decided the trip she planned could wait. Newquay would still be there the next day.

CHAPTER 26

Ed dropped Fat Boy off at Laura's around nine o'clock and the fickle bastard didn't even bat an eyelid when he left. He was far more interested in begging for a piece of toast Raechael was eating and was rewarded for his persistence. Laura had both Ed and Emma's mobile numbers and he told her to call if there were any problems. Not that there would be any. Fat Boy was well trained and would come when called and walk to heel. What could go wrong?

The journey to Tintagel was torturous. They were stuck behind a couple of old farts, who refused to go above 30mph all the way. Due to the narrow winding roads, Ed was unable to overtake and they parked up in the town, with Ed somewhat agitated. Emma said she wanted to see the infamous King Arthur's Castle she read about on the internet before leaving. This despite Ed telling her the legend was a load of old bollocks, dreamt up by the Cornish Tourist Board to drag a few more tourists in. Emma told him he was just a cynical, old git with no imagination, which was probably true. The castle itself was pretty unimpressive, due to the fact there wasn't a great deal left of it. However, if you used your imagination, you could tell it would have been magnificent in its day, a point he made to Emma to prove his imagination wasn't that limited.

After visiting the castle they walked across the clifftop and sat down to admire what was left of the castle from a far, Emma taking plenty of photos on her mobile phone.

'I thought you'd love all this knights in shining armour stuff, right up your street, isn't it? All the chivalry and damsels in distress,' she said teasing him 'I think you would've fitted in quite well - my very own, Sir Lancelot.'

Ed laughed and put his arm around her shoulders. 'Sir Lancelot was the sly old dog, who shagged King Arthur's missus, Guinnevere. Some mate he turned out to be. Maybe with my track record I'm more like Arthur.'

'You're so unromantic,' she told him. 'Having said that, what were you up to with Laura in the kitchen last night? Serenading her at the sink.'

'Just having a laugh,' he said defensively.

'Well, you shouldn't lead her on. I had a nice little chat with her yesterday and she's got a real crush on you so don't encourage her, if you don't feel anything for her. OK?' she said sternly.

'I didn't lead her on. It was just a bit of harmless, larking around. She's out of my league anyway, even if I did want anything more.'

'How the hell did you come to that conclusion? You're a millionaire and not too bad looking. You're no Brad Pitt but you're not ugly and she's in a wheelchair. How can she be out of your league?' she replied, staring at him with a look of incredulity.

'She's bloody gorgeous. I feel like Quasimodo standing next to her! Of course she's out of my league. Money and wheelchairs have nothing to do with it. Just assume the wheelchair is a temporary thing, like she said it was. What then? Is she really going to want to be hanging around with an ugly bastard like me? Get real, she could have the pick of anyone she wanted,' he said, giving her a look that said she must be stupid. 'Anyway, it's not an issue. I like her, of course I do, but that's it.'

'You haven't got a clue about women, have you? That's why you missed the boat with Chris and that's why you'll miss the boat with Laura. You're also a crap liar. I've seen the way you look at her. You're just terrified of making the same mistake you did the first time round. Just because you had one bad experience, it doesn't mean it's going to happen again,' she said forcefully.

'There was never a boat to miss with Chris. We've never been anything but good friends. We tried to be more, as you know, and it didn't work. Being with Chris would be a nightmare, we'd end up killing each other with niceness and end up old and bored and there is no boat to miss with Laura either,' he replied sternly, choosing not to comment on her views of his disastrous marriage.

'OK, have it your way but don't say, I didn't tell you so, when you end up breaking her heart,' she said, ending further conversation.

They set off back up the incredibly steep slope that led back to the town, in search of somewhere nice to have lunch. Ed was thinking about the conversation they just had. Was he lying to Emma and, more importantly, to himself? He wasn't sure. Yes he did like Laura, a lot, if he was honest, but did he want anything more? He didn't know but she had hit a nerve with her perception of his reluctance with relationships. Deep down, there was an element of truth there. Not that he would admit to it. He was a bloke, after all; so he did what he did best and buried it under the carpet and left it there to fester.

They found a nice bistro and after seeing the extensive menu, what they thought was going to be a light lunch, turned out to be a gut buster. Ed was contemplating a tuna sandwich and a cup of tea but couldn't resist the French onion soup or the sound of the spit roasted chicken, with jacket potatoes and seasonal vegetables. The knickerbocker glory was just completely unnecessary but fantastic. They both walked out and could almost feel their arteries clogging up with the cholesterol they just consumed. Emma insisted on paying, which Ed thought was a nice gesture but amusing as it was money he had given her in the first place, but thanked her anyway. They decided the best way to ease the bloated feeling they were both experiencing was to take a long walk along the clifftops.

CHAPTER 27

Laura and Fat Boy were having a great time. As soon as Ed left, she set off for the mini-market with Fat Boy and brought a box of dog biscuits, while Fat Boy sat obediently outside. She spent most of the morning sitting on the floor in the caravan, feeding him biscuits and was covered in dog slobber and ginger dog hair, not that she minded; neither did Fat Boy.

In the afternoon she decided to go for a walk with Fat Boy, leaving her mother to read the newspaper in a deckchair outside the caravan. She set off, Fat Boy walking obediently at her side, and headed for the clifftops, feeling a lot happier than she had in a long time, thanks to Ed. Her relationship with her mother had improved tenfold and was almost back to how things were before her accident. What he said to her that night in the restaurant she had no idea but whatever it was, it had changed things dramatically. She was sure it was more than telling her mother she had a nice bum; that much she did know. She would ask him next time she saw him. She knew it was difficult for her mother and was aware she had to stop herself from trying to do everything for her but at least now she would wait for her to ask for help, which she knew her mother was secretly pleased about when she did.

Her thoughts turned to Ed, as they seemed to do a lot these last few days. She had never met anyone like him; even her mother liked him, which is more than could be said for her ex-fiancé, Greg. She never liked him and at times found it hard just to be civil to him, as she didn't think he was good enough for her daughter. Maybe she was right, although she still had strong feelings towards him, despite the fact he broke off their relationship at a time when she needed him most. It was difficult for him, she knew. He was under a lot of pressure at work and she was just an added burden, one he had trouble dealing with; it wasn't his fault. Who would want the burden of a disabled partner? Nobody, who was she kidding? Emma had told her Ed was the sort of person who could see beyond the superficial, but who was she trying to kid? Why would a millionaire want a cripple to hold him back? Sometimes, like last night, she thought perhaps there was something there, some spark, but she put that down to wishful thinking. No, he was just a nice, happy-go-lucky person, who flirted with everyone, even her mother. She was pretty sure she was nothing special to him.

She turned down the track that led to the clifftops, working purely on autopilot, absorbed in her thoughts, when she heard a loud, blood curdling yelp from Fat Boy, who was walking obediently behind her. The yelp soon turned into a pitiful howling. She turned to see Mack standing there, smiling with an evil glint in his eyes, blood dripping from the knife he held in his hand. Fat Boy was on his side and she could see blood spreading out in a pool from his stomach. Laura could only look, mesmerised by the spreading pool of blood, as Fat Boy's howling abated to a low whimper. It was when Mack chuckled and grinned even more broadly, displaying his mouthful of decayed teeth that her blood turned to ice and she screamed and screamed.

Mack calmly walked towards her and wiped the knife on her sleeve as she continued to scream and shake uncontrollably, having never felt so frightened in her entire life.

'Tell that fucking boyfriend of yours, he's next,' he said, leaning close to her face and grabbing her jaw, squeezing hard. His breath was putrid and she tried to back away from him but he just leaned closer, grinning. He then pulled away and in the same fluid movement tipped her chair over, leaving her in a crumpled heap on the track. He picked up her wheelchair and threw it as far as he could before jogging off, laughing manically.

She crawled towards Fat Boy, her useless legs dragging behind, her knees grazing painfully on the track but she didn't care, she just wanted to get to him to see if he was still breathing. She put a trembling hand under his front leg, into the equivalent of an armpit on a human, hoping that the same principles applied to dogs, for checking the presence of a pulse. She felt a faint pulse but the dog wasn't moving and his breathing was barely perceptible, but at least he was alive. She sat up, pulled her legs towards her and took off her socks to use as a makeshift pad and after sliding towards the dog, applied pressure to the wound in his side, cradling his head in her lap, sobbing uncontrollably.

The old man had seen what happened and turned and ran back to his cottage as fast as his old legs would carry him and rang for an ambulance, before heading back to Laura armed with an old sheet and a blanket.

'I'm Amos,' he said softly and put the blanket around her shoulders. He then tore the sheet in half, with a strength that belied his frail appearance and used it to run a bandage around Fat Boy's middle, pulling it tight and using Laura' socks as a pad underneath to try and keep as much pressure on the wound as possible. He then retrieved Laura's wheelchair and sat with her, putting a protective arm around her shoulders.

'Is that Fat Boy?' he asked. 'I thought I recognised him,' he said after Laura nodded. 'Don't worry love, dogs are quite strong creatures, he'll be OK,' he said convincingly but was far from convinced himself and knew his chances were slim, judging by the amount of blood he appeared to have lost.

The ambulance finally arrived, pulling up behind them. Two paramedics emerged and hurried towards Laura. The first lifted Laura to her feet and put her in her wheelchair, asking her if she was ok and if she had any injuries.

'We'd better get you to hospital anyway, for a quick check. Just to make sure,' he said.

'What about, Fat Boy?' she asked.

'We can't take him. I'll phone a vet for you,' he said apologetically

'I'm not going anywhere without him. Take him with us, you can't leave him there he'll die!' she screamed at him.

'Sorry love, we can't take him. I not allowed to,' he said softly.

'In that case, I'm not going. Just take him to the vet. How can you leave him there to bleed to death? Do something. You can save him, please!' she begged him, tears flowing freely down her cheeks.

In the end he relented. He put Fat Boy on a stretcher and into the back of the ambulance with Laura and blue lighted it to the veterinary surgery in Padstow.

Ed and Emma were driving back from Tintagel, having walked off their excessive lunch. Ed was ready for a pint and wished he wasn't driving, as there were several nice pubs in Tintagel they could have gone to but, as one was never enough, they agreed to head back and go straight for the clubhouse. They were a few miles from Padstow when his mobile started ringing. He turned off the radio and hit the answer button, seeing that the caller came up as Laura.

'She's missing you already,' Emma said, giving him a nudge in the arm. Ed gave her a terse smile in return.

'Hi Laura,' he said answering the call. 'Don't tell me, Fat Boy's being a complete pain in the arse and you want me to come and get him?' he said cheerily.

'Hi Ed, it's Raechael,' she said solemnly 'Where are you?'

'We're just on our way back. What's wrong? You sound very serious,' he asked, slightly concerned.

'Laura was attacked but it's OK, she's fine. Just very shaken up,' she said, but it was obvious there was more. 'Ed, it's Fat Boy, he's at the vets in Padstow. He was stabbed. He's not in a good way but I've spoken to them and they're doing all they can but he's in a serious condition...'

Ed had turned pale, he felt physically sick and was shaking with rage and feared he was about to lose Fat Boy. The road was too narrow to pull over and stop so he put his foot down, to give him something to concentrate on.

'Ed. Are you still there?' she asked.

'Yeah, I'm here,' he said quietly 'Laura's OK, isn't she?'

'Just very upset but no real physical harm was done. It was the same man you had the altercation with in the clubhouse the other night but I suppose you have already guessed that,' she informed him.

'I did and I'm gonna do what I should have done in the clubhouse and break his fucking neck!' he said so angrily that it made Emma, sitting next to him, jump 'Sorry about the language, Raechael. Look, I'm nearly in Padstow now so I'm hanging up and I'll pop round later. Bye,' he said curtly.

Ed couldn't remember the last time he had been this angry. His knuckles were white as he gripped the steering wheel like a vice, speeding towards the vets. Emma took one look at his face, which was full of hatred, and was shocked at the malice there. She had never seen him like this and it frightened her. She put a hand on his thigh to try and comfort him but he continued to glare straight ahead with his mad eyes.

Ed pulled up outside the vets, walked round the car and took a deep breath, preparing himself for the worse.

'You OK?' she asked, giving his hand a squeeze. He nodded and walked in clinging on to her hand, almost painfully. They were told to take a seat in the empty waiting room and after what seemed an infinitely long wait, a tall, grey-haired man, with a ruddy face came out to see them. His face was almost expressionless, one practised over years to give nothing away, while delivering good or bad news without emotion. Ed looked up at him, urging him to speak.

'Mr. Case?' he asked, extending his hand. 'David Peters, I'm the surgeon here.' Ed gave him a nod and steeled himself for the bad news, which was about to be delivered. 'Fat Boy is in a bad way, Mr. Case. He's lost a lot of blood but fortunately the knife missed his vital organs but there was some damage internally, which I've managed to repair. He's still very weak and he's not yet in the clear. I'll be totally honest with you, it could go either way. The next few hours are critical. Hopefully, he won't pick up any secondary infections. I cleaned the wound up as much as I could and he's on an antibiotic drip so it's a matter of wait and see. He was lucky that your friend had the foresight to try to stop the flow of blood, while the ambulance arrived and even luckier she persuaded the paramedic to bring him here. Otherwise, it might have been a different story; as it is, there is still a chance.'

'Can I see him?' Ed said quietly. The vet looked at him and nodded and asked him to follow him through. Emma shook her head and remained seated, giving him a weak smile of encouragement, not having the stomach to go in with Ed. She knew she would burst into tears the instant she saw him and that wouldn't help matters.

Fat Boy looked pathetic, laying there with tubes in each of his legs, obviously heavily sedated. Ed walked over and stoked him, willing him to live.

'Don't let him die,' he said weakly 'He's all I've got left.'

The vet patted him on the shoulder and led him back out. 'We're doing all we can for him, Mr. Case. The rest is up to him.'

Ed gave his credit card details to the receptionist and turned to the vet and asked him to do everything possible, whatever the cost was. He nodded and led them out into the street, where Ed roared at the top of his voice and slammed his fist against the wall, sideways, not knuckles first; he wasn't that dumb.

'Don't worry mate, I'll buy you another hamster,' one of two youths said as they walked by, the other laughing at his joke. Ed grabbed both by their collars and slammed them against the wall, lifting them off the ground, his eyes boring into them, with a look of absolute hatred. Emma put a hand on his arm, which was trembling with pent up rage and told him in a soft voice to put them down. He let them go gently and they hurried off, telling him he was fucking mental and needed locking up. For what he wanted to do to Mack, he probably would be, too.

'You OK?' Emma asked, genuinely concerned.

Ed looked down at her and shook his head 'I'm scared,' he said and pulled her into him and hugged her. When she looked up, her face was streaked tears, as was Ed's. 'God, I'm going soft,' he said embarrassed. 'He's only a dog,' he added, with a weak smile.

'No he's not. He's you're best mate and you know it,' she said sniffing.

'Come on. Let's go and see how Laura is,' he said, getting behind the wheel of the car and wiping his eyes, before driving off at a more sedate pace than arriving.

CHAPTER 28

On arriving back, the first thing Ed did was to down a bottle of beer from the fridge, quickly followed by another, belching loudly when he finished it. Emma sat there nursing a glass of wine, not knowing what to say or what to do. Each time she thought of saying something, it seemed totally inadequate so she remained silent. Ed got himself a third beer and sat down next to her on the sofa, putting an arm around her shoulders, more for his benefit than hers.

They sat that way until they finished their drinks. Ed deciding he couldn't put off seeing Laura any longer and dreading it. If it hadn't been for him, none of this would have happened. Raechael was going to go ape-shit, he thought, and he would be an unwelcome visitor. How did he always manage to end up screwing things up? It seemed like everything he touched turned to shit.

'Bollocks,' he said quietly. 'Shall we go?'

'You go, I'll stay here. I don't feel like being sociable,' she said. Ed nodded and set off to face the music.

Ed tapped lightly on the caravan door and braced himself for an ear-bashing at best and physical abuse at worse; both of which he felt were more than justified.

'Come in,' Raechael said softly, closing the door behind him. 'How is Fat Boy? I take it you've been to see him?'

Ed nodded. 'Not good. It's touch-and-go but there's a chance he'll be OK,' he replied, close to tears again, thinking about it.

Raechael threw her arms around him and gave him a hug, which was far better than the verbal or physical abuse he was expecting.

'I thought you'd be mad at me,' he said.

'Really, I'm not that bad, am I?' she asked.

'No, but if I hadn't got into a fight with Mack, none of this would've happened. How is she?'

'You know. You're what my mother used to call a rough diamond. I know you mean well. It's not your fault what happened,' she said softly. 'Why don't you go and see her? She's in bed, resting. She's very upset about it and, for some reason, she thinks it's all her fault,' she said, shrugging. Ed smiled back at her and wandered off to see Laura.

'Go away. I don't want to see you,' she said as he walked into the room.

'Well, that's no way to treat a friend. How are you?'

'I'm fine. How's Fat Boy?'

'Well, if it hadn't been for you and your first aid and persuading the paramedics to take him to the vets, he would be dead by now. As it is, he's still got a chance, thanks to you.'

'It wasn't just me,' she said, explaining the help given by Amos and refusing to set foot in the ambulance unless they took Fat Boy. Ed could imagine her doing that, if their first encounter was anything to go by. 'I'm really sorry,' she added

'Come on, it wasn't your fault. If it was anyone's, it was mine. I never realised Mack was such a nasty bastard or I wouldn't have let you go off with Fat Boy. To be honest, I'd forgotten all about him until today. It should be me apologising to you. I take it the police have been round?'

'I spoke to a PC at the hospital, before they ran a few tests to make sure everything was OK. Don't look so worried, nothings any more broken than it already was. I've got a couple of grazes and a few bruises but I'll live. There was more damage to my wheelchair. It's got a few scratches and one of the footplates is bent but the wheels still go round,' she said.

'Are you wearing anything by the way?' he asked her.

'Strange question. Haven't you got other things on your mind?' she said, giving him a seductive smile.

'I was going to give you a hug but I didn't want Mrs. Robinson out there coming in and catching us in a possible compromising position,' he explained.

'Well, in case you haven't noticed I'm a big girl now and as for my mother, she likes you so you don't have to worry about her.'

'I had noticed, that's what I was worried about,' he said. 'So Mrs. Robinson, sorry, I mean your mother likes me, eh?' he said teasing her.

'Don't even go there,' she said in mock horror.

'Good looking woman your mum. Still goes in and out in all the right places, too. You think I might be in with a chance?'

'You are wrong in so many ways, Ed. Are you going to give me that hug or what?' He did.

'You lied, you're not wearing anything,' he said, his hands touching the bare flesh of her back, making her giggle. 'You are pure filth,' he told her, making her giggle more. 'I'd better go and leave you to rest and go cheer Emma up, she's just as upset as I am.'

'Ed, that man said to tell you, you're next, by the way, so be careful.'

'I will. I just hope the police get him before I do, because right now if I get to him first, I'm going to tear him from limb to limb,' he replied and meant it.

'Just be careful,' she said as he got up. As he did get up she let the sheet fall revealing part of her areolas.

'Jesus Christ!' he said, rushing over and pulling it back up. Laura just laughed and gave him a pout. He liked her. Nice norks too, he thought as he walked out of the room.

Raechael was waiting for him as he walked out and was smiling broadly.

'Were you ear-wigging by any chance, Mrs. Jacobs?'

'Who me?' she said innocently. 'Of course not. Listen, my daughter is very fond of you, Ed. If you break her heart, I will break your nose,' she said very matter of fact.

'Wouldn't dream of it, Mrs. Robinson, er sorry, Mrs. Jacobs,' he said and turned to leave.

Raechael pinched his bottom and blew him a kiss as he walked to the door, whistling Simon and Garfunkel's Mrs. Robinson and was rewarded with the tea towel being thrown at him. All was well and he left much less troubled than when he arrived but was still full of sadness and anger. It was beer time.

CHAPTER 29

Ed sat down and filled Emma in on all the details of his visit to Laura and Raechael. She was just as surprised Raechael had given him a warm reception. Ed left out a few details, which he knew would provoke further discussions regarding his love life, or lack of one, to be more precise. A fortuitous knock on the caravan door, which he locked behind him, saved him from further probing in any case. Ed answered the door and was greeted by DCI Bob Brown and another officer introduced to him as DS Phil Reynolds.

'Sorry to hear about Fat Boy, Ed. I really am,' Bob said with genuine sorrow 'How is he?' Ed explained the situation, giving Laura, Amos and the paramedics a lot of praise. 'Good,' he said in a professional manner. 'So it was the same scumbag you had a run in with the other night?' Ed nodded. 'That's what I thought. Next to the infamous, Black Cockle Strangler, he's next on my shit-list. Turns out the old boy he robbed a week ago ended up in intensive care and died yesterday, so he's wanted for murder as well as assault, carrying an offensive weapon and cruelty to animals. You certainly know how to pick 'em. But rest assured, we'll get him.'

Ed stared at him coldly. 'You want to make sure you get him before I do, because if I get to him first, you'll be having me up on a murder charge.' Bob could tell he meant it. He knew from Jacqui he was more than capable in a scrap. He had never witnessed it first-hand but was impressed from what he knew. Would he take it to another level though? He didn't think so but wasn't sure. Ed had a look in his eye he hadn't seen before and it worried him.

Bob nodded sympathetically and asked directions to Laura's

caravan. Ed told him, and he left to interview her, leaving Phil as chaperone.

Bob returned, knocking and not waiting to be let in. 'Bloody hell, that Mrs. Jacobs a bit of alright! Very tasty indeed. The daughter's a stunner too, bloody shame about the wheelchair though, are you two…?' he said enthusiastically, leaving the question open.

'Don't you bloody start. No. Wouldn't that be batting above my average?' he said referring to the comments he made when first meeting Emma, making her laugh.

'Quite right. Well above your average, I'd say. Seems to be a hobby of yours,' he said with relish. 'You didn't tell me that scumbag told Laura he was coming for you next. Did it slip your mind?' Ed gave a shrug, not thinking it was important and hoping he would give it a try so he could rip him apart. 'Because that, sunshine, puts a different complexion on things entirely. You're going to have police protection, a DCI no less.'

'I don't need police protection,' Ed protested.

'You're getting it and you're not having a say in the matter. The protection is to stop you doing anything bloody stupid, not to stop you getting stabbed. Is there anywhere Emma can go? I don't think it would be a good idea for her to stay here.'

Ed looked at Emma, who suddenly looked frightened. He wasn't impressed with Bob's lack of tact. 'I can give Chris a call. I'm sure it would be OK for her to stay there. That OK with you Emma?'

Emma nodded and Ed picked up the phone and explained the situation to Chris, who was full of concern for Fat Boy, and said she would be delighted to have Emma for as long as she liked. Emma went and packed her clothes, emerging a few minutes later with the huge suitcase they purchased only a few days ago in Debenhams, looking pale and worried. Ed walked her out to the police car and gave her a hug and promised to phone her in the morning. Phil got behind the wheel and drove off with her. He didn't know why but he had a sinking feeling she wouldn't be coming back. Great, yet another monumental cock up.

Bob opened a couple of bottles of beer and was scouring the cupboards for a snack. He looked pleased when he came across a large bag of peanuts, which he emptied into a bowl, took back to the living room and placed on the coffee table. Being shy was not one of his virtues.

Bob was very interested in Raechael. After his opening line of 'Tell me about the lovely Mrs. Jacobs, then,' Ed told him how he met Laura and Raechael and how she was so frosty and how she changed after their meal at the Harlyn Inn. Bob was lapping up every detail and seemed very pleased she was single. Ed laughed and said it would be quite amusing if he and Laura got together, Bob could be his father-in-law, in years to come. Bob shook his head and said she had suddenly lost all her appeal.

'So, how's the Black Cockle Strangler case, coming along? Have you made any progress yet?' Ed asked.

'Absolutely bloody nothing. Not a single thing from forensics, no eye witnesses, nothing. He's either very careful, very lucky or both. We still don't have any links to any of the victims and there are no apparent motives. The only link is they're all young, single and live alone. They're all murdered in the same way, left in exactly the same way and he puts painted fucking seashells on their tits.'

'The black paint is normal black, gloss paint for wood, right?' Ed asked.

'Correct and we've done a check on black paint sold in the region. We've checked CCTV and eliminated everyone so far. We're not bloody stupid.' he said, clearly frustrated.

'Yeah but it's normal black gloss for wood, which could've been stuck in a shed for years or months. How many people do you know who use black paint?' he asked rhetorically. 'Not many. I've never been in a house and seen black paint. The only use for black paint is to paint a front door, garage door or window frames in old houses. So my theory is, you need to have a look at all the houses and garages with doors painted black and check out the owners and eliminate them; simple. Don't worry about your fancy profilers, finding out why he's putting black shells on their nipples, because it's a gimmick. At least I think it is, to throw you off the scent.'

Bob studied him for a while considering what he said before committing to a response. 'You might have a point there about the paint. But you're wrong about the shells; too simplistic. They're there for a reason, we just haven't found out yet.'

'May be he has strong religious beliefs and doesn't like topless girls and so he covers them up; black signifying death, and therefore, symbolic in some way.'

'Too easy. It's something deeper than that.' The conversation about the killer continued until late or, to be precise, until Bob had quaffed the last beer and finished off the peanuts and, finding the fridge empty, declared it time to turn in.

CHAPTER 30

Ed was up early on account of Bob's snoring, which was so loud it could be heard clearly from the adjacent bedroom. Annoyed at being woken up and, to make matters worse, alone with no Emma curled up next to him, he got up, dressed and went in search of coffee. The absence of Fat Boy was palpable and filled Ed with a sense of loneliness he hadn't experienced since the death of his parents. His mood wasn't improved with the appearance of Bob, walking into the dining area in just his boxer shorts, scratching his balls and demanding coffee.

After making Bob a coffee, Ed showered, more for the solitude than anything else, not wanting to engage in conversation with Bob, whose presence was more like an intrusion. He felt a guilty thinking like this, knowing that Bob didn't have to stay over and keep him company, even if his reasons were for Ed's own good.

Any guilt soon evaporated when, freshly showered and changed, he walked back into the dining area to find Bob tucking into a hearty fry-up, of the standard he could never achieve. What really irked him was Bob's failure to make him a fry-up and, worse still, leave nothing in the fridge for him. Bob gave him a look of incomprehension and shrugged, telling Ed he would have done him a fry-up but there wasn't enough. The man was all heart. Ed settled for another coffee.

Bob made a call to arrange a lift, then showered and shaved. No doubt using Ed's soap and razor; he would change them both later. The thought of using a bar of soap that had been rubbed around Bob's scrotum was something he didn't wish to consider. Looking slightly more presentable and smelling of Ed's best aftershave, Bob walked outside with Ed to wait for his lift. It was then that they noticed the graffiti, sprayed in black aerosol across the side of the caravan 'YOUR NEXT'.

'Not very articulate is he?' Bob said, commenting on the schoolboy grammatical error 'but at least we know we aren't looking for an English teacher.'

'As a guard dog goes, you're about as much use as Anne Frank's drum kit! It's sprayed right across the outside of the room you were sleeping in,' Ed said to provoke a reaction, still pissed off with not getting a fry-up.

Bob shrugged. 'I slept like a baby last night, must have been all those beers you made me drink.' Ed snorted his derision at the remark and chose to ignore it. 'Bastard's taking the piss.' Bob said angrily. 'I'm gonna throw the book at him when I get hold of him,' he added.

'Unless I get there first,' Ed added venomously. Bob shot him an angry look and patted him on the shoulder, which was the nearest Bob ever got to showing compassion.

After Bob departed, Ed sat in the caravan drinking coffee, watching the news on TV. It was more of a distraction than for the want of catching up with all the doom and gloom, which passed as current affairs, but it wasn't working. He needed fresh air.

Normally, walking around the coastline of North Cornwall would be the ideal tonic for Ed but the absence of Fat Boy bounding along beside him made it a joyless experience. He turned and headed back to the caravan. He checked his watch and it was still only half-past-nine; the day was dragging. He decided it was late enough to call Emma.

'Hi. How was your evening?' she said, picking up after a couple of rings. Ed hoped she had been waiting for his call.

'Crap. Bob drank all the beer, scoffed all the peanuts and went to bed. Got up, used up all the bacon and eggs and buggered off. So bloody terrific. Yours?'

'Great, Chris has been so nice. I'm going to do some painting in her studio today. I think it will be nice and therapeutic for me,' she enthused, making Ed rather jealous.

'That's good,' he said keeping his voice cheery. 'Do you want to do lunch later?' he asked expectantly, not liking the pause before she answered

'Can we do it tomorrow? Once I get painting, I just like to get on with it and get as much done as I can,' she replied.

'Yeah that would be good,' he lied. 'I'll come down tomorrow morning. I've got a few things to do in town tomorrow so I'll come and meet you at the shop at around midday.'

'Good. Are you OK, Ed?'

'Of course I am. Just a little worried about Fat Boy. I'll give the vet a call later and get an update. Not that I'm expecting much progress,' he said. What he really wanted to say was that he was he was feeling lower than a snake's scrotum and really needed to be with a friend. But he was a bloke so he lied to hide his vulnerability.

'Right, see you tomorrow, then. Bye.'

Ed phoned the vet next and was informed there was little change in Fat Boy's condition. He was still very weak but stable. He wasn't expecting to be told he had made a full recovery and was bouncing round the walls like a puppy but would like to have heard something a little more positive. At least his condition hadn't deteriorated so there was some positive to take from the brief exchange.

Ed fired up the computer and browsed the Internet for what he wanted. If painting was therapeutic for Emma, then a bit of online shopping might cheer him up. He found what he wanted and then rang the helpline number and managed to persuade the woman on the other end of the phone that it was an urgent requirement and he would happily pay extra to have an express delivery. Eventually, she rang him back and informed him the earliest it could be with him would be Thursday and there would be no extra charge, which pleased him.

Feeling slightly better than he had first thing, Ed wandered over to see Sue at the clubhouse, knowing once in a while she had problems with graffiti and might have something to clean up the side of his caravan. She did and after a nice chat and some strong filter coffee, he was back scrubbing the off the graffiti with the sun beating down on his bare back. Whatever it was she had given him was good and it came off with ease. Unfortunately, it made the rest of the caravan look filthy and he felt obliged to give the whole thing a good clean, which took him up until lunchtime. Right now, killing time was the name of the game, anything to stop him from getting bored. If he got bored, he would either get maudlin or angry, which was worse because he would then go off in search of Mack. Not that he didn't intend to but he needed to be calmer and in control before he confronted him. When he did, he would give him a pasting like he had never experienced in his life. Ed was going to inflict some serious damage and to hell with the consequences.

He wandered over to see Laura and Raechael, hoping that they would be in. He didn't want to spend any more time alone and he couldn't think of anyone else he would like to spend time with. Luck was on his side and Raechael answered the door and invited him in.

'We had a visit from your friend DCI Brown last night but I suppose you know that?' Raechael said nonchalantly but in such a way, it made Ed suspicious.

'Don't I know it. He drank all my beer, stayed the night, ate me out of house and home and cleared off to work.'

'Oh, he seemed like a very nice man to me,' she said. Ed noticed she touched her hair. Did that mean she fancied him, or Bob? Ed suspected the latter and, despite being pissed off with Bob, thought he might put in a few good words for him.

'Take no notice of me, he is. He's very good at his job, too. A little unorthodox from what I've heard from Jacqui but he means well.'

'You two are very alike then,' she said. Ed couldn't work out if that was a compliment or not.

'Maybe,' he said reluctantly. 'What are you two up to for the rest of the day? Want to keep me company on the beach?' Raechael agreed but Laura was reluctant. 'What's the problem?' he asked.

'This is the problem,' she said, gesticulating at the wheelchair.

'No, it's not. It's an excuse.'

'I don't want to go. Everyone will be staring at me. It'll be embarrassing for me and for you,' she said sulkily.

'Of course they'll be staring at you, you're gorgeous. Now, I'm off to put my trunks on and if you're not ready in your bikini by the time I get back, I'm going to wheel you down there naked, so get a move on.'

'You're such a bully,' she told him angrily but the look on her face said otherwise.

CHAPTER 31

The slope to the beach was fine for walking down but not exactly wheelchair friendly. Ed carried Laura down to the beach. He put her down in what he thought would be a good spot to sunbathe in and went back and retrieved the wheelchair. Towels down and Ed was looking forward to a few hours in the sun. Laura laid on her front and unhooked her bikini top and asked Ed to put on some suntan lotion. Ed's mind slipped back twenty years to the time he was almost in the exact same spot, oiling up Chris. The memory made him smile and he hoped that Laura didn't try the same trick. He was sure the result would be the same.

Ed asked Laura to return the favour a little later, when he felt it was time to get some sun on his back. He was glad he was on his front as the way she caressed his back was extremely sensuous and was having an amazing effect on a certain part of his anatomy he didn't want to share with the rest of the beach.

'Ok, who's up for a swim?' he said, poking Laura in her side. What he really meant was come on, Laura, we're going for a swim.

'I can't,' she replied.

'What, you can't swim?' he asked, thinking everyone knows how to swim.

'Of course I can. I do it all the time as part of my physiotherapy. It's, well, well, I don't want to, OK?'

'Ah, embarrassed, right?' he said mockingly.

'Yes, if you must know,' She replied tersely.

'You know, if you worry about what other people think all the time, you're going to end up very bored. Do you want to go for a swim?' he said, almost as an order.

'Yes, I suppose so,' she replied. That was all Ed needed to hear and scooped her up and carried her down the beach into the water. When the water was up to his chest and lapping at her backside, he let her go. The water was cold, as it hadn't the chance to warm up over the summer months, but it was refreshing after having the sun beating down on their skin for the last hour. They splashed about and swam for a while, until they began to get cold. Laura swam up to him and put her arms around his neck and he carried her out to the beach.

'Anyone want an ice cream?' Ed asked 'There's a van on the beach down the next bay.'

'I'd love one Ed, but it will have melted by the time you get it back,' Raechael said, shaking her head like he was stupid.

'OK. Care to take a bet on that?' he asked with a grin, already with a plan in mind. They settled on a pound bet. Ed didn't care how much it was, a bet was all about proving a point and he set off down the beach towards the ice cream van, half a mile or so in the distance.

Half an hour later, everyone on the beach looked up amazed as the ice cream van came round the rocky outcrop, with Greensleeves chiming away and Ed hanging out the window grinning like the village idiot. It had taken a lot of persuasion with the vendor but he finally wore him down, that and the promise of a hundred quid. He had seen the lifeguard jeep running up and down the compacted sand, where the tide had gone out earlier, so knew it would be safe but he had to convince the vendor, who wasn't quite as convinced as Ed. The hundred quid swung it eventually, as did the promise of a beach full of customers.

Ed thanked him and jumped out to be the first customer and walked back smugly to Raechael and Laura and proudly presented them with their cones.

'You owe me a quid, Mrs. Jacobs. Cough up,' he said smugly.

'That's cheating.' she told him but she was obviously impressed. 'How the hell did you manage that?'

'A little bit of friendly persuasion and, at the end of the day, he couldn't resist the lure of a beach full of customers. That and the hundred quid I offered him by way of a bribe,' he said laughing.

'You gave him a hundred pounds to win a one pound bet.'

'Yep and it was worth every penny, just to see the look on your faces. It's not about the amount; it's all about the winning.'

'At this rate, you are going to die a very poor man,' she said seriously.

'But I'll die a very happy and very smug one, too. Now cough up loser,' he said raising his hand to his head and making the L sign with his thumb and index finger, like he had seen the kid next door make to his father. At the time he didn't know what it meant but asked him the next day. Clearly the boy's father didn't know either, as if he did, Ed was sure he would have had a few stern words with him.

The ice cream vendor departed very happy, having just sold over a hundred pounds worth of ice creams, snacks and sweets. He was driving back down the beach, rubbing his hands together in glee to the sound of Greensleeves.

After seeing Rachael and Laura safely back to their caravan and saying his goodbyes, Ed headed back, showered and changed. He headed over to the clubhouse, where he sat in the restaurant and ate what was the equivalent of a supermarket sad meal for one, only with waitress service. He didn't eat a great deal of it. It was a case of feeling he should eat, having eaten nothing all day and it was something to do. Raechael invited him to dinner, which he would have loved to have taken her up on, but didn't think he would be much company. He made the excuse he had taken up far too much of their time together already, over the last few days. Raechael nodded and told him Laura would be very disappointed as he reached the door. Just as he was leaving, she put her hand on his arm and told him he was very good for her daughter, getting her to overcome her self-consciousness and fears and kissed him on the cheek. Ed was quite touched and smiled, before walking back to the empty caravan.

CHAPTER 32

Ed was up, showered and shaved, before the sun had dragged itself over the horizon. He was starving and decided to walk into Padstow and have a huge breakfast and a general wander round before meeting Emma for lunch. He walked quickly over the undulating clifftops arriving in Padstow just before eight o'clock, securing a window seat in the cafe on the harbour front. He ordered double everything with toast and a mug of tea and sat there watching the world go by. Not that there was much doing that time of the day but it was a pleasant enough way to pass the time. He thought about going to see Fat Boy but decided to phone instead and was told he was much the same. He was stable and making steady progress but was still a bit weak and they advised him not to visit, as getting him over excited might not be a good idea. Christ, they treated them like humans, which wasn't a bad thing he supposed.

He killed some time by going to the bank and looking round all the tourist traps. He had covered nearly every inch of the town, before stopping at the florist and purchasing two large bouquets, one each for Chris and Emma. He was a little early as he walked into the arts and crafts shop Chris owned but he couldn't think of anything else to do.

'Hi Simon,' he said to the shop manager as he walked in, 'Is Chris out back?' He nodded and told him to go through, remembering not to ask about Fat Boy, having been briefed yesterday by Chris. Ed found Chris in her office, working away on some paperwork. She was pleased to see him, loved the flowers and walked with him to the studio upstairs, where Emma was working on what Chris described as a real masterpiece.

They walked into the studio, where Emma was hard at work or at least Ed assumed she was but to him, appeared to be just staring at her painting. It looked finished to him but she added a few strokes here and there and stood back, looking at it intensely. The rustle of the cellophane from the flowers broke her concentration and she turned round looking irritable. Ed gave an apologetic smile as she rushed over and gave him a hug and a kiss on the cheek. He looked down to check that there was no paint on his shirt and was relieved to find it clean.

'They're lovely. Are they for me?' she asked, looking at the huge bouquet he was holding.

'Actually, they're for Chris but I thought you would like to see them before I gave them to her,' he joked, before handing them over to her. 'I like the picture,' he told her. It was brilliant and something he would willingly pay for to have hanging on his wall. She looked pleased that he liked it and grinned broadly.

'I've been making jewellery too,' she said enthusiastically, almost childlike. God, he missed having her around. He still had that strange feeling something had changed and things just wouldn't be the same again but kept smiling, pleased she seemed so happy. A quick look at Chris confirmed what he thought he already knew, as she gave him a quick smile and wouldn't look him in the eye.

They left Chris and headed round the other side of the harbour, to a nice bistro just set back off the main harbour road. It was a small, intimate place with soft lighting and equally soft music, barely audible in the background. They ordered and sat drinking their wine, waiting for their food to arrive. They got all the preliminary conversation out the way, on how Fat Boy, Laura and Raechael were. He then told her about his day on the beach, making her laugh when he got to the ice cream van part. She told him how great Chris was and how she was enjoying her painting, all building up to the big one, Ed thought.

'Chris said, I can stay with her as long as I like,' she said nervously 'She's been so nice. She's like the big sister I never had.' Ed nodded. He knew exactly what she meant, she was like the big sister he never had, too.

'I know. She's only a year older than I am but she's the same with me,' he said sadly. 'And are you going to stay?' he added. She nodded.

'I feel really ungrateful about it. After all you've done for me and for all you've given me. Not just buying me clothes and meals but making me feel like I was something special and not worthless, like I felt when we first met. Are you sure you're OK with it?'

'Of course I am. I was beginning to wonder what to do with you. We couldn't really stay in a caravan forever, could we? And you can't go back to Cambridge so I look on it as Chris doing me a favour,' he said, not believing a word and neither did she. 'I will miss having you around. God, it's horrible without either you or Fat Boy; it's depressing if you really want to know but I'm happy you're happy.'

'I can't come back,' she began. 'When we first met, you made me feel safe and that's exactly what I needed and still do. What happened to Laura and Fat Boy frightened me and knowing that idiot is going to come after you at some time scares me and I've spent far too long being scared. Do you understand?'

Ed nodded. It wasn't that many years ago he felt the same and Chris came along and hauled his sorry arse out of despair. She was kind and compassionate but also gave him a bloody good shake and encouraged him get on with the rest of his life. 'I've been there, remember? Look, being with Chris will be good for you. She has a knack of making people feel good and bringing the best out of them. You couldn't be in better hands.'

'What are you going to do? She asked.

'Well, as soon as Fat Boy gets out of doggy hospital, I'll stick around a few days until he's stronger and take him home, I suppose. To be honest, I hadn't really thought of that yet.'

'What about Laura?' she said with a glint in her eye.

'Don't you start. I've got her bloody mother trying to match make as well, now. She keeps telling me how good I am for her daughter and if I break her heart, she'll break my nose,' he said with a smile. 'Have you said anything to her?'

'No, I haven't. I had a nice chat with Laura but not Raechael. Perhaps you need to wake up and smell the roses. We can't both be wrong, can we?' she said gleefully. Ed did his usual and shook his head and took a long drink of wine.

The food and ambiance was excellent but Ed could see that

Emma was itching to get back and finish her painting. She insisted on paying for lunch, telling him it might be her last chance of buying him a meal, which didn't do much to lift his spirits. They walked out hand in hand and headed back to Chris's shop and Emma's beloved masterpiece.

CHAPTER 33

Ed fell to the ground, almost dragging Emma with him, as his hand tightened around hers, due to an excruciating pain in his side. It took him a few seconds as he knelt on the pavement to realise he had either been punched or stabbed in the kidneys. He tentatively put a hand to his side to check. He pulled it away quickly and was relieved to find there was no blood. He was just severely winded and having trouble catching his breath, which came in short gasps. Emma dropped to her knees beside him with a look of panic on her face.

'What's wrong with you?' she asked on the verge of tears.

Ed looked over his shoulder and saw the retreating Mack, smirking and giving him the middle finger. 'Bastard!' Ed hissed in between breaths, trying to stand, eventually overcoming the pain and managing to get to his feet. He breathed deeply through his nose and exhaled through his mouth a couple of times and stretched.

'Mack,' he said, his eyes blazing with hatred, which frightened Emma even more than Ed suddenly dropping to the floor; she knew this meant trouble. Ed turned and tried to run as fast as he could in pursuit of Mack, who, not hampered as Ed was, began to put distance between them.

There were only two places he could go, around the harbour to the ferry that took tourists across to Rock on the opposite bank of the Camel Estuary or up the slope and onto the coastal path. Ed had a feeling it would be the ferry. He glanced over to where the small, green boat was moored, which was filling up with passengers. If Mack got there soon he would be home and dry. He tried to coax a little more speed out of his body but it was like trying to run with a stitch. Emma was keeping pace beside him with ease, and was pleading with him to stop. No chance. The adrenaline had kicked in and he wanted him. He wanted revenge for Fat Boy.

He saw Mack jump on the ferry as the deck hand was about to cast off. Ed continued to pound painfully down the harbour but he was too late. The small boat pulled away, just as Ed arrived seconds after. He looked at the boat a few yards out from the harbour wall and wondered if he could do it. Could he jump and land on the boat? He readied himself and was just about to sprint to the end of the harbour wall and launch himself off when Emma grabbed his arm.

'Ed, don't be so bloody stupid, you'll kill yourself!' She was close to tears, her eyes watery and slightly puffy and she looked so frightened it stopped him in his tracks.

'You're right,' he said giving her a hug. 'There's another way. Come on,' he said and started to jog back the way they had come. By the time he reached the other side of the harbour, he was breathless and stood there with his hands on his hips, looking around, finally finding what he had come for.

Colin walked over to Ed and shook his hand. 'Hello mate, long time no see. How are you?'

'Still running those speedboats of yours, Colin? I need to get over to Rock in a hurry,' he said grinning at his own genius.

'No problem. Just you or are they coming along?' he said pointing at Emma and Chris, who saw them run past the shop and came to see what was going on.

'Just me, Colin. Do you reckon you can get there before the ferry does?' he asked excitedly.

'Yeah, maybe. There are restrictions on how fast I can go 'til I'm out of the harbour but there might be a chance. If not, I won't be far behind it. What's the hurry, anyway?' Ed told him as they walked down the steps to the waiting speedboat. He jumped in and Colin fired the powerful engine. Seconds before he pulled off, Emma jumped in beside him and gave him a look that told him not to argue. Colin cruised out of the harbour and as soon as he was clear, pulled the throttle open. They instantly picked up speed, skimming across the waves. Ed held on tightly, remembering the last gonad-busting trip he took in one of Colin's speedboats.

They made up ground on the ferry quickly, but they were too far behind to catch it. By the time they caught up with it, it had already stopped. The deckhand ran out the gang-plank and passengers started to disembark onto the beach. Colin slew the powerful machine round pulling up directly behind the ferry and grabbed hold of it, allowing Ed and Emma to climb on board. Ed pulled out his wallet but Colin just waved his hand at him and sped off back to the harbour.

Mack saw all this from the shore and began jogging down the beach, Ed now in hot pursuit and gaining ground. Mack looked over his shoulder and Ed thought he saw a look of panic in those evil eyes. Mack stepped up a gear to try to lose him. Ed wasn't going to lose him this time. The pain in his side was gone, the adrenaline was pumping through his veins and he was pissed off. Mack veered up the beach and headed for the dunes beyond. His progress slowed, due to the fine, dry, shifting sand and Ed felt he could almost touch him. That is until he too, hit the dry sand. Then it was as if he was in one of those agonising dreams, where you are running away or after someone and no matter how fast you go, it seems as if you are treading water, only this was no dream.

Out of breath, Mack eventually stopped in the bottom of a huge, bowl-shaped dune and stared back at Ed, as he too slowed to a stop and caught his breath. The two of them stood there, several feet apart, staring at each other, breathing heavily, both wanting to catch their breath before the inevitable conclusion. Mack was the first to speak.

'Fancy your chances, do you? I hope you put up more of a fight than the spastic did or your dog come to that,' he mocked, trying to provoke him.

'You're an evil bastard. I'm going to enjoy tearing you apart,' Ed spat back, receiving a mocking laugh in return.

'In your fucking dreams. I'm going to cut you up, just like I cut your pathetic, little dog up. I really enjoyed hearing him howl in pain. Pitiful it was. Fucking shame really, looked like a nice dog. Oh well, what a bastard,' he said laughing.

'You'll need to do a better job on me, because he's still alive and if you don't do a better job, I'm going to fucking kill you and that is a promise.'

'I will, don't worry and when I'm done, I think I might have a piece of her for myself. Looks well tasty and I reckon she's gagging for it,' he said, looking at Emma, who was standing a few feet behind him.

'Emma go and stand over there,' he said, pointing to the top of the dune. 'I don't want you getting in the way.'

'Come on cunt, what are you waiting for. You scared or something?' Mack taunted him again. Ed looked up to make sure Emma was far enough away so in the unlikely event he did lose, she had a good head start on Mack. Well, you could never be certain of these things. Emma was joined by Bob and Phil. Chris called Bob just before Ed boarded the speedboat. They commandeered Colin's second boat and been seconds behind them. Bob insisting he was the police and harbour restrictions weren't applicable, hence arriving so soon. Bob stood there with a protective arm around Emma, who had tears rolling down her cheeks. Bob nodded and Ed stepped forward towards his enemy to seek his revenge.

'I want you to video this, Phil. Right?' Bob said, as Ed walked towards Mack with a look of absolute hatred, etched on his face.

'Right Guv,' Phil said and pulled out his mobile phone and started recording.

CHAPTER 34

Ed got within striking distance and immediately lashed out with a powerful jab that split Mack's grinning lips and loosened a tooth. Before he could recover, he jabbed again with the left, catching him on the cheek. Ed was satisfied the smirk had been replaced by a look of fear.

Bob was almost dancing on the spot, like an over-excited schoolboy. 'I hope you're getting all this Phil, this is fucking awesome!' he said

Ed, having scored so easily, followed up again, firing left and right-hand jabs into Mack's face, dropping in a few body punches and relishing the pain he was clearly inflicting. Mack threw a few punches back but they lacked power and Ed didn't even feel them as his adrenaline levels were so high.

'This is better than anything I've ever seen on Sky Sports.' Bob shouted excitedly 'Jacqui said he was a bastard in a fight but I never expected this.'

'I'm so glad you're enjoying yourself, he could get hurt,' Emma said hysterically.

'Don't be daft, love. That scumbag's hardly laid a finger on him,'

Ed was enjoying himself, letting go with combinations of jabs to the face and body, wearing his opponent down, just like he had in the ring all those years ago. It was almost too easy but he didn't want it to be over too quickly. He wanted the bastard to suffer, to atone for his dog and for Laura. Mack lashed out and caught him on the jaw, causing Ed to step back, which gave Mack an advantage. He came forward, raining down blows but they were wild and uncontrolled. Ed managed to block most of them, although some got through and he could feel a trickle of blood from his nose.

He recovered his composure and after blocking a roundhouse, he delivered a powerful uppercut to Mack's ribs, knocking the breath out of him and causing him to almost double over. Ed was quick to pounce on the advantage and battered Mack's head and face with a series of left and right hand hooks, smiling as he watched his head rock from side to side with each blow. He finished the combination with an uppercut, catching him squarely on the jaw and knocking him to the ground.

'Fucking hell, this is almost better than sex!' Bob exclaimed.

'Aren't you going to stop it now?' Emma asked and received a look from Bob that suggested she was mad.

'Get up you bastard,' Ed hissed, kicking Mack's foot. He bent over and grabbed the front of his T-shirt. Mack turned and threw a handful of sand in his eyes. Ed couldn't open them and was rubbing them furiously and shaking his head to clear them.

'The dirty bastard,' Bob said, stunned at such poor sportsmanship. Ed was still blinking away the sand, when Mack got to his feet and from somewhere produced a lump of old driftwood and began to swing it like a club, ginning with malice. All Ed could do was to take a step back but Mack came at him fast and swung the wood. Ed managed to get an arm up to protect his head as the wood came crashing down. His arm took the brunt of the power, before it smashed into his temple, splitting his eyebrow open. The wood splintered on impact and Mack threw it to the ground.

Ed was dazed. His left arm was numb, blood was trickling into his left eye and his head was swimming. He still had sand in his eyes and was blinking myopically, trying to stay upright, knowing if he went down he would lose and that was unthinkable. Mack let loose with the first blow. Ed brought his arms up in front and bowed his head, like they taught him to do when he was boxing. All he could do was ride the storm and hope his head cleared.

'Bob, stop it. He's going to kill him!' Emma pleaded, almost hysterically, while Phil carried on filming.

'He's OK. This is classic; it's like watching Ali. Well it would be if he was black. Ali used to cover up like that and let his opponents punch themselves out. Then he would come off the ropes and batter them. This is fantastic. That boyfriend of yours is good. You should be proud of him.'

Ed was feeling anything but like Ali, as Mack hit it him with everything he had. Ed stopped a lot of the blows from getting through but was thankful Mack was so full of anger he had no control over his punches. He just swung wildly, hoping that one would get through. When they did they hurt, especially when Mack hit him on his damaged eyebrow, forcing the splinters deeper into his flesh. Ed hissed in pain.

The pain brought him to his senses and although still slightly dazed by the blow, he lashed out with an uppercut catching his opponent on the nose, making it bleed. Seeing his opponent step back, Ed let his guard down and breathed deeply, thankful for the respite.

Mack smiled at him and from his back pocket produced his flick-knife and began waving it to and fro in front of him, like he had done in the club. 'Time to go meet your dog, you fucker' he said, the smirk back on his evil face. Ed blinked out the last of the sand and stood his ground. His left arm was still next to useless, still numb. He had movement but little feeling. He was just glad Mack was left-handed or he really would be in trouble. There was no way he would be able to disarm him with his left-hand but at least it wasn't a gun, or he really would be in the brown smelly stuff.

Mack looked at him and grinned through his split lips, shook his head and switched the knife to his right hand, now laughing. Ed stood there as he stepped forward wafting the knife. He flexed his fingers and although he could move them very little, there was a little feeling in them. He knew what he had to do.

As Mack took the final step towards him, Ed looked up at Emma and smiled, winked with his good eye and shrugged. Mack lunged powerfully with the knife, which was aimed at Ed's stomach. To Ed, everything seemed to go in slow motion. He saw the knife come towards him and turned slightly, angling his body away from the blade. His left arm came down and grabbed Mack's forearm pushing the knife down and stepping forward in the same movement.

The knife pieced Ed's thigh. The pain was like nothing he ever experienced. He pulled Mack in further and head-butted him on his nose, which flattened with a sickening squelch, like a peach being hit by a hammer. Blood exploded from his nose. Ed, spurred on by this success, kneed him hard in the balls, causing Mack to double up in pain and grab his genitals, pulling the knife from Ed's leg as he did so. With blood flowing freely down his leg, Ed edged forward, fighting through the pain and delivered clubbing right-hand blows to Mack's head and face. He knew he had him beaten now, as he swayed from side to side on the verge of falling. Just as Mack was about to fall, Ed turned his body to put his full weight behind his next punch. He hit him with an uppercut so powerful, Mack's head snapped backwards, knocking him off his feet onto his back, where he stayed.

He saw Bob and Emma run down the hill, followed by Phil, who was still filming, on Bob's instructions, of course. Ed looked down at his leg and saw his once beige chinos were now red and soaked with blood. He walked over to Mack, who still hadn't moved and kicked him viciously in the ribs, relishing the two cracks that he heard.

'That was a bit unnecessary, wasn't it?' Bob said to him, tutting.

'That was for my trousers. Look at the bloody state of them, they're ruined,' he said with as much bravado as he could muster.

'That, my friend, was absolutely awesome. Better than bloody sex that was. I think I may even have a hard on!' he informed Ed. 'Right, lay down there and put your leg in the air.'

'Have a heart, Bob. My arsehole is about the only part of me that isn't bloodied and bruised. Be gentle for Christ sake,' Ed said grimacing

'I was thinking more about stopping the bleeding. Do I look like a bloody poof? Now, do as you're told.'

'Bollocks to that. I won and I'm walking out of here,' Ed said defiantly.

'Don't get any blood on my nice blue flag beach, you stupid, proud bastard.' Bob shouted, as Ed walked off with his arm around Emma for support.

Ed hobbled slowly towards the road with Emma beside him. Blood was still flowing down his left leg, saturating his trousers. Emma said nothing, knowing he would take no notice anyway, if she told him to stop and do something to abate the bleeding, despite being concerned he might bleed to death. They eventually reached the road where he sat down painfully and waited for the ambulance to arrive, which they could hear approaching in the distance.

'Doesn't it hurt?' she asked.

Ed grimaced and looked across at her. 'Just a lot. It's feels like a really bad paper cut that's been hit with a sledgehammer,' he told her.

'Paper cut. Nasty,' she said, trying to sound light-hearted but was alarmed at the amount of blood he seemed to be leaking. His trouser leg was now sodden.

'The bastard's ruined my trousers,' he said, feeling light-headed and looking rather pale.

'Your eye looks quite nasty, too. It's got splinters in it and I think it'll need stitching.'

'Shit. I didn't realise he hit me that hard. Those splinters are the insides coming out,' he said jokingly.

'I'm glad you find it amusing,' she said sternly. 'I was worried bloody sick. I thought he was going to kill you.'

'Nah, I'm bloody immortal. I think I must be down to eight lives now, though. I don't feel too clever, if I'm perfectly honest. I'm cold,' he said, despite the day being blisteringly hot. There was genuine concern in his voice. Emma moved closer and put an arm round him and they sat huddled together, waiting for the ambulance to arrive.

Fortunately, two ambulances arrived, which Ed was thankful for as he didn't want to share with Mack. He might be tempted to give the bastard another kicking on the way to the hospital. He made it into the back of the ambulance and lay down on the stretcher. The paramedic cut his trouser leg open and looked at the wound. He could tell by the look on Emma's face, who was sitting opposite, it wasn't good.

CHAPTER 35

At the hospital, he was left in a cubical and within a few minutes a nurse arrived with a doctor. Either they knew he had BUPA or it was a slow day in the NHS. His only previous experience at accident and emergency hadn't been a pleasant one. He waited hours before a nurse came and dragged him away to be patched up, concerned by the amount of blood pooling by his feet, or because she thought he might be health and safety risk, more likely.

'What happened to you, then?' the nurse asked, whose name badge identified her as Claire.

'Got into a slight altercation with a guy on the beach,' he replied lamely.

'Don't tell me. You should see the other bloke,' she said, laughing at her own joke.

'You really should,' Ed replied, smiling. 'I think he's probably in one of the other cubicles. With any luck, he looks a lot bloody worse than I do.' She regarded him strangely and walked out, only to return a few minutes later.

'You must be so proud of yourself?' she said venomously.

'I'm not proud of myself but I'm not sorry either. That guy is wanted for the murder of a pensioner, and on a more personal level, he stabbed my dog and tipped a friend out of her wheelchair. So before you get all anti with me and inflict more pain than is absolutely necessary when you stitch me up, have a think about it,' Ed said defensively. She was clearly giving the matter some thought.

'He's telling the truth,' Emma interjected to help her make her mind up, which it seemed to do.

'OK. I'll be nice to you then,' she said, giving him a quick smile, before cleaning the wound with what felt like battery acid, making his eyes smart.

'Jesus Christ.' Ed cried out in agony.

'Don't be such a baby,' she admonished 'I've got to do your eye next, so brace yourself.'

A doctor came eventually and checked him over. His leg was stitched, as was his eye, once they had cleaned it and removed the splinters. Next he was sent to X-ray to have his arm checked for fractures, which thankfully showed it was not broken, just severely bruised, as was his head. He was informed they would need to keep him in for a few days for observation and rest, which he wasn't best pleased about and played the BUPA card. No way was he staying in a mixed ward, full of coffin-dodgers and snotty-nosed kids. I'll have a nice room all to myself, with a shower and à la carte dining, he told them and that's what he got.

His nurse was an immense black woman, with a friendly disposition and rather a lot to say for herself or, in other words, opinionated but nice with it. Ed was feeling pretty miserable and did his best to wind her up. She gave as good as she got, which passed the time.

'What do you want for supper, Ed?' She asked him, handing him an extensive menu – one of the perks of going private.

'I could murder a beer but I can't see it on the menu, Annie.'

'That's because you ain't allowed any beer, James and it's Anita not Annie,' she scolded.

'Well, in that case, get me some potato skins and I'll make some moonshine, using the vase and the bed frame and it's Ed not James,' he replied, enjoying the banter.

'Just order you food. You've gotta eat to keep your strength up,' she said sternly.

'What have you got in mind for me, then?' he said smiling, making her laugh.

'Ed, I eat little boys like you for breakfast. By the time I was finished with you, you'd be in intensive care,' she said, chuckling away to herself. Ed looked at her and decided she was probably right.

'In that case, I'll have the chicken breast and boiled spuds please. That should keep me going 'til breakfast,' he said winking at her.

She snatched the menu away from him, turned and walked out the room, her massive buttocks bouncing like two hippos in a sack.

His food, when it arrived could best be described as hot. It looked like chicken but tasted bland and Ed struggled to get it down but did so, as he knew he would incur the wrath of Sister Freeman, although she didn't like him calling her Sister, on account of him being too anaemic to be a brother. He needed to get out of this place and hoped he would be given the all clear in the morning. He was going stir crazy and he'd only been in a few hours. Do anything you like, Mr. Case, as long as it's swallowing antibiotics and doesn't involve getting out of bed, which left watching TV or re-reading the newspaper, both of which were boring. He was hoping for a visitor or two, armed with beer and his iPod but he was told no visitors until tomorrow, which made him think he could be in for at least another day yet. Deep joy.

CHAPTER 36

He had been watching her for two days now, having singled her out amongst many, on the basis she was flirtatious and in his view, therefore, promiscuous. The way she acted disgusted and offended him. Whores like her needed to be taught a lesson, one he was more than willing to deliver.

It was becoming too easy. He easily passed off unnoticed in a crowd and relished knowing what he knew about himself and the fact nobody suspected. He was above and beyond the law. This time he would make it interesting and give the police and the press something to think about.

His intended target was just like all the others, young, blonde, lived alone and was filth, just like all the others. Once inside the house it was easy. It was just a case of making small-talk about the weather and the recent murders. He was barely able to contain his excitement. When she went to the kitchen to put the kettle on he followed her out, crept up behind her and put the chloroform-soaked handkerchief over her face. After a brief struggle he lowered her to the floor. He pulled his latex gloves from his briefcase and carried her upstairs, quickly stripping her, leaving her naked on the bed. He undressed himself and put his clothes in his briefcase, laying the black boiler-suit at his feet.

Once the cord was securely round her neck, he retrieved his camera and took numerous photographs from every angle, not rushing and spoiling his shots as he had the first time due nerves and over excitement. His excitement was already mounting, reaching its peak, his erection painful. He fondled her breasts and between her legs, becoming much bolder, knowing he would not be caught, could not be caught. He was too clever, far too clever.

She began to stir on the bed so he put the cloth back over her face, ensuring she would sleep a little longer. He wanted more time.

He set the camera to movie and angled it on the bedside table, ensuring that nothing would be missed. He parted her legs and knelt between them, pushing his fingers deep inside her, his free hand working up and down his penis. When the girl began to stir he leaned forward and massaged her breast roughly, pinching her nipples hard to awaken her. When she awoke and regained sufficient awareness, he grinned at her malevolently. She pulled in a deep breath and was about to scream. He pulled tightly on the cord at her throat, before the scream had a chance to leave her body.

She thrashed wildly, tearing at his hands, throwing her body from side to side, which just increased his excitement as he watched her panic, her eyes bulging, her tongue protruding from her mouth. He ejaculated in huge gouts as the life drained from her body and became still. It was then he leaned forward and gently caressed her face before gouging her eyes out, placing the bloody orbs on the bedside table.

He pulled on his boiler-suit and left her there, returning to his car to get the tarpaulin, which he wrapped her in and deposited her in the boot. He drove calmly and within the speed limits, not wanting some over-exuberant patrol car stopping him before he reached his destination, which was back to the same beach as his first victim. What fun he would have as the police tried to make a connection and formulate patterns. Placing patrols on the beach where he left his second victim, trying to pre-empt his next move. He knew what his next move was already and it wasn't there.

He parked up and waited to make sure the coast was clear. When certain it was, he donned his ski mask and retrieved the body from the boot and carried it slowly and steadily towards the beach. He stopped and listened every few yards, as was his routine, continuing only when he was sure he was still alone. Eventually, he reached the beach and dropped his burden onto the sand.

Allan volunteered to drive the babysitter home, as he always did. The first time it was out of a sense of duty but now it was to get her somewhere dark and indulge in extra-marital sex. Pauline was only seventeen, barely legal with an amazing body. She was so lithe and supple and was willing to experiment and try anything, which was more than could be said for his wife, who since the kids arrived, had turned her back on him in the bedroom. Therefore, his actions were justified or so he told himself.

This night she protested it was the wrong time of the month. Allan was so horny he didn't care and parked the car and taken her down to the sand dunes anyway, after all even a hand job or a blow job was better than nothing. It was whilst Pauline was giving him the best head he'd had in years, he heard a rustle from the beach below. The thought of being caught red handed, literally as was the case tonight, filled him with dread. Pauline was OK for one thing but he had no intention of ruining his marriage over it.

The sound continued and he became more worried, his penis went limp. Pauline looked angrily at Allan and was about to vent her disappointment, when Allan put his finger to his lips and whispered to her to be quiet. He got to his feet slowly, pulling his trousers up and looked over the dune to the beach below. He saw the killer laying the body out and watched both fascinated and horrified. He was torn between doing the right thing and ignoring it. His conscience wouldn't allow him to ignore it so he shouted out and started to run down the dunes.

The killer panicked and looked up startled, like a rabbit caught in the headlights of an approaching car, before taking flight. The oversized flip-flops were thwarting his progress and he kicked them off, running on the wet sand where the tide had ebbed to gain the advantage. He looked over his shoulder and saw his pursuer had stopped by the victim and was no longer a direct threat. He was however, on his mobile, which meant trouble. In a blind panic he doubled back and raced back to his car, no longer worried who saw him, now afraid. Once behind the wheel, he slammed the car into gear and sped off.

Allan stayed and waited by the body until the police arrived, despite his concerns. Firstly, how he would explain to the police why he was on the beach at such a late hour and secondly, how he would explain his late return to his wife. The only consolation was he had done the right thing. He would worry about everything else later. Hopefully, by that time, he would have thought of a feasible lie to spin when he arrived back home.

Bob was ecstatic and could hardly believe his luck. His first break through. His team assembled quickly and their enthusiasm initially non-existent, due to the late hour of the callout, soon became fever pitch. The flip-flops were retrieved and would be used to extract DNA, as would the tarpaulin. Allan was able to give a good description of height and build but not a great deal else. He was allowed to go but would be required to give a formal statement in the morning.

Plaster casts of the footprints in the wet sand were taken. These along with the wear on the flip-flops, would indicate they were not looking for someone with size twelve feet, more like a size nine or ten. Traces of semen were present on the victim's abdomen and would also be used for DNA testing. Later, further analysis, would show that the body had been sexually abused. This, coupled with the gouging out of her eyes, was a new development and one Bob didn't like. Either the killer was gaining confidence, discovered more perverse pleasures or both, this worried Bob. The absence of black cockles was, he hoped, only because the killer had been disturbed. A worrying thought crossed his mind, there may be a second killer out there, one more evil than the first but he pushed that thought to the back of his mind.

CHAPTER 37

Morning came and the nurse woke him up to shovel another couple of bloody pills down his throat. Ed wasn't best pleased about this, after a sleepless night due to the pain in his leg and a headache, as the painkillers wore off. The nurse, who wanted to take his temperature, was a grumpy, sour-faced woman, whose name Ed didn't even bother to read off the badge. To show his displeasure, Ed rolled over and showed her his arse for her to insert the thermometer into, which she was unamused by and gave him a ticking off. Miserable cow. Next was the blood pressure check, which she wrote down on a chart and refused to tell him if it was good, bad or indifferent.

She thrust a menu in front of him and curtly asked him for his order. God she was miserable and stood there impatiently, tapping a pen against her notepad. Ed very, very, slowly read every word on the menu, smirking. He settled for toast, which he munched whilst watching GMTV. It was eight o'clock in the morning and he was bored, bored, bored, bored, bored.

Relief came at lunchtime, in the shape of the same sour faced nurse, to give him more pills and perform the same temperature and blood pressure checks and get his lunch order. It's funny how boredom makes you hungry, Ed mused. You could be working away on a project, such as wallpapering or laying a floor and not think about food all day. Sit there in an armchair, watching daytime TV and you'd be ravenous within an hour and be reaching for the chocolate biscuits. Ed settled for the bangers and mash, which he was sure were made from cardboard but it relieved the boredom. He needed to get out of here and quickly.

That afternoon he had visitors. Chris, Jacqui, Raechael and Laura walked and wheeled their way into his room, smiling happily until they saw the stitches over his eye and the black bruise, which ran the length of his arm.

'They told us no visitors yesterday when we rang,' Chris explained, feeling guilty. Ed was just pleased for the company, as long as it wasn't the wicked witch of the west, who marauded as a nurse in her spare time.

'We would have been here earlier, if it wasn't for Laura taking so long to get ready,' Raechael said, teasing her daughter.

'Well, it was well worth the wait,' Ed replied, causing Laura to blush and smile broadly at the same time. She did look good, too. Perfect make-up to go with perfect hair and a tight T-shirt that left little to the imagination. 'No Emma? Ed asked.

'Oh, she had to go to the ladies,' Chris said. Ed knew she was lying. She always was a crap liar and he stared at her intently.

'I've got some clean clothes for you, for when you leave,' Chris said, putting a carrier bag down on the floor beside the bedside table. 'I heard the ones you were wearing got a little dirty,' she said, more as a question than a statement.

There was a light tap on the door and Emma walked in, with a big grin on her face and sporting a new, slightly shorter haircut. 'Hi,' she said, looking round 'I've brought someone to see you.'

Fat Boy walked in and, on seeing Ed, jumped on the bed and started licking his face and ears, whimpering and wagging his tail furiously, before lying down beside him on the bed and thumping his tail on the mattress. Ed was overcome and buried his head in the dog's mane and made a huge fuss of him. When he sat up he wiped away his tears. 'I think I've grown allergic to him,' he said, embarrassed by his reaction to seeing him again, partly because he didn't think he would see him again.

'I think it's catching,' Raechael said wiping away her own tears, as was everyone else apart from Bob, who had just walked in behind Emma.

'Christ almighty! You'd think someone had died the way you lot are carrying on. Is this the same bloke who knocked ten shades of shit out of that scumbag on the beach yesterday? You need to get out of this place. It's turning you bloody soft,' Bob said for the benefit of everyone. Ed looked and was sure Bob's eyes were just a little more watery than they normally were but was in no position to comment.

'Did anyone think to smuggle in any beer for me, by the way?' Ed asked, looking at every one. Judging by the blank looks nobody had.

'Are you wearing anything under that sheet?' Laura asked, referring back to the conversation they had the other day, making him smile.

'Of course I am. I've got on my white, leather, Gucci posing-pouch,' he replied.

'Liar,' she told him.

'I'm a millionaire, that's what I wear. Why do you want to know, anyway?'

'I wanted to give you a hug to say thanks for the wheelchair.'

'Oh, I'm glad that came. I'd forgotten all about that. You did say your one got damaged and I felt responsible. I hope it's OK? I thought a red frame might look quite cool. It did on the website, anyway and looks OK from here.'

'It's great, really comfortable. You didn't have to but thanks,' she said, wheeling herself to the side of the bed and putting her arms around his neck. Ed pulled her up and hugged her.

'Are you really wearing a leather posing-pouch?' she asked.

'Of course. Would I lie to you?' he replied innocently. Laura reached over and lifted the sheet up and peered down.

'You liar. That's gross,' she cried.

'I think you'll find that's a beauty.' Ed told her, laughing loudly

'Not that, your stitches. There's nothing wrong with the other thing,' she said and looked quite impressed or that's how Ed read it, anyway. Everyone else just shook their heads in pity, with the exception of Bob who clearly thought it was amusing.

The door opened and in walked Nurse Anita Freeman. Ed quickly pulled the sheet over from the other side of the bed and covered Fat Boy. Unfortunately, the dog's tail was poking out the bottom and was still wagging dementedly but it was too late, anyway.

'Ed, what's that dog doing in my hospital?' she shouted. Even Bob looked scared.

'Have a heart, Annie. It's Fat Boy. He's just got out of hospital and wanted to see his dad.'

'He's got 'til I come back,' she said kindly. 'And then he's out of here,' she followed up with, before turning round and walking out.

'Bloody hell and you're paying for this?' Bob exclaimed, blowing out a long stream of breath.

'She's actually, OK,' Ed said in her defence. 'We've actually been having quite a good laugh, which is more than I can say for some of the others. I'm sure they're on day release from Colditz.'

'Think I'll take my chances with the NHS,' Bob declared.

Annie took her time coming back, almost an hour in fact and told him again the dog needed to go, as the doctor would be round shortly to take a look at him. He might even be able to go home today if the doctor was happy, which cheered him up. Bob said he would wait outside with Fat Boy, as he needed to make some more calls to catch up on the latest developments with the murder case. He seemed a lot happier and was even upbeat about getting a result in a few days.

Laura let him know that Fat Boy would be staying with her and Raechael and seemed to be happy about that. Raechael said she would come and pick him up, once he had the all clear from the doctor, which he thanked her for but knew he would get a taxi, rather than impose. When they left him, Ed felt a little happier but knew the boredom would set in quite quickly. He hoped the doctors would be round soon and give him the thumbs-up.

'I think she's more than a little sweet on you, Ed,' Annie told him.

'And who would that be?' he asked, acting dumb.

'You know who I'm talking about – Laura. If I had someone look at me the way she looks at you, I'd.... Well, I'd eat them for breakfast,' Ed gave her his best puppy dog look, trying to make light of it. 'It ain't working,' she said giving him a serious stare. 'Are you and her going to get it together?' she asked.

'You ask a lot of questions, Anita but I don't think so. Once bitten twice shy,' he replied lamely.

'So you have one bad experience and that's it? You don't strike me as being a quitter.' Ed gave her a quick summary of how it worked out with his ex-wife. Annie just stood there nodding and smiling throughout.

'So, are telling me, if you fell off your bike and hurt yourself, you'd leave it at that, walk away, frightened in case you fell off again? Maybe, I overestimated you, Ed. I've been married three times. The first was an abusive alcoholic, the second ran off with a girl half my age and now I've been happily married for five years. He ain't perfect but then he's a man. What man is? If I'd taken your attitude, I'd be on my own and would have missed out on a chance to be happy. That what you want?'

Ed felt uncomfortable talking so openly to someone who was almost a complete stranger. 'You're looking at me like I'm holding a gun to you head,' she said. 'What's your problem, Ed. Don't you want to be happy?'

'Of course I do but it's a bit more complicated than that, isn't it?' he replied.

'Because she's in a wheelchair? Ed, she's beautiful and I can tell she loves you and would do anything for you. A woman knows these things and you're gonna throw it all away because she's in a wheelchair. That's sad Ed, real sad,' she said, shaking her head. Ed shrugged in self-defence and looked at his hands anywhere but at Annie, who was staring at him. 'Well, I've got work to do. I can't stand around here sorting out your love life. I've got better things to do. You're gonna end up a very sad and lonely man, if you don't put the past behind you and take a chance once in a while. Think about it,' she said and left, shaking her head in despair.

The doctor came by at around six that evening, after Ed had eaten another bland, disappointing meal and declared him fit enough to leave. He advised him he might want to use a stick to take some of the strain of his thigh muscle, after seeing Ed hobble to the shower. Ed nodded but had no intention of using one, pride wouldn't let him. He dressed and left the room, leaving the clothes he wore when he arrived in the bin beside the bed. There was a florist by the main reception so he bought a large bunch of mixed, flowers and wandered off to find Annie. She seemed quite pleased with them and told him, again, to think about what she had said.

CHAPTER 38

Ed was sitting alone in the caravan with Fat Boy, having collected him yesterday evening from Laura and Raechael. Raechael gave him a ticking off for not calling her so she could collect him from the hospital, as he expected her to. The flowers he bought for them both stopped any further admonishment, as he hoped they would. They had a few drinks in the clubhouse, where Sue was fussing over him, like a mother would, as were Raechael and Laura. Although it was nice of them, it was tiring. His leg was painful and even the short walk to the clubhouse wore him out. He would get a stick tomorrow to see if that helped. Pride was one thing but pain was another and easily outranked pride.

In the morning he drove into Padstow, which again was hard on his leg due to constant gear changing. There were a lot of things he needed to buy and got most of what he wanted but would need to go farther afield for some of them. He paid Chris and Emma a visit. Emma was still working away in the studio, now on her second painting. The first having been completed and was standing on an easel in the corner. It was really good. The detail was amazing and captured the movement of the waves perfectly. He could almost feel the breeze and smell the sea air. She seemed pleased that he liked it, especially when he told her he would happily pay for it, if it was hanging in a gallery.

He drove to Wadebridge and, after eventually finding somewhere to park, walked round the shops and struck lucky, getting the last item on his list. When he finally arrived back at the caravan, he was knackered. He tried out the walking stick he purchased in Padstow and found that it did ease the pain but he felt like a right twat using it. Still, if it helped, what did it matter what he looked like? If anyone took the piss he'd give them a thump, or maybe not. His knuckles were still bruised and slightly painful from pummelling Mack, who had a head like a lump of breezeblock.

There was a knock on the door and after shouting come in and nobody entered, he limped over to the door with the aid of his stick. He opened to door and looked own on Laura, who looked immaculate as usual, if not a little sad. He put his stick down, hobbled down the two steps, lifted her out of the wheelchair, carried her inside and sat her down on the sofa. She didn't seem to want to let go of his neck, either that or she'd been playing with superglue and her fingers were stuck together, so he sat down facing her.

'Mum wants to know if you'd like to come over for dinner this evening?' she said flatly. 'I think it's fish.'

Ed sniffed a few times. 'Thank God for that. I thought maybe you had a personal hygiene problem.' he said grinning, receiving a weak smile for his efforts at humour. 'OK. What's up with you, today? You don't seem too happy.' Laura shrugged and stared at him with her sad brown eyes. 'If you don't tell me I'll tickle you,' he said putting his hands on her waist.

'Just a bit fed up.' Ed frowned, encouraging her to say more. 'I have good and bad days. Today is a bad day and I'm just fed up with people staring at me like I'm some kind of freak,' she said, shrugging again. 'God, I hate being a bloody cripple.' Ed smiled at her and chuckled. 'Well, I'm glad you find it amusing,' she added.

'I don't but I have a theory, if you want to hear it?' she did. 'Who's been staring at you?'

'Everybody, men, women, children, everyone. Just don't tell me I'm lucky and there are people worse off than I am because I don't want to hear it.'

'Well, there are. Every day I see some poor sod in a wheelchair, being pushed around because they can't wheel themselves along and probably needing help doing everything else, but that's beside the point and, as you said, you don't want to hear that. You can discount children, because they're just curious or envious as they have to walk everywhere.' She was giving him a look that asked where this was going. 'Getting back to the point though, women are jealous.'

'Jealous?' she interrupted 'Oh yeah, every woman I know would love to be a freak in a wheelchair so everyone could stare at them and pity them.'

'I don't mean like that. I've seen the way women look at you. I know I'm a bloke and like most, I probably wouldn't notice a bank robbery if I walked within a yard of it. I can however, spot a cleavage or a mini-skirt a mile away and I do notice other things, believe it or not. It's just easier to pretend I'm completely unobservant. Women stare at you, not because you're in a chair but because you're beautiful and they're jealous. I've seen it in the club. It's either that or it's because you're with me but I can't see that.

Men stare, partly for the same reason and because of the massive hard on they get when they see you, which takes up all the available slack in their skin and draws the eyelids back. Have a look at the lunchbox next time a bloke stares at you.'

'OK, how come, if I'm as beautiful as you say I am, I haven't got an army of blokes queuing up to take me on a date, smart arse,' she said but a little less angry than when the conversation started.

'Ah, now that's an easy one. It's because you're beautiful and most men are intimidated by that. When Bob first met Emma, the first thing he said to me, was I was batting well above my average, and that's how most blokes think. Chris is one of the best looking women I've ever met. She hasn't got a husband or boyfriend. Why? Because a bloke would be in a pub and say to a mate, I think I'll ask her out for a date or buy her a drink and his mates will all say to him, 'she's out of your league pal' and he won't bother because he doesn't want to be rejected. On the other hand, he might say sod that. Have a few more beers for Dutch courage and by the time he's had the balls to speak to her, he's pissed. She thinks he's an arsehole and it's over before it's even started. It's the way things are and the way things will always be,' Ed was quite pleased with having put his argument across so well and sat smiling, just inches from her face, as her arms were still round the back of his neck. He waited for her to come back with a counter argument.

'That's rubbish. I've had plenty of men come up to me in a bar and buy me a drink so that's that argument blown out the water,' she said pleased.

'I bet most of them were pissed or cocky twats?' Ed replied.

She thought about it and nodded 'A lot were but not all of them,' she said defiantly. 'So, you wouldn't buy me a drink in a bar, then?'

'Of course I would but then I'm a cocky twat and would probably be pissed too.' Which was probably a very truthful answer 'Anyway, I thought I did a few days ago?' he added

'Only as an apology and I was in my wheelchair so it doesn't count. What about if I wasn't in a wheelchair?'

'Honest answer? Probably not.' She gave him a quizzical look. 'Laura, you're without doubt, the most beautiful woman I've ever met. When I see you come into a room, I get that feeling in my stomach like I've just remembered I've left the gas on. When you smile, I have to remind myself to breathe again. Well out of my league so no, I wouldn't.' Where he hell did that come from, he thought, feeling slightly embarrassed.

'Is that what you think?' she said softly. Ed nodded. 'That's the nicest thing anyone has ever said to me,' she added in almost a whisper. Ed shrugged as she lunged forward and kissed him. Ed was expecting a peck on the cheek or lips but her mouth opened and her tongue was in like a weasel down a rabbit hole. What could he do but respond? Anything else would have been bad mannered. When she finally pulled away Ed was breathless not to mention aroused.

'That was...unexpected,' Ed told her.

'Didn't you like it?' she asked looking a little taken aback. Ed stared at her wide-eyed in reference to their earlier conversation.

'Like it. It was bloody fantastic! I can't remember the last time my teeth felt so clean either,' he replied.

A cough from behind, made them look up and turn round. 'Hi, I was just going to the shop and wondered if you needed anything? I take it you'll be coming to dinner?' Raechael said, with an, I've been here a while, look on her face. Ed knew she had, as he saw Fat Boy look up from his bed but hadn't made the connection.

'Of course I will. Thanks, Mrs. Jacobs. I'll bring the wine. What time do you want me over?' he asked.

'Well, I'm sure Laura would like to have you as soon as you're ready,' she replied. Ed wasn't sure if there was an intended innuendo in there or not so decided to let it go. Raechael was grinning, which made him wonder.

'Is it OK if I bring a friend?' he asked.

'You mean, Fat Boy? Of course, I was expecting you to. You don't need to ask,' she replied.

'I'd better go, too and make myself presentable,' Laura told him, although she looked pretty good to him already and couldn't see how it could be improved upon but what did he know. He carried her out of the caravan to the wheelchair that never made it inside and watched her wheel away with her mother.

CHAPTER 39

Ed showered and shaved again, not wanting to be too much of an ugly duckling compared to Laura and Raechael and wandered over armed with a carrier bag full of wine, a smelly retriever and a walking stick. If Ed didn't think she could have made an improvement on her appearance earlier, he was mistaken and stared wide-eyed at her and adjusted his crotch, when he walked in, making her laugh.

The food was amazing. Raechael was definitely a great cook. The sea bass was done to perfection and was washed down with the three bottles of white wine he had brought with him, so they started on the first of the reds.

'Nice wine, Ed,' Raechael commented.

'I get it online by the case. It works out cheaper. I had it on a business lunch once, when I was working and don't buy anything else now,' he replied.

'You're a millionaire and you try to save a couple of pounds on a bottle of wine? That's quite amusing,' she said laughing.

'It's two hundred pounds a bottle,' he told her, not bragging that he could afford such an expensive wine but just to see what the reaction was, which was amusing. He took great delight as she sat there lost for words. 'The white was only fifty pounds a bottle. You haven't just quaffed six hundred pounds worth of wine. I have a relatively cheap lifestyle and this about my only extravagance.'

'I just hope I don't acquire too much of a taste for it,' she replied and seemed slightly shocked.

'Well, why don't you adopt me and you can, and I can have your great cooking every day.'

'Aren't you a little old to be adopted, Ed? And come to that,

I'm a little too old as well, and wouldn't it put my daughter off limits?' she said with a glint in her eye, which clearly embarrassed Laura and Ed come to that.

'Ed, help me into my wheelchair please. I need to use the loo and get away from my interfering mother, who thinks she's being funny,' she said in mock annoyance.

He helped her into the wheelchair and when she was out of sight Raechael leaned across the table. 'I think my daughter is very fond of you, Ed. How do you feel about that?' she said, very direct and to the point.

'I think you know how I feel about your daughter, Mrs. Jacobs. I think you were in my caravan a little longer than you let on earlier?' Ed said questioningly.

'I was,' she said, smiling broadly. 'I thought that was very sweet what you said to her. I hope you meant it?' Ed nodded. 'Good,' she said adding no more, leaving Ed wondering what it was all about.

'Here comes the sexiest thing on wheels, with the exception of the Lotus Elan,' Ed said making Laura smile more broadly. He helped her back into her chair. 'You smell nice. Got a new air freshener in the toilet?

'It's Channel No5, actually.'

'Must be quite wealthy using that in the toilet or did you just need something a bit stronger than Airwick, for that one?' Ed asked.

'You are so gross sometimes,' she said, giggling regardless.

They retired to the more comfortable sofa at the other end of the caravan and finished two of the three bottles of red Ed brought and Laura fell asleep on Ed's shoulder. Ed carried her to her bedroom and laid her on the bed. He kissed her on the forehead and left her snoring quietly for Raechael to deal with later. Ed helped Raechael with the dishes, despite her protests it would still be there in the morning, which gave her another chance to renew her interrogation about his feelings towards her daughter, the wine making her a little bolder.

'So, where were we?' she said mischievously. 'So, do you think you and Laura have a future together?' she asked, making Ed squirm.

'I hardly know her, Raechael,' he replied and knew it would be an unacceptable answer, even before he said it.

'Come on Ed, you can do better than that. Don't be shy.' Ed hated being put under the microscope like this but the wine was helping a little, although he seemed to be sobering up pretty quickly. 'I've seen the way you are with her. You're good for her. Today for example, she was miserable all day and a few minutes with you and she was the happiest I've seen her in a long time. You make her feel good about herself and forget about her problems. What's the problem, Ed? I don't have you down as someone who would be bothered about her being in a wheelchair. Or are you?'

Ed took a deep breath and tried to formulate an answer. 'Not as such. What bothers me is that I don't want to spend all my life wishing she was something she's not. I know her condition may or may not be temporary and I'd be gutted it if it was a permanent condition but I could live with that. What worries me is, if she does make a full recovery is she going to want me around? She could have the pick of anyone she wanted with looks like that. Is she really going to want to be with Mr. Bloody-average? That's what bothers me.' Raechael took a step towards him and rested her hands on his arms.

'Is that what's really bothering you?' she said, shaking her head. 'You've got a very low opinion of yourself, haven't you? You're better than anything she's ever brought home for me to meet. My God, the last one was so full of himself it was unbelievable. I hated him from the first minute I met him. He treated her so badly and she put up with it. It was quite a relief when he broke off the engagement after her accident. It broke Laura's heart but secretly I was extremely pleased. It's not what you look like. It's what you are that counts. Why not just throw caution to the wind and make a go of it. If it doesn't work out, so what?' Ed shrugged and Raechael gave him a hug.

'You're probably right. I don't have a very good track record with relationships and I don't want to go through what I did with my ex-wife again. It was messy and, well, let's say I didn't cope too well but you know all that,' he eventually replied.

'Ed.'

'What?'

'Do you mind taking your hands off my backside,' she asked

him.

Ed smiled sheepishly 'Sorry, didn't even realise I was touching it. It's very nice though,' he said removing his hands. 'If only you were thirteen years younger. Not that I'm superstitious mind you.'

'Ed, go home and think about what I said.' She kissed him goodnight and he and Fat Boy made their way slowly and painfully back.

CHAPTER 40

Ed hadn't slept well, on two accounts. His leg had been throbbing painfully and he had been thinking about last night's chat with Raechael. He knew she was right, and thought, what the hell; maybe he would give it a go. He decided he would go over and see Laura later that morning, invite her for lunch and take it from there.

At a little after eleven-thirty, Raechael opened the door for him and let him in. Her first words were 'don't ask,' as he walked in to a full caravan. Laura wheeled herself over and introduced him to everyone. 'This is my best friend Charlotte,' she said, pointing to an attractive young girl, slightly on the chubby side, with the most enormous breasts Ed had seen in a long time. 'This is Greg.' He was tall, athletic and handsome, as well as bronzed and looked like something off the cover of a GQ magazine. Ed hated him immediately. 'And this is Charlotte's boyfriend, James.' He also looked like he had dropped off the same front cover as Greg but didn't look quite as greasy and obnoxious as Greg did, so he gave him the benefit of doubt.

'Hi,' Ed said, giving them what he hoped was a friendly smile. 'I take it that's your Lexus outside, then? Nice car.' It wasn't but he wanted to appear congenial, despite being pissed off his dinner plans looked to have been screwed up.

'That's mine,' Greg informed him proudly. 'Of course, in my job, I need a good car to impress the clients. Wouldn't be good for business, turning up in a Mondeo would it. What do you drive, Ed?'

'Mondeo actually,' he replied not the least bit embarrassed. A car was something to get you from A to B so he went for practical every time.

'Nothing wrong with them, they just don't float my boat,' Greg said smirking. 'I take it your job isn't customer facing then?'

'Not at all. I'm between jobs at the moment. I took voluntary redundancy a while ago and nothing has come up yet or nothing that seems to float my boat,' he replied, hoping his slight piss-take of making inverted commas in the air with his fingers around his 'float my boat' comment would be recognised.

'Bad luck. We're just having a glass of wine before we go to lunch. Want a glass? It's a nice one. Might be a bit rich for you though,' he said still smirking.

'Why's that, is it a Merlot? I normally go for something a little lighter.'

'No, it's a Shiraz actually. It's just that it's thirty quid a bottle so don't suppose you'd go for something in that range, what with being out of work.' Ed wanted to knock that smirk clean off his face but smiled politely.

'If you prefer Ed, there's some of the wine left, you brought over last night?' Raechael said, stepping in before Ed could reply.

'OK, I'll take some of that one. I know that one's more in my price range,' Ed replied. Raechael was struggling to suppress a laugh. Greg wanted to know what it was, probably only so he could take the piss, but that was OK with Ed. 'It's a Chateaux Palmer Margaux. I buy it in bulk off the internet to save a few pounds a bottle. It's nice but you certainly wouldn't find it in the thirty pound a bottle section,' Ed told him, deliberately misleading him to think it was just a bottle of Chateaux Collapso and it worked.

'I guess when you're on benefits, you need to look after the pennies. Me, I think, what's the point in not enjoying the finer things in life, when you earn over a hundred grand a year. That's what money's for, isn't it? Most people only dream of earning what I do and probably wouldn't know what to do with it if they had it,' Greg said proudly and seemed to be enjoying laying it on thick to impress everyone and belittle Ed.

'Having an income like that would certainly give me nightmares,' Ed replied, whose income through interest alone was way in excess of that. He looked over a Laura, who seemed uncomfortable with either the way the conversation was going or uncomfortable Ed was there at all, which, he couldn't work out. Either way, he felt like he'd been kicked in the teeth.

'We're down for the bank holiday,' Greg began. Ed didn't even realise it was a public holiday weekend. 'Thought we'd surprise Laura and take her out to lunch; Charlotte's idea, really. Can you recommend anywhere, Ed?'

'Well, there's a McDonalds and a KFC in town,' Ed started and Raechael had a coughing fit. 'But a man of your means wouldn't want to go there and if you're out to impress a lady, then why not try Rick Stein's. That's what Padstow's famous for these days. It's a little more expensive than some of the other places but I'm told the food is good. Haven't been there myself though so I can only go on what I've been told.' Ed was laying on the poor relation bit a little thick, which Greg seemed to relish. He hadn't been to Rick Stein's on account of not being a huge seafood lover and for no other reason, but Greg didn't know that. 'It gets quite busy as well, so if you haven't booked, you might want to get there early.' Ed hoped that might spur the obnoxious prick into leaving and fortunately it did.

'Well, in that case, we better get going. I'd hate to disappoint anyone. Still, I'm sure I could grease a palm or two and get a table,' he said with a smug grin. Ed wasn't so sure.

'I'm so sorry, Ed. They turned up completely out of the blue,' Raechael said, once they'd gone.

'I can see why you like him so much,' Ed replied 'What a tosser. It was working with people like him that made me take redundancy. I could see myself getting too much like them. What a self-centred, arrogant prick.'

'As I said to you earlier, I can't abide the man. Laura was always besotted with him though. I'm really sorry, Ed. After all I said last night and this happens,' Raechael said genuinely disappointed.

'It's not your fault, Raechael. Maybe she'll see him for what he is and that'll be it. Funny though, I took on board what you said last night. I thought, she's dead right, and came over here to take her to lunch and suggest making a go of it. Bollocks.' Ed said in frustration.

'It was quite funny though, he didn't know you were having

fun at his expense. I could hardly keep a straight face. Not that it's any consolation.'

'Yeah, too far up his own arse to see it,' Ed said happily. 'Well, if I can't take your lovely daughter to lunch, can I take her equally lovely mother to lunch?' he asked.

'I'd love to, as long as it's not McDonalds or KFC.'

They settled for a pub lunch in St. Merryn, both having burger and chips, as a gastronomic tribute to McDonalds. The burgers were homemade, fat and succulent, as were the chips. The buns the burgers came in were full and plump, unlike those from the burger chains, which looked so appetising in the pictures on the walls but in reality, looked like they had been run over by a steamroller, before being wrapped in greaseproof paper and handed over by a bored, dribbling teenager. Raechael didn't appear to have much of an appetite, which was to Fat Boy's benefit, who thought Christmas had come early, when presented with half a burger and a handful of chips.

'What's up, Raechael?' Ed asked.

'Nothing. I'm just really annoyed about Greg turning up like that. It's going to end in tears, I know it is. It was Charlotte's idea. She probably thought she was doing her a favour but no good is going to come of it.'

'Well, part of me hopes you're right but if that's what she wants, then I hope she's happy,' Ed replied but wasn't convincing.

'Really?' she asked.

'No. I hope she sees right through him for the self-centred, conceited, smug, arrogant bastard that he is.'

Raechael nodded. Ed's phone rang and the display identified the caller as Bob.

'Hi Bob. Whatever it is, it wasn't me. I've been on my best behaviour since leaving hospital.'

'Where are you?' he demanded, rather than asked.

'I'm having lunch with an extremely attractive, young lady, if you must know, down in St. Merryn. Why, what's it to you?'

'We need to talk. Get your arse back to the clubhouse, now. I'll be there soon and you owe me a few beers. Who's the friend?'

'Raechael, Mrs. Jacobs. But how do you work out I owe you a beer?'

'Raechael? You mean the gorgeous mother of the girl in the wheelchair? Don't tell me, you're giving her one?'

'Of course I'm not. Why, are you jealous?' Ed asked, knowing Bob was quite taken by her the last time they met. Bob chose to ignore the jibe.

'You owe me… let me think. Not arresting you for ABH, GBH, assault, bleeding on a blue flag beach and foul and abusive language for starters. I make that at least 5 beers you owe me so get your arse up that clubhouse, now. I'm thirsty. Oh, and bring Raechael with you. Got it?' He then hung up.

'That was Bob. DCI Brown,' he added, when there was no recognition from Raechael. 'He wants us back at the clubhouse, now. Not sure why, apart from it's my round but he asked for you as well.'

'Oh. DCI Brown's a very charming man.'

'Really? He said something along those lines about you, although not quite so eloquently put,' Ed replied, thinking a little bit of shit-stirring could be fun to see how Raechael liked it. To his disappointment, she didn't seem to care.

'Really,' she said coyly, touching her hair, as they walked back along the beach. Bloody hell, if Emma was right about the hair business, then Bob could be in with a chance. What a horrible thought. She linked her arm through his and seemed in a hurry to get back.

They strolled back along the low clifftops, taking in the views of the beach and the distant coastline, which curved raggedly around the headland. Ed looked down the beach and did a double take. He stared intently at the sand dunes and could see a figure sitting there, aiming a pair of binoculars along the beach. From his angle, Ed couldn't see what the figure had his binoculars trained on but there was no mistaking who it was. Ed knew instinctively it was Pete, from the grey hair and blubbery lips. The beach below was crowded, with it being a public holiday, so the binoculars could have been trained on anyone. He was sure Pete wasn't a budding ornithologist and thought it suspicious. Could he be the Black Cockle Strangler? It would explain his more than unhealthy interest about it, when they met on Friday. Not to mention, there was something a little creepy if not disturbing about him. Ed made a note to inform Bob. Perhaps he could check him out.

CHAPTER 41

Bob was sitting at one the bench tables outside the clubhouse with DS Phil Reynolds, both with empty glasses.

'What's with the stick, you big girl's blouse?' Bob shouted as Ed approached.

'They say short-term memory goes as you get older. But to give you a quick reminder, I was stabbed a couple of days ago,' Ed said sarcastically. 'It hurts like hell and the stick takes a bit of the strain off it.' Bob sniffed derisorily.

'Well, you look like a tart. Mine's a lager and the same for Phil. Be careful in there, the bloody lights went out while I was getting served.' Ed asked Rachael what she wanted, threw his stick on the floor and hobbled towards the bar, muttering he could manage.

'So, why did you drag me away from my lunch, then?' Ed asked, when he returned from the bar with a tray of drinks, two of each to save making another trip. He knew how Bob could get through them when he was in the mood.

'Oh that. I just wanted to tell you your mate, Mack, escaped from the hospital earlier today. We're out there looking for him and he shouldn't be hard to find but, as you know, I've got a murder investigation on the go, so it's not our number one priority. So keep an eye out.'

'How did that happen?' Ed asked but wasn't overly concerned. Even with a bad leg, he was confident of still being able to give him a good kicking.

'We had a bobby outside 24x7 but he escaped via the window. The ward he was in was on the ground floor. I'm telling you, just in case he comes looking for you. Ordinarily I wouldn't be worried, especially after seeing what you did to him but he does have access to a gun, in case you forgot. If he's got any sense, he'll be as far away from here as possible but he does seem to be a particularly vindictive bastard so be careful.'

'Nice job you done on him,' Phil chipped in. 'Impressive to watch, I must say. I've got it all on DVD; when I get round to it, I'll give you a copy,' he said cheerily.

'Thanks Phil. Take your time with that. I've got enough reminders already,' he said, rubbing his leg. Phil nodded.

'Two broken ribs, dislocated jaw, three missing teeth and a nose that's as flat as a kipper's tit. I'd say that was a hell of a job you done on him. Bloody marvellous to watch. I'd heard you were a bit handy in a fight but that was something else,' Bob said a little too enthusiastically.

'Bob, it's not something I'm proud of. Can we change the subject? How's the Black Cockle Strangler case coming along?' Ed asked.

'Better but not sure we're any closer to nailing anyone yet. We've got plenty of DNA. We know his approximate height and weight. We know the previous footprints were a red herring, as he was wearing over-sized flip-flops. We now know, rather than a size twelve, he's actually a size ten. We got an unconfirmed report of a red Volvo estate driving erratically around the same time but other than that, we've no suspects. We'll get there though but I'm worried if we don't get him soon, he'll strike again and God knows what we'll find. The last one was particularly nasty compared to the first three.' Bob was thinking about the state of the last body, with the eyes gouged out and semen traces all over the abdomen. He had seen at lot in his time but this one was particularly chilling.

'Well, you know my theory. What do you reckon, Phil?' Ed asked.

'What's your theory? It seems like everyone has one so I might as well hear yours,' he said in friendly manner. Ed told him his theory about the black, gloss paint being uncommon and would only be used by someone with a black front door, window frames or garage door. Phil nodded and actually looked interested.

'I think you might have a good point there,' he replied. Bob just shook his head in despair.

'Also, I was thinking about this. How come, when I assume

everyone is being so vigilant; I mean most young women would be concerned and very aware of what's going on, right? So why is it, this guy seems to be able to go around and pick up victims with what appears to be such ease? My theory is he's somebody someone trusts or someone who can mingle easily, such as a lifeguard or even a copper.' Ed knew Bob wouldn't like that suggestion but what the hell.

'Are you saying, you think it's one of our own doing this? You are so far off the mark. No bloody way,' Bob said defensively.

'Not saying it is but I reckon it's someone who can melt into a crowd. You tell me, who else can do that?' Ed replied, not happy that Bob wouldn't even consider it as a possibility. Phil on the other hand seemed to like the idea and was nodding and even gave him a thumbs-up.

'I'm off now, boss,' he replied. 'Technically, I'm still on duty and I've got a load of paperwork to get through. Cheers for the beer, Ed,' he said and left. He only drank one of the pints Ed had bought so Bob knocked it back, slamming it down hard on the table top, looking at Ed and shaking his head. He wasn't happy.

'Your round, I think, Sherlock.' No, he definitely wasn't happy. 'Here comes your beautiful daughter, Mrs. Jacobs,' he added. Ed looked up to see Greg and James walking towards them, followed by Charlotte and Laura, wheeling herself along at the back. That in itself got Ed's back up, Greg, not even having the courtesy to push or at least walk with Laura. Raechael wasn't slow to pick up on this.

'Now, be nice to him, Ed,' she said in a whisper, putting a hand on his knee. 'I don't like him any more than you do but do it for my daughter.'

'OK, but I'd rather rip his head off,' he said turning to face her. 'But if he starts being smug, all bets are off.' He turned back and smiled at the new arrivals. 'I was just going to get a round in. What do you want?' he said, forcing a congenial smile.

'Don't worry, I'll get these, mate. Don't want you spending all your dole cheque in one go,' Greg replied, laughing. Ed bit his lip and started counting to ten, just to keep Raechael happy. She put her hand back on his knee and whispered, 'easy Ed.'

'Dole cheque? What the hell are you on about, he's bloody loaded!' Bob boomed. Ed cringed.

'What? You told me you were unemployed,' Greg said, confused.

'Greg, you assumed I was unemployed. I said I took voluntary redundancy, there is a difference,' Ed replied, trying not to sound as smug as Greg usually was.

'You bloody lied to me, you prick,' he replied indignantly.

'Greg, I didn't lie to you. You've just got your head so far up your own arsehole, you couldn't see what I was getting at.' The look on Greg's face was a picture and it encouraged Ed to continue. 'The wine you scoffed at is two hundred pounds a bottle but you assumed, because I buy it on the internet by the case, it was cheap. When I said your salary would give me nightmares, it would. It's significantly less than my annual income from interest alone. You assumed, I thought your income was an amount I could never dream of earning. You know, having money is great but it doesn't make you better than anyone else, you should remember that. How you conduct yourself and what you do with your money makes you a better person. Being rich doesn't mean you have to be a complete arsehole. You should remember that as well.' Ed stopped. Feeling he had lectured enough. 'So I'll ask again. Anyone for a drink?'

'You bastard. I bet you knew as well didn't you, Raechael? It would be just like you, you never did like me.' Ed tensed but Raechael put a hand on his knee again. 'And what about you, Laura, I bet you knew as well, didn't you?' Laura nodded. 'Well, that's just fucking great. I thought better of you but you're just as bad as that bitch of a mother of yours. You know what? You deserve to be in that fucking wheelchair!'

Everyone was silent in complete shock. Even Bob was shaking his head in disbelief. Ed was livid.

'Raechael, can you take your hand off my knee? I'm going to kill the bastard. Excuse my French.'

'That's quite alright Ed. You go and kill the bastard,' Raechael replied, smiling sheepishly at him. Ed laughed and called her potty mouth, before standing up and limping towards Greg.

'Greg, I think an apology would be a good idea. Preferably by the time I've walked round the table,' Ed said, menacingly, eyes ablaze with anger.

'I'm not apologising to anyone,' he said defiantly 'How dare they humiliate me like that.'

When Ed had walked past James, he got up and followed him a pace behind. Ed stopped brought his elbow back sharply into his solar plexus then flipped his forearm up, smashing his fist into his nose. James hit the floor like a sack of shit and stayed there with his hands pressed against his bleeding nose, struggling to catch his breath.

Ed continued, hardly breaking his stride and stood in front of Greg. 'Last chance to apologise, before I rip your head off,' he said, looking up into the taller, more handsome, more tanned face of Greg.

'Fuck off and die,' he spat. 'I'm a black belt in karate so watch it.' Ed almost laughed out loud.

'Well excuse me for not quaking in my boots but I'm a black belt in No-can-do so that makes us even. Now is your last chance to apologise of your own free will, before I make you. Of your own free will would be much more pleasant for you.' Greg looked a little worried and shook his head in a final act of defiance, before Ed shrugged and kicked him as hard as he could between the legs and followed up with a right hook, as he was falling to the ground. Greg was lying there clutching his throbbing testicles as Ed pulled him up to his knees so he was facing everyone. 'Apologise to the ladies, Greg,' he said calmly and hit him on the top of the head with the knuckle of his index finger, when he refused, making him gasp in pain. A neat trick he learnt from a friend in the prison service. It seemed to have the desired effect and Greg mumbled a very insincere sorry. Ed put a foot on his chest and pushed him to the floor, telling him if he wasn't crawling to his car in the next thirty seconds, he would kick his arse all the way to Exeter.

'You need a bloody sign round you neck stating, dangerous when provoked,' Bob told him as he made his way back to the table.

'Very funny,' Ed replied. 'He bloody deserved that. I think that's just about the nastiest thing I've ever heard anybody say,' he added by way of justification.

'Quite right, Ed. It was a terrible thing to say,' Raechael said in his defence.

Ed apologised to Charlotte, who didn't seem that bothered and gave him a shrug Ed would have been proud of. Laura on the other hand looked sulky. Ed bent down and looked her in the eyes, ready for a tongue lashing or a slap. Laura leaned forward, thanked him and gave him a kiss, before putting her arms around his neck so he could lift her out of the wheelchair.

Raechael and Bob left together after a couple more drinks, using the old excuse of leaving the youngsters to enjoy themselves. Ed winked at Bob and received a middle finger for his trouble, as he and Raechael headed off, leaving him with Laura and Charlotte and her unbelievably large breasts.

It turned out their lunch was a complete disaster from the outset. The town was packed and it took the best part of an hour to find somewhere to park. When they did find somewhere, it was on the outskirts of the town and Greg was annoyed at having to hold on to Laura's wheelchair to stop her careening out of control down the steep slopes into town, which he was obviously embarrassed about. When they finally got to Rick Stein's it was already full. Greg had tried bribing the Maître d' and was very impolitely told where to go, much to the amusement of everyone else in the queue behind them. They finally settled for a small bistro down one of the narrow streets off the harbour that was just about accessible to wheelchairs. Greg, once again, was embarrassed at having to help Laura over the step into the premise. He sulked all through the meal and was rude to all the staff and left without leaving a tip, despite the food and service being excellent. Laura was rightfully annoyed, even before they got back and after what he said to her, she hoped she never set eyes on him again.

The trip down for the public holiday had been Charlotte's idea as a surprise. As she didn't drive, she persuaded James and he invited Greg to make up a foursome. There was never any intention of Greg trying to win back Laura's affections, which pleased Ed and he had to concede, yes he was jealous, much to Laura's delight and she teased him mercilessly. Ed wasn't too bothered, as it obviously made her happy so that was fine by him.

The afternoon turned into evening and the drinks kept flowing. Charlotte wanted champagne, which was when it started to get messy. Charlotte was drinking it like water and was soon pissed as a fart, much to the amusement of Ed and Laura. When she fell off the bench, landing on her back, with her skirt over her face, flashing her knickers to the world, laughing like a hyena, they decided to call it a day. Ed walked over to the chip shop and got three portions of cod and chips and gave them to Laura to carry, as he supported Charlotte back to Laura's caravan. He gave up half way and carried her. She was certainly no lightweight and Ed's bad leg was in a lot of pain by the time they arrived.

They sat Charlotte on the floor, propped up against the back of the sofa, where she sat eyes closed, mumbling something neither of them could understand, while stroking Fat Boy. Ed and Laura sat on the sofa and ate their fish and chips out of the paper. Ed remembered he hadn't fed Fat Boy so gave him Charlotte's fish and chips as a substitute, as she was now snoring loudly, still propped up against the sofa. Ed and Laura lay together on the sofa like a couple of teenagers, unfortunately just talking, until Laura fell asleep on him again. Ed lay there looking at her until he too nodded off, only to be woken by Bob shaking him. Ed opened his eyes and got them into focus.

'Come on, sleeping beauty, you've got a guest, I'm staying with you tonight,' he said grinning. Ed looked at his watch. It was just after eleven. He gave Raechael a hand by carrying Charlotte into Laura's room. Fortunately, Laura was just tired and not out for the count. He offered further help, getting Charlotte under the covers but Raechael said she could manage. Ed argued she was quite heavy and was concerned Raechael could suffer serious injury, should she get hit by one of Charlotte's enormous breasts. She smiled and told him to go home and look after Bob. What a delight that would be; a night of Bob snoring and waking up to find the entire contents of his fridge missing. Still he was a mate so it was OK.

Bob went to the fridge as soon as he got inside the caravan. Ed was sure that he didn't really want a beer and it was just a reconnaissance mission, to see what there was for breakfast. The way he nodded as he closed the fridge door was a complete give away.

'So where did you get to with the lovely Mrs. Jacobs, then? Ed asked.

'We went for a stroll along the coast and along the beach and had dinner at the pub, if you must know and don't look at me like that, it was all above board. Don't judge me by your own devious standards,' he came back with defensively - a little too defensively for Ed's liking.

'Good looking woman, Mrs. Jacobs,' Ed said grinning at Bob. 'She quite likes you, too. Said you were a very charming man. I nearly choked on my chips when she said that. It's OK though. I put her straight and told her you were more like Keith from Eastenders, only in a suit,' Ed said, pleased with the analogy.

'Funny bastard. She told me you and Laura are getting on really well.' Obviously, he was now going tit for tat. 'Only you're too bloody scared of the past to make a commitment. Funny isn't it, you go around kicking the crap out of anyone who upsets one of your friends or gives a woman a hard time but you're too shit scared to get into a relationship.' Bob felt a little guilty but made a promise to Raechael, he would do what he could to push Ed in the right direction. The problem with Bob was he only knew one way and it wasn't called tactfully. 'What's wrong with you? You've got a beautiful, young girl, almost throwing herself at you and you're standing there like a spare prick at a wedding, with your thumb up your arse, bleating on about the past.'

If Ed was shocked he didn't show it. 'You're dead right, Bob. I know I am but I can't help it. You don't know what happened with my ex-wife, do you? I know I've told you what she was like but you don't know the full story,' Ed said calmly and told him the whole story he told Emma on the trip down. When he finished Bob sat there staring at him.

'Didn't realise you were such a sensitive, little soul,' he replied. 'You never told me all that before.'

'Until I had a run in with Emma on the way down in the car, I hadn't told anyone, ever. Now I've told everyone, including you. So, now you know. It still gives me nightmares thinking about it. I know it was years ago but I don't want to go through that again.'

'Fair point,' he replied. 'Don't think Laura's in the same league as your ex though, do you? She's not after your money, just your body. Think about it Ed, you don't want to end up a sad, lonely, old bastard like me, do you? I'll see you at breakfast, all this talk about relationships has made me tired. Later Ed'

'It must be love, Bob.'

'Fuck off, Ed.'

CHAPTER 42

Ed climbed into bed, tempted to set his alarm to make sure he was up and about before Bob. His intention to make as much noise as possible, wake him up and to scoff all the bacon, sausages and eggs. Quite how he would manage four eggs, half a dozen sausages and nearly a full packet of bacon was another matter but was buggered if he was going to let Bob get there first, like last time. It was a bit childish but so bloody what.

In the end, it didn't matter. Ed was woken up by the sound of the Clash, belting out Tommy Gun on the iPod docking station. He tried to ignore it but it was followed by White Riot and by this time was wide awake. He got out of bed and dressed, already in a foul mood, which didn't improve when he got a whiff of bacon frying.

Ed walked out the bedroom and stared daggers at Bob, who looked up and smiled back. 'Come on, sit down, breakfast's nearly ready,' he said grinning, as if he knew Ed was thinking he was only cooking enough for himself. That got Ed's back up, too.

'You're up early.' Ed said grumpily, having been woken up and outsmarted by Bob.

'Too much beer. Woke up with a bladder like a duffel bag and couldn't get back to sleep, so I thought I'd make a start on breakfast. Good selection of music by the way, I might bring a few blank discs with me next time and download some of it. Didn't have you down as a punk? A bit before your time, I would have thought?'

God, he was bloody chatty this morning, Ed thought, and decided he preferred him grumpy and obnoxious. He thought about making a point that nobody used blank disk these days but new a conversation on flash drives and other external storages devices would be lost on him.

'So was Tchaikovsky but you'll find the 1812 on there somewhere and the Beatles, Stones just about everything from Abba to the Zutons. I'm into my music. Didn't have you down as Clash fan either?' Ed said, mellowing a little.

'One of the greatest bands ever. Saw them live a couple times in the late seventies along with the Stranglers, Sex Pistols, and the Damned. I used to be young once, you know.' Ed was impressed and nodded enviously. 'Thought any more on what I said last night?' he said, placing a plate in front of Ed, which was on a par with Emma's.

'Looks good. I'm impressed,' he told him.

'Of course it is. I've had plenty of practice. It's how it is when you're old and live on your own. Something you may end up like, if you don't get your act together. Now stop avoiding the question,' he replied.

'Answer me one thing before I do. Did Raechael put you up to this?' Ed stared him in the eyes, looking for a nervous twitch or some other indication of a lie. Not that he would get one. Bob was an expert at playing poker face, which he had honed from years of interviewing suspects and hard men, who would exploit any weakness shown.

'She did. For some reason, Raechael thinks the sun shines out your arse. God knows why but she does and thinks you're perfect for her daughter, despite your many shortcomings. Thanks to you, I spent most of my time with her yesterday talking about you and how bloody wonderful you were. How well you treated her and her daughter and how happy you make her. She also made me promise to have a word or two with you, to get you to do something about it. Come on Ed, shit or get off the pot.'

It was an honest answer, which Ed wasn't expecting and was probably the longest string of sentences, he had ever heard him put together.

'Without wanting to avoid the question,' he began and Bob stared daggers at him. 'What do you think? Honestly.'

'I think you'll be mad not to. Why is my opinion so important all of a sudden?' he said narrowing his eyes in suspicion.

'Well, I think it's important that you consider me a worthy son-in-law,' Ed said bursting out laughing.

'You can be such an arsehole. Just because I think you should make a go of it, doesn't mean to say I think you deserve her. But as it happens, I do. Now stop taking the piss and answer the question.'

'I think so. I realise what you said last night was true. I need to get on with my life and if it all goes wrong; so what. I'll go over there later and have a word. I just hope Raechael's right and I don't end up looking like a plum.' Bob nodded and grinned. 'I also hope that Charlotte isn't hanging around all day. I've never met anyone who can drink as much champagne as her. I would say I don't know where she puts it but I think it's bloody obvious. I think she's like a bloody camel and stores all her alcohol in her humps,' Ed said, chuckling at his own joke.

'As it happens, camels don't store water in their humps, they're fat reservoirs,' Bob told him matter of fact, which impressed Ed. 'But you're right, she's got a bloody rack on her, don't get too many of those to the ton, that's for sure. Anyway, I think you're doing the right thing.'

'I bloody hope so. Anyway, are you working today?' Ed asked, more to change the subject, than wanting to know.

'Nope. Today I am taking the lovely Raechael to the Eden Project. She's never been there and I need to keep her out of your way,' he said, giving Ed a wink.

'That's handy, anyone would think you'd planned all this,' Ed replied

'Maybe. It must be your lucky day, my son. Right, I haven't got time to sit here chewing the fat, I need to get home and make myself look presentable for my own date.'

'Bob, before you do go, there's something I forgot to tell you. It might be nothing but then again…'

'Don't tell me you've got another theory?' Bob said sarcastically. Ed smiled back sheepishly. 'Well, come on, I haven't got all bloody day.'

'OK. Last Friday in the clubhouse, there was a guy in there called Pete. I've never seen him before but he's friendly with Jacqui. If you asked me he looked a bit creepy. You know, the sort of guy who hangs out in playgrounds, that kind of stuff,' Ed said uncertainly.

'And you think because he looked like a kiddy-fiddler, he's our man? Stop wasting my time, I've got a date and I don't want to be late,' Bob replied curtly and stood to leave.

'Hang on Bob, there's more.' Bob sat back down, gave an exasperated sigh and shot Ed a bored look. 'I'm only trying to bloody help, you know,' Ed replied angrily. 'I saw him on the beach yesterday, sitting in the sand dunes with a pair of binoculars.'

'Well, that's it then. I'll send out a squad of her majesty's finest to round up Pervy Pete and charge him with impersonating a paedo and owning a pair of fucking binoculars.'

'Sometimes you can be a right arsehole. Just listen, will you. On Friday in the clubhouse he seemed very interested in the Black Cockle Strangler case, more so than anyone else did. He looks a bit dodgy and I'm pretty sure he wasn't skulking in the sand dunes doing a bit of bird watching. You only get bloody seagulls down there and you don't need a pair of binoculars to see them. You just need to open a packet of crisps and you'll have half the gull population of Cornwall shitting on your beach mat.' Ed sat back and stared hard at Bob, hoping he would take his outburst seriously.

Bob nodded. 'OK. You might have a point. I'll get someone to pay Jacqui a visit and find out who he is and check him out. See if he has any previous.' Ed nodded his approval. 'And thanks Ed,' he added as he got up and left for his date with Raechael.

CHAPTER 43

The basement was lit only by a single 30 watt bulb, which hung shade-less and covered in dust in the centre of the low ceiling. It gave off barely sufficient light to penetrate all corners of the room but that didn't bother him. There was sufficient light for his needs and its dinginess helped to focus his dark thoughts.

He gazed around the small room or his killing room as he preferred to call it, as this was where his dark thoughts surfaced and festered and became reality. The walls are festooned with press cuttings and pictures of crime scenes. The once beautiful, tranquil beaches, turned ugly by the whores who frequented them, he was now cleansing, making them a place of beauty once more. Places to be enjoyed by decent people with morals, like he had.

Between the newspaper cuttings was his own work; the real photographs behind the headlines that nobody would get to see. This was his very own private collection, showing his victims at various stages of his ritual. Eyes bulging as he pulls the garrotte tighter around their necks, the fear in their eyes palpable. Others of him masturbating over the prone women, rendered unconscious by the chloroform. His favourite, a full length photo of his last victim takes pride of place. He is kneeling between her legs, fingers deep inside her shaved vagina, semen splattered across her stomach, her eyes gouged from her face, which are just visible on the bedside table. The wonders of modern technology with video and high resolution cameras built into tiny little mobile phones and with editing apps to extract stills from video footage, making his work so much more pleasurable.

He frowns as his eyes land on a small passport sized photo of an 80's female pop star, clearly out of place on his wall of death.

Where it all began, he muses. His mind wanders back to his school days, back to when he was a teenage boy, with a fixation on an iconic 80's singer. He heard one of her songs on the radio and fell in love with the voice. After seeing a photograph of her, he fell in love with the beautiful face and lithe body. He bought the entire back catalogue of her work and became an avid fan; his bedroom walls covered in posters of the love of his life. His classmates teased him mercilessly but he didn't care, they didn't understand. They were too narrow-minded to do anything but follow the crowd and wouldn't consider any music, unless it was deemed to be cool or trendy.

Then one day his entire life fell apart. Brian Hicks found an image on the internet of the star posing topless for a lads mag with her nipples painted in black make-up. Brian had printed a copy and taped it to the blackboard for everyone to see. The whole class laughed and taunted him before he ran from the room in tears.

The photo changed everything. He knew then that every woman, no matter what they looked like or how they acted, possessed a dark side. Under the surface they were all duplicitous whores. That evening he stripped his walls bare and destroyed all the music he had collected over the years. He was distraught. How could the object of his affections have let him down so badly?

The pain he felt inside was immeasurable and he needed to find a channel for it. It came in the shape of Brian Hicks. The next day he hid in the bushes near to his house and after Brian passed by, he crept out silently and smashed him over the head with a heavy branch from a tree. Brian fell to the floor unconscious, where he kicked him black and blue and left him bleeding and needing hospital care.

At school, the taunting soon stopped, when anyone who did taunt him was dealt with violently. He had a growing reputation as someone to keep clear of. It was suspected he was Brian's attacker but never proven and nobody had the courage to accuse him for fear of getting similar treatment.

The girls kept well clear of him due to the hateful looks he gave them and his violent mood swings. There was also a particularly nasty incident with Julie Kelly at a party. Julie was worse for wear, having consumed almost two litres of cheap cider and was flirting with everyone. Most of the males just laughed it off, as Julie had a reputation as being easy and they heard she once gave a guy herpes.

She took him to one of the spare rooms and stripped to the waist. She dropped to her knees and pulled his trousers down and started to suck his flaccid penis. After a few minutes and not getting an erection, Julie had laughed at him, calling him a faggot and a virgin. He responded by punching her in the face and making her nose bleed. His erection was instantaneous and he was shocked at just how aroused he had become. He threw her onto the bed and lifted her skirt up but was unable to sustain his erection. Julie laughed in his face and goaded him, until he hit her again, rekindling his erection.

The only way he could sustain an erection was with acts of violence. He squeezed her breasts viciously and pinched the nipples while kneeling between her legs, causing her to whimper in pain. The sight of blood from her nose and the red marks across her breasts was a major turn on and he soon reached orgasm. He left Julie on the bed, bruised and crying with semen splattered across the front of her knickers. He smiled at the memory and wondered what had become of Julie Kelly.

He managed to sate his sexual appetite for violence against women by amassing a huge collection of hard core S&M pornography. There were also certain underground clubs that catered for his needs but after getting carried away during one session and leaving a female member with a broken rib, after a near death by asphyxiation experience, his membership was revoked.

He looked again at the photograph of his teenage fantasy that for so many years had been locked away in a dark corner of his mind. Manacled to the past, where pain and anguish couldn't intrude on the present. Until she burst into his life again after appearing on a reality TV show. How could she do that? Intruding into his life, smiling beguilingly and portraying herself as sweetness and light, when underneath her soul was black, stinking and corrupt. The memories flashed back with such intensity it made him cry out in pain. Brian Hicks and his classmates taunting him. Julie Kelly, laughing at him as she kneels between his legs. Brain Hicks, unconscious on the pavement, blood oozing from the back of his head, his face a mass of bruises. Julie Kelly on the bed with a bloody nose, angry welts across her breasts and abdomen. Sweet revenge.

He connected his phone to the USB socket of the computer and waited excitedly for the images to be transferred to this PC. Once complete, he opened the new folder and set the software to view the photos as a slideshow. All the images were of the same girl, clad only in a pale blue bikini, her dyed, blonde hair tied back into a plaited ponytail. The photos were taken in the beer garden of a pub, just across the road from the beach and on the beach itself. Most of the occupants around her had the decency to cover up with shorts and T-shirts or lose fitting beach dresses but not her. Oh no, she wanted to be noticed. She flirted with the boys, leaning forward to emphasise her cleavage, touching them when talking to them. Her nipples were visible under the thin material of her bikini top, which she felt no shame over. He guessed her age at only 18, already she was corrupt and worthless. She knew the boys were staring at her and revelled in the attention; a knowing smile played on her lips. Soon the time would be right and he would wipe the smile from her pretty face and ensure her sluttish behaviour would no longer have to be tolerated.

The girl, he knew, was approximately five-feet-six-inches in height and of average build. Her chest he estimated at 36B. He zoomed in on her left breast on the computer until he thought it was approximately life size. The image was slightly pixelated but he could still see the outline of her nipple and areola. He lifted a shoe box from the floor and removed the lid. He looked at the contents and extracted a cockle shell, painted in black, gloss paint and held it up to the image. The shell was about 2.5 inches in diameter and looked just about big enough to cover her nipple. He delved into the box and bought out a second shell of similar size and put the pair of them into a small, silk-lined, necklace box. He gazed at the shells thinking how much nicer they would look on the pale dead skin of his next victim.

CHAPTER 44

Ed wandered over around mid-morning to see Laura, hoping that the champagne sponge with enormous breasts was long gone, which unfortunately she wasn't. When he arrived Laura was sitting in her wheelchair, hair pulled back in a severe ponytail, wearing her glasses, looking very much worse for wear. Charlotte was slumped on the sofa, wearing what he guessed was a borrowed towelling robe as it barely met in the middle. Her hair was a mess, the remains of yesterday's make-up smudged across her face.

Fat Boy wandered in and put his nose up the back of Charlotte's dressing gown, his cold wet nose causing her to cry out in alarm and the robe to part at the chest, revealing an impossibly deep cleavage. It wasn't a pretty sight. She sat up and pulled it back together but it only just covered her modesty. Fat Boy renewed his attack and went in for the kill seeing her chunky thighs on display. Charlotte saw this coming and grabbed his head before he could reach his goal. Fat Boy put his head in her lap and contented himself with having his head stroked, for now at least.

Charlotte had been trying to call James all morning, or since she got out of bed, which equated to about thirty minutes, and been unable to contact him. She was concerned about getting back to London so Ed volunteered to drive her back to her hotel and said he would come back and take Laura to lunch. On that basis, Laura decided not to come as she needed to get ready.

Charlotte, dressed in yesterday's clothes, with more than a couple of stains from the previous night's binge, sat in the passenger seat looking rather sorry for herself. Ed just hoped she didn't start vomiting all over the car. They arrived at the hotel in Rock and walked up to reception to get her key. The receptionist told her Greg and James paid for the rooms and left an hour or so earlier. She didn't look happy. Ed couldn't believe they just left without letting Charlotte know. He guessed they were still sulking from their encounter with him yesterday afternoon and Charlotte staying behind with Laura was seen as a betrayal in some way. Even so it was a little harsh, Ed thought. Ed accompanied her to her room where her bags were, still unpacked from when they arrived yesterday. He felt rather sorry for her and said he would drive her somewhere she could catch a train to London easily. She seemed to perk up at this idea and asked him nicely if she could grab a shower before heading off, promising to be quick. Ed said it was OK but it wasn't really. There was no way he would get back in time to take Laura to lunch. He rang Laura on his mobile and explained the situation. She seemed happy enough but made him promise to take her out for dinner instead.

Ed was sitting, reading the numerous tourism leaflets left on the dressing table, when he heard Charlotte exit the bathroom. He put the leaflet down and turned round to be confronted by Charlotte, wearing only a skimpy pair of knickers, standing inches from his face.

'Bloody hell, Charlotte, put some clothes on for Christ sake.' he said, a little shocked and more than a little intimidated.

'Don't you like them, Ed?' she replied, pushing them forward for greater effect.

'No, it's not that, they're very… impressive,' he managed to say, pushing his chair backwards.

'Oh, don't tell me you're gay?' she enquired, looking disappointed.

'No, I'm not gay. You just took me by surprise that's all. Now get dressed I need to get back and take your best friend, Laura, out for lunch,' he replied, dropping a subtle hint.

'You're boring. Laura wouldn't mind. Most men I know would die to get their hands on these,' she said indignantly.

'Well, I've only got little hands and I'm in hurry so come on, get dressed.'

'Your loss,' she said, stretching over to the dressing table to pick up the hair dryer, nearly knocking Ed's head off with her left breast as she did. She dried her hair and remained naked for what seemed as long as possible to Ed, before finally getting dressed and repacking her bag. 'Last chance.' she told him as they were leaving. Ed ignored the comment and pushed her through the door, rather pleased he had resisted the very strong temptation to cop a good feel of her breasts, just out of curiosity, of course.

Ed drove out towards the A30, not really knowing where to drop her off. In the end, he opted for Exeter, as it was the only place he could remember the train stopping, when he used it once as a young lad, before he passed his driving test. The only other option he knew of was Penzance but, for reasons unknown, and he would later come to regret, decided on Exeter. He knew there was a station in Bodmin, which was only a few miles away but decided it was probably a bit mean dropping her there, where she would most likely have to change at least once, to get back to London.

He had only travelled a few miles on the A30, when he hit traffic. Not just a little traffic but stationary traffic. Once again, Ed had completely forgotten it was a public holiday and people were heading back home. Despite spending a lot of time in Cornwall, he only knew one way in and one way out and that was the A30 so he was buggered. He pulled his phone out and called Laura to tell her he might be some time. She seemed to be OK with this, although he detected a slight undertone in her voice, which suggested it wasn't really. Charlotte tried to cheer him up by suggesting he could play with her breasts to while away the time, which was rather sweet of her. Ed thanked her but declined her kind offer.

'Just how big are they, Charlotte?' he asked, curiosity getting the better of him, which seemed to please her.

'Thirty eight double G,' she informed him proudly. Ed now knew just what fitted into those crash helmets tied together with elastic he had seen in the Debenhams lingerie department last week and nodded, clearly impressed.

'That's big! That would be like me having a ten-inch dick,' he replied.

'What size is it then?' she asked, relishing the way the conversation was going.

'Dunno. I've never measured it,' he lied. Not wishing to discuss the size of his manhood with a stranger. 'I suppose it's average size, whatever size that is. It's not as big as the ones you see in porn films though. Christ, some of those blokes have dicks like Popeye's forearm.'

Charlotte's hand shot towards his crotch, like a striking cobra and grabbed a handful of his crown jewels. 'I'd say it was a good size,' she said smiling and kneading his crotch. Ed tried his hardest to tear her hand away, without doing himself any serious damage but she was like a bloody barnacle, once she was latched on to the rudder, that was it. Despite himself, he was only human after all, within a few seconds had a lazy lob on. Charlotte pleased with the reaction went at it with renewed vigour. He managed eventually to prise her off and left his left hand there, guarding his genitals from further assault. 'Well, at least now I know you're not gay,' she said giving him a salacious look. 'You sure, you don't want me to finish you off?' She asked, giving him a look of disappointment when he declined.

'What's up with you, are you on heat this week or something?' he asked exasperated.

'No, I just like cock,' she replied happily, making Ed laugh.

The traffic eased and eventually started moving and within a few miles Ed was making good progress on the outside lane. Charlotte was good company despite being a nymphomaniac and amused him with various stories about office Christmas parties and bedding various members of the senior management team at the bank. She knew she had a reputation but didn't care. She couldn't help herself. She just liked cock and a lot of it. The only sour point of the whole journey was when she put her hand on his knee and gradually slid it up to his thigh and gave it a squeeze, right on his stitches. Ed screamed like a girl and cursed. Charlotte thought it was funny and offered to kiss it better but again, Ed declined.

They eventually hit the outskirts of Exeter and followed the signs to the station. Progress was painfully slow but eventually he pulled up outside, breathing a sigh of relief. His leg was hurting, not just because of Charlotte's unwanted attention but the constant use of the clutch was taking its toll. He asked Charlotte if she had money for a ticket and after looking in her purse found she only had twenty pounds and some shrapnel. Ed pulled his wallet out and gave her a hundred pounds, hoping it would cover the cost of her ticket. He didn't have a clue but knew from buying season tickets to London years ago, that the rail companies were all robbing bastards. Charlotte assured him she would pay him back, but Ed said not to worry, knowing that her payback probably meant some kind of sexual favour. Not a bad alternative really but after the stories she told him during the journey, not worth the risk.

Ed gave Laura a quick call to say he was on his way back and this time there was definitely a hint of annoyance in her voice. He explained the traffic and completely forgetting it was a public holiday and promised to be back in time to take her to dinner. Unfortunately, he didn't bank on getting lost in the centre of Exeter for over an hour. He cursed not investing in a satnav, despite all the horror stories he had been told by friends who did have them, such as getting sent up dirt tracks and getting stuck in thick mud or driving endlessly around one way systems, as the software was out of date. Eventually, he found someone who gave him directions and another thirty minutes later he was back on the M5, unfortunately travelling towards London and stuck in another bloody jam. Ed pulled his phone from his pocket to put back in the cradle to make a call and dropped it. It landed on the gear stick and fell to pieces, the battery disappearing under the passenger seat and the other two halves, a piece in each foot-well. He cursed and drove on, turning round at the next junction and heading south.

He eventually pulled up outside his caravan at just after eight o'clock, tired, thirsty, so hungry he could eat his own feet and his leg throbbing painfully. He retrieved his stick from the back, along with the various parts of his phone and hobbled over to see Laura, who was out. He walked into the clubhouse and saw her sitting there with Bob and Raechael. She seemed to be having a good time without him. Ed crept in and walked round to the restaurant and stole a plastic rose off the nearest empty table. He never realised they were plastic until today as they looked so realistic but it would do as a peace offering.

He walked over to Laura and presented her with the rose. 'You think that gets you off the hook, do you?' she said, giving him a stern look. Ed thought it was time to go for the sympathy vote.

'Sorry Laura. The traffic was a nightmare. I completely forgot it was a public holiday. Then I got lost in Exeter and ended up going towards London. My leg is killing me, I've had nothing to eat or drink all day and all so I could do you a favour and get Dolly Parton's nymphomaniac lovechild to the station. Give me a break.'

Laura gave him a look that said she was deciding whether or

not to be angry with him or not and then finally made up her mind, which was neither. She obviously wanted to make a point. 'Luckily, mum came home and we had fish and chips or I'd have starved to death waiting for you.' She smiled and added a thank you for taking Charlotte back and asked him if he wanted a drink. Ed nodded and Bob said good as it was Ed's round. Ed got up painfully and got the round in and a packet of crisps, which got Fat Boy's attention. Just as he sat down the lights went out once more, to the now customary chorus of boos.

'Anyway, what do you mean Nymphomaniac?' Laura asked him. Ed explained the events in the hotel and during the entire journey to Exeter. Laura thought it was funny, Raechael looked quite shocked and Bob gave him a look of envy – clearly a tit man.

'What about lunch, tomorrow? Third time lucky,' he asked Laura, who declined, telling him she and Raechael were going out for the day, sightseeing and shopping. Raechael suggested Ed come along. The idea of spending the day with Laura appealed to him but he declined on the grounds he had no intention of stopping them shopping 'til they dropped or having a bit of mother and daughter time together. Laura seemed disappointed, which was good, as it meant he wasn't entirely in her bad books and the frosty reception was wearing off.

'How was your date, I mean day at the Eden Project?' he asked Bob, who narrowed his eyes at the deliberate play on words and muttered fine and it was none of his business. Raechael began to tell him all about it, until Bob's phone rang. Bob looked at his phone clearly not happy his day off had been disturbed but answered and walked off to a quiet corner. When he returned he looked pleased.

'It would appear we have a breakthrough,' he told them and for some reason gave Ed a dirty look. 'It seems, DS Reynolds has been a busy boy, following up on a few leads and we might just have a suspect.'

He apologised to Raechael for cutting short their evening and thanked her for a lovely day, even leaning over and kissing her, much to Ed's amusement who smiled, said 'That's nice,' and winked at Bob, who shot him an icy glare and strolled purposefully out the clubhouse.

CHAPTER 45

Phil had been busy since leaving the clubhouse the previous afternoon. He was inspired by Ed's views on the Black Cockle Strangler, in spite of these being readily dismissed by his boss. He went straight back to the station and pulled a few favours, managing to get a list of the names and addresses of lifeguards and surf instructors in the area, as well as, firemen and anyone related to the health service, such as, doctors, nurses and ambulance men. He also compiled a list of all male police officers, which was much easier as all the details and contact numbers were readily available. He was able to narrow that down quite quickly and significantly, as he thought it unlikely that the Chief Superintendent or the Assistant Chief Constable were likely suspects. He was positive the Chief Super was gay and the ACC was a decrepit, old fart, who couldn't punch his way out of a paper bag, let alone strangle a fit and healthy young woman.

After plotting all the addresses on a map, he set off in his car to look at them. Most of the lifeguards and surf instructors lived very local as did the majority of his colleagues, with the exception of one or two that lived around the Bodmin area. He concentrated his search locally, working on the premise he could cover ninety-five percent of his list quite quickly this way. It was however, slow and frustrating work as he drove around the estates and villages, stopping to view the colour of the doors and windowsills of the addresses on his list but so far got his list down to three possibles.

When he saw a maroon Volvo estate parked at the kerb a short distance from one house, his heart skipped a beat. A sighting of a red Volvo estate had been reported going at speed, the night the last body had been found. Maroon was close enough to red to not be a coincidence, surely? After consulting his list, to put a name to the address, he was shocked to find it belonged to a fellow officer and immediately wanted to dismiss the idea he could be implicated. Professional pride dictated that he should follow it up and he took the registration of the Volvo to check out later. The house itself was an end of terrace with a garage attached to the side, which had its wooden doors painted black. Surely, finding a serial killer wasn't going to be this easy?

After completing his check of all the remaining properties on his list, Phil headed back to the station. Rather than put in a vehicle registration check, which would arouse suspicion, he checked the station records for cars authorised to use the station car park and found that the maroon Volvo was listed as being authorised. The name of the officer, matched the address. He had one more check to make but that would have to wait until morning, as it was almost midnight.

Phil slept poorly, his mind continually mulling over the possibilities of solving the biggest and most notorious crime the area had seen in many a year. Surely, this would ensure the promotion to Detective Inspector he had been pursuing for the last three years was in the bag? He did however, have a major problem, one that was basically illegal and could result in the evidence not being admissible. Every police force asked officers who came into contact with crime scenes and crime scene evidence to provide DNA samples, in order that they could be eliminated from investigations. This was not obligatory and many refused, on the grounds of infringement of their human rights. However, all new recruits had to provide a DNA sample as a condition of employment, despite being heavily criticised by the Human Genetics Commission. The DNA of police officers was kept separately from the national database and searching of this was strictly off limits. Phil had plenty of contacts and knew he could pull in a favour but it would cost him a bottle of scotch, which was a small price to pay if it proved successful.

Phil made the phone call from his personal mobile in the station car park. His contact Adrian Walker refused point blank, telling him it was more than his job's worth, and as well as being illegal, was also morally wrong. Two bottles of scotch sealed the deal. Phil gave him the case reference for the DNA samples found on the latest victim and the name, rank and collar number of the officer he wanted the check made against. Adrian said he would call back later, once the office was quieter and nobody would see what he was up to. The wait was agonizing and made worse by the appearance in the office of his number one suspect but that gave him another idea.

Outside the house, Phil waited patiently for his accomplice to arrive. Darren sauntered up to him casually and smiled, before getting to work on the lock, which he opened in seconds. Phil shook his hand and slipped the fifty pounds they agreed on into his shirt pocket. He had known Darren for years and arrested him at least half a dozen times for being in possession of stolen goods and breaking and entering. His father before him had been much the same, although a little better at keeping out of the reach of the law and passed on his lock picking skills to his son, so he could continue the family business. Phil felt a little sorry for him, as with a father like that, he never stood a chance, and tried as much as possible to persuade him to look for more gainful employment. Asking him to pick a lock for him was, therefore, more than a little hypocritical, not to mention illegal but Phil felt it was justified.

Once inside he put on his surgical gloves and started his search of the house. He started upstairs and was disappointed to find the bedroom yielded no evidence to suggest he was on the right track. Downstairs was equally uninspiring, finding absolutely nothing to link his suspect back to the murders. He wandered into the kitchen, which again proved to be another blank, until he turned to leave and noticed a door behind the opened kitchen door, which he assumed led to the cellar.

Phil was about to turn the handle but noticed it was locked with a padlock. He cursed his bad luck and was about to leave, when he had second thoughts. Fuck it, nobody would know, he thought, and dug in his pocket for his Swiss army knife and started working on the screws securing the bracket. His hands were trembling with anticipation, which didn't help. Sweat was beading on his forehead but eventually he completed the task and pushed the door inwards, revealing a steep, narrow staircase. He located the light switch just inside the door, turned on the dim light and descended.

Just as he began his descent, his mobile phone rang, frightening him to death in the eerie silence of the house. He saw the caller was Adrian, who muttered 'It's a match. You owe me,' and hung up. Phil's pulse quickened, his head began to swim with the possibilities of what he might find. What he did find in the small room at the bottom of the staircase sickened and shocked him. The walls were covered in photographs of the four victims in various poses, before and after death. Interspersed with the photographs were newspaper articles of each of the victims, like a hideous shrine. There was also a computer, with a digital camera attached to it on a small desk at one end of the room and above it a huge monitor. Phil walked over and moved the mouse and the screen burst into life, revealing a grotesque photograph of the last victim. She was lying naked on the bed, with her eyes gouged out and semen across her abdomen and chest. Phil had seen enough and wanted to get out, he had the evidence he needed and raced back up the narrow staircase, fighting back the bile that was rising in his throat.

Once at the top, he managed to put the bracket back on with shaking, sweaty hands. He cleaned up the fresh sawdust on the floor that resulted from taking the screws out and headed back out onto the street, where he stood breathing deeply, trying to control his shaking and swallowing back the vomit that was threatening to erupt onto the street.

He sat in his car for some time, trying to decide what to do. Officially, he wasn't on duty today so he headed home, he needed a drink. He knew what he achieved today was monumental but all of it was unauthorised. He knew Bob would understand his actions but would be mightily pissed off, with both this and the fact Ed had been right. In fact, Ed being right was probably going to irk him more than the fact Phil had gone solo on this. Eventually, he plucked up enough courage to make the call to Bob.

CHAPTER 46

'You did what!' Bob bellowed 'Jesus Christ, Phil,' he added, running a hand through his hair, unhappy Phil made an illegal check of the Police DNA register and enlisted the help of a petty crook to break into the house. Phil looked sheepish, knowing that his actions could have compromised the case. 'Good work, though. Although, it pisses me off no end that Ed was right on the mark. He's gonna be bloody unbearable when he finds out. Right now, I need to think how we're going to wrap this one up, without either of us earning a bloody suspension. I'll make up some cock-and-bull story for the Chief Super and I want you to keep an eye on Murphy's place. The last thing we need now is him going off and killing someone else. Let me know the minute he leaves his house.'

Thirty minutes later, Bob was sitting in the study of Chief Superintendent Clatworthy's house, feeling very uncomfortable. In the end, he told him the truth, which was a first for Bob but he couldn't think of any other plausible lie to cover up Phil's maverick approach. Of course, Bob laid it on thick, elaborating even on Phil's description of what he found in the cellar but Clatworthy was no fool, despite his appearance, and waved his hand dismissively, telling Bob he 'got the picture and there was no need for fabrication.' He even managed a barely perceptible grin.

Clatworthy ran a hand over his chin, contemplating what Bob just told him and what to do next. He tapped his pen nervously on the desk in front of him, studying Bob, who stared back poker-faced. Below the surface he was a bag of nerves. Both his and Phil's arses were on the line and he wished to God Clatworthy would stop tapping that bloody and pen and say something.

Eventually, he stopped tapping his pen and spoke.

'So, you're telling me that DS Reynolds, in the course of following up his investigations, which were fully authorised by yourself?' he asked, raising an eyebrow. Bob nodded at the rhetoric question and Clatworthy continued. 'Noticed a car matching the description of a car being seen speeding away from the scene of the crime and became suspicious. He knocked on the door and, when there was no reply, went round the back and found the back door open?' Bob nodded again enthusiastically at the Chief Super's slant on things. 'On entering the property, DS Reynolds found the door to the cellar open and discovered the shrine to the macabre. Is that correct?' Bob nodded again. 'Anything else I should know?'

Previously, Bob's opinion of Clatworthy had been he was a doddery old fart, just seeing out his last few years before retirement and not wanting to rock the boat or tarnish his record. Not that there was much of a record to tarnish. He had never been much of a copper and just got lucky with promotions, right place, right time, rather than hard graft and results: a typical pen-pusher in fact. Now, however, he was seeing him in a different light and liked the way he fabricated a feasible story out of what was potentially a disastrous situation. Bob guessed even Clatworthy was getting pressure from above to get a result. It spurred Bob to tell him the whole truth.

'Well, Sir. There is one other thing I forgot to mention. DS Reynolds called in a favour and had Murphy's DNA checked against the sample found on the last victim and got a match.' There his conscience was clean, just a matter of waiting for the fall out.

'And of course, this was with your full knowledge?' Clatworthy said in a way that meant Bob had no option but to agree.

'Of course, sir.' Bob replied, knowing this meant if the shit hit the fan, he was right in the firing line.

'Good and obviously you came to me and based on the evidence presented, I authorised it.' Bob nodded again, this time more enthusiastically, pleased with the way things were going. 'Of course, I shall deny all knowledge of this, if things get a little uncomfortable and you will take full accountability for this. Do I make myself clear, DCI Brown?'

'Perfectly, sir,' Bob replied, now thinking what a slippery bastard he was but knew that's the way things worked. Clatworthy left the room, telling him to wait and returned a few minutes later.

'I have spoken to the Assistant Chief Constable, who is, as you would expect, pleased we have this one wrapped up. It would seem as the suspect is one of our own, it will be much easier to ensure certain... procedural discrepancies can be over looked. However, he has warned me, if any of this becomes public knowledge, he will deny all knowledge, as will I. Therefore, the buck stops with you. Now, do what you need to do and get Murphy in. I want him charged so we can arrange a press conference for first thing in the morning.'

Bob thanked him and stood to leave, relishing the thought of wrapping the case up.

'One last thing before you go, DCI Brown,' Clatworthy said, stopping Bob in his tracks. 'Good work, Bob, please pass on my thanks to DS Reynolds.' Bob nodded and left a very relieved man.

He made a call to Phil and told him he would meet him at Murphy's house and to round up the troops. An hour later, Murphy was in custody in interview room one, looking apprehensive and sweating profusely, while his house was being pulled apart, inch by inch by the scene of crime team.

Bob and Phil conducted the interview, which in the end was a lot easier than either of them expected. Murphy confessed within minutes and broke down in tears, crying like a baby, which Bob found embarrassing but strangely satisfying. After he regained his composure, the interview resumed. Murphy recalled the events of each murder, providing every minute detail of each one, obviously relishing every minute. It was almost as if he were reliving the brutal slaying of each victim. An hour later, Bob called a halt to the proceedings. He needed some fresh air, feeling nauseous just being in the same room as Murphy, and walked out to the car park, taking a deep lungful of the crisp night air. He was joined by Phil, who lit a cigarette and inhaled deeply, letting out a long stream of smoke. Bob asked him for one, despite having given up two years ago and relished the familiar burning sensation as he inhaled. They both stood in silence smoking, neither wanting to interrupt the others private contemplation on the interview and Murphy's beatific confession, which was unnerving.

The interview continued into the small hours of the morning, until Bob finally called it a day. He was tired, both physically and mentally and needed sleep and to be away from the oppressive and claustrophobic interview room.

'Just one thing, Murphy,' Bob asked after the interview had been terminated and the tape recorders switched off. 'Why?' he said regarding him coldly.

'Because they were filth, of course.' Murphy replied as if the answer should be obvious. 'The way they acted was disgusting, like common whores. They were an affront to common decency and needed to be taught a lesson in propriety.'

'What about the cockle shells, what were they all about?' Phil asked.

Murphy smiled and shrugged 'Just a ruse, really. I liked the idea of being given a name. You know, like Jack the Ripper, the Boston Strangler and so forth. I wanted to become infamous. I wanted people to know my name and to remember me and fear me.'

'Why paint them black?' Phil probed further.

'Why not?' he asked rhetorically. 'They look so much nicer painted and black is rather fitting, don't you think? Black like their souls,' he said, grinning insanely. 'Also it was the only colour paint I had around the house, unless you count white emulsion but that didn't seem very appropriate. White is a pure colour and not fitting for those cheap whores.'

'You're a fucking sick bastard, Murphy!' Bob spat at him and left the room, with Phil following closely behind. Murphy bowed his head and squeezed his eyes shut. He thought about telling the truth but knew that Brown and Reynolds wouldn't understand; they were too narrow-minded. Not that it mattered, not now. It was over. He looked across at his solicitor, who stared back with a look of contempt. Murphy smiled and gave a low chuckle that built into uncontrollable laughter.

Back in the car park, Bob scrounged another cigarette from Phil, before heading home to get a few hours sleep, ahead of the press conference in the morning. There was also an interview to finish and the unenviable task of making sure all the volumes of case notes were in order. More importantly, there was the small matter of the post case piss-up he would need to organise. He would also attempt to get a few quid out of the Chief Super for behind the bar. He was usually quite forthcoming but he could afford to be. The worse part of tomorrow would be facing Ed. When he found out he was spot on with his views on the case, right down to the fact the cockles were just a gimmick and the black paint was only because it was available, he would be unbearably smug, because he himself had dismissed his ideas immediately.

CHAPTER 47

Once again, Ed had a night of interrupted sleep. This was partly due to the wound on his leg, which throbbed painfully, despite the painkillers he had taken. Additionally, he experienced a recurring dream, reminiscent of the 1960's TV series The Prisoner, where Patrick McGoohan is chased by a large white ball. In Ed's dream he was pursued by two balls, which would back him into a corner. When he opened his eyes, he was confronted by Charlotte, wearing nothing but a red, satin thong, smiling salaciously, asking him if he wanted to play with her breasts. She would walk slowly towards him, caressing her breasts as Ed tried to shrink further into the corner. Her breasts seemed to double in size with each step until Ed was enveloped in her cavernous cleavage. Ed woke up sweating and gasping for air on several occasions. No matter how hard he tried, he couldn't shake the dream off and would awake after the same dream with the same suffocating result. In the end he gave up on the idea of sleep and taken Fat Boy for a walk, albeit a slow one. Fat Boy seemed to be making an excellent recovery all considered, which was more than Ed could say for himself.

After a few cups of coffee and a revitalising shower, Ed and Fat Boy jumped in the car and headed towards Padstow and the vets, where Fat Boy was due a check up. His stitches weren't due out for another few days yet but the vet insisted on coming back after a week, just to make sure the wound was healing and there were no secondary infections. It also gave Ed an excuse to see Jacqui, Chris and Emma. He rang Jacqui first and asked her if she wanted to go for lunch somewhere. She declined as she had a busy day ahead but suggested he bring some sandwiches over and they could catch up in her office. Ed was disappointed but happy with the compromise and brought sandwiches and cakes. He entered her office via the back of the building, not wanting to intrude on any customers she may have waiting in the parlour, if he entered through the front door.

'You look stressed out,' he told Jacqui, after emptying the contents of his carrier bag onto her desk.

'Thanks, you certainly know how to make a girl feel good. I am as it happens. I didn't realise the job would be so hard when I agreed to take over from my dad,' she replied as she selected a chicken salad sandwich and began extracting it from the plastic sleeve.

'I'm surprised you did. I thought you were happy being a copper. Bob was well pissed off when you jacked it in. In fact, I remember you telling me once, there wasn't a chance in hell of you taking over the family business. You were only a flat-chested, gangly teenager at the time though,' Ed told her smiling. 'What made you change your mind?'

'Thanks for the reminder, Ed,' she said and looked as if she was going to say more but remained silent.

'You turned out OK, though; filled out in all the right places,' Ed said, trying to redeem himself. 'You didn't answer my question though.' Jacqui studied him and after finishing a mouthful of sandwich, eventually answered.

'I was diagnosed with angina and needed to do something less physical and a little less stressful,' she told him.

'Bloody hell, Jacqui. Why didn't you tell anyone?' Ed said concerned.

'Same reason you never told anyone you tried to top yourself a few years back,' she said, staring at him. 'It's my problem and I'll deal with it. I don't need everyone making a fuss. It's not life threatening, at least not yet. It may get worse but at the moment it's intermediate. There, now you know and I haven't told anyone else so keep it to yourself. I don't want anyone making a fuss and treating me like an invalid,' she said, giving him a terse smile.

'So, you're not about to end up in one of your own boxes, just yet?' Ed asked, trying to lighten the mood.

'Of course not. I gave up the police because chasing after criminals became a problem. I couldn't keep fit enough and I'd look a right idiot chasing after a suspect and having to stop when I got a pain to take a hit on my GTN spray, wouldn't I? Dad wanting to go abroad was an opportunity to drop out without raising any eyebrows and anyone asking too many questions. Turns out, this is just as stressful as the police, dealing with grieving relatives every day. At least in the police you only experienced that once in a blue moon.'

'Sorry for being a nosy sod,' Ed said, apologising lamely, not really knowing what to say. Jacqui dismissed him with a smile and a wave of her hand. 'You know, I said years ago you had a cute angina, nice norks too!' Ed said making her smile, which was a good sign.

'Very funny. Just don't tell anyone, especially Chris, you know what she's like,' she said seriously. Ed nodded, although it would be a difficult secret to keep. 'Anyway, changing the subject, how are you and Fat Boy after your fun on the beach?'

'Fat Boy's doing OK.' Ed replied and gave Fat Boy the crust of his sandwich, who had thumped his tail on the floor expectantly at the mention of his name. 'We've just been back to the vet and he's pleased with his progress. No secondary infections and his wound's healing nicely. He seems to be doing better than I am, for sure. I need a bloody stick to get around but it's getting better.'

'By the way, how's it going with Laura?' she asked grinning. 'I had dinner with Chris and Emma last night and Emma seemed to think you and Laura were quite close.'

Ed was about to answer when his phone rang, definitely a case of saved by the bell. He looked at the caller display and it showed as an unknown number. Ed answered it anyway.

'Ed, it's Phil Reynolds, how are you?'

'I'm fine,' he replied. 'How did you get my number?'

'I'm a copper, I can get anything I like if I need it,' he replied laughing. 'I asked Bob for it if you must know. Where are you?'

'I'm at the undertakers in town. Wasn't feeling too good so popped in just in case,' Ed replied 'It's OK though, I'm feeling a lot better now, thanks. Just wind.'

'Right, seeing Jacqui, then? Lucky man. How do you fancy a quick beer? I've got something to tell you,' he asked. Ed could detect the excitement in his voice.

'I'm having lunch, actually. Can it wait until a little later?' Ed asked.

'I'll tell you now. I can only have a quick lunch break as things are a bit busy. We got the strangler, full confession, the lot. You'll like the next bit. His house had a black front door and it was the only colour paint he had in the house. It gets better, he did it for a gimmick, just like you said and he was one of ours, just like you said. Bob is so pissed off about it,' Phil enthused, chuckling down the line, which was infectious. 'We're having celebratory drinks at the clubhouse tonight so make sure you're there. I want to buy you a beer or two and ask Jacqui along, we could use a bit of glamour. In fact, ask Chris as well, if you see her. If Jacqui turns me down, I'll have a crack at Chris.'

'Who was it? If I'm allowed to ask.'

'Head-banger Murphy. Your best mate. I'll give you the details tonight. Assuming, you don't hear it on the news first.'

'I can't wait to see Bob. He must be sick as a pig, no pun intended. Give him a very smug grin from me when you see him.'

'Funny, he said you'd have a face like you'd just rogered the neighbour's cat. See you tonight,' he said, before hanging up.

He related the conversation to Jacqui, who was surprised the black cockle shells were a gimmick and nothing more meaningful, more so than she was the strangler was Murphy.

'Phil asked for you personally to put in an appearance tonight,' Ed told her, looking for a reaction and adding 'I think he likes you,' just for good measure. Jacqui touched her hair and blushed slightly, making Ed laugh.

'Don't think I'm busy tonight,' Jacqui said coyly.

'Good, I'll pick you up at seven,' Ed said walking round the desk and kissing her goodbye. Fat Boy trotted out after him, leaving a rather large wet patch on the carpet, where he dribbled constantly during their lunch.

Ed purchased a couple of boxes of handmade chocolates from the confectionary shop and walked the short distance to Chris's shop, with Fat Boy's nose pressed hard against the carrier bag they were contained in. When he entered the shop, Chris was actually behind the counter and came round to greet him with a hug.

'I thought you'd forgotten about me,' she said with a pout. 'Too busy with Laura, I suppose,' she said grinning at him.

'Give it a rest, Chris. You're as bad as Emma and Raechael, the nurse at the hospital, Jacqui and even Bob's on my case now. It's a bloody conspiracy, now leave me alone,' Ed said light-heartedly, although it was beginning to feel very much like a conspiracy; not that it was getting anywhere. It seemed the odds were stacked against him.

'That bad, eh? Let's go upstairs and grab a coffee. Emma will be pleased to see you,' she said and was right. Emma rushed up to him, dragging him off to the studio.

'Well, what do you think?' she said pointing at one of her completed paintings, which was now framed.

'It's fantastic. I love it. You're really good; I'd be happy to have that hanging on my wall; it's perfect.' It was a typical Cornish coastal scene, in oil but extremely detailed, every rock and every wave had been painstakingly given life. Ed peered at it and marvelled at exactly how much detail and work had gone into it. 'It's definitely something I'd buy. How much are you going to sell it for?' he asked.

'I'm not. I'm giving it away to you as a present. It's a thank you for all you've done for me. You do like it, don't you? You're not just saying it to make me happy, are you?' she asked, looking nervous.

'No, it's brilliant. You've got a real talent. I can't accept it, though. You want to sell it and make some money out of it.'

'I've already finished another two. Now I know what I want to do, it's really easy. It's like anything else once you've done it once, you get quicker,' she said enthusiastically.

'OK, if you're sure. I really do like it. Thanks,' he said giving her a hug. 'Have you sold any yet?' he asked.

'Not yet. Chris had a word with a friend who owns one of the galleries in town and he said he would take some to sell so I can get more exposure. He really liked them and thinks they are very marketable and should sell for around seven hundred and fifty pounds. If they do start selling, we can then put the price up,' she said excitedly.

'She's got a real talent, Ed. You should see some of the jewellery she's made. I've sold every piece so far. I just wish I could prise her away from her painting more often, to make some more,' Chris said enthusiastically.

'Just keep her away from the Absinth and don't let her cut her ear off. And don't let her do any of the modern shit you don't know what you're looking at,' Ed told her.

Ed handed out the chocolates, which Emma opened immediately to have with their coffee. Ed declined, he had never been a big chocolate lover but suggested Fat Boy could have his and Emma duly obliged, which briefly abated Fat Boy's dribbling. He told them of his call from Phil and Murphy's arrest had been as a result of Ed, telling him his theory. Chris called him a smug bastard, to which Ed just nodded smugly to prove a point. Emma said she thought Murphy was a bit shifty and there was something funny about him but didn't have him down as a sadistic killer.

'There's a bit of a celebration at the Clubhouse tonight. I said I would pick Jacqui up at seven so I can pick you up too, if you like? Assuming you'll be coming. Bob will be there Emma,' he said trying to get even for her match making efforts with him and Laura, knowing she had a soft spot for Bob. Ed couldn't see what the attraction was but Emma seemed to find the craggy, older man look, quite appealing.

'We'll be there,' Emma said, looking at Chris, who nodded. 'Will Laura and Raechael be there?' Ed filled her in on the developments of the last couple of days with Raechael and Bob, which was greeted with a lot of surprise. 'So you've not made any progress with Laura? Ed, you're such a let-down.' she told him.

'It's not through want of trying. It's like everything's against me,' he told her and gave her a rundown of his two failed attempts to take Laura to lunch.

'Charlotte sounds like a handful,' she said laughing.

'More than a handful. I asked her and she said she was a thirty-eight double G. How scary is that!' he said shuddering at the memory.

'I'm surprised she manages to stay upright with those,' Emma quipped.

'From what she was telling me, she doesn't stay upright for long. She's a self-confessed nymphomaniac. She told me and I quote "I just like cock." That's even more frightening than the fact she is a double G. Anyway, the bottom line is, I've got nowhere with Laura. Maybe it's not such a good idea.' The look that Emma gave him suggested he was wrong. 'Look, I'm going to head back and get cleaned up and I'll be round at seven,' he said. Emma quickly ran out, returning to present Ed with her painting. Ed headed back to the car, looking forward to a good night out. He would call Laura when he got back and make sure she would come, although he suspected Bob had already invited her and Raechael. He was in for some shit when he saw him. Ed laughed to himself as he put the car in gear and headed home.

CHAPTER 48

He pulled up outside Jacqui's house and sounded the horn. A few minutes later she closed the front door and jumped in the passenger seat. Ed looked at her and smiled.

'You OK?' he asked.

'Ed, don't start. Just because I've got a minor condition it doesn't mean I'm disabled,' she said tetchily. 'This is exactly why I haven't told anybody about this.'

'Sorry. Just concerned about your wellbeing,' he said cheerily.

'The way you're carrying on, I'm going to outlive you by about forty years so shut up, if you know what's good for you,' she said with a smile.

'You look very nice, by the way. Making a special effort for Phil, by any chance?'

'Might be. Got a problem with that? He's quite a nice guy and between you and me, I used to fancy him when we worked together. At the time, I didn't think it was a good idea to get involved with someone from work, certainly not in the same department. What do you think of him by the way, is he suitable?' she asked mockingly.

'Not my type but he seems like a nice bloke and from what he said on the phone earlier, he seems quite keen on you,' he said, which seemed to please her and he noticed she toyed with her hair. Maybe there was something in that after all. He'd definitely have to watch out for the hippy in the pub when he got home though.

They picked up Chris and Emma, drove back to the caravan park and parked outside his caravan.

'Are we going straight over or stopping for a glass or two at yours?' Chris asked.

'More like a bottle or two with you lot but no, haven't got time. I said I'd be round to pick up Laura and Raechael at half past,' Ed replied.

'That's nice. Luscious Laura's still keen on you then, is she?' Chris teased him.

'Dunno. She was a bit frosty last time I saw her but she's coming because Bob invited Raechael. Now that is a strange combination. To think that cheeky bastard said Emma was batting above my average. A case of the kettle calling the pot black, if you ask me,' Ed replied a little bitterly.

'I think he's rather handsome in rugged, older-man sort of way but then I like a face with a bit of character,' Emma announced.

'You need to get laid more often, you're getting desperate,' Ed said, trying to wind her up and succeeding.

'Now who's calling the pot black? Last time you saw any action, we still had a conservative government,' Emma said, laughing at her own joke.

'A real friend would help me out,' he said blowing her a kiss.

'Not my type, too young and nowhere near rugged enough,' she replied. 'In any case, you're already spoken for and here she comes.' Right on cue, Laura and Raechael exited their caravan, made their way down the ramp and they all headed to the clubhouse.

Phil was the first to greet them, shaking Ed's hand furiously, then putting his hands on his cheeks and kissing him plum on the lips.

'That's a much more enthusiastic welcome than this lot gave me, come on you've pulled,' Ed said, slightly shocked.

'Sorry about that, I've had a few already and if it wasn't for you, we wouldn't be here. Not sure if you're just a lucky guesser or just a lucky bastard and to be honest I don't care,' he said handing him a pint.

'Modesty dictates I should say I'm a lucky guesser but it was bloody obvious, wasn't it?' Ed said jokingly.

'I don't care, it was spot on and right now I'm the toast of the station and I reckon should just about seal my promotion to DI.'

'Congratulations by the way. I must admit I was surprised it was Murphy. I thought it might be a lifeguard really but in a way I'm bloody glad it was him. I only met him a couple of times and I thought he was a twat. As my grandmother used to say "I wouldn't piss up his arse, if his kidneys were on fire." '

Bob joined them and said hello and kissed everyone, bar Ed, which was fine by Ed, one kiss from a bloke in a night was more than enough.

'You must be pleased with yourself?' he sneered at Ed.

'As it happens, I am just a bit. Didn't I tell you, it was someone with a black front door, who had a drop of paint left, was either a copper or a lifeguard? I also recall saying the cockles were just a gimmick and you all laughed or dismissed it. Too bloody right I'm feeling pleased with myself,' Ed said, beaming from ear to ear. 'To be honest, I'm just glad you caught him. You've been a miserable bugger since I got here so it's time to lighten up and get back to catching a few of those sheep shaggers you're always on about.' Bob held out his hand for Ed to shake, which he did. Bob even gave him a man hug or pat on the back as the case may be and genuinely thanked him. He then put his hand in his pocket and bought another round of drinks and ushered them over to some spare tables at the front of the stage, which he reserved earlier.

It seemed like most of the station was there and most were half drunk by the time they sat down, thanks to the generosity of Chief Superintendent Clatworthy. Phil made a point of manoeuvring himself so he ended up seated next to Jacqui and immediately began a conversation with her. Bob did the same with Raechael, leaving Ed, Emma, Chris and Laura to fight over the remaining places. Emma and Chris did their own manoeuvring and ensured that Ed was seated next to Laura with Emma beside him, to make sure he made an effort and to coach him from the side-lines. Fat Boy squeezed in under the table in front of Ed, where he could curl up and sleep if there was nothing to eat on offer.

Ed leaned closer to Laura to hear himself speak over someone singing Dire Straits "Walk of Life", and asked her how her shopping trip was.

'She was bloody miserable all day, Ed,' Raechael leaned over from the other side and told him. 'I think she was missing you.'

Laura gave him a shrug and an embarrassed smile. 'Were you?' he asked.

'Maybe, just a bit,' she said still smiling. 'I was feeling guilty about being hard on you the night before. Sorry but I was pissed off. I was looking forward to lunch and you didn't turn up and I spent all day on my own, bored.'

'Would you like to come to lunch with me tomorrow?' he asked.

'That was a very formal request.'

'It was meant to be. Well, do you?' he asked again.

'What, like a proper date?' she asked smiling broadly.

'Yes. Like a proper date. If you want to that is,' he said, knowing what the answer would be. She grabbed him by the back of the head and pulled him towards her and kissed him passionately, raising a chorus of cheers.

'I take it that was a yes, then?' he said, relishing the taste of her lipstick on his lips.

'Of course I do, stupid,' she replied.

'Who said romance was dead,' Bob piped up.

'You should try it sometime, Bob,' Ed replied.

'I would but I think her mother would slap me if I tried to snog her daughter and you'd probably kick the shit out of me come to that, you evil bastard,' Bob replied happily 'Now go and get the beers in.'

Ed did better than that and came back with a round of drinks, followed by Lisa carrying a tray with six bottles of Champagne and Sue carrying a tray of glasses. Ed was a happy man.

The champagne didn't last that long with Chris around, ably supported by a bunch of her majesty's finest, all with thirsts you could photograph. Beers and shorts were appearing from all directions and Ed was feeling a slightly drunk but wasn't alone. Ed put his name down for Karaoke and got up and gave a fair, if not depressing fist, of Elvis Costello's "A Good Year For The Roses".

'Fuck me, Ed. It's supposed to be a party not a bloody funeral,' Bob told him.

'I thought it was lovely,' Raechael told him. 'Take no notice of him. He's just jealous because he can't sing.'

'Can't sing. I'm bloody marvellous. If he gets up and belts out a proper song and not a soppy, bloody ballad, I'll get up and show you what I'm made of. Deal?' Bob announced much to everyone's delight.

Ed relished the challenge. He flicked through the song list on the table and, keeping it hidden from everyone, filled out one of the slips and handed it to the host, who looked at it, nodded and gave him a look that said it was a good choice. After a rather drunk WPC finished a fairly bad rendition of Gloria Gaynor's "I Will Survive" – yes it was that time already; Ed took the stage and belted out, Golden Earring's "Radar Love". It wasn't the best he had ever sung it but, considering the amount of beer and champagne he had pushed down his neck, it was passable and even got a reasonable round of applause.

'Not bad,' Bob said grudgingly and handed his own slip of paper to the host, who looked at him and shook his head in dismay.

'Can't wait for this,' Ed said.

'He might be quite good. You never know.' Laura said but without much conviction.

Bob took to the stage and the room went silent. Phil got out his phone and started recording. When the intro came over the sound system, Ed's jaw dropped. Bob launched into, "I Fought the Law" by the Clash and was giving it some right welly. At one point he even started playing air guitar. He was good, Ed had to admit, although not to Bob, of course. It was as Bob was milking the standing ovation from his friends and colleagues, he was joined on stage.

Bob's eyes narrowed and he bared his teeth, staring daggers at Mack, who crept onto the stage unnoticed from the left. The clubhouse fell into a deathly silence. Ed smiled, taking great pleasure in Mack's appearance. His eyes were still puffy and swollen, making his small, round eyes appear even smaller and yet somehow sill menacing. His face was a mass of purple and yellowing bruises and his nose was just a pulped mess. Ed was pleased he made such a good job of it, only regretting not going further.

'I don't know why you're fucking smiling. You're about to die you cunt!' Mack spat at him with pure hatred. He turned fully to face Ed, grinning and displaying his rotten teeth well, those Ed hadn't knocked out. It was then Ed noticed the gun he had been concealing, which was now pointing directly at him. 'Thought that might wipe the fucking smile of your face,' he said, grinning insanely. If asked, Ed would have said he was cool, calm and collected but he was, by his own admission, feeling physically sick.

'You're a vindictive bastard, aren't you?' Ed said, standing up and taking a swig from his bottle of Budweiser, trying not to look too frightened, which was easier said than done. Fortunately the beer and champagne was giving him a bit of bravado and was going some way to stop his legs shaking. 'You do realise most of the people in this room are police? Shooting me probably isn't the smartest thing you'll ever do.'

'Like I give a shit.' he spat. 'I'm already fucked for killing the old man. Handy he had this,' he said waving his gun. 'I'm gonna get a stretch either way so I might as well go down knowing I evened the score with you.' He turned quickly pointing the gun at Bob, who was edging closer. 'Don't move any fucking closer or you'll go first, pig,' he shouted, which had the desired effect; Bob stopped in his tracks. 'You know, I might even have a bit of fun first,' he said directing his attention back to Ed. 'Might kill one of your mates first, just for a laugh and to watch you fucking suffer a bit. Got any preference?' he said laughing manically. Ed just stared at him, trying to think of something to do. 'Come on, cat got your tongue? What about the pretty little one or the blonde one? Maybe I'll shoot your little spastic friend. Might even be doing her a fucking favour, putting her out of her misery,' he said grinning. Ed bristled with rage.

'If you've got any sense at all, you'll shoot me first, because if you don't, I'll be up on that stage so fast, you won't get another chance and I swear, I'll tear your fucking head off,' Ed said, full of pent-up anger, eyes blazing.

'Hit a nerve, did I? And you think I'm sick. At least I'm not shagging a fucking cripple.' he shouted, which only enraged Ed more. That and the fact he felt completely impotent, unable to do anything. He turned and smiled at Laura, who was staring straight ahead, with tears rolling down her cheeks.

Ed drained the last of his Budweiser, more for something to do, while he thought of something useful he could do. He held his free hand up and shielded his eyes from the harsh stage lights. 'Lights are a bit bright,' he said glancing at Bob, hoping he might get the message but he was just staring intently at Mack, also wondering what he could do. He knew one of Bob's colleagues would have phoned the emergency services and an armed response unit would be on the way but probably too late. Ed picked up a pint from the table just to his left and took a swig and put it down on the floor in front of him. Mack glared at him intensely.

'What the fuck are you playing at?' he hissed.

'Putting my beer down. Don't want that bugger nicking my last beer' he said pointing at Phil. 'Can't trust these coppers,' he said smiling and hoping Bob was getting all this. 'Might be the last beer I ever have,' he added.

'Put the fucking bottle down, too.' Mack shouted 'I don't want you throwing it at me,' he said, as if he had got one over on him, knowing what Ed was thinking and having out smarted him, which couldn't have been further from the truth.

'This?' Ed said nonchalantly. 'Sorry, too much Karaoke, thought it was a microphone. You never close your eyes anymore, when I kiss your lips,' Ed sang into the bottle, grinning after singing his one line. He then dropped the bottle into the pint glass in front him, shattering it. 'Oops. Must be the bright lights,' he said with a shrug. He looked over at Bob, who gave him an almost imperceptible nod before dropping the microphone he was holding into his own pint, at his feet.

There was a loud bang and the clubhouse fell into darkness. Ed made to sprint forward as Mack fired. Ed saw the muzzle flash and stopped dead. Feeling no pain and realising he wasn't hit, he lunged forward. Just as he reached the stage the second shot was fired, stopping him a second time. In the muzzle flash he could see the outline of two people lying prone on the stage but little else. Ed leapt onto the stage, just as the lights came on.

Bob was kneeling next to Mack, checking for a pulse. Mack himself was unmoving with the gun in his mouth and hand clutched tightly around the trigger. A pool of blood was spreading out across the stage, from the back of his head and from his mouth. Bob stood and pulled Ed away to the right of the stage, putting an arm around him and patting him on the back, letting him know the ordeal was over.

Screams from below startled them. Turning to see what the commotion was, they jumped from the stage and ran to where they had been sitting a few minutes earlier. Bob pushed everyone out of the way with Ed following close on his heels, taking advantage of the space Bob made to get to the source of the screaming. When he got there Phil was trying to pull Chris away, who was on her knees in front of Jacqui, with her head in her lap. Jacqui was slumped in her chair, her head resting on her chest, with a crimson stain in the centre of her white blouse. Phil eventually got Chris to her knees and began walking her away, giving Bob a shake of the head. Ed knew then Jacqui was dead and felt sick to the stomach, knowing it was all his fault. The look of utter hatred that Chris gave him confirmed that.

Bob began to take control of the situation, moving everyone out of the way and barking orders to the other members of the force gathered around him. Raechael wheeled Laura quickly away. She turned around to look for Ed, who was standing trance like, staring at Jacqui, as the reflected blue lights from the ambulance and police cars from outside danced across her face.

CHAPTER 49

Ed was outside, sitting on the ground with his back against the clubhouse wall, Fat Boy beside him. He was smoking what must have been his third or fourth cigarette. Dried tears streaked his face. Bob emerged from the clubhouse and sat down next to him.

'Didn't know you'd started smoking again?' he said, helping himself to one from the box beside Ed, which he took from a table on his way out.

'Could say the same for you?' he replied morosely. 'I only smoke when I'm pissed or pissed off,' he added.

'Me too,' Bob replied, blowing out a long stream of smoke. 'Fuck, fuck, fuck and fuck! I need a drink.'

'Me too. I'll go and get a bottle of something. Not scotch though, I hate that stuff,' he said, getting to his feet. A few minutes later he was back, sitting next to Bob.

'What the bloody hell is that you've got? Looks like a girl's drink,' Bob said in disgust.

'Grand Marnier. I like it. If you don't, tough shit,' Ed said angrily, taking a long pull on the bottle and handing it over. 'Try it. You never know, you might like it.' Bob took a long swig and swallowed.

'It's not bad. A bit sweet but it's got a nice kick and hits the spot. Cheers.' He handed the bottle back. Ed took another large swig. 'I know exactly what you're thinking and it wasn't your fault, you know. Don't go blaming yourself,' he said, putting a hand on Ed's shoulder. 'What you did back there was the right thing to do, bloody clever if you ask me. It's not your fault that stupid bastard couldn't shoot straight. I know what you're like and I know you were trying to get him to shoot you or at least at you. It was a bloody stupid thing to do if you ask me but bloody brave.'

'Oh yeah, really clever. One of the best friends I've ever had got killed. Well done Ed. Give yourself a big, pat on the back,' he said bitterly. 'Now what you did was brave and it could cost you your job.'

'How do you work that one out?' Bob asked, shooting him an angry look.

'Bob,' he said exasperatedly. 'I may be a bit of a fuck-up but there's nothing wrong with my eyesight. I was only standing a yard away. I saw what you did.'

'You saw nothing,' Bob said menacingly. 'What you saw was me trying to take the gun from his mouth before he blew his own head off. It was dark, you were drunk and you weren't thinking straight. If you think you saw something other than that, you're mistaken. Got it?' Ed looked Bob in the eyes.

'Bob, I know what I saw and thanks. Prison was too good for him and if you hadn't done it, I would. I'll swear blind if I have to you were trying to stop him blowing his own brains out but be honest with me.'

'OK, you're right. Happy now? I did it because you're a mad bastard, and I know if I didn't, you would've done, and you would be the one up on a murder charge. I did it to save you from yourself. Ask me again and I'll deny it. You know and I know and this conversation never happened. Got it?' he said in an angry whisper, leaning close to Ed's face.

'Thanks Bob. I think I probably would have killed him, you know,' Ed said as a matter of fact.

'I know and no jury in the world would let you off. Think about it. He knifed your dog and you went after him and beat him to a pulp on the beach. OK, you were provoked when he punched you in the kidneys but you chased him in a bloody speedboat just to get even. When he turned up tonight, they'll just see it as you being vindictive not the other way round. You could get a good lawyer to plead your case, but you wouldn't get an ounce of sympathy. Some bugger had to do something. I could see it in your eyes you weren't taking any prisoners this time. You can be a stupid bastard at times.'

Ed shrugged and was saved from answering by the approach of a police officer he hadn't met before.

'Mr Case?' he said looking down at him. 'We need a statement from you and then you can go home,' Ed stood and walked off to provide them with a few lies.

The interview was with a DCI Morris from Bodmin, who Ed thought was a bit of a jobs-worth. The questioning was direct and, to Ed, seemed like they were out to lynch Bob. Ed gave him a rundown of the chain of events leading up to the culmination of Jacqui's untimely death, which he was asked to provide as background information. Morris constantly checked his notes and nodded so Ed guessed, Emma, Chris and Laura had already been interviewed. Ed gave an account of the evening and made it perfectly clear what he saw. Morris was thorough and tedious, asking the same questions over and over again. Was he was sure of what he saw and could he have been mistaken? Eventually letting him go, advising him a formal statement would be required at a later date.

'Well?' Bob asked when he re-joined him sitting by the wall, still smoking and drinking. Ed lit a cigarette and took a swig from the bottle.

'I told them the truth, of course. When the lights went out, you ran across the stage and wrestled him to the floor and tried to stop him blowing his brains out. I told him a dozen times in a dozen different ways. If I have to, I'll swear on the bible it's the truth. I'm an atheist and if doing that is a sin, well who cares. I don't think I'll be going to heaven, anyway. If there is such a thing as heaven and hell, well, I'm destined for an afterlife of hellfire and damnation downstairs.'

'Thanks, I owe you one.' It came out almost begrudgingly but Ed knew he was being sincere.

'Actually, there is something you can do for me,' Ed said smiling.

'Why don't I like the sound of this? Go on.'

'Well, it's not illegal if that's what you think; quite the opposite actually. It's just that I don't have the stomach for it.'

'Just tell me, for fuck's sake, before I change my mind.'

'Well, it's like this…'

Ed walked back into the clubhouse hoping to find Emma and Chris but was disappointed to find they had already left. Phil told him Chris was inconsolable and had been taken home in a squad car. Ed was wondering if he should call but decided he would do that tomorrow. Chris gave him a look of utter disgust as they passed earlier. He thought it best to give her some time. Hopefully, by tomorrow she would be a little more approachable. Laura and Raechael were just leaving and Ed jogged to catch them up. Raechael gave him a sympathetic look and made her excuses that she needed to see Bob, leaving them alone.

'Wanna go home?' he asked her. Laura nodded and Ed pushed her along, walking in silence, Fat Boy trotting behind. When they reached her caravan, she invited him in for coffee but Ed declined.

'Want to come in and not have coffee, then?' she asked, giving him a weak smile.

'I don't think I'd be much company to be honest. Are you OK, by the way?' he asked, genuinely concerned.

'Fine. A bit shocked that's all. I'm just glad that evil bastard's dead,' she said venomously.

'You and me both. He's bloody ruined my holiday. He was a right nasty piece of work. What he said about you really pissed me off. I only wish I could've got hold of him before he shot himself.'

'People have called me worse. How are you, though?'

Ed shrugged. He didn't know how to put how he felt into words. He was bloody angry and at the same time grieving at the loss of one of his oldest and dearest friends. He leant down and pulled Laura up and hugged her, relishing the comfort of being close to someone.

'Are you sure you don't want to come in for coffee?' she asked.

Ed shook his head. 'I'll call you tomorrow. Don't we have a lunch date?' he said sadly. Laura nodded and returned his smile before opening the door, leaving him standing alone.

CHAPTER 50

In the morning, after a sleepless and tearful night, Ed still felt numb from grief. It had been a few years since he felt like this, since the loss of his parents and it wasn't any easier to cope with. He stood in the shower for a long time, eventually slumping down into a sitting position letting the scolding water cascade over him. He rested his arms across his knees, hung his head and wept, silently. Eventually, he pulled himself upright, stepped from the cubicle, wrapped a towel round his waist and walked out to slump on the sofa.

By mid-morning he had shaken off his melancholy mood and decided he needed fresh air and stimulation. He tried picking up the phone and dialling Emma's number but each time he cancelled the call. Somehow, he couldn't face being told that a call to Chris would be as welcome as rusty razor blade at a Brit Milah and gave up trying to pluck up the courage. His leg was aching, probably through tiredness but decided he didn't need the stick, better to push through the pain, hoping it might ease, once the stitches were removed in a couple of days. That reminded him Fat Boy's stitches were also due to be removed. He seemed to be coping with his much better, lucky bugger.

Ed sat down at his favourite spot looking out over the rock pools, watching the tide creep slowly up the beach, which was relaxing and helped clear his mind. His telephone rang startling him, breaking the almost near silence, with the exception of the waves pounding the beach below. He looked at the number and saw that it was Phil, having programmed him in after his last call.

'Hi Phil,' he said, trying to sound cheery but failing miserably.

'Hi Ed. How's it going?' was his monotone response.

'To be honest Phil, I feel like a right shit. I can't shake off the feeling that it was my fault. I just want to turn the clock back two weeks and do everything differently. Only it's a bit late for that now. You can't be feeling too great yourself. I know you and Jacqui were quite close in a way.'

'We were. I always had a soft spot for her but, you know, working together it was kind of frowned on to get your honey where you make your money, to coin a phrase. Left it too bloody late, didn't I? I wouldn't go blaming yourself, though. That's the reason I'm ringing. We've had the ballistics report back. It turns out the barrel of that pistol was as bent as a nine bob note. On top of that, the barrel was full of crap and probably hadn't been cleaned since World War II and the bullets were filthy. He probably had more chance of winning the lottery than shooting you with that thing. It was just bad luck he hit anyone, let alone Jacqui.'

'Thanks Phil, I appreciate the call but I can't say it makes me feel any better knowing that. If I hadn't tried to punch his lights out that night in the clubhouse, none of this would have happened. Simple as that.' Ed let out a long sigh and sniffed, knowing he was close to tears again.

'Pull yourself together. It was just another case of wrong place, wrong time. You can't blame yourself for everything. I for one don't believe in the butterfly effect. Come on, get over it.' Ed nodded, completely forgetting he was on the phone. 'You still there?'

'Yeah, I'm here. Look, thanks for letting me know, Phil. I really appreciate you trying to help. I'll see you around.'

'I've been round to see Chris this morning, if you're interested?' he said, not adding anything, tempting Ed to continue the call.

'How is she? She was in a bad way last night. I've been meaning to phone her all day but after the look she gave me last night, I don't think I'll get a warm reception.'

'She's OK, just a bit shaken up. Emma's doing a good job of looking after her. She's quite tough that one,' he said in genuine admiration.

'Yep. She's had a hard time of it recently so she knows the kind of thing Chris is going through.'

'You should give Chris a call. I'm sure she'd appreciate it or maybe go and see her. She could probably do with a friendly face or two. Anyway gotta go, lots of work to do. I just wanted to tell you about the ballistics.'

Ed hung up and thought about what Phil had told him. OK so the gun was shaped like a banana and it was just a horrible fluke, but the bottom line was he was the catalyst for the whole thing and no matter how hard he tried, he couldn't see past that. He sat there staring out to sea, legs dangling over the ridge of the gently graduating slope of the cliff, stroking Fat Boy, who had adopted the same pose. How he wished he could turn back the clock as he remembered the good times shared with Jacqui over the last twenty years, of which there were plenty. It didn't help.

'Hi Ed, want some company?'

Ed turned around to see the welcoming face of Laura. She looked melancholy but still as beautiful as ever.

'Of course,' he tried to say enthusiastically, standing up and giving her a hug. She put her arms around his neck and he lifted her from her wheelchair and put her down next to where he had been sitting, sat down himself and embraced her. 'To be honest I could use the company, it might help me shake off the blues.'

Laura said nothing, knowing whatever she said wouldn't make much difference but kissed him on the cheek and smiled broadly at him, which did help.

'I told you, it wasn't your fault,' she said, after Ed had given her the update from Phil. 'Don't keep torturing yourself over it. It was an accident, they happen. The driver, who knocked me off my bike didn't mean to do it. It wasn't his fault I had a tumour and dislodged it, leaving me in a wheelchair. It happened; nobody was to blame. Just like last night. He could have shot anyone or nobody, it just happened. Please don't shoulder all the blame,' she said, staring at him earnestly.

'I know, you're right but it's so difficult. What really makes it worse is the look Chris gave me, that really hurt. God, I'm a walking disaster. Seems like everything I do turns to rat shit,' he said and blew out hard and stared at the sky, forcing back the tears that were there, stinging his eyes. The slap across his face wasn't particularly hard but took him by surprise.

'Pull yourself together, Ed!' she said harshly 'Wallowing in self-pity isn't going to get you anywhere. Put yourself in Chris's shoes and just imagine how she felt afterwards. Her best friend since school, shot in front of her eyes. Of course she's going to be pissed off and look for someone to blame. She's probably sitting at home right now, feeling exactly like you are, regretting taking it out on you like that. I bet you haven't even phoned her, have you? I thought not,' she said when Ed shook his head. 'Well do it. Don't let his drag on and on and leave it until it's too late. Come on, get your phone out and do it now. Sorry about the slap, by the way,' she said giving him a sheepish grin.

Ed looked at her, shocked at how forceful she was and smiled at her. Not that he should have been surprised, as it was no different from how she behaved when they first met. Although only a week or so ago, it seemed a lot longer; a lot had happened in that time. He had certainly grown very fond of her that was for sure. Laura coughed and reminded him to make the call. Ed picked up the phone and dialled, this time not hanging up.

Chris answered and despite seeming a little low, as would be expected under the circumstances, she was civil and understanding. She told him that Phil had been round and explained about the pistol and scolded him for being such an idiot for trying to get himself shot. She also apologised for the look she gave him and assured him she didn't blame him. Ed felt so relieved and his mood improved considerably. He suggested coming to see her in the afternoon. She said she'd like that, telling him to bring Laura along. He said he would ask her and put his hand over the phone and did just that and told her she would be coming. When he hung up he was actually smiling.

'Yes I am looking down your top before you ask,' Ed said as he pushed Laura back towards home. Fortunately, she didn't seem too bothered and didn't give him another slap. 'Bollocks. I was supposed to be taking you to lunch,' he said, having completely forgotten.

'There's always tomorrow,' she said, looking up at him and smiling.

'Yeah right. We've been saying that for four days now and today was supposed to be an official date,' he said, reminding her of their conversation last night.

'So you can take me on an official date to see Chris and Emma. I'm not really hungry anyway.'

'Me neither. Maybe I'll take you to dinner tonight, he replied, adding 'Unless you're busy or have another date perhaps?'

'Oh yeah, I've got them lined up by the dozen, because I'm such a catch,' she said cheerfully enough but he could tell there was some bitterness there.

'I think so,' he said, without hesitating, surprising himself.

'In that case, you get to go to the front of the queue.'

'If I'm not, I'll just do as they do in Germany and push in. I might even leave a towel on your lap, just to make sure I'm first every day.'

'There won't be too many of those left, will there? What are your plans anyway?' she asked with a hint of sadness in her voice.

'I don't know. Fat Boy has to have his stitches out in a day or so as do I, assuming the doctor says they can come out, which I might as well have done here. Then there's the funeral and after that I don't know. When are you going home?'

'Next week is our last week. I think probably next Friday to give us the weekend at home to get straight, before going back to work; something you wouldn't know about.'

'Well, I won't be sticking around after that, then. Not much point really. Emma's all sorted now with Chris and seems to be settled. She doesn't need me anymore and she'll be good company for Chris too, so they're both alright. If you and your mum are gone, then I might as well go back home myself, as there's nothing to hang around for.'

'Will you keep in touch, after you go?' she asked.

'Of course I bloody will, stupid. And you only live a few miles away so I might even come and pay you the odd visit, if you like.'

'Really?' she asked and seemed surprised.

'Of course I will. Your mum's a fantastic cook. Where else am I going to get the best sea bass in town? You're so dumb,' he teased.

'Bastard,' she replied with a smile.

CHAPTER 51

Ed parked up in the courtyard at the back of the shop and knocked on the door. Emma opened it and smiled. Fat Boy gave her a cursory sniff, hurtled by her and ran up the stairs to be the first to greet Chris. Ed carried Laura up the stairs and then went back down for the wheelchair. In the living room, Chris was sitting at one end of the sofa, with Fat Boy curled up next to her, with his head in her lap, tail thumping quickly and nervously, knowing he shouldn't be on the furniture. Emma suggested to Laura, she might like to see her paintings and left Chris and Ed alone. Ed ordered Fat Boy down and took his place next to Chris, giving her a hug. Chris was the first to break the silence.

'Ed, I'm so sorry about last night. I was wrong to take it out on you. It wasn't your fault and you shouldn't blame yourself. It was just one of those things.'

'I'm just glad you're still speaking to me. I was worried sick that things would never be the same again between us. You've got Laura to thank for that. You know she slapped me round the face, told me to get a grip and to give you a call.'

'Well, she's the first person I know to lay a finger on you and not need hospital treatment. It must be serious,' she said with a knowing look. 'Going OK on that front, is it?'

'Well, we still haven't managed to have that lunch date, four days running now but I'm sure we will soon.'

'Pretty girl, isn't she?' she said rhetorically 'Seems to like you a lot. I think she might even be a little bit in love with you,' she added, grinning at Ed's obvious embarrassment. 'What about you, how do you feel?' Ed shrugged and felt compelled to add more after Chris frowned at him.

'She's nice,' he replied.

'Nice? Come on, you can do better than that. What do you really feel?' Ed laughed.

'I like her. OK, I like her a lot,' he added after receiving another one of her looks. 'She's good looking, good company and I'm really happy but I've not even been on a first date yet so what can else can I say?'

'Same old Ed,' she said exasperatedly. 'Do something soon or you might end up regretting it.'

'Again,' Ed replied, looking directly at Chris, who wasn't slow to pick up on the inference and shook her head sadly.

'A long time ago, Ed and a lot of water's flowed under the bridge since. Just don't get cold feet with Laura, OK?'

'OK.' he replied.

'Come on, let's go and see Emma's paintings,' she said and slapped him on his thigh, right on his stitches. Ed winced 'Sorry, forgot,' she said with a chuckle.

Ed parked the car outside his caravan, having spent a nice afternoon chatting and having three women generally teasing him. Emma was quick to fill the gap left behind by Jacqui, despite only knowing him a matter of weeks, throwing in the odd hint about him and Laura making a go of it, for good measure. Laura was slightly embarrassed as was Ed but she seemed to like the idea of Emma and Chris doing their best to match-make.

In the evening they ate a takeaway curry, which Ed picked up on his way back from walking Fat Boy, along with a box of dried food and a couple of tins for the dog as he wasn't risking giving him curry, not after the last time. Ed was a bit drunk and left the carton on the floor and fell asleep in the armchair. When he came down in the morning the smell was horrendous as was the kitchen floor, covered in several piles of runny dog shit. No, he wasn't making that mistake again, especially not in a caravan.

He unbuckled his seatbelt and rubbed his aching thigh, giving Laura a quick smile. Her hand moved across and replaced his on his thigh. 'Does it hurt?' she asked quietly.

'Just aches a bit every now and again. Driving doesn't help, especially round these bendy roads, having to change gear so often,' Laura leaned over and kissed him on the lips and before he knew it they were kissing passionately.

'God, I feel like teenager again,' Ed said chuckling.

'You're not going to put your hand up my skirt and see how many fingers you can get up my fanny are you, and then go bragging to your mates?' she said making him laugh and blush at the memories of doing exactly that once or twice; boasting with friends to see who held the record for how many and how far up.

'Only if you want me to?' he replied. 'Personally, I'd like to think my technique has improved a little since those days, although I might do, just for a trip down memory lane.'

A thump on the roof of the car scared them both half to death and set Fat Boy barking. Ed jumped out the car, ready to give someone a piece of his mind and came face to face with Bob, grinning like an oversized schoolboy, with his arm around Raechael's shoulder; all that was missing were the grey shorts and matching cap. If Ed was to search his pockets he was sure he would find a conker and a catapult.

'Your face is a picture.' he said laughing. 'I'm not sure if you look guilty or pissed off. Give you a fright, did I?' Ed made light of it but could have killed him. 'I saw you pull up as we were coming back from the pub. Thought you might like a nightcap as you obviously haven't had a drink.'

'Your place or mine?' Ed asked. 'I'm ok with either; as we're here, my place?'

It wasn't the end to the evening he had in mind but it was enjoyable all the same. All he wanted to do was to have a bit of time alone with Laura, just for a change, but it seemed it wasn't meant to be. Bob was in good spirits, despite officially being on a leave of absence, pending an internal inquiry over the shooting incident. Unofficially, he was still working on wrapping up some paperwork from old cases and also unofficially, been cleared of any wrongdoing. Whether it was because, despite his roguish behaviour and unorthodox, politically incorrect ways of working, he was actually well respected or because Mack was a nasty piece of work who would be missed by nobody, or a combination of both, nobody involved in the subsequent investigation seemed to work too hard on trying to pin a murder charge on him. To Bob, it gave him a few days holiday to spend with Raechael, which suited him after the stress of the Black Cockle Strangler and of course, living with the guilt of killing Mack; the latter being easier to cope with, on account of Bob not having a conscience.

Bob made it clear he was staying the night, not that Ed offered. Ed would have preferred he went and stayed with Raechael. He could then have Laura as a guest but as he didn't know how to broach the subject, he left it at that. Raechael suggested she and Laura go home, as it was late. She wanted to make it known to Bob, although she was fond of him, she didn't want to sleep with him or not yet anyway. Ed suggested Bob and Raechael leave first, initially saying by the time he got the wheelchair out and Laura into it, they would be holding them up. In truth, Ed didn't want to see Bob snogging Raechael goodnight, not after a curry and a few glasses of wine, it could be dangerous.

CHAPTER 52

Ed was up early the next day, in spite of a late night, once again having difficulty sustaining sleep. Nightmares of Charlotte's massive chest replaced by vivid dreams of Jacqui, slumped in a chair with blood oozing from her chest. In his dream she lifts her head, smiles, points an accusing finger at him and says 'It's all your fault.' Ed would wake, soaked in sweat and fighting for breath. Eventually sleep would come, only for the dream to recur. A shrink would probably have a field day with him, he thought. Filling his head full of crap about some syndrome or another and charge him a fortune for telling him what he already knew. No matter how hard he tried and how hard other people tried, he still felt responsible. Ed hoped that time would stand up to its reputation of being a good healer and what he was experiencing wasn't going to eat away at him like cancer. He'd been there once before and didn't want to go back there in a hurry. He finally gave up on trying to sleep, got up and took Fat Boy for a walk along the beach, where he sat down to watch the sunrise, trying to block out the morning chill and the lingering memory of his dreams.

When he got back to the caravan, Bob was up and about and thankfully making a fry-up. He was either hungry or he was making enough for two; fortunately it turned out to be the latter.

'You were up early,' Bob commented, with a mouthful of fried egg, which wasn't the pleasantest of sights.

'Bad dreams,' Ed replied. Bob nodded as if he knew what the dreams were about.

'They'll pass,' he said reassuringly.

'What about you? Having any trouble sleeping?' Ed asked, knowing if he murdered somebody, he would definitely have a very troubled conscience.

'No, as far as I'm concerned, I done you a favour and the tax payer, therefore, my conscience is clear. Anyway, he took his own life, didn't he?' He gave the last part as a statement rather than a question and Ed took the hint.

'Lucky you, I'm bloody shattered. Good fry-up by the way, thanks. Working today or spending some time with the lovely Raechael?' Ed asked.

'A little bit of both. Got a few things to clear up with the Murphy business and this afternoon, I'm going to take Raechael for lunch. What about you?'

'Off to buy a suit for the funeral on Monday. I don't have one here. Never thought I'd need one. I might give Chris and Emma a shout see if they want to go shopping.'

'What about Laura? From what I saw last night, you seemed to be getting on famously,' he said grinning.

'Absence makes the heart grow fonder, so they say,' Ed replied 'but I'll go over and say hello before I go.'

'So you can get reacquainted with her tonsils more like.'

'I was hoping to get acquainted with a lot more than her tonsils last night, until some twat started banging on the roof of my car. Thanks to you, I'm still walking round with testicles the size of water bowsers.'

'I know the feeling,' Bob replied. 'Anyway, cheers for the bed but I've gotta go. I cooked so you can do the dishes,' he said picking up his jacket.

'Bob. Do you want a spare key for this place?' Ed asked.

'Are you suggesting me and Raechael use this place like a cheap motel?' Bob asked rather indignantly.

'Am I bollocks. I'm asking if you want a spare key, in case I'm not here for any reason and you're too pissed to get a cab home. Even you wouldn't stoop that low, would you?' Ed said to try to rattle him a little. It didn't work. Bob seemed to be in a buoyant mood and wasn't going to be lured into being riled.

'Give me some credit you cretin. And thanks for the offer but I can call out one of the uniforms to get me home if I need to. Perks of the job.'

'Bloody hypocrite. I thought you were all for saving the tax payer money a minute ago.'

'Like I said, perks of the job. Might see you later or not. Don't wait up.'

CHAPTER 53

It was the day of the funeral and Ed was driving into Padstow contemplating the last few days. Fat Boy was curled up in the back sleeping. He eventually managed to find a suit, in Bodmin, and just made it back in time to take Laura on their lunch date. Fifth time lucky wasn't what sprang instantly to mind. In his haste not to keep his date waiting, he was nearly run off the road by an old fart in a 4x4 who seemed to think he needed and was entitled to more road than was strictly required. OK, Ed was driving a little too fast for the narrow lane but the old fart had the reaction time of a sloth on cannabis. Fortunately, there had been a gate set back slightly from the road, enabling Ed to swerve at the last minute to avoid a collision. He arrived a few minutes late but Laura didn't seem to mind. They had a nice walk to the pub, both looking forward to their first date proper. When they arrived, Raechael and Bob were already sitting in the beer garden, looking over the menu. Ed tried to make as if he hadn't seen them but it was too late and they ended up on a double date. It was pleasant enough but not what either of them had in mind. The penny seemed to drop with Raechael and after they finished eating, she made an excuse to leave. Bob on the other hand wasn't quite so aware and tried to insist they stay for another drink. Considering Bob was a detective, he was a bit slow on the uptake and Ed wondered how he managed to get where he was today. Unless of course, as with the recent serial killer, he relied on this underlings to do the thinking for him, a bit like the cartoon character, Hong Kong Phooey, who only solved a crime with the help of Spot, the police station cat.

Once Raechael and Bob left, Ed and Laura gave them a few minutes head start and walked back. They stopped and sat on the beach, propping themselves up against a sand dune, to people watch and just spend time together. For Ed it was a great way to take his mind off the recent events and the forthcoming funeral, which he really wasn't looking forward to. Once it was over, perhaps he would be able to draw a line under it and try to move on, although he knew it would be imbedded in his memory forever.

That night they ventured over to the clubhouse, at Ed's request. It was the first time since the shooting and Ed had argued he couldn't avoid it forever. They made sure they sat well away from where they were the night Jacqui was killed but both found it difficult to relax. When the lights went out, as was the norm, the memories of that night flooded back and lingered long after they came back on. In the end, after only a couple drinks, they went for a stroll in the warm evening air. They sat down on the clifftop and listened to the waves crashing on the rocks below, as the gibbous moon moved across the sky, reflecting on the calm water below.

They spent a great deal of time together and even Ed, cynical as he was, realised they had become quite close. The relationship had not yet developed past anything other than frequent kissing and cuddling and Ed wasn't sure why this was. It certainly wasn't a lack of desire. She had a fantastic figure and was beautiful beyond Ed's wildest dreams. He would've liked nothing more than to get naked and physical with her but for some reason he held back. Laura found it frustrating, both physically and mentally. She wanted a more hands on relationship and was beginning to wonder if Ed was reluctant to take it further because he was still scarred by the painful memories of his ex-wife or if it was because of her disability. She didn't want to broach the subject, for fear of spoiling what they did have. However, she was conscious that the clock was ticking and had less than a week left together. Perhaps she would take matters into her own hands, quite literally and vowed to do so as soon as the funeral was over, which might also be a factor in Ed's reluctance to commit.

Ed pulled up in the yard behind Chris's shop and let Fat Boy out, telling him to be on his best behaviour and not to jump up at anyone. Fat Boy gazed up at him, not understanding a word of what was said. Chris opened the door, dressed in a black suit and her hair tied up in a bun at the back of her head.

'You look nice,' Ed said, unsure if that was the right thing to say or not but said it anyway.

'Liar. I've been crying all bloody morning and I know what I look like,' she said attempting a smile.

'OK. You've got eyes like two blood oranges with big bags under them and your only redeeming feature is that you smell good,' Ed replied grinning.

'I think I preferred you lying to me. Coffee or something stronger?'

'Coffee please, I'm driving.'

'Really? I assumed you'd be having a few drinks after or do you have a hot date tonight?' she teased.

'I haven't arranged anything so I could leave the car here and get a cab back, if that's OK with you? I must admit I've been running on autopilot all morning and just jumped in the car.'

'No problem. Just leave me the keys before you go, in case I need to move it.'

'Good, cancel the coffee. I'll have a red wine.' As Chris left the living room to fetch some wine, Emma walked in and gave him a hug.

'She's been a bit of a mess this morning so no bad jokes, OK. I know what you're like,' Emma said earnestly. 'Anyway, are you OK?'

'I've not been sleeping too well, since the night in the clubhouse. I keep having bad dreams and can't get back to sleep again. Apart from being knackered, I'm OK.' Ed told her about this recurring nightmare and how vivid they were.

'Still blaming yourself, then?' she said, not expecting anything from Ed other than a shrug; he duly obliged. Emma shook her head in dismay. 'It wasn't your fault and nobody's blaming you. What you need is a distraction,' she said firmly. 'How's it going with Laura?' she added, grinning at him.

'Great. Couldn't be better,' he said, not elaborating further.

'Have you? Well you know...' Ed knew what she was implying but was enjoying watching her struggle to say it.

'Have I what?'

'Have you slept with her yet?' she asked blushing.

'No. I've got no further than a snog,' he said smiling back at her.

'Really, waiting until you're married? That's sweet,' she teased.

'Waiting for the right moment and a bit of time alone, which I don't seem to get, because it seems everywhere I go, bloody Bob's there, fawning over Raechael. If it goes on any longer, I'm gonna have to start buying larger pants, if you get my drift.' Ed informed her making her laugh. Chris came in with the wine and looked at them with a raised eyebrow, wondering what the joke was.

'Ed was just telling me how he was getting on with Laura, which isn't very far by the sound of things.'

'What you haven't, you know?' Chris asked as tentatively as Emma did.

'No, I bloody haven't and don't remind me. I'm seriously worried if our relationship does progress further, as soon as she lays a finger on me, my cock's going to explode, like one of those joke cigars.'

'Too much information, Ed. You're gross,' Emma told him. Chris agreed.

After a couple of glasses of wine, they left for the church, which was only a short walk away. Ed left Fat Boy outside and he seemed content to lie in the sun, watching the entrance until his master returned. The church itself was not large and was fairly full. She had only a handful of relatives there, including her mother and father, who had flown back from Spain. The rest were her many friends and old police colleagues.

Ed knew this wouldn't be a traditional funeral as Jacqui hated all the hymns and prayers. He was still surprised when Frank Sinatra came over the speaker system, singing 'The Impossible Dream' as the pall bearers carried the coffin in. The vicar gave a nice eulogy, most of which had been provided by Chris, who was now crying silently next to him. Ed had packed a couple of packets of tissues and handed one of them to her and put an arm around her shoulder. He hated it when women cried, as he never knew how to react. Fortunately, the service was brief and ended with Ruby Turner belting out, 'Stay With Me Baby', which was Jacqui's favourite song. Shortly after it started, just about everyone in the church was reaching for their tissues and handkerchiefs or accepting the offer of one from the person next to them.

They gathered around the grave and the coffin was lowered and the vicar began the burial service. When he recited the ashes to ashes, dust to dust part, Ed immediately wanted to sing funk to funky, we know Major Tom's a junky and put it down to nerves. He was just glad when it was all over.

Everyone was invited back for drinks and nibbles at Chris's place but only a few family members and close friends took up the offer, around twenty in all. The place was crowded but not claustrophobically so. Ed was wandering around, mingling and was dreading meeting Jacqui's parents but they were OK and didn't seem to hold Ed responsible, which was a relief. In the main, most people were talking about how much they hated funerals. Ed was inclined to agree but the one previous had been fantastic as it was his ex-wife's. His only regret was she was cremated and not buried so there was no grave to dance on, whenever he felt in need of a bit of cheering up. He kept that opinion to himself.

As the drink flowed, the conversations turned to more general topics. Everyone seemed to have forgotten or put to one side why they were actually gathered there in the first place. Maybe it was just Ed but he couldn't think of anything else and decided he needed a bit of space. He took Fat Boy for a quick walk and rang Laura to say he might be later than expected. When he returned, he grabbed a glass of wine and made his escape to the studio, to admire Emma's paintings. He slumped down onto the floor with his back to the wall and stared at Emma's latest piece of work. It was another seascape showing a watery sunset, reflecting off the calm sea and, like the others she had painted, was brilliant. His thoughts turned to Jacqui and of the many good times they shared over the past twenty years, trying to fight back the tears that were stinging his eyes, eventually giving up and letting them spill down his cheeks.

Chris walked in to the studio, carrying a newly opened bottle of wine and sat down next to him and filled his now empty glass.

'I saw you sneak out earlier and thought you might be in here,' she said softly.

'I just wanted a few minutes on my own to think. I can't get that bloody, stay with me baby, song out of my head. It always did give me a lump in the throat. Was that your choice?'

'No, she had it all written down in her will. She made it out last year after taking over the business.'

'When I went round to see her the other day, she told me the reason she gave up the police was because she was diagnosed with angina. It just coincided nicely with her parents deciding they wanted to go to Spain,' Ed told her, waiting for a reaction from Chris.

'Really? She never told me,' Chris said, hurt her best friend had kept something this important from her.

'The reason she didn't tell you or anyone was because she didn't anyone to make a fuss and treat her differently. I just managed to wheedle it out of her and was sworn to secrecy. Guess it doesn't need to a secret be now.'

'I suppose not. I know that you slept with her, as well, when she was in London,' she told him. Ed stared as her not knowing what to say. 'I knew, anyway. Well, I could tell something was up, when she came back and said she'd seen you. It's not a problem. I don't know why you kept it from me.'

'Don't know really. It wasn't something that was planned, it just happened a bit like with you and I, but at least she didn't tell me it was like sleeping with her brother,' Ed replied, trying to make light of it. Chris laughed at the memory.

'Come on, let's get back and be sociable,' she said, standing up and pulling Ed to his feet, giving him a hug.

CHAPTER 54

Ed knew something wasn't right, the minute he opened his eyes and looked at the unfamiliar surroundings and not being able to place where he was. Emma was lying beside him smiling

'Morning Tiger.' she said, kissing him on the cheek.

'Oh shit,' Ed said quietly. 'We didn't... I mean... you know?' Ed asked completely flustered.

'You mean, you don't remember?' Emma said, pretending to be hurt by his lack of memory.

'Er... No. The last thing I remember was sitting on the couch drinking wine,' Ed said apologetically, desperately trying to recall the bits in between the couch and waking up.

'That's because it was the last thing you did. That is until you fell asleep and started snoring. Chris and I had to carry you to the bedroom,' she said, still grinning broadly. Ed moved his hand under the covers and discovered he was naked.

'I see you weren't the perfect gentleman that I was,' Ed said embarrassed.

'I told you I wouldn't be,' she said laughing.

'I hope you were suitably impressed?' Ed said grumpily. Emma pretended to think about it for a while before telling him she wasn't. 'Thanks. After all I've done for you and you don't even have the courtesy to lie to me to make me feel good,' Ed said feigning indignation. Ed gave her a sly look and pulled back the sheet, to find as he suspected, she too was naked. Emma shrugged and gave him a so what look.

'See anything you like?' she asked. Ed ran his hand over her calf up to her thigh and lingered on her hip, before caressing her buttocks and moving on over her waist and further, cupping her breast.

'No, nothing. 34B if I'm not mistaken and I prefer a C cup to be honest,' Ed replied flatly.

'You're mean and if you don't like the size of my breasts, get your hands off,' she told him. 'The last thing I want is for that thing to go off like an exploding cigar,' she said in reference to yesterday's conversation, making Ed laugh. 'Anyway, we don't want to leave the tank empty for Laura, do we?' Ed gave her a weary smile.

'Very droll. So nothing happened last night, then? Ed asked.

'You snored and farted a few times but no, nothing happened,' she gave him a serious look before adding. 'I'm waiting for the results of an aids test, if you must know. Chris said it would probably be a good idea, as Danny and his friends were all users and well, after what happened...' Ed leaned over and gave her a hug

'I didn't think about that. When are you expecting the results?' he asked concerned.

'Today. Jacqui had a few friends in the labs at the hospital and pulled in a favour to get them fast tracked. I'm sure I'm clear but better to be sure,' Ed looked her in the eye and could tell it was just bravado. 'Do you love Laura?' she asked out of the blue, taking Ed completely off guard.

'Er... I dunno? Strange question to ask,' he replied flustered.

'Oh, come on, Ed. It's a simple enough question. How do you feel about her?'

'She's nice and we get along well together,' Ed replied, thinking it was a good answer. Emma clearly didn't and frowned.

'Do you get butterflies in your stomach when you see her for the first time each day? Ed nodded. 'Right, and do you think about her a lot, when you haven't seen her for a while?' Again, Ed nodded. 'Good, and when you are together, do you feel the urge to hold her, kiss her and hug her all the time?' Ed nodded again. 'When she laughs or smiles, does it make your heart race?' Ed nodded. 'OK, and does the thought of never seeing her again, make you feel sick?' Ed nodded again 'Right, that's it, questions over. I think we can safely say you're in love. Next thing is you need to tell her, because I know for a fact she loves you. She told me.'

'She never told me,' Ed said, surprised by this revelation.

'You can be so dumb at times. Of course she's not going to tell you, in case she frightens you off, because she doesn't know how you feel, because you never tell anyone how you feel. Now get out of here and go and tell her.' she said, shaking her head.

Ed jumped out of bed forgetting his nakedness and stood there looking for his clothes. 'Emma, what have you done with my clothes?' he asked, looking confused.

'Oh, they're around somewhere, you just have to look,' she replied. Ed found a sock on the back of a chair, which was a start and soon located the other one on the wardrobe door handle. He was spinning round, frantically trying to assemble the rest of his clothing without much luck, whilst Emma lay back in the bed laughing at him, which wasn't helping matters. He found his shirt under the bed and put that on and found his suit hanging up inside the wardrobe. His shoes were on a shelf, barely visible due to a large stuffed teddy bear being placed on top of them. By the time he dressed, he was sweating.

'Thanks Emma,' Ed said sarcastically and leaned across the bed and kissed her goodbye.

'Ed,' she called, just as he was walking out into the hallway. He turned and gave her a quizzical look. 'Nice cock, by the way,' she said, giving him a wide smile.

'Yeah, very funny. Grow up and get yourself a pair of tits,' he said smiling back and receiving a pout in return.

Today was the first day in around three weeks the sun was not shining. The sky was dark and brooding; rain didn't look to be too far away. Ed wasn't bothered, as he drove down the narrow winding lanes with Fat Boy curled up in the boot, on his way to meet Laura. Emma was right, he needed to tell Laura how he felt about her and try and make a go of their relationship. She would be going in a few days and not seeing her after was not something he wanted to consider. Emma was right on that front. The thought of not seeing her again did make him feel sick inside. Whether that was love or not was another thing but if it wasn't, then perhaps it was something pretty close.

He parked the car beside his caravan, let the dog out and went into the caravan. He made sure Fat Boy had fresh water and gave him some breakfast before leaving him behind, knowing Chris had already taken him for a walk, first thing and headed over to see Laura.

CHAPTER 55

'Where have you been? I've been trying to get hold of you all night and all morning,' Laura berated, as soon as he sat down.

'Don't ask,' he replied happily, retrieving his mobile phone from his jacket pocket and seeing it was switched off. 'I think Emma must have switched it off.'

'You're still wearing your suit. Did you stay over?' she asked.

'Don't go there. I had a few too many, fell into a deep sleep and got put to bed. I would have been here sooner but Emma hid my clothes all round the bedroom and it took me bloody ages to find them all, while she lay there laughing,' he told her shaking his head and smiling at the memory.

'Are you telling me you slept with Emma?' she said quietly. Before Ed could explain, she jumped to the conclusion he had. 'You bastard.' She shouted 'I thought we had something special. Well, clearly I was mistaken, I hate you!' she shouted before spinning round in her chair and wheeling herself out the caravan, slamming the door behind her, leaving Ed stunned.

A minute or so later the door opened and he expected to see Laura but it was Raechael.

'Oh hello, Ed,' she said, surprised to see him. 'Where was my daughter going in such a hurry?'

'I was explaining why I didn't make it back last night and she didn't let me finish. Now she thinks I slept with Emma and thinks I'm a bastard and hates me,' Ed said wearily.

'And did you?' she asked as she put her groceries on the table. Ed explained what happened, making it perfectly clear he only shared a bed and nothing else. 'So that's it, is it? You're just going to sit here feeling sorry for yourself?' she asked rhetorically.

'Look, she's a bit hot headed, probably gets it from me. She didn't mean what she said. Why don't you go and tell her? That's what she wants you to do.'

'It sounded very much like she meant it to me and doesn't want anything to do with me,' Ed replied sadly.

'You don't know much about women, do you? Of course she didn't mean it. She wants you to go running after her. Go and find her, Ed.' Ed shook his head not comprehending the complex nature of the fairer sex.

'Wouldn't know where to look,' he said sulkily.

'Where would you go, Ed? That's where she'll be,' she replied, giving him a smile of encouragement. Ed knew exactly where he would go to be alone and stood to leave. He kissed Raechael and set off with purpose through the camp site.

As he set off to find Laura, the rain started. It was only a very light drizzle but one look at the dark, brooding clouds told him it was going to pour down and would probably continue for most of the day.

He could see Laura, sitting, looking out over the cliffs in the very spot she found him sitting a couple of days ago, completely oblivious to the rain. He silently thanked Raechael and walked towards her.

'You'll go rusty sitting there in the rain,' Ed said quietly, as he approached and stood next to Laura.

'Piss off and go annoy someone else. Someone like Emma, perhaps,' she said bitterly.

'Laura, I've come to explain. You didn't let me finish earlier and jumped to conclusions.'

'Oh, that's nice of you. Come to explain you slept with Emma because she can give you what I can't. How very nice of you but save your breath and leave me alone,' she spun her chair round and was about to set off, until Ed grabbed the wheel nearest him to stop her, pulling her round to face him.

'Will you just shut up and hear me out. If you still feel the same afterwards, fine. I'll leave you alone and let you get on with the rest of your life,' he said angrily. Laura was still trying to wheel herself away and thumped the back of his hand hard, crushing his fingers on the wheel. That was the final straw for Ed. He was determined to have this conversation, no matter what and spun her chair back round hard to face him and began rocking it from side to side.

'If these stupid legs of mine worked, I'd kick you right in the balls,' she said angrily, making Ed smile, which only made her angrier.

'You've got two choices. Sit there and I'll tip you out so you can't run away or you can grab hold of me and you won't end up on the floor. Either way this wheelchair is going over so take your choice.'

He continued to rock the wheelchair from side to side, picking up momentum each time, until the angle became acute enough for him to push it all the way. At the very last minute Laura grabbed him round the neck and he carried her down the gentle incline of the cliff, towards the beach.

'Put me down you bastard. I hate you!' she shouted at him

'No you don't. I'm your best friend, remember. And I have no intention of putting you down until we've have had a nice walk along the beach and you've let me explain.' he replied smiling at her, which didn't help abate her anger and if anything, increased it further.

'No you're not. I hate you and I hate Emma,' she yelled.

'Right now, I'd say Emma is probably one of the best friends you'll ever have, apart from me that is,' Ed said, striding down towards the sand. He was doing well until he hit the green stuff: a thin blanket of seaweed on the flat surface of a sea-worn rock, sloping towards the beach. When Ed hit it, he began sliding immediately and was unable to stop, due to the leather soled brogues he was wearing that had absolutely zero traction. Worse still, he was picking up speed and heading for a very large rock pool. Laura stopped shouting at him and looked over her shoulder, then back at Ed and gave him a terrified look. Ed gave her a nervous grin back before saying 'Brace yourself,' as he zipped off the edge of the rock and splashed into the rock pool.

The water was up to his waist and was freezing. Laura escaped lightly with only her feet, claves and buttocks getting a soaking.

'You stupid bastard, now look what you've done! I'm bloody freezing.' Ed laughed and kissed her on the lips as he waded over to the side of the pool and put Laura down. He climbed out, shivering. Just to add to his misery, the rain started coming down heavier, as he carried Laura back up towards the clifftop. He stopped under a slight ridge putting her down, hoping that the overhang would give them some shelter from the rain.

'Right, time for you to listen,' he said forcefully. 'I slept in the same bed as Emma because I fell asleep in the living room. I've not been sleeping well lately and was absolutely knackered. Two bottles of wine was enough to knock me out cold. When I awoke, I was in bed with Emma on account of there only being two bedrooms. Emma stripped me naked for a laugh, because when she fell asleep the night we went out for a meal, I was the perfect gentleman and put her nightdress on first before taking her clothes off, to preserve her modesty. She said then, if the boot was on the other foot she would have a good look. That's what she did for a laugh. Nothing sexual took place. The fact of the matter is, she's waiting for the results of an aids test, because of what when on before we came here.' Laura looked at him blankly, all the earlier anger and bitterness erased from her face.

'Oh god, I feel awful. God, how could I be so stupid. I'm so sorry, Ed. You must hate me now,' she said, tears welling up in her eyes.

'The reason I'm here now,' Ed said in a softer voice, 'is because of Emma. She persuaded me to try and tell you how I feel about you.'

'How do you feel about me?' she asked.

'I think you're a pain in the bloody arse, right now but I want, that is if you want as well, to try and make a go of this relationship, as in a couple, an item, boyfriend girlfriend, kind of thing.'

'Of course I want to,' she said, throwing her arms around him and kissing him passionately, hands everywhere. Ed responded and was just about to enjoy a grope, when he was interrupted.

'Excuse me, sir. Is that your wheelchair up here?' a voice from above said.

'Shit,' Ed said under his breath. 'Yes, it is. Thanks, I'll come and get it later.'

'Are you sure everything is OK, sir? It's the police. We were called after a couple reported a possible abduction.' Laura giggled.

'It's OK, officer. I think there's been a misunderstanding. Apart from being wetter than an otter's pocket, everything is OK, honest.' They could hear approaching footsteps and a few seconds later the face of a young constable was peering down on them.

'Hello, sir, madam. Are you sure everything is Ok? The caller seemed quite positive when they dialled 999.'

'Officer, everything is fine. Well, actually, no it's not fine. I was just about to have a nice grope and you interrupted me,' Ed replied, making the young constable blush. Laura leaned over and began kissing Ed. The constable backed away embarrassed, muttering his apologies for disturbing them.

The mood broken, Ed picked Laura up and carried her to her wheelchair, which had since been up-righted by the policeman.

'I suppose we'd better head back and get out of these wet clothes before we die of pneumonia. I'm bloody freezing, too.'

'If Mum's not around you might have to give me a hand getting out of mine,' Laura informed him giving him a salacious look.

'Right, better get back quick, before she goes out, then,' Ed said and began pushing her along at a run.

CHAPTER 56

There was a note on the table from Raechael when they arrived back. Ed was exhausted from the run back and Laura was shivering from the cold. The note was addressed to them both, making Ed smile at her confidence he would win the battle of wills with her daughter. It read "Gone shopping back later, good luck. Mum."

'All that running and we missed her,' Ed said, leering at Laura.

'What a shame. You'll have to help me out of these wet clothes then,' she said, grinning at him. Ed was only too happy to oblige and took off his own sodden jacket and hung it over the back of a chair. He bent down and picked Laura up and carried her to the bedroom sitting her down on the bed. He was shaking and didn't know if it was from the cold, excitement or nerves or all three.

'Are you just going to stand there staring at me or are you going to help?' She asked looking up at him with her alluring brown eyes, making Ed's heart skip a beat. Laura lay back on the bed and unbuttoned her trousers. Ed knelt down, pulled them off and began looking round the room for a hanger. 'Ed, just throw them on the bloody floor and get on with it, will you,' she said unbuttoning her blouse. Ed didn't need any more encouragement than that and began stripping himself. When he was finally naked, he picked Laura up, kicked back the sheet and laid her down with her head on the pillow and lay next to her.

'What about taking precautions?' Ed asked, tentatively.

'Well, I'm on the pill and I don't have any sexual diseases and I've had plenty of blood tests recently so I know I haven't got aids.'

'Well, I might have a couple of rubbers in my wallet and they might even still be in date,' Ed replied. 'I had an aids test after the wife was killed, just to be on the safe side. It's been so long since I last got lucky, the only thing you're likely to catch of me is a nasty case of dust mites,' he replied apologetically.

'Ed, shut up,' she said and began kissing him.

It wasn't the best sex either had experienced, due to a combination of nerves and, for Ed, being a bit ring-rusty. The exploding cigar fear wasn't an issue but it wasn't long after she started giving his crown jewels some attention that he ejaculated and felt the need to apologise, despite Laura thinking it was funny. Ed was quite surprised at how energetic Laura was and had serious concerns when the use of her legs returned, he wouldn't be able to keep up with her. However, the second time they made love it had been much slower and more intimate than the first, which was pure lust.

They were laying there exhausted facing each other, Ed grinning like the cat that got the cream, when Raechael walked in.

'Oh sorry, I didn't realise…' she started. Ed turned and smiled at her.

'Er, Raechael, I know what you're thinking,' Ed began and Raechael did her best to suppress a smile. 'And well, it's exactly what it looks like,' Ed said, beaming from ear to ear.

'Good,' she said. 'By the way your clothes stink of seaweed,' she said lifting his trousers up and sniffing them.

Ed brought her up to date making her laugh.

'So, of course, I had to help Laura out of her wet things and my own and that's when she took advantage of me.'

'Whatever. Anyway, would you like a cup of tea?' she asked, as if it was the perfectly normal thing to do, when you caught your daughter in bed with her boyfriend.

'Well, unless you can rustle up one of those tinfoil blankets they give you after running a marathon a cup of tea will be fine. I feel half knackered. Your daughter's a bit of a tiger in the sack, Mrs. Jacobs.'

'Too much information, Ed,' she said walking out. Laura slapped him playfully on the arm and began kissing him. They were still kissing when Raechael came back in with the tea and biscuits. 'Put him down, Laura,' she said, placing the teas on the bedside table and sitting down on the bed beside Ed, which made him nervous.

'Mind the wet patch, Mrs. Jacobs,' Ed said with a grin.

'Ed, you're gross,' Laura said giggling.

'What I meant was that's where you were sitting in your wet trousers, but I like the way you're thinking,' Ed replied, although neither believed him, despite the innocent look he was sporting.

'I was going to ask if you wanted me to nip over and get you some dry clothes?' she asked, adding 'Or do you intend to stay here long enough, that these ones will have dried out?' Before he could answer she leaned across and gave them both a hug and told them how pleased she was for them. Ed said he wouldn't mind some dry clothes if it wasn't too much trouble. Raechael got up to leave and turned and smiled at them.

'Oh and take your time, Raechael,' Ed added, giving her a wink as she left, shaking her head at his cheek.

CHAPTER 57

That evening Ed invited Raechael and Bob over for dinner, which he spent all afternoon preparing. The next day everyone was still alive so he considered it to be a success, not that much could go wrong with melon and Parma ham, followed by chilli con carne. The next few days went by in a blur for Ed, knowing his time with Laura was limited, despite her persuading Raechael to stay on until Saturday. It didn't take much of an effort, as she was clearly keen to spend more time with Bob. Ed and Laura spent most of the time in bed, as she thought after so long on the wagon, Ed needed the practice. Ed didn't disagree.

Ed booked a table the Harlyn Inn for Friday night, to have a farewell meal, with Chris, Emma, Bob, Raechael and Laura. Compared to the previous meal there two weeks ago, the evening was uneventful. Sarah the waitress with the perpetual smile was waiting on them, at Ed's request, when he booked the table. The manager, who Raechael tore to pieces last time, kept a safe distance and left Sarah to it without interference. Once again, the champagne flowed and a good time was had by all. When Ed went to the gents after the main course, Bob followed him in and told him he had a favour to ask.

'I need you to have Laura stay with you tonight,' he mumbled, slightly embarrassed. Ed wasn't slow on the uptake but thought he'd make Bob earn his favour.

'Why's that, then?' he asked, finding it hard to suppress a grin.

'Do I need to bloody spell it out, you tart?' Bob said, knowing Ed was taking the piss.

'You want me to have Laura stay over so you can get your leg over with Raechael?' Bob stared daggers at Ed and nodded. 'OK.'

Ed said, turning to walk out 'You got enough change, Bob?' Ed said, tossing a two pound coin to him and pointing to the condom machine on the wall. 'I think they're about three quid these days and you only get two. Use them wisely Bob,' he said, laughing as he walked out.

'Funny bastard,' Bob shouted at him as he left.

After the meal, they walked back to Ed's caravan for a nightcap as they had the last time, only slightly more sober, although only just. Seated on the sofa, a glass of wine in one hand and Laura's hand in the other, Ed was a happy man.

'What are you grinning at, Chris?' Ed asked.

'You,' she said still grinning. 'I can't remember the last time I saw you so happy.'

'It was probably when he was giving someone a good bloody kicking,' Bob announced, laughing at his own wit. Ed didn't even bother coming back with a witty retort and just carried on smiling. 'Bloody hell, it must be love, he hasn't answered back,' he added.

'Do you think I'll need to buy a new hat soon?' Chris asked 'It's been ages since I went to a good wedding.'

'Very funny. We've only been an item a couple of days, one step at a time,' Ed replied.

'What happens after tomorrow?' Chris probed further, enjoying Ed's discomfort.

'Not sure. Haven't given it too much thought, really. St. Albans is only a few miles away from my place. I'm sure we'll manage to work something out,' Ed replied.

'You seemed to be managing pretty well on Tuesday,' Raechael chipped in.

'Mother!' Laura cried 'You're getting a bad as he is,' she said, nudging Ed in the ribs.

'Have you ever been married, Chris?' Raechael asked. Ed gave Bob a nervous glance.

'No, I was engaged once but it didn't work out,' she replied. 'Since then, I just don't seem to have met the right person.'

The truth was that Bob and Ed had been out for a few beers and during the walk between pubs, noticed two guys having an altercation in an alleyway. Bob's policeman instinct kicked in and they both wandered down the alley to investigate. It turned out one of the men was Chris's fiancé Paul and the other man was accusing him of sleeping with his wife. Ed asked him if it was true and he nodded so Ed broke his nose, told the other guy to carry on and left. In the morning he went to see Chris and found out it was over as Paul had confessed. He knew if he hadn't, Ed would have informed Chris. It saved Ed the dilemma of should he tell her or not and was grateful for that. Since then, Chris had a few relationships but none amounting to much, which in Ed's view was a bloody waste.

'What about you and Bob?' Chris asked Raechael, who was smiling broadly.

'That depends on Bob, doesn't it?' she replied, very noncommittally, raising her eyebrows at Bob. Ed was pleased to see Bob squirming.

'Any chance of a refill, Ed?' he asked, ignoring the question. Ed thought about pressing him for an answer but got up to bring another couple of bottles of wine from the kitchen. 'Have you got a DVD player, by the way?' he asked. Ed pointed out the big silver box underneath the TV to him. 'I've got something I want to show you,' he said, switching the TV and DVD player on and slipping in a DVD, he produced from his jacket pocket.

The DVD started up and Ed saw himself squaring up to Mack on the beach. Ed looked around nervously but everyone else seemed captivated. Emma was the exception, who shuddered at the memory. The fight commenced with Ed giving Mack a battering and standing over him telling him to get up. When Mack threw sand in his eyes and lumped him with the plank of wood, Chris, Raechael and Laura almost jumped out of their seats. Ed winced at the memory and was surprised at the force with which he hit him. Bob played it through to the end and by this time everyone was sitting there wide-eyed and slack-jawed. Ed was wondering what the point in all of it was.

'Right, a question for you,' Bob announced. 'And tell the truth, I've got fifty quid riding on the answer. Did you or did you not, deliberately get yourself stabbed in the leg?'

'He was waving that knife around like a lunatic, it could have gone anywhere,' Ed replied, evasively and deliberately not giving an answer. Bob rewound the DVD to just before Ed was knifed and put it onto slow motion.

'Look at this,' he said to everyone. 'Just before you get knifed, you shrug and start smiling and I even think you wink at us. I think, you knew exactly what you were doing,' he continued, as the slow motion showed just that. 'Well?' he asked again. Ed looked around the room and saw that all eyes were on him.

'Yes,' he replied receiving a gasp from Laura. 'I didn't have much bloody choice, did I?' he said moodily 'My head was still spinning and my left arm was numb and next to useless. He was going to do some me serious damage, the way he was wafting that thing around. I thought it would be safer in my leg, than slicing me across the belly. Happy now?' Everyone was staring at Ed, making him feel uncomfortable.

'I think he was bloody brave,' Laura said, breaking the silence.

'Bloody stupid,' Emma replied.

'Perhaps a little foolhardy but not stupid.' Bob said, coming to his rescue but probably only because he needed Ed to do him a favour tonight. 'And Phil owes me fifty quid.'

Bob ejected the disc and threw it to Ed. 'That's a present from me,' he said proudly.

'Tell Phil, if I see this on YouTube, I'm gonna kick his arse,' Ed replied. 'Talking of presents, I've got a something for everyone. Kind of going away presents,' Ed opened a cupboard under the TV and pulled out a pink gift bag with Barbie on it and handed it to Bob, who glared at him when he pulled out a bottle of Grand Marnier.

'Very funny, I hope you kept the bloody receipt.' he replied.

'You drank enough of it the other night. I thought you'd like that?' Bob put it back in the bag and put it down by his feet. 'OK don't bloody sulk,' Ed said and walked off to the bedroom and came back with a large box containing half a dozen different bottles of single malts and handed it to Bob, who was like a kid in a sweet shop as he fawned over every bottle.

'This is more like it,' he said, then frowned. 'Jesus Ed. Glenmorangie thirty-year-old, that's about two-hundred quids worth and Glenturret twenty-one-year-old, that's gotta be another hundred. I don't know what to say.'

'Well, just don't go quaffing them all in one go. If you want to get pissed and pine over Raechael, go and buy a bottle of supermarket blended, these are for savouring,' Ed replied, unable to help but get another dig in. Not that Bob seemed to care as he pawed over every bottle.

Ed went to the bedroom again and came out with two more boxes and gave one each to Raechael and Chris. 1995 Krug Vintage Champagne for Chris and Chateaux Palmer Margaux Burgundy for Raechael, knowing she liked it. While they were thanking Ed, he reached into the cupboard under the TV and pulled out a small flat box and handed it to Laura, who opened it slowly and smiled broadly at the contents.

'Where the hell did you manage to get this?' she said, holding up a heart shaped sapphire pendant on a gold chain.

'Argos. Like it?' he said smiling.

'Liar, I can tell from the box it's not and it's beautiful.'

'Said I'd buy you one the first day we met. I like to keep to my word. Oh, nearly forgot,' he said and handed Emma a card. 'I didn't know what to get you, so I got you a card.'

Emma look slightly disappointed as she opened the card but stared open mouthed once it was opened. 'I can't accept this.' she announced.

'Of course you can. Anyway, there's a charge if I cancel it so just cash it. I really didn't know what to get you. I know you left everything behind in Cambridge so there's plenty you do need and I want you to have it so you can make a fresh start,' he told her solemnly. Chris leaned over and looked inside the card over her shoulder and smiled.

'What the bloody hell is it? Bob asked.

'It's a cheque for a hundred thousand pounds,' Emma said quietly.

'Bloody hell. If you don't want it, I'll swap you for my whisky,' Bob said.

'You'll end up a very poor man at this rate,' Raechael told him. Ed shrugged. He had more than enough to see him out. He was just glad Emma hadn't read the card out, which was quite sentimental, for Ed at least.

After Laura handed round her necklace for everyone to look at, Ed put it round her neck but left the matching earrings in the box. It looked good on her and she seemed rather pleased with it and couldn't stop touching and looking at it. Ed brought her a mirror so she could see it properly and she stared at it for a long, long time.

'Well, I don't know about anyone else but I'm just about all in and need some sleep,' Raechael told everyone; Bob immediately offering to walk her back. He gave Ed a hard stare as he got up. Chris rang for a cab for her and Emma and said they'd walk back with them. Ed volunteered to walk with them and wait to make sure the cab turned up. Fat Boy needed to go out anyway and he could carry Chris's champagne. Laura said she would stay a bit longer and gave her mother a knowing look.

After saying goodbye to Raechael and Bob, who was in a rather good mood and hopeful of a night with Raechael, Ed walked to reception and waited with Chris and Emma, until their cab arrived. Emma gave him a hug and told him she would miss him and once again, tried to give him the cheque back. Ed refused and told her if she didn't want it, to buy some shares. Emma gave him a sad smile.

He felt more than a little sad walking back to the caravan, as he would miss Emma but cheered up at the prospect of knowing Laura was waiting for him. During the walk back, he glanced over at Raechael and Laura's caravan and caught a glimpse of the silhouetted figures of Bob and Raechael kissing through the thin curtains, until the lights went out. Ed chuckled to himself and finished the rest of his short journey with a smile on his face.

When he arrived back at the caravan, Laura was already in bed waiting for him, which was a good sign in Ed's book.

'You sure you want to stay the night?' he asked, slipping into the bed next to her.

'Of course. Why wouldn't I?' she asked, somewhat surprised at the question.

'Just asking. You know, I snore and fart a lot and probably have a hundred other nasty habits, I don't even realise I have?'

'I don't care. I love you warts 'n' all. Now shut up,' she said and kissed him.

Ed awoke with a stretch and an extremely loud fart, which woke Laura up.

'Jesus Christ, Ed. You're disgusting and you stink. That's really unfair you know I can't run away,' she said jokingly.

'Warts 'n' all you said. Warts and all,' he reminded her.

CHAPTER 58

Ed was driving back home, with Fat Boy in the boot and Laura in the passenger seat, having persuaded him to take her back to St. Albans. Not that it took a great deal of arm twisting, Ed wanting to delay the inevitable as long as he could.

When the phone rang, he switched off the radio and pressed the answer button to take the call from Bob and put a finger to his lips, for Laura to be quiet.

'Hi Bob. Missing me already?' Ed asked cheerily.

'Funny bastard. Thought I'd give you a call to give you the good news,' he replied.

'Congratulations. Do I get to be best man?'

'Do you want to hear what I've got to say or not, you cretin?' He took the silence to be a yes. 'I just had a call from my old mate in customs and excise about that favour you asked me. Looks like you were right on the button with that one.'

'Are you going to elaborate on that or what?' Ed asked impatiently.

'Your friend Danny, turns out to be a bit of a naughty boy. He got raided last night and they found several kilos of cocaine, ecstasy by the bucket load and various other amphetamines, which would be worth several hundred thousand pounds on the street.'

'Nice one. I take it he's going to be doing a few years for that?' Ed replied happily. Laura just looked confused.

'I should say. Not only that, they found a young girl, drugged and tied to the bed, being shagged stupid by one of Danny's mates, while he was filming it all. It was quite a big operation by the sounds of it. Webcams all over the place, streaming live over the internet and an entire room full of DVD equipment to produce illegal porn. Pretty nasty stuff most of it. The evil little shit apparently abducted the girl they found there, kept her drugged and made her do stuff I don't even want to think about, let alone talk about. It should be hitting the press later today so keep an eye on the news. I thought you might want to know.'

'Thanks Bob. I hope that bastard goes down for a long time. Just do me a favour and don't tell Emma. Let her find out on her own. I don't want her to know I had anything to do with it. OK?'

'Of course I bloody well won't. We had a deal, didn't we? Anyway, haven't got all day to gas with you. Take it easy and I'll see you soon,' he replied and hung up before Ed had a chance to say goodbye.

'What was all that about?' Laura asked. Ed thought about it for a minute and decided he might as well tell her.

'Just tying up a loose end. I asked Bob to have a quiet word with some of his friends about Emma's charming ex-boyfriend, rather than take matters into my own hands. Surely you didn't think I'd let something like that go, do you? Looks like I had a right result.'

'You know, you're quite a vindictive sod, really,' Laura said light-heartedly.

'I prefer to think of it as being protective towards my friends,' Ed said. 'Vindictive is a little harsh, don't you think?'

'Maybe,' she replied.

'Good,' Ed said and turned the radio back on and allowed himself a smug grin.

Laura noticed the absence of his wedding ring as he reached over to turn the radio on and smiled to herself. That morning when Ed had taken Fat Boy for his morning walk, he stood at his favourite spot on the clifftop and hurled his wedding ring as far as he could into the sea, deciding now was as good a time as any to move on.

.

THE AUTHOR

John Morritt was born in England a long time ago, but in 2013 he
made Thailand his new home.
John is the author of a book series featuring the likable Ed Case,
who somehow seems to invite trouble. "Black Cockles" is the
series debut novel, followed by "Nine Lives" with "Inglorious"
being the third installment.
His stand-alone novel, "Vengeance" explores the darker side of
human nature.

For more information visit www.johnmorritt.com

Other books by the Author

<u>NINE LIVES</u>

(Ed Case: Book 2)

When Soho club owner Johnny Gold, tells Ed "I could use someone like you." Ed jumps at the opportunity of a job as a bouncer. Little does he know that he is entering a world of sleaze and corruption that will put his life in danger, because Johnny has a hidden agenda. It is only exotic dancer TJ, who stops him walking away. But even TJ has a secret.

After Johnny frames Ed for murder, he flees the club in an maelstrom of violence and is pursued the length of the country by two of Soho's most ruthless gangs, because Ed has something that belongs to Johnny and they all want it back – at any cost.

Surviving a terrifying orgy of death and violence, Ed heads back to London believing his ordeal is finally over, unaware that his real nightmares are just beginning.

INGLORIOUS

(ED Case: Book 3)

Enjoying a quiet life after moving to Cornwall, Ed and TJ couldn't be happier. Their tranquillity, however, is shattered when a bitter resident drags up their past - a violent and tragic past they dearly want to forget.

When Ed unearths a 150-year-old mystery while renovating their house, and as they set about investigating it, they uncover damning details that takes a terrifying turn, exacerbating the resident's hostility towards them.

Their situation becomes worse when Ed's friend, DCI Bob Brown, asks him for a favour. Ed knows it wouldn't just be a case of 'give Roly a knuckle sandwich and job done'; life is never that simple for Ed.

With recent events and his fragile mental health, Ed is caught in a situation where he has to choose between breaking his promise to TJ to stay out of trouble, or help Bob. There is only one outcome and soon Ed finds himself drawn in the criminal underworld of ex-London gangster Harry Daniels.

VENGEANCE

At the tender age of five, Peter Edwards witnesses the horrific death of his father by a drunk driver. Twenty years later, the nightmares that tortured him for a few years after the accident inexplicably return to haunt him, leading to the breakdown in his relationship with his girlfriend, Janet, and destroying his teaching career.

After a particularly graphic nightmare one night, Peter vividly recalls the face of the killer. He is filled with anger so strong, that he becomes consumed with avenging his father's death.

Though many dream of revenge, they lack the courage to act. Not Peter Edwards. An eye for an eye, a tooth for a tooth he tells himself as he embarks on a terrifying trail of vengeance.

16772333R00174

Printed in Great Britain
by Amazon